REESE WITHERSPOON

GONE BEFORE GOODBYE

HARLAN COBEN

GRAND
CENTRAL

NEW YORK   BOSTON

Copyright © 2025 by Harlan Coben and Reese Witherspoon

Cover design by Alan Dingman and Albert Tang
Cover images by Getty Images and Shutterstock
Cover copyright © 2025 by Hachette Book Group, Inc.

Grand Central Publishing
Hachette Book Group
1290 Avenue of the Americas, New York, NY 10104
grandcentralpublishing.com
@grandcentralpub

First Edition: October 2025

Grand Central Publishing is a division of Hachette Book Group, Inc. The Grand Central Publishing name and logo is a registered trademark of Hachette Book Group, Inc.

The publisher is not responsible for websites (or their content) that are not owned by the publisher.

The Hachette Speakers Bureau provides a wide range of authors for speaking events. To find out more, go to hachettespeakersbureau.com or email HachetteSpeakers@hbgusa.com.

Grand Central Publishing books may be purchased in bulk for business, educational, or promotional use. For information, please contact your local bookseller or the Hachette Book Group Special Markets Department at special.markets@hbgusa.com.

Print book interior design by Marie Mundaca

Library of Congress Control Number: 2025940630

ISBN: 9781538774700 (hardcover), 9781538779361 (signed edition), 9781538779354 (special edition), 9781538774717 (ebook), 9781538775158 (large print trade paperback), 9781538775028 (international trade paperback)

Printed in the United States of America

LBK

10 9 8 7 6 5 4 3 2 1

GONE BEFORE GOODBYE

ALSO BY REESE WITHERSPOON

NONFICTION
*Whiskey in a Teacup: What Growing Up in the South
Taught Me About Life, Love, and Baking Biscuits*

CHILDREN'S BOOKS
Busy Betty
Busy Betty & the Circus Surprise
Busy Betty & the Perfect Christmas Present

ALSO BY HARLAN COBEN

NOVELS

Play Dead	*Live Wire*
Miracle Cure	*Shelter*
Deal Breaker	*Stay Close*
Drop Shot	*Seconds Away*
Fade Away	*Six Years*
Back Spin	*Missing You*
One False Move	*Found*
The Final Detail	*The Stranger*
Darkest Fear	*Fool Me Once*
Tell No One	*Home*
Gone for Good	*Don't Let Go*
No Second Chance	*Run Away*
Just One Look	*The Boy from the Woods*
The Innocent	*Win*
Promise Me	*The Match*
The Woods	*I Will Find You*
Hold Tight	*Think Twice*
Long Lost	*Nobody's Fool*
Caught	

*To the many military doctors and nurses who have
placed themselves in peril to help save every soul they could.
Thank you for your courage and compassion.*

GONE BEFORE GOODBYE

TriPoint, North Africa

I don't hear the scream.

The nurse does. So does the anesthesiologist. I am too deep in the zone, the zone I can only enter in an operating theater, when a sternum is cracked open like this, and my hands are inside the boy's chest.

This is my home, my office, my sanctuary. I am Zen here.

More screams. Gunfire. Helicopters. An explosion.

"Doctor?"

I hear the panic in her voice. But I don't move. I don't look away. My hands, the oldest medical instruments known to mankind, are inside the chest cavity, my index finger palpitating the pericardium. I am totally focused on that, only that. No music is playing. That's weird in an operating room nowadays, I know, but I relish silence in this hallowed space, even when we've done heart transplants that last eight hours. It annoys my staff. They need the diversion, the entertainment, the distraction—and that's the problem for me. I want no distractions. Both my bliss and my excellence come from that singular focus.

But the sounds invade.

Rapid gunfire. Another explosion. Louder screams.

Getting closer now.

"Doctor?" The voice is shaky now, panicked. Then, because I'm clearly not listening: "Marc?"

"Nothing we can do about it," I say.

Which is hardly a comfort.

Trace and I arrived in Ghadames eight days ago. We flew into Diori Hamani airport, where we were met by a young woman Trace and I knew named Salima, if that is her real name, and a burly driver who never introduced himself or said a word to us. The four of us traveled northeast for two long days, sleeping in a safe house near Agadez and then tents under the stars in Bilma. We left the driver in northern Niger, traveling through the desert by night, until we met another car.

Salima and Trace have eyes for one another. I'm not surprised. Trace is the pure definition of a "playah." Even surrounded by death . . . well, maybe that's just it.

When you're close to death, that's when you feel your most alive.

Salima kept us moving north, straddling the border between Algeria and Libya. East of Djanet, a half dozen heavily armed militants stopped us. They were all young—teens, I would guess—and tweaking from some sort of potent narcotic. They were called the Child Army. Blood was in the air. Wide-eyed, they grabbed me first, then Trace. The young militants made me kneel.

They put a gun to the back of my skull.

I would be first to die. Trace would watch. Then it would be his turn.

I closed my eyes and pictured Maggie's face and waited for someone to pull the trigger.

The Child Army didn't shoot us, obviously. Salima, who speaks at least four languages fluently, fell to her knees and talked fast. I don't know exactly what she said—Salima wouldn't tell us—but the child soldiers moved on.

More screams. More gunfire. Closer now. I try to hurry.

I didn't tell Maggie the truth about how risky this last mission was on so many levels, not because I thought she would worry but because of the promises we had made to one another—she would have insisted on coming.

That's how Maggie and I are built.

You wonder what makes a hero? There's altruism, sure. But there's also ego and recklessness and thrill-seeking.

We don't fear danger. We fear normalcy.

Trace, wearing a surgical mask, pokes his head in. "Marc?"

"How much time do we have?"

"They've burned down the north side of the camp. Dozens are already dead. Salima is moving everyone out."

I look at the nurse and the anesthesiologist. "Go," I tell them.

"You can't save him," the nurse says to me, as she pulls away. "Even if you finish in time, even if he could somehow survive the surgery, they won't let him live."

I don't know who "they" are. I don't know the justifications, the origins, the history, the factions, the tribes, the warlords, the fanatics, the extremists, the innocents. I don't know who the good guys or the bad guys are, why these people are in this refugee camp, what side is the oppressor or what side is the oppressed. It's not that I'm not political, but for Maggie and Trace and me, it can't matter.

I continue to work on my patient, a fifteen-year-old boy named Izil. I hope everyone I treat is an innocent, but I doubt it. It just can't be our job to figure out who is on what side. Our job, not to get too grandiose, is to save their lives. They say, "Kill them all and let God sort them out." It's close to the opposite for us—save them all and let God . . . You get the drift.

I'm not being "both sides" here. I'm being "no sides."

"Everyone out," I say. "I want the room cleared."

"Marc," Trace says.

Our eyes meet over the surgical masks. Trace and I have known each other a long time. We did our surgical residency together. We have provided medical aid in humanitarian crises like this one across the globe. He is one of the most gifted cardiothoracic surgeons in the world.

Trace says, "I can help you close."

"I got it."

"We'll wait."

I shake my head, but he knows.

"Leave me an ambulance," I say. "They won't shoot up an ambulance."

We both know this is no longer true, not in today's world.

We should never have come. I shouldn't have allowed it. I should have taken care of business and said goodbye and flown home.

I should be with Maggie.

I don't say goodbye to Trace. He doesn't say goodbye to me.

But this will be the last time I ever see him.

Seconds later, it's only Izil and me in the room. I hurry, stupidly thinking I can make it. I am closing the boy's chest when the doors burst open.

Armed militants storm in. I don't know how many. They all have that crazed look in their eyes. I have seen that look before. Too many times. I saw it just a few days ago east of Djanet.

And sometimes I see it when I look in the mirror.

I close my eyes and picture Maggie's face and wait for someone to pull the trigger.

CHAPTER ONE

Baltimore
ONE YEAR LATER

Maggie McCabe shouldn't have come.

"Where are you?" Marc asks.

Maggie looks down at her husband's face on the phone screen. "I told you."

"Johns Hopkins?"

"Yes."

"You on the quad?"

"Yes."

"Where we met," he says. "Orientation week of medical school. You remember?"

"Of course I remember," Maggie says.

"I knew you were the one the moment I saw you."

"Don't make me gag."

"I'm trying to boost you up."

"It's not working."

"So what are you doing?"

Maggie flashes back to her first time on campus, all dewy-eyed and fresh-faced, as they say, full of hope and optimism and vim and vigor and all that nonsense. How naive. But then again, when your world falls apart—when you had everything and even understood and appreciated that you had everything and never took any of it for granted, not for a second, knew how lucky you were, and because you were so grateful, you somehow naively expected karma to reward you, or at least leave you be—you learn in the hardest of ways that fate is fickle, that life is chaos and no one gets out unscathed, that you can have everything one moment and have it all snatched away so easily...

"I'm throwing myself a little pity party," she says.

"Stop. Go inside."

"I want to go home."

Marc frowns. "Don't do that."

"I'm not ready."

"Yes, you are. Please? I want you to go. Do it for me."

"Seriously?"

She looks up at the white cupola sitting atop Shriver Hall and blinks back a tear. An hour ago, she'd reluctantly put on a long-sleeve, navy blue, mid-calf-length formal dress. Not black. That would be too morbid. Navy seems like a safe bet—respectful of the occasion, but not trying to pull attention. In fact, she would rather melt into the floor than be anywhere in the vicinity of conspicuous on this particular night.

"Maggie?"

"I'm here."

"Go inside. It would mean a lot to me. And your mother."

"Wow," Maggie says.

"What?"

"You never used to be this sentimental and manipulative."

"Sure, I was," Marc says.

Her voice is soft. "Sure, you were." Then: "This sucks."

"What?"

"Nothing, never mind."

Twenty-two years ago, Maggie had graduated from these esteemed halls with every kind of honor they could bestow upon a medical student. She did her surgical residency at New York-Presbyterian, became a renowned reconstructive surgeon, served her country on the front lines in Afghanistan and the Middle East as a Field Surgeon 62B, married Marc, moved with him overseas to heal the underserved.

Marc's voice from the phone: "Hello?"

"They'll stare."

"Of course they'll stare," he says. "You're smoking hot."

Maggie frowns. Some things never change.

"Go," he says again.

She nods because he's right and disconnects the app. Her phone case features two M&M candy characters, the Yellow M&M guy holding flowers to the Green M&M woman. Marc had given her the phone case as a half-serious/half-gag gift. Maggie & Marc. M&M. Marc bought M&M pillowcases. He bought M&M throw pillows. Marc thought it was adorable. Maggie thought it was pure cringe, which, of course, only encouraged him.

"Maggie?"

She startles at the sound of the voice and drops her phone in her purse. She turns and sees her old classmate Larry Magid, a dermatologist. The last time she'd seen Larry was five years ago in Nepal when he'd flown over to help her and Marc with an outbreak of Hansen's disease, more commonly known as leprosy. They both ended up working out of the same hospital, even working out of the same floor, so he was intimately familiar with her current woes.

"Hey, Larry."

He squirms. "Are you here for... I mean, uh, are you going...?" He semi-gestures toward the building.

"Sure," Maggie says.

"Oh."

"What?"

"Nothing."

"They've named a scholarship in my mother's memory," she says.

"Right, I heard."

"So that's why I'm here."

"Right. Gotta go. Mickey will be waiting for me."

He hurries away as though, Maggie is tempted to shout out loud, she has leprosy. She wants to grab her phone, get Marc on again, and whine, "See what I mean?" but the phone is already in her bag and now she's a little annoyed so to hell with it.

Maggie hesitantly trudges up the same steps she'd enthusiastically marched up to get her diploma two decades ago. The banner pinned above the door reads:

SCHOLARSHIP RECOGNITION EVENT

WELCOME BACK, JOHNS HOPKINS ALUMS!

The hall is buzzing. The music, a string quartet of current students, plays Mozart's String Quartet No. 19 in C Major. Her hands at her sides, Maggie can't help half consciously moving her fingers along with the music, as though there's a violin in her hand. There are something like five hundred people—physicians and scholarship winners—milling about the esteemed hall. You know it's a medical event because too many men are wearing bow ties. That's a big look with doctors, mostly because regular ties hang loosely and get in the way during exams. Her father, an army surgeon who also saw combat as a Field Surgeon 62B—in his case, in Vietnam—always wore bright flowery ones. He claimed it let his patients see him as a bit goofy and thus comfortingly human.

When Maggie finally enters the grand hall, the room doesn't stop or go silent or any of that, but there is definitely some hesitation in the air.

She stands there for a few long seconds, feeling beyond awkward, as though her hands were suddenly too big. Her face flushes. Why had she come? She looks for a friendly or at least familiar face, but the only one she sees is from the poster on an easel up on the dais.

Mom.

God, her mother had been beautiful.

The photo they'd blown up had been taken for the school directory five years ago, Mom's last year teaching here. This was right before the diagnosis, something she hid from her two daughters for the next three years, until she finally called Maggie at their new clinic in Ghana and said, "I'm going to tell you something if you promise you won't come home when I do. Your work is too important." So Maggie promised and Mom told her and they both cried but Maggie kept her promise until her sister Sharon called and said, "It's almost time." Then Maggie kissed Marc goodbye at Dubai International, told him to finish up and come home soon, and flew home to sit vigil with Sharon for her mother's final days.

Maggie locks eyes with her poster-mother because right now it is the only friendly face in the room. She holds her head high as she walks toward the dais. She hopes that it's narcissism on her part, but conversations seem to halt or at least quiet as she passes. Murmurs ensue, or again maybe that's just in her head. Still she does not look away, does not let herself use her peripheral vision. Her eyes stay on her mother's, but she feels the stares now.

A familiar figure steps in her way and says, "Surprised you'd show your face."

It's Steve Schipner, aka Sleazy Steve, another reconstructive surgeon like herself and yet hopefully nothing like herself. He has over a million followers on an Instagram account where he displays "before and after" photos and calls himself the Boob Whisperer. She and Steve graduated in the same class and did a surgical rotation together at NewYork-Presbyterian/Columbia University under the tutelage of Dr. Evan Barlow. Steve is that guy who can't say good morning without making it sound like a sleazy double entendre, ergo the nickname.

He lives in Dubai now and specializes in, to quote his profile bio, "ambitious influencers looking to enhance their social media hits, their lives—and their cup size."

"Yeah, well, I'm full of surprises," Maggie says.

He looks around, notices the hostile stares. "At least I'm happy to see you."

"Thanks, Steve."

"You seen Barlow?"

"Have you?" she asks.

"Nope."

"I doubt he'll be here."

"I heard he was showing up," he says. "I want to talk to him about a sweet partnership deal and..." He stops, turns, gives her the full-wattage smile. "Oh, guess where I'm working now."

She doesn't want to, but it would be worse not to play along. "I heard Dubai."

"Yes, but *where* in Dubai?"

"I don't know, Steve. Where?"

He leans in and whispers. "Apollo Longevity."

Maggie tries to keep her face blank. It takes some effort.

Steve continues: "Isn't that where you and Marc used to—?"

"I'm not involved anymore."

Maggie tries to process this. Apollo Longevity is still active. Even now. Even after all that's happened.

That's not a good thing.

Steve looks her up and down, his gaze crawling all over her like earthworms after a rainstorm. "You look good, Mags." He arches one eyebrow, before he adds, "*Real* good. *So* good."

Maggie makes a noncommittal noise like "Uh-huh."

"*So* toned, *so* fit," Steve continues, doing a bicep curl to illustrate the point. "What do you do, free weights? Pilates?" Another eyebrow arch. "Sweaty, hot yoga?"

She shakes her head. "Do these lines ever work, Steve?"

"All the time, Mags. You know why?"

"You don't have to tell me," Maggie says, "but I bet you will."

He leans in toward her ear. "Because I'm a rich, successful forty-seven-year-old surgeon now. I can pull much younger tail than you."

She makes a face. "Did you just say 'younger tail'?"

"You're not too good for me," he says. Then he adds in a cruel whisper, "Not anymore."

With that, Steve oozes away.

Steve's trail of ooze leads to a cluster of their old classmates in the right-hand corner. She knows them all, but when she looks over, they all huddle up and do their best to pretend they don't see her. Part of Maggie is furious and wants to confront them, but a bigger part—a more honest part—wonders whether she'd be part of that eye-avoidance huddle had another classmate been this shamed instead of her.

Screw it.

Maggie heads straight into the heart of the huddle and says, "Hey, everyone."

Silence.

She looks from face to face. No one meets her eye.

"Stephanie," Maggie says to an old friend who is staring at her champagne as though it holds a secret, "how's Olivia?"

Olivia is Stephanie's daughter.

"Oh, she's, uh, she's doing well."

"Did my recommendation letter help?"

Maggie knows that it did. She'd written the letter a year ago, when her name opened rather than slammed doors, and she knew of course that Olivia had gotten in, but right now Maggie is not in the mood to let anyone off the hook.

"Stephanie?"

Before Stephanie can answer, another classmate, Bonnie Tillman, takes Maggie's elbow. "Can we talk privately for a moment, Maggie?"

Bonnie is an ophthalmologist in Washington, DC, and still (and forever) their class president. Her helmet of hair is firmly shellacked into place. She forces up a smile. It's a big effort to hold it. They say it takes seventeen muscles to smile and forty-three to frown. In Bonnie's case, it's clearly the opposite.

They move through a set of old glass doors onto a terrace.

"We all feel bad about your recent troubles," Bonnie begins in a voice that couldn't be more condescending without some kind of surgical help, "but it doesn't excuse what you did."

Maggie says nothing.

"This event," Bonnie continues, "is for esteemed physicians."

"It's for graduates."

"You know better."

Silence.

"Your medical license was revoked," Bonnie continues.

"Suspended," Maggie corrects. "Pending a review."

"Oh, so you're innocent?"

Maggie says nothing.

"You should leave."

"I don't think I will."

"It's unfair to your mother's memory."

"Excuse me?"

"You don't own her memory, Maggie. Not on this campus. She meant a lot to many of us students. Your being here? It's a blemish on her memory."

"I was asked to present the scholarship," Maggie says.

"That was before."

"No one rescinded the invitation."

"No one thought it was necessary."

"So who's doing it?"

Bonnie straightens her spine.

"Wait, you?"

"The administration thought it best."

"But my mother always thought you were a stuck-up tight-ass bitch, Bonnie."

Bonnie's eyes widen as though she'd been slapped. "Well!"

Maggie says nothing. Bonnie recovers.

"Either way," Bonnie says, "you should leave. Your being here sullies the reputation of our class."

Bonnie spins to leave. Maggie closes her eyes, opens them, stares out. "Bonnie?"

Bonnie stops and turns back to Maggie.

"My mother never said that. I'm sorry. That wasn't fair. She always spoke well of you. You're a good choice to do this."

Bonnie swallows. "I'll do my best. I promise you that."

She leaves Maggie alone on the terrace. From inside, someone starts clinking their champagne flute with a fork to get people's attention. The crowd quiets. Someone asks people to gather around so they can begin. Maggie stays out on the terrace.

Bonnie is right. She shouldn't be here.

She stares out at the foliage. From behind her, someone closes the glass doors so that she no longer hears what's going on in the room. That's okay. She is tempted to reach into her purse and contact Marc again, but that's an awful crutch and just makes her feel worse.

"Hello, Maggie."

The man wears a bespoke tailored suit of cobalt blue with a tie so perfectly knotted that one assumes he had divine help. His hair is gray, parted perfectly on the left. Maggie knows that he's in his early seventies—he'd been a classmate of her mother's and she'd been invited to his seventieth birthday party a few years back, but she'd been overseas and couldn't attend.

"Hello, Doctor Barlow."

"You haven't been my student for a long time, Maggie. Can't you call me by my first name?"

"I don't think I can, no."

Evan Barlow smiles. He has a good smile. He looks, to quote a sleazy classmate, so toned, so fit. She almost asks him if he does sweaty hot yoga. Evan Barlow heads up the Barlow Cosmetic Center, perhaps the most prestigious and discreet cosmetic surgery firm in the country. When celebrities want the work done so that no one knows, they trust Evan Barlow.

They stand now side by side, staring out at the quad. "Do you know this is my first time back on campus since I graduated?" he says.

"Really?"

"Yes."

"So why are you back?"

"I think you can guess."

"Mom?"

"I loved her, you know."

"I didn't know that."

"She and your father are both gone, so I can admit it now."

"I thought you two just dated for a few weeks."

"We were in our second year. But she broke my heart."

Maggie frowns. "Haven't you been married three times?"

"Four," he says.

"And isn't your current wife like thirty years old?"

"Thirty-two," he says, spreading his hands. "See what a broken heart does to a person?"

Maggie can't help but smile. Barlow does the same.

"Your father was such a good man, a much better choice for her. So I settled for friendship. But..." He shakes his head. "You get old, you get sentimental and philosophical. I'm trying to be glib, but I'm also revealing a truth." When he smiles at her, she flashes back to surgical rounds at NewYork-Presbyterian, what a generous teacher he'd been to her, how exhausting and exhilarating it was just to be in his presence. Evan Barlow had been a pure hit of crackling energy. You wanted to be around that.

As though reading her mind, Barlow says, "You're the best student I ever had. You know that. You're a surgeon, so you have the ego to know that what I'm saying is true."

"Correction: I *was* a surgeon."

She squeezes her eyes shut. She feels his hand on her shoulder.

His voice is so gentle. "Maggie?"

The tears push into her eyes. "I'm so sorry."

"It's okay."

"I let you down." She opens her eyes. "I let *her*"—no need to say who *her* referred to—"down."

"You didn't," he says. "Wait, okay, sorry, that's condescending. You did. I won't lie. May I speak frankly? You did mess up. Big-time. That's why I'm here."

"I'm not following."

"I don't need a scholarship ceremony to honor your mother's memory. I can do it in a much more concrete way." Barlow holds up his hand. "Wait, I'm not saying this right. Let me start again. I came tonight to see you."

"Me? Why?"

"I have a favor to ask."

When he doesn't immediately continue, Maggie says, "Go ahead."

"I'd like you to come by my office on Monday."

"This Monday?"

"Yes. Ten a.m."

"You have a Barlow Center in Baltimore now?"

"No, but maybe soon. Right now, they're in Palm Beach, Los Angeles, and New York City. I'd like you to come up to New York City. I'll arrange a private car to drive you, and I have a suite reserved at the Aman."

"I don't understand. Why do you want me to come to New York?"

"I can't tell you that."

"Why not?"

"I just...it's not my place."

Maggie makes a face. "Then whose place is it?"

"It's an intriguing offer. That's all I can tell you right now."

"I don't have a medical license anymore."

"I know. The offer is a tad"—Barlow looks up as though searching for a better word but finally shrugs—"unusual."

"Can't you just tell me now?"

"I can't, no."

She thinks about it. "If you don't mind me saying, Doctor Barlow, this is all a little weird."

"I know."

"More than a little weird, in fact."

"It is, I admit that. Look, I know you and Sharon are having serious financial difficulties—"

"How do you know that?"

"—but I'll write you a check right now for twenty thousand dollars. Just to show up."

He reaches into his suit pocket and pulls out a pen and...

"Is that a checkbook?" she asks.

"Yes."

"What is this, 1987? Who still carries around a checkbook?"

Barlow can't help but smile. "I wanted to be prepared."

He starts scribbling on the check.

"You don't need to do that," she says.

"No, I do. You should be compensated for your time."

"Don't," she says a little more forcibly. "I'm going to say it again: You're being weird."

"I know." He puts the checkbook back in his pocket. "Do you trust me, Maggie?"

In truth she trusts no one anymore. Well, almost no one.

"One more thing," he says.

"What?"

"I'd appreciate it if you didn't tell anyone about this."

"I have to tell my sister."

"It would be better if you didn't."

"I'm living with her. I just can't vanish to New York City."

"Sure, you can." He hands her a card. "I'll have someone text you to arrange the car pickup."

"I'd rather take Amtrak," Maggie says.

"If that's what you prefer. There'll be a reservation under your name at the Aman hotel on Fifty-Seventh Street starting tomorrow night. We'll be in touch about the details for Monday."

Maggie takes the embossed business card, looks at it, looks at him. Dr. Evan Barlow runs one of the most successful high-end cosmetic surgery practices in the world. He is worth millions and reeks of it. She tries to read his face. It's smooth, professional, handsome, full of gravitas.

But does she also see fear?

"What's really going on, Doctor Barlow?"

"I can't say more, Maggie. Take it or leave it."

"And if I leave it?"

He shrugs. "It was nice to see you."

Barlow kisses her on the cheek and heads to the door.

"How did you know I'd be here?" she asks.

Something crosses his face, something she can't read. He gives his head a small shake and turns the knob.

"You'll find out all on Monday," Barlow says, and then he heads back inside.

CHAPTER TWO

Marc says, "You'll hem and haw, but we both know you're going to go."

He's right. Again.

Maggie is walking across campus. She'd stayed long enough so it would not appear that anyone had run her off, but as soon as the speeches were done and the mingling began again in earnest, Maggie slipped out.

"So," Marc continues, "what do you think Doctor Barlow wants?"

"I was hoping you'd have an answer," Maggie says.

"Hmm, let me do a quick search on him...whoa."

"What?"

"Did you know Evan Barlow is on the Forbes list of richest doctors?"

Maggie makes a face. "Forbes has a list of richest doctors?"

"Top one hundred, yeah."

"And Barlow is on it?"

"Number forty-two. Net worth estimated at nearly a billion dollars."

"He makes that as a doctor?"

"Not really, no. He makes it as, I don't know, I guess you'd call him a medical entrepreneur. Barlow Cosmetics is a major brand. Plastic surgery is still their mainstay, but they've gotten into home remedies and beauty products. Ironic."

"What?"

"None of the richest doctors made their money seeing patients. It's either from pharmaceuticals or insurance or patents. A few doing biotech, pushing the bounds of medicine, as their slogan says."

"So what does Doctor Barlow want with me?"

On the too-small screen, Marc shrugs. "He was your favorite teacher, right?"

"Yes."

"Your mentor. Close to your family."

Maggie nods. "He told me tonight that he'd always been in love with my mother."

"So maybe that's it. Maybe he just wants to help you out."

"How?"

"Give you a job at Barlow Cosmetics."

"But I lost my license. I can't do surgery."

"You could still do some other kind of work for him."

"Like what? I'm only good at one thing." Maggie sees the smirk on Marc's face. She sighs and rolls her eyes. "Don't say it."

Marc smiles. "What?"

"Just don't."

"You mean about you only being good at one thing?"

"Stop."

"Okay, okay," he says, raising his hand in mock surrender. "But I still think it's most likely Barlow knows your situation and wants to help."

Because her head is down and her eyes are on the screen, Maggie nearly bumps into a group of students walking in the other direction. One of them mutters something about watching where she's going, and she offers a sincere apology because, to be fair, she hates when people are walking with their heads down and eyes on the screen.

"What else do you see?" she asks.

"He opened the first Barlow Cosmetic Center seventeen years ago. Supposedly it's cutting-edge and state-of-the-art."

"What's the difference between those?" Maggie asks.

"What?"

"They always say that in ads. 'Cutting-edge and state-of-the-art.' Aren't they the same thing?"

"Cutting edge refers to the most recent and advanced tools or platforms in a particular field. State of the art refers to the best technology or techniques made up of the most modern methods."

Maggie makes a face. "You just looked that up."

"I did, yes."

"He wasn't a billionaire when we were at Columbia," she says. "He did cleft lift and palates, burns, reconstructive surgery. Worked almost exclusively with the underserved."

"Like you," Marc says.

Maggie shakes her head. "Like us."

"I never did a cleft—"

"You know what I mean."

"I do, yeah. Either way, all that is probably in his past. My guess is, Barlow does mostly breast augmentation and facelifts now. The details on his practice are pretty secretive."

"He's got some famous clients," she says. "They probably demand discretion."

"Probably."

She thinks about it and then figures, *Why not?* "I saw Sleazy Steve."

"Did he hit on you?"

"Yes, but he can pull younger tail now."

"Younger tail?"

"Apparently that's a thing." Then she says, "He said he works at Apollo Longevity." When there's no reply, she says, "I thought it closed down."

"It still has its original mission: longevity. Blood spinning, ozone therapies, cell regeneration, stem cell, EBOO therapy." He grins. "All cutting-edge *and* state-of-the-art."

"But WorldCures is out?"

"There is no more WorldCures, Maggie."

Just like that. Matter-of-fact as can be.

"Right," she says. "I know."

"So when are you going up to New York?"

"Tomorrow morning," she says. "I'm going to call your dad at Vipers, see if he's around."

"Have you seen him recently?"

"Not since he and the gang road-tripped through here last month."

"How's he doing?"

"You know Porkchop," she says.

Marc doesn't say anything, just waits.

"He's good," she lies.

Maggie turns the final corner. Up ahead is the saltbox colonial she grew up in and where she now resides with her sister Sharon and nephew Cole.

"Maggie?"

"Yes?"

"I have a bad feeling about this."

She stops. "About the meeting with Barlow?"

"Yes."

A cold finger traces down her spine. "What makes you say that?"

"Nothing. I mean, no facts or anything."

"Just a bad feeling?"

"Yes."

"Except," Maggie says, "you don't work off feelings."

No reply.

When Maggie sees her nephew step out of the house, she hits the red disconnect icon and drops the phone in her pocket. Cole pops on a huge smile when he sees his aunt. It's been a tough year for the kid—too much death, divorce, and debt for a fifteen-year-old boy—but Cole always manages a smile for his aunt and his mother. Maggie doesn't know whether the smiles are authentic or not. She suspects not. Cole is so damn kind and perceptive, Maggie suspects that he sees the stress his mother and aunt are under and does his utter best not to add to it.

"Hey, Aunt Maggie."

She gives Cole a hey back. He starts a gangly, endearing trudge toward her. It tweaks her heart, the humanness of his sputtering movements, his youth and vulnerability.

"How's Mom?" Maggie asks.

His face falls. "She's at the kitchen table again."

"It'll be okay," Maggie tells him. Then: "She'll be okay."

"Your being here, with us—I know it's not your responsibility—"

"It's my responsibility," Maggie says.

Cole nods, forces the smile back onto his face. The honk of a horn draws their attention. A car pulls up with a bunch of teens hanging out the windows. They call to Cole, who looks an apology at her, but Maggie smiles and waves him off.

"Go," she says.

"You sure?"

"I got this."

Cole does the gangly trudge toward the car, though this time with more speed. Maggie watches, glad for this bit of normalcy. Her nephew deserves this. The back door opens and swallows him whole.

When the car vanishes down the road, she takes out her phone and calls Vipers. She hears the ringing of the retro black payphone in the corner of the bar with a sign reading OUT OF ORDER so no patrons use it. This is Porkchop's version of a Batphone. Her father-in-law, Porkchop—yes, that's what everyone, even his son, calls him—redefines old school. He doesn't own a mobile phone or computer. For that matter he doesn't own a house or car or television. Porkchop once told her, "All I own is a motorcycle and the open road," and when she made a face, he shrugged and said, "I read that on a matchbook in some biker bar in Sturgis."

When the phone is picked up, a woman speaks. She sounds somehow both young and like she's seen it all. "Vipers for Bikers."

Maggie can hear the customary background racket of the biker bar. "Bat Out of Hell" is on the jukebox, one of Porkchop's favorites, Meatloaf right now rocking that when the night is over, he'll be gone, gone, gone. Maggie and Marc played the song at their wedding, she and Marc and Porkchop and Sharon standing in a circle on the dance floor, shouting every lyric at the top of their lungs until Marc pulled her close and the world vanished and the song softened for a moment and Marc sang along that she's the only thing in this whole world that's pure and good and right. And then they stared at each other until the song picked back up again and she's reminded that Meatloaf is really singing about their last night together and the stanza ends with him screaming, "We'll both be so alone."

"Is Porkchop there?"

"No."

Maggie can see the scene—that jukebox in the corner, the sawdust on the floor, the collection of neon beer signs, the heady smell of worn leather, diesel fuel, and testosterone.

"Can I leave a message for him?"

"Depends. You one of his old ladies?"

"Old ladies," Maggie repeats. "Did Porkchop tell you to say that?"

"Yeah."

The man never changes.

"Tell him it's Maggie."

The woman doesn't bother with an "Okay" or "I will." She just hangs up.

Maggie puts away her phone and enters the house, nearly tripping over a pair of Cole's sneakers the size of small canoes. "Hello?"

"In the kitchen," Sharon calls back.

The house is stuck somewhere in the...Maggie wasn't even sure of the era. Seventies? Eighties? When you grow up in it, you don't get how dated your own home is, and of course there is nothing wrong with that. The green-beige curtains are too heavy with tassels. The Persian carpets are pattern-complicated and threadbare. The antique "knickknack cabinet"—that's what Mom had called it—has dozens of small, silver-framed photographs, most of them black-and-white, along with various cheesy figurines like Hummel children—boy in apple tree, girl with umbrella, that kind of thing. They had always been there, as far as Maggie knew. She didn't remember her parents ever buying or putting one up or moving one or changing any. None of the knickknacks seemed to hold any particular significance to her parents. They never talked about where the Hummels came from, but Maggie assumes, knowing her parents, that someone had gifted them or they'd inherited them and their fate was either storage in the basement or placement on the knickknack cabinet.

It wasn't that her parents were cash-strapped or, to be more blunt, tacky, but it was more that the "Doctors McCabe" couldn't be bothered. Mom and Dad didn't care about the dated wallpaper or the worn shag carpeting. Her parents were wonderful and kind and distracted; they were readers and healers and academics. They spent their money on books and experiences, not upholstery or décor. She could still see them in this living room with their friends, maybe fueled by a little too much alcohol, the debates lasting into the wee hours of the morning in the days when disagreeing was considered a good thing, when differing viewpoints were welcomed because they challenged and honed your thinking rather than producing anger and scorn.

But Maggie isn't in the mood right now for that kind of...Was it nostalgia? What do you call a longing for critical thinking and common sense and decency?

Maggie's family history is still told via framed photos on the fireplace mantel—she and Sharon at their dance recital when Maggie was eight and Sharon was six, various graduations, weddings, births, you know the deal. We have all seen it before. Maggie stops at the largest photograph—a horizontal group shot from her and Marc's wedding. She and Marc are beaming in the center. Next to Maggie is Sharon, her obvious maid of honor. Next to Marc is his best man, Trace Packer. Trace could have been on either side of them, really. Trace had met Maggie first, serving with her as a Field Surgeon 62B in combat for two tour duties.

When she introduced Trace and Marc, the two men hit it off immediately. Eventually the three of them—Marc, Trace, Maggie—would create WorldCures Alliance, one of the world's most dynamic charities, specializing in providing medical services for the most impoverished.

In the photo, Maggie's parents are on the far right, looking heartbreakingly alive and healthy. Now that she looks again, does Maggie see hesitancy in her mother's body language? Or is that "had I but known" projection on her part? Porkchop, Marc's father, is on the far left. All the men wear matching tuxedos, except for Porkchop, who did don the bow tie and piqué bib white shirt but kept on the leather biker jacket and the smile-skull jewelry, and Maggie would have wanted it no other way.

As though on cue, her phone rings. The incoming call simply says PAYPHONE.

"Hello?"

Porkchop's gruff voice barks. "What's wrong?"

"Nothing," Maggie says, still looking at Porkchop's image in the old wedding photograph. "Well, except that whoever answered your phone is referring to fellow women as your 'old ladies.'"

"What, you prefer my 'girlfriends'?"

"Not really."

"What then? My 'hotties'? 'Main squeezes'? 'Love monkeys—'"

"Did you say 'love monkeys'?"

"My bae, my boo, cuddle muffins—"

"Please stop."

"Some of the youngins call them 'shorties,'" Porkchop continues. "That better?"

"No," Maggie says. "And never use the term 'youngins' again."

"It's cute when I say it."

"Yeah, it's really not."

"Sooooo," Porkchop says, dragging out the word, "this has been a fun icebreaker. What's wrong, Maggie?"

"Can't I call to say hello?"

"Sure."

Silence.

"I'm coming up to Manhattan tomorrow," Maggie says.

"Taking the Amtrak?"

"Yes."

"Time?"

"The seven fourteen."

"I'll pick you up. You'll tell me all then."

Porkchop disconnects the call. Maggie's eyes travel across the wedding photograph again, her mind blank and everywhere all at once.

From the kitchen, Sharon calls out, "Maggie?"

She wrestles her eyes from the photograph, inhales, and, taking a cue from her nephew, forces up a smile. When Maggie enters the kitchen, Sharon is sitting at the table, per what Cole said, her laptop open, papers strewn as though someone had dropped them from a great height. There is an open bottle of red from the Château Haut-Bailly. Just seeing it leads to a deep pang in her chest that has nothing to do with her sister's recent desire to drink to excess.

"What are you doing?" Maggie asks.

Sharon looks up. "Coding to enable a hyperdimensional generative interference through stochastic gradient descent optimization of artificial intelligence by leveraging—should I continue?"

"Please don't."

Sharon takes off her reading glasses. "So how was the event?"

"Pretty good, actually."

"Liar."

Sharon is a genius. For real. Maggie had been a top student—high school salutatorian (damn Stuart Kleinman beating her for the valediction spot by .003 GPA points), driven from a young age to be a physician like her parents—but her sister Sharon had been a true polymath, what teachers and administrators used to call "academically gifted" or "overly advanced" or most commonly, "child prodigy." Sharon could have graduated high school at the age of eleven, but the truth is—a truth her parents both understood early on—child prodigies don't make it long-term. Think about the ones you knew growing up. Where are they now? See? They end up paralyzed by anxiety or abandon too many hobbies or spiral into self-doubt and self-hate or . . . Who knows?

They crash and burn.

Her parents, understanding this, encouraged excelling, but they insisted on routine and normalcy. Dad loved to quote Flaubert on the subject: "Be regular and orderly in your life, so you may be violent and original in your work."

But it was never easy for Sharon. Her brain couldn't—still can't—slow down. Her neural signaling and power impulses and transmission synapses, whatever—they all ran too hot. Brain activity is commonly referred to as electrical, and hers would surge until the fuse blew. She couldn't ease up or pace it. Even the smallest mistake would cause Sharon to obsess, blow it out of proportion, self-flagellate.

"Who gave out Mom's award?" Sharon asks.

"Bonnie Tillman."

"Oh, good. Mom liked Bonnie."

"Don't rub it in."

"What?"

"Never mind. And Mom never liked her. She said she'd make a great doctor."

"Same thing to Mom," Sharon says, which was true.

Sharon too had served in the military, albeit for a clandestine branch of the army, breaking codes and developing AI, refining advanced reconnaissance software. At some point, Sharon and her husband, Tad—Cole's father—turned to doing tech work privately, building an app that could in fact change the world. Sharon had designed a more advanced "humanoid AI" in the hopes the device might enhance and improve well-being through constant and immediate access to experts. Would you like to speak to your physician at any hour? Sharon's anthropomorphic AI version of your favorite doctor is always available for a chat. Care to consult your attorney twenty-four seven, though this version of them has the wisdom of a thousand attorneys? Sharon's app can do that. Do you sometimes need an emergency session with your therapist, maybe in the middle of the night, but of course, they aren't available? Well, the AI version is there for you twenty-four seven, and for a small fee...

You get the gist.

On a practical level, the possibilities are an endless wow. But the moral implications started to weigh on Sharon, slow her down. Tad, who saw the dollar signs and realized, perhaps correctly, that someone might beat them in this global race, didn't like that. He stole their patents by having Sharon sign papers she didn't understand, and then he ran off with his assistant. The subsequent divorce had been brutal. Sharon tried every legal avenue to remedy the situation, but Tad's father was a powerful federal judge, and if you think our legal system is about truth or fairness or equality, you're either not paying attention or delusional.

Now Sharon is in heavy debt with no recourse.

Kind of like Maggie.

Yes, the McCabe Girls, raised by the Doctors McCabe to excel and be so accomplished, have been sidelined by enormous financial burdens, legal peril, and yes, scandal, with seemingly no options left.

Except, maybe, perhaps, who knows, Maggie's old mentor in New York?

"Tell me the truth," Sharon says. "How was the event really?"

"So many students adored Mom."

"I meant for you?"

"Oh." Maggie thinks a moment: "Shit."

"Sorry," Sharon says.

"Yeah, it's okay."

"Can't say we're surprised."

"We are not, no," Maggie says. "Doctor Barlow was there."

"Oh, that must have been nice for you."

"It was," Maggie says. "He told me he was in love with Mom."

"I bet he wasn't the only one," Sharon says.

"Yeah."

"What?"

"Nothing," Maggie says with a head shake. She scans the papers on the table. They aren't scientific research—they're bills. "What's up with this?"

Sharon puts on the half-moon reading glasses again and peers over the top of them. "I'm calculating our financial options."

"And?"

"And we have to sell the house."

"Not yet."

"Mags, it's just a house. You get that, right? An inanimate object. A corporeal entity. Inert matter. Wood, bricks, mortar. It's not . . ."

"Mom and Dad," she finishes for her sister. "I know. Look, I'm going to New York tomorrow. Let's talk about it when I get back."

That gets Sharon's attention. "What's in New York?"

Maggie had planned to tell her about Barlow's invitation, even though Barlow had insisted she not, but now that the moment is here, she is suddenly hesitant. She isn't worried about betraying Barlow's trust—her sister trumps an old mentor—but it suddenly feels like the wrong move to drag Sharon into this until she knows more.

Sharon mistakes the pause for something else. "Are you, uh, meeting someone?"

"What? No."

"It's okay—"

"Sharon—"

"Okay, never mind. Did you see any guys from your class at this thing?"

"Sleazy Steve."

Sharon makes a face. "Eww, gross."

"Right?"

"So why are you going to New York City?"

"To see Porkchop."

Sharon pins her with a gaze. "What else?"

"What do you mean, what else?"

"It goes without saying that we all love Porkchop," Sharon says, "but he'd road-trip down here if you need to see him."

Maggie sighs. "Just . . . There's a possible business situation."

"What kind of business situation?"

"God, you're nosy."

"I prefer 'inquisitive.'"

"Can you be okay with me saying 'I don't want to tell you yet'?" Maggie asks.

"If you can be okay with me saying, 'I worry a little.'"

"Don't worry."

"I'd never judge you, Mags."

"I know." Then: "Also there's nothing to judge."

"What about Trace?"

Maggie feels the cold travel down her spine again. "What about him?"

"Is he back? Will you see him in New York?"

"Trace is still overseas," she says. "Bangladesh, I think."

"Trying to resuscitate WorldCures?"

Maggie shakes her head. There is zero chance of resuscitation. Sharon knows that, which makes the comment weird, but Sharon can be that way. Maggie McCabe, the face of WorldCures, is a pariah now. The funding is gone.

"In other news"—Sharon lets loose a deep breath—"I signed up for a dating app."

"Good for you. About time."

"The app is called Melody Cupid. It matches you by musical taste."

Maggie puts her hand to her mouth. "Oh God."

"What?"

"You have terrible taste in music."

CHAPTER THREE

When Maggie gets off the Amtrak at New York City's Moynihan Train Hall, Porkchop is already waiting by the tracks.

Porkchop is not playing with a phone. He's not shuffling his feet. He just stands there with Zen-like patience, an older version of his surgeon son. Porkchop looks like what he is—a lifelong biker. He's got the salt-and-pepper beard, green bandana holding back the long hair, leather jacket, faded blue jeans with splashes of motor oil discoloring them. His silver belt buckle is a skull and crossbones. His skin is tan and weathered from years on the road, his face handsome and hard, like something carved into stone.

Porkchop meets her eye and gives the slightest of nods. If he'd been wearing a cowboy hat, he would have tipped it at her. She hurries over, trying not to run, and Porkchop spreads his thick arms wide to welcome her. When he hugs her, she vanishes for a moment. Her eyes close. Porkchop is a big bear of a man. He makes her feel small and safe, and since those feelings don't come often, Maggie just settles into that for a few moments. He holds her close and stays silent. Porkchop exudes both calm and electricity.

Like his son.

There is the faint whiff of Marlboros—Porkchop has always been a smoker—and here that familiar smell deepens her comfort. She almost asks him for a cigarette, even though she hasn't smoked in ten years.

Once they step back, Porkchop asks, "Where are you staying?"

There is no reason for the normal "how are you, how was the trip" type pleasantries with Porkchop; the embrace took care of those.

"Aman hotel."

"Whoa. Classy."

"Yes."

"I thought you were broke."

"I'm not paying for it."

Porkchop arches an eyebrow, and she sees the echo of his son when he does. "Oh?"

"It's a business proposition," she says.

"Oh?"

"Stop that."

Porkchop grabs her overnight bag, and they start for the door. "Want to tell me about it?"

"I do not," Maggie says.

"Then should we head to Vipers?"

"It's a little early, no?"

"We do a nice brunch now."

"Seriously?"

"Tourist trade, my dear. The gang is anxious to see you."

Vipers for Bikers is partially what it sounds like—a biker bar located in the shadow of MetLife Stadium off Route 17. Back in the day, it was a hardcore biker bar/strip joint with the moniker, written out in neon flickering script, Hotties on Hogs. Porkchop had bought Hotties when it went bankrupt eight years ago and gentrified it into a touristy cosplay biker bar/restaurant called Vipers for Bikers.

"That's nice," Maggie says. "And I want to see everyone." Then she puts her hand on Porkchop's arm. "But I need to stop at Trace's apartment before we go."

She waits for Porkchop's reaction, but she doesn't get much of one. "Why?"

"Because I always do that when I'm in the city."

"Uh-huh."

"And maybe we can get a beat on where he is."

"Bangladesh."

"Do we still believe that?" Maggie asks.

Porkchop doesn't reply.

They exit the station onto a packed Eighth Avenue. Madison Square Garden in all its coliseum-like splendor is across the street. Porkchop's bike is parked on the corner of 31st Street. Maggie is surprised when she sees it isn't a Harley-Davidson.

"Since when do you ride a BMW R 18, Porkchop?"

"Since they started sponsoring me."

"For real?"

Porkchop nods. "I get a free bike, free gas, plus a grand a month."

"Sweet," she says.

"I also prefer the BMW's shaft transmission over the belt transmission of a Harley. Makes for a smoother ride. The BMW has three ride modes—rain, roll, and rock—whereas the Harley only has one."

"They tell you to say that?"

"And exactly that," he replies with a grin. "Took me three weeks to memorize it."

Two young bikers guard the BMW. Both wear a patch with the Serpents and Saints logo on their upper right sleeve. Serpents and Saints is Porkchop's . . . She would call it a motorcycle "gang," but that brought up Hells Angels connotations and that didn't come close to fitting anymore. Maybe thirty years ago. Not anymore.

The Serpents and Saints logo is a mean-looking, black-and-gold, heavily fanged snake with a halo over its head. Marc had a tattoo of it on his upper right quadriceps, albeit a far more cartoonish version with a goofily smiling serpent who looked about as mean as Snoopy. Instead of black and gold, his Serpent and Saint was garish orange and purple; instead of an intimidating glare, his serpent had a silly, exaggerated wink.

The tattoo, Marc had explained in bed, was the result of a late-night drunken visit to a New Orleans parlor on Mardi Gras when he was nineteen.

"It's kind of ugly," she'd told him.

"Don't worry, my love. Only you'll see it. Unless you think I should wear a Speedo."

"Only I'll see it."

One of the young bikers is tall, thin, long-haired, white. The other is short, round, buzz-cut, Black. Together, they look like a bowling ball heading toward a pin. Porkchop takes two helmets from the Pin and hands her one. Maggie straps it on and hops on the back of his bike.

"Pinky will drop your bag at the Aman."

Pinky, she now sees, is Bowling Ball. Porkchop, Pinky—the members like nicknames. Pinky takes her suitcase. Porkchop gets on the front of the bike. Maggie wraps her arms around his waist and feels the hum as Porkchop starts up the engine. When Marc had first introduced Maggie to his father, it had taken her a little time to get used to riding on the back. It wasn't that Maggie didn't trust Porkchop's driving—it's just that she hated to be in any situation where she wasn't in control.

Now she relishes it. No talking. No music. No podcast. Nothing but the feel of the world being washed away by the wind.

Porkchop cruises them up Eighth Avenue. They turn west to Riverside Drive and then back north. Fifteen minutes later, Porkchop pulls up to the front of their old apartment building in Washington Heights, four blocks from NewYork-Presbyterian medical center. For a long moment, she and Porkchop just stand there, both of them straddling the bike.

"Porkchop?"

"It's fine. Go. I'll wait here for you."

She watches Porkchop for another moment, but he is already fiddling with something near the throttle. As she turns toward the entrance, the doorman greets her with a wide smile. "Doctor Maggie!"

"Hey, Winston."

Winston looks as though he wants to hug her, but decorum is what it is. She wants to reach out too, but she isn't sure she can handle another hug right now. They both stand there for an awkward second before Winston's smile fades away.

"I'm sorry about..." He stops. "Just about everything."

"Thank you."

"You still have Doctor Trace's key?"

"I do," she says, showing it to him. "Have you seen him at all?"

"Not in many months," Winston says. "Doctor Trace's mailbox got all filled up. We emptied it out, put everything in a box for you. It's in his apartment."

"Thanks."

Maggie stays quiet as the elevator dings its way up to the eighth floor. They had all moved in at the same time. Maggie and Marc had taken a two bedroom on the fourth floor. Trace had grabbed a one bedroom on the eighth. They'd chosen this building because it was reasonably priced and had doormen and, most importantly, it was walking distance to NewYork-Presbyterian medical center. All three of them had crazy hours doing their surgical residencies.

She unlocks his door and enters. She expects the place to smell stale, but it doesn't. There is almost no dust, and Maggie wonders whether Trace hired a housekeeper. Probably. At Camp Arifjan in Kuwait, the team used to tease Trace for being such a neat freak. Maggie had at first seen Trace as more hyperorganized, an überpreparer, someone tightly wound in a way that made him focused, detailed, a great surgeon.

The furniture is modular, beige, functional; everything about the place screams, "A man lives here alone." There are two items on display with any flair or prominence—and they stand side by side on his acrylic dining room table. The first is a model of the human heart signed by two legendary cardiothoracic surgeons credited with creating the first artificial heart, Michael DeBakey and Denton Cooley. It's the kind of anatomy model you might find in any doctor's office or biology class.

The second item, displayed under Plexiglas next to the DeBakey-Cooley model, is an inoperative (though it would definitely be described as cutting-edge and state-of-the-art) prototype of, per the engraving, **THUMPR7-TAH**—what they'd all hoped would eventually be the next generation in making artificial hearts more permanent and efficient.

Maggie stares at the device, pushing away the bad flashback. The THUMPR7 had been developed and registered by WorldCures Alliance—that is, Marc, Trace, Maggie. She hadn't wanted that—her name attached—because though she had trained in cardiothoracic surgery and assisted Marc and Trace plenty of times, she'd opted to make reconstructive and trauma surgery her official specialties.

The TAH stands for Total Artificial Heart, but the THUMPR7, despite its blend of robotic design, DNA coding, and stem cell research, remained a distant pipe dream.

Maggie knows that better than anyone.

On the wall, there is a framed color photograph taken by war photojournalist Ray Levine on what had been one of the worst combat days for Maggie and Trace. From his embedded perch on the ground in Kamdesh, Levine had gotten an almost surreal shot of Maggie and Trace furiously working to save two soldiers while their medevac UH-60 Black Hawk copter hovered above the ground. The sky above them is striking blue, the blood on their hands striking red, and something about the composition made it appear that Maggie and Trace were somehow defying gravity, that there was no way they wouldn't tumble out of the copter in the next second or two, that the only thing preventing disaster had to be some kind of divine hand keeping them up in the air.

Maggie remembers it all too vividly. Trace's soldier survived. Maggie's did not.

Only two hours after that mission ended—right after they showered and cleaned up—Trace came to her tent and said, "Come on, let's go."

"Trace . . ."

He held up the bag of lollipops. "Now."

Trace did this almost every time, especially when the mission had been particularly bloody. He grabbed a jeep and drove Maggie to the local town. When they pulled in, Trace shouted, "I'm here!" Children came running out from everywhere, squealing with delight. They already knew Trace—and his beloved lollipops. He started passing them out, smiling, nodding for Maggie to do the same. Several adults came out to greet them and offer them food. Maggie passed, but Trace told her she was being rude. He devoured everything, to their hosts' delight. Then he played some kind of exhausting tag game with two boys. More children came out. Trace made funny faces and farting noises—mouth-to-palm style—and they all howled with laughter.

Maggie just watched in awe.

Trace.

That night, after they got back to camp, she and Trace lay under the stars, the smell of thyme and cedar in the cool desert air. For a long time, neither spoke, comfortable in the silence. Then Maggie whispered a truth into the dark sky:

"The dead don't leave us."

Not ever. The dead stay by your side, as though you held on too hard as they tried to pull away and something had broken off. The man dying in Ray Levine's photograph was named Greg Steeple. He'd been twenty-one years old and had a mother and a father and two younger brothers and a fiancée named Claire.

"And yet," Trace whispered back, "we'll always long for this thrum in the blood."

That is what they don't warn you about when it comes to combat.

It's terrifying, it's awful, it's the worst thing imaginable, you wish it on no one.

But it's also addictive.

She can't get the faces of the dead out of her mind.

But she also can't get the memory of the adrenaline spike out of her blood.

The unspoken part of what makes it hard for combat soldiers to come home isn't the flashbacks or the fear of returning—it's almost the opposite. It's the sudden quiet, the cloying calm, the suffocating safeness and sameness of normal life. One moment you're ducking bullets, half hanging out of a moving helicopter, your hands working inside a warm abdomen to keep some kid like Greg alive—and then, what, you're supposed to go back to your suburban split-level and do laundry and pick up your kids from soccer practice and sit in too much traffic on your way to work?

It would be easy to say they—she, Marc, Trace—created World-Cures Alliance for purely altruistic reasons. That had been a good story—three combat doctors who saw a need and eschewed the comforts of home to save the needy and revolutionize health care, but that felt too much like spin to Maggie. It's not that you are not genuinely concerned about your patients—you acutely are—or don't believe in your mission—they did—but the terrible secret, the secret she and Marc and Trace shared, is that you do it to be special. To paraphrase Eminem, a normal life is boring. The idea of going home to the kids, the laundry, the car pool...no, not for, pardon the play on words, M&M.

Scratch the surface of a person doing good works, and you'll find someone who fears the mundane and conventional.

There is only one other framed photograph in the room—a slightly faded color one of a smiling ten-year-old Trace Packer on the Jersey Shore with his matching-smiling mother, Karen. Genetics. There is no doubt that these two are mother and son. In the photo, Karen wears the stunning square-cut emerald ring that always adorned her finger. A family heirloom, Karen had once explained to Maggie, given to her by her own grandmother. Years later, at Karen's funeral, Trace clutched the green emerald in his hand for the entire ceremony. Maggie never forgot that image—Trace, sitting in the front pew by himself, opening and closing his fist, staring at his mother's glistening square-cut emerald, as though the gemstone had some magical power that could bring his mother back to life.

Trace has a floor-to-ceiling redwood wine rack on the one wall that would get no sunlight. She checks the bottles. All reds from Château Haut-Bailly, a Bordeaux from the Pessac-Léognan appellation. Maggie knows it well. Trace, a true Francophile whose second love after medicine is French wines, had invested in it—count on Trace—and she and Marc had visited the vineyard not long before she returned to Baltimore to take care of her mother. Maggie remembers that trip to Bordeaux so vividly. It was after a particularly grueling month in a huge refugee camp in Kakuma. They needed the break before heading to Dubai, but neither she nor Marc handled their spirits well. Trace arranged for his "closest pals" what he labeled "a palate pilgrimage"—a fancy term for a tasting where everyone gets overserved—and it had been fabulous and delicious and then she and Marc both got sloppy and laughed too much and, man, that had been a night.

No need to go there right now, Maggie thinks.

The pain never goes away. The pain never lets you go. You just learn to live with it.

Maggie forces herself to turn away, and when she does, she spots the cardboard box loaded with mail. She drops to her knees and thumbs through it. Junk mostly. Trace had set up automatic bill pay on most everything—utilities, rent, cable, internet, whatever—so it's mostly ads from real estate agents ("Look What Sold in Your Neighborhood!"), discounts for food takeout, and furniture catalogues.

There is also a letter from Wells Fargo Bank.

Hmm. Maggie takes hold of it and lifts it into view. It's thin—one page or two at the most—so it's not a financial statement. She wonders whether she should open it, but of course, that's why Trace had asked her to stop by whenever she was in town—to make sure everything was in order and copacetic. She doesn't want to look as though she's invading his privacy, but does she just ignore this?

It's probably an ad for a credit card or something.

Except it doesn't feel like that. It feels like something important.

She slits the envelope. There is only one sheet of paper.

It's a bill for a safe deposit box.

Maggie's first thought is Trace's mother's square-cut green-emerald ring. Karen's emerald, she remembers, had been appraised for over twenty thousand dollars. It isn't like Trace wore it. He'd have wanted to keep it safe. Where better?

But—check that—it's a bill for *three* safe deposit boxes. Two of them are ten inches by ten inches. One is three feet by six feet.

A little much for a piece of jewelry.

She reads both the front and the back of the bill to see where the safe deposit boxes are kept. Oddly enough, it doesn't say. She looks at the postmark—the bill was mailed two weeks ago from San Francisco. That's probably the main headquarters for the bank. Is that where he keeps the boxes? She doubts it but maybe. Had she ever heard Trace talk about San Francisco? Not that she can remember.

So now what?

Do the smart thing, she figures. Maggie snaps a photo of the bill, scrolls to Trace in contacts, and texts him the image with a quick note:

Want me to pay it or will you handle?

No reply. Then again, there hadn't been one in a very long time.

Maggie stares at the bill from the bank for another moment before putting it back in the envelope and dropping it into the cardboard box. She then does a quick walk around the apartment, turns the faucets on and off, flushes the toilet, makes sure the windows are locked. Everything seems in place. She wonders about the keys to Trace's safe deposit boxes. Does Trace keep them here, in a drawer somewhere?

Does it matter?

Her phone buzzes. She looks down and sees a text from Dr. Barlow.

> **Barlow:** Pickup tomorrow at 8AM. Black Mercedes Maybach with tinted windows.
>
> **Maggie:** No need. I'll make my own way to your office.
>
> **Barlow:** Better we drive you.
>
> **Maggie:** You're on Park Avenue and 51st. It'll be a nice walk through the park.
>
> **Barlow:** No.
>
> **Maggie:** No?

There's a delay and the three dancing dots seem to sputter before the next text pops up.

Barlow: Pickup tomorrow at 8AM. Black Mercedes Maybach with tinted windows.

She sighs. No reason to press it right now. She makes sure to turn off all the lights and heads back down.

———————

Back on the street, Porkchop leans against his bike, doing the Zen patient-waiting thing again.

"Anything?" he asks.

She'd planned to tell him about the safe deposit boxes, but what's the point? "All good," she says.

Porkchop shakes his head.

"What?"

"First you don't tell me why you're here. Now you won't tell me what you found in the apartment."

Porkchop was seventeen years old when he became a father with Marc. Yes, seventeen. Marc's mother had been Porkchop's high school math teacher. She was thirty-six and married with three kids when she got pregnant by her student. She wanted to abort. Porkchop didn't like that. He convinced her to go to full term—there may have been some threat of public exposure involved—and give Porkchop custody of Marc.

So yes, Maggie's dream man had been raised by a single teen dad in a motorcycle gang. It made for a strange yet wonderful upbringing.

Porkchop says, "Spill it."

"It's a big nothing."

He beckons with both hands for her to go on.

"There was a bill for some safe deposit boxes," she says.

"Do tell."

She does. Porkchop listens without reacting. When she's finished,

Porkchop scratches his beard. "Why wouldn't you want to tell me about that?"

"It wasn't that I didn't want to tell you," she says. "It just seems irrelevant."

"Hmm."

"So what do we do now?" Maggie asks.

Porkchop gives her a charismatic grin and wiggles his eyebrows. "We get shit-faced drunk at Vipers."

CHAPTER FOUR

When Maggie's alarm goes off the next morning, she sits up fast—
too fast, her head reeling in protest. A jackhammer batters her
skull from the inside. Her heart thumps deep in her chest. She flashes
back to the night before, at Vipers, sitting on that cracked-leather stool,
the floor sticky from spilled beer, Bob Seger's "Night Moves" on the
jukebox, the bar loud and growing hazier, old friends embracing her,
regaling her with familiar stories of Marc as a precocious child, stories
she's heard a dozen times before and had always relished. But not
tonight. She tried so hard to listen, to engage, to give her full attention
to every single person who approached because they deserved that
at the very least, but even as she tried to hold on, Maggie could feel
herself slipping away into her own personal darkness. She drank her
whiskey neat—Porkchop was currently endorsing Laphroaig 10 Year
Old Islay—the weathered faces surrounding her, getting too close,
blurring, becoming one indistinguishable mash. Then other faces
emerged in their stead, dozens, maybe more, faces with pleading eyes,
staring up at her with the blend of hope and despair that only a doctor
witnesses. Marah, Joseph, Ahmed, Seema . . . And then, in the end, the
last face, always the last face, was Kabir's. She tried to comfort them,
tried to stop the bleeding, tried to understand what they were saying
to her. But they were speaking a foreign language, their pained words

drowned out by mortar fire and the roar of helicopter rotors and the screams.

Give me another chance, Maggie thinks. *I'll fix them.*

And sometimes, in her dreams, she gets that chance. The big do-over. They are alive. All of them. She can save them if she moves fast enough. She feels a sudden joy, a rush of hope, an odd clarity and focus and even peacefulness, and then something outside the dream—the alarm going off, Sharon calling out to her, Cole slamming the front door, whatever—pulls her away. There's this brief, horrible moment where Maggie is still in the dream, rising out of that cusp between sleep and consciousness, when the faces begin to fade away, dissolve, and Maggie realizes with cruel certainty that this is not reality, that this is a dream, that she will soon wake up to a world where the dead will always be dead.

Enough, she tells herself.

Maggie throws her feet off the bed and onto the floor. She takes a few deep breaths, lets her pulse slow down. She tries to remember the last time she drank too much, and an outdoor bar in Juba on a hot South Sudan evening comes to mind. Trace kept buying rounds of Araqi, a delicious date-based liquor, and Maggie and Marc kept imbibing. There had been lots of laughs as there always are after too much horror. Trace had a girl with him—Maggie couldn't remember her name because Trace always had a nameless girl with him and then the girl would be gone and there'd be another. Trace doesn't like attachments. Or more likely, he can't do them. On the surface, Trace gives off that sort of healable fragility, that vulnerability that draws in every woman who thinks they can fix him, but whatever is broken inside of him stayed broken.

Where is Trace Packer right now?

No clue.

Maggie blinks. It takes her a few moments to get her bearings.

She's at the Aman hotel.

She stumbles out of bed, flicks on the light, enters a ginormous bathroom. On her right is a too-inviting pink-crème bathtub the approximate size of a Cadillac Escalade. On her left is a black-stone shower room—room, not stall—with an array of showerheads. Maggie chooses the shower, in part because she fears that if she sinks into that bathtub with its potpourri of bath crystals and bath teas and bath salts and bath oils and bath pillows, she may never be able to extract herself.

She strips out of the oversize T-shirt she slept in last night. The T-shirt is from the Vipers gift shop. Porkchop had given it to her. Across the chest, it reads:

I DON'T SNORE. I DREAM I'M A MOTORCYCLE.

Hard to escape the dad jokes with Porkchop.

Maggie turns on the showerheads, all of them, full blast. She steps into the middle and lets the sprays blast away at her skin from every direction. The water pressure is excellent, almost piercing her skin. She doesn't want to move. She thinks back to her time overseas, how she'd yearn for a hot shower, how she realized that one of life's greatest and most unappreciated luxuries was a hot shower. If you think about it, no human on planet Earth had even experienced a hot shower until, what, a hundred years ago maybe? She once googled it—because that's how her brain works—and hot showers were not common until the 1970s.

"Enjoy the smaller moments," her father had often told her. "That's where life is lived."

So she does—at least for right now. After some time passes, when she realizes that she must regretfully turn off the sprays and step out of her black-stoned cocoon, there are plush Frette robes and thick towels. The hotel phone rings, a gentle gong, letting guests know that there is an incoming call but not wanting to disturb their serenity.

Maggie answers. The voice on the other end of the line probably does voice-overs for hypnosis apps. The voice asks what food or beverage she "craves" for breakfast, promising an arrival in five minutes.

"Coffee," she says. "Black. Strong."

"The Florentine omelet is a specialty."

Maggie passes. Just the coffee.

Her mobile phone jangles in the stillness. It's Porkchop. She answers on speakerphone.

"Good morning," she says in a quiet voice.

"Why are you whispering?" he asks.

"Something about this room is making me stay quiet."

"You quiet? Must be a miracle room."

"Are you being a wiseass?"

"Just a little." Then he adds, "You okay?"

"I'm good."

He waits.

She sighs. "It was just a lot, you know."

"I do."

"I wasn't really prepared for that."

"That's on me."

"No, it's not," she says.

"Everyone was happy to see you."

"I know I sort of zoned out."

"You did, yeah."

"I hope I wasn't rude."

"You're family—no such thing as rude," Porkchop says. "How are you feeling now?"

"Pretty hungover."

"Same."

"Wait, you?"

"I'm not as young as I used to be, Mags."

Pinky had been the designated biker. He drove her back last night.

She feels weird about having too much to drink, but again, her issue had been pills, not booze, and boy, that sounds like a pathetic loophole. So did the idea that she had "issues" with pills and not an "addiction." She had stopped taking them cold after the...What does she call it? Incident? Accident? Catastrophe? Could she have done that—stopped the pills cold—if it had been a real addiction? She doubts it, but does it matter? The damage was done.

She isn't sure what to say next, but Porkchop takes over, asking in a quasi-mocking tone whether she's on her way to her "big, secret meeting."

"I need to get dressed," she says.

"Call me when you're done."

"You don't have a mobile phone," she reminds him.

"I'll be by the payphone. Are you sure you don't want to tell me what this meeting is about?"

"Bye, Porkchop."

She hangs up and throws on black jeans, boots, a denim shirt, and a blazer. It's a massive mind melt that never seems to have a clear answer: Never be too provocative but never be too stuffy...Oh, but have a sense of style and always know what's trending so you don't appear, gasp, out of date—always trying to find the right balance between feminine and practical.

Utterly exhausting.

Maggie props up her phone on the bathroom vanity as she starts her makeup. She hits the icon and waits. When Marc's face appears, Maggie says, "I saw your dad yesterday."

"How is he?"

She chooses a little avoidance because she doesn't want to go there right now. "Vipers is doing great. You ought to see what he's done with it."

"Did you both get drunk?"

"No." Then: "Yes, of course."

Marc smiles. "I'm glad you two have each other."

Which is an odd thing to say.

"How long until your meeting with Evan Barlow?" he asks.

Maggie checks the clock on her phone. "Shoot, I'm running late. Talk later."

She takes one last look in the mirror, shrugs, pockets the phone, and heads into the corridor. She reaches the fourteenth-floor atrium. The elevator doors are already open and waiting for her. The Mercedes-Maybach is parked at the quieter entrance on 57th Street. The chauffeur wears a black suit, black tie, and completes the look with a peaked newsboy cap. He holds the back door open.

"Hi," she says. "I'm Maggie."

"I'm Alou."

She sticks out her hand and meets his eye. "Nice to meet you, Alou."

He hesitantly shakes it. "Yes, ma'am."

The windows are fully tinted, so no one can see in. She slides onto the plush leather in the back. The seat's heater is already on full blast. There is a woman in the front passenger seat. She turns and gives Maggie the full-wattage smile.

"Hi, Maggie, I'm Dawn! I'm your Barlow concierge!"

Dawn speaks in exclamation marks, which are not welcome this early in the morning ever, never mind after a night at Vipers with Porkchop. Maggie looks back at Alou before he closes her door. He shrugs as if to say, "Yeah, this is how it is."

"Hi, Dawn."

"Many of our patients demand total confidentiality!"

"I'm not a patient, Dawn."

She blinks and the full-wattage smile flickers but stays strong. "Oh, I know. We just thought you might want to experience the service. Plus, well, I was asked to assure your ride is comfortable and discreet."

"I appreciate that. Where are we going?"

"To see Doctor Barlow, of course."

She turns to face forward. The car starts up. Maggie stays quiet for a moment. When they start heading north on Madison Avenue, she leans forward and says, "Isn't Barlow Cosmetics south of here?"

"That's the public office," Dawn says. "We think of it as our storefront. Most of the elite surgeries are done in, shall we say, a more private location."

"And that's where we're going?"

"That's where we are going, yes."

"Can you tell me where specifically?"

"I never remember the address. It won't be long. Would you like a Minus 181 mineral water?"

Ten minutes later, the Mercedes heads into a garage under a Dolce & Gabbana. There are cars lined up to be parked, but Alou circles around them and veers down a ramp. They drive two floors down and pull up to an elevator with its door open.

"Here we are!" Dawn exclaims in a singsong voice.

Maggie tries to open the door, but it won't give. "I think my door is locked."

Dawn turns to her from the front seat. "First, do you mind leaving your phone here?"

"Pardon?"

"We don't allow phones on the premises. Company policy. For the privacy of you and all our patient—" Dawn stops, corrects herself. "I mean, visitors. Don't worry. Your phone will be safe with Alou."

"And if I don't want to give up my phone?"

Dawn's reply is a disappointed-schoolteacher frown. "I'm afraid we can't make exceptions to this policy."

Maggie debates making a stink or calling Dawn's bluff, saying something like, "Okay, fine, take me back to the hotel," but really, what's the point? She powers down her phone and places it on the seat next to her. Alou opens the back door. Dawn escorts Maggie into the elevator. She presses the button for the eighteenth floor. Maggie stands and watches the light dance upward. Dawn does the same. Maggie has questions, but she sees no point in asking them right now.

The doors open, and it almost feels as though Maggie were back in the Aman. The medical offices—assuming that's what these are—feel more like an upscale spa. Soothing sounds are playing. No one is wearing white—that would be too loud and disconcerting—and so the staff mills around in light-sage surgical garb. Dawn opens a door and invites her to enter. After Maggie does, Dawn gently closes the door behind her.

The room has wall-to-ceiling windows with spectacular views of the Manhattan skyline. Funny. Maggie loves nature—she has experienced every sort of mountain, desert, ocean, valley, canyon, night, day, sunrise, sunset, whatever view imaginable—but something about the skyline in a great city works best for her. She never tires of them. Maybe it's because city views change. They are man-made, not divine, so she can relate to them more on some base level. Or maybe, more likely, it's because you are not alone with this view: It isn't just rock or brick or stone or vegetation—there are people out there, thousands or even hundreds of thousands of them, and they all have hopes and dreams and a spiritual vibrancy and connection that nothing in nature can duplicate.

Man, Maggie thinks, *I'm in a mood.*

"Maggie."

Dr. Barlow enters from the side door, wearing the light-sage scrubs and a surgical cap, though she doesn't think he just got out of surgery or is headed into it. He greets her with a hug and a buss on the cheek. "Sorry for the whole cloak-n-dagger bit, but I thought you might like to see how we handle our more discerning patients."

"It's quite an operation," Maggie says.

"It feels like overkill, I know, but—" Barlow shrugs, waves his arm to have her take a seat on an off-white leather couch. "Some patients will do anything to make sure no one knows they are undergoing a procedure. A few years ago, we had a big-name celebrity who didn't want the tabloids to find out she was getting a rhytidectomy. You know how it is. So to disguise herself, she came to our midtown office in a—I can't believe I'm even saying this—in a burqa."

Maggie frowns. "Wrong in so many ways."

"Exactly. So now we offer greater privacy in this location. We have recovery suites, guest apartments—you get the point. Again, not all our patients want this. In fact, I would say fewer than ten percent purchase the security package. But it's a service we have to offer."

She was getting a bit impatient. "Doctor Barlow—"

"Evan, please."

"Evan, why am I here?"

"You'd find this place intriguing, Maggie," he continues, as if she hadn't spoken. He's staying on a script, she figures, so she'll just have to hang on for the ride. "As you know, we at Barlow Cosmetics are constantly pushing the boundaries. Refining and updating our procedures. We make them less invasive. Fewer scars. Shorter recovery time. You've always been a risk-taker, Maggie. It's what drew you to the military. It's what drew you to provide care in some of the most dangerous countries on the planet. You were never one to color in the lines. Perhaps that led to your..."

He falters here. Maggie helps him.

"Downfall?" she tries. "Destruction? Ruin?"

Barlow shakes his head. "Seems too harsh."

"But apropos," she says.

"I have a question for you."

She waits.

"When the medical board crucified you, why didn't you fight the charges?"

"Because," Maggie says with no hesitation, "I'm guilty."

Barlow isn't sure what to say to that. "So you plan on never doing surgery again."

He says it like that, a statement not a question, and the idea is so unfathomable. Never, ever again do the only thing she ever wanted to do? It breaks her heart anew.

"Looks like," she says, slapping on the brave face. "I might still be able to do research for you, but I think having my name connected to Barlow—"

"I don't want you to do research."

"What then?"

He stares at the window. She joins him. "I work with a select few clients who will pay a premium for complete discretion. A very high premium."

"Yeah, you've made that pretty clear."

"One particular client..." He stops, rubs his chin, considers his words. "I'm going to bring someone in in a moment. He demands complete confidentiality. There can be no record of this meeting. There had originally been a request to have you sign an NDA, but without a recording of this meeting, you'd have nothing to back up any claims."

"What kind of claims?"

"It's not like that."

"Not like what? What exactly is this?"

"Look, I've said too much. You're safe. I promise. I only have your best interest at heart. I think you know that. So let me bring him in. Listen to his offer with an open mind. If I didn't believe this was something you should do, I would never have brought you up here."

Barlow moves back to the side door and opens it. A large man fills the doorway. He almost seems to duck to get inside. When he's fully inside the room, the man struggles to button the blazer on his suit.

"Maggie McCabe," Barlow says, "this is Ivan Brovski."

Brovski is bald and broad. He has no neck, his bullet-shaped head comes straight up from his shoulders. His suit looks expensive and tailored and yet it doesn't fit, because this guy wasn't built to wear a suit. Brovski manages a no-teeth smile and stretches out his hand for her to shake. She obliges. His hand swallows hers whole.

"Nice to meet you, Doctor McCabe," Ivan Brovski says.

There is a hint of a Russian accent, but it is fainter than she would have imagined. He's studied English for a long time. Judging by his accent, probably in London.

Barlow says, "I'll be in the next room if I'm needed." He can't get through the door and close it behind him fast enough.

Maggie is standing. Brovski is standing.

"What can I do for you, Mr. Brovski?"

"I am a liaison for a very wealthy man," Brovski says. "My client is in need of certain medical procedures."

"What kind of medical procedures?" Maggie asks.

"You, Doctor McCabe, are a renowned reconstructive surgeon," he begins, "a recognized expert in several surgical subfields, including cosmetic and facial reconstruction. You graduated summa cum laude from the University of Pennsylvania before attending Johns Hopkins medical school. You've done residencies and fellowships at some of the country's most elite hospitals, and even under the tutelage of our mutual friend Doctor Evan Barlow at NewYork-Presbyterian. Both of your parents were physicians. Your father, Clark McCabe, spent his career as a military doctor, mostly serving gravely war-wounded soldiers at Walter Reed. You followed your father into the military, where you served two full tours in heavy combat, earning you the Medal of Honor, the Distinguished Service Cross, and a Silver Star. You've also been awarded, along with your surgical partner Doctor Trace Packer, the Jackson Foundation award and, perhaps most impressively, a Purple Heart when you both took shrapnel from an IED in the Wardak Province of Afghanistan. After you served, you, Doctor Packer, and your husband, Doctor Marc Adams, created a rather noble charitable entity—"

Maggie holds her hands up. "Yeah, okay, I get it. You googled me, I'm flattered. Why am I here?"

"My employer needs discreet cosmetic surgery done."

"Can you be more specific?"

Brovski rubs the top of his head. "We need you to perform surgery on two people. Cosmetic procedures, as I said. My employer will tell you the specifics when you meet."

Maggie looks left, then right. "Is he here?"

Brovski does the no-teeth grin again. "No."

"So what's the plan here, Ivan?"

"We fly you to a private location."

"Where?"

"Someplace"—he takes his time—"out of the country."

"I'm going to need more than that."

"There is a place called Rublevka. It's—"

"—a suburb outside of Moscow," she finishes for him.

He arches an eyebrow. "You've been?"

"No, but I've heard of it."

Rublevka is the epicenter of the Russian oligarchs, perhaps the wealthiest residential area in the world. Lenin and Stalin had dachas there. Khrushchev and Gorbachev had summer residences.

Brovski nods. "When you were in college, you took a course called Modern Russian History with Professor Taubman. I nearly forgot."

"Do you know when I got my first hickey?"

"What?"

"I bet your researchers missed that. Seventh grade. A game of spin the bottle with Mitch Glassman. You can stop with the 'I know all' intimidation tactics, Ivan. I'm a military brat who grew up military trained, so I know the program. Get on with it."

"Fair enough," Brovski says, amused. "But I think you see what we are after. We are looking for an expert surgeon who is willing to travel to Russia and perform highly confidential cosmetic procedures. We think that expert surgeon should be you."

"What's your client's name?"

"I can't reveal that at this time."

"Is it a name I'd know?"

"I don't know what you know," Brovski says, "but I can tell you that my client values his privacy."

Maggie takes that in for a moment. "You must be aware that my medical license has been revoked."

"Yes, of course," Brovski says. "It's why you're perfect."

"Foreign doctors typically need to meet MIMC licensing to operate in Russia—"

"Done."

"What?"

"It's done," he says. "MIMC has already issued your permit. What else?"

"I'd need two surgically trained nurses and one anesthesiologist."

"Done."

"I'd need extensive operating equipment and a sterile environment."

"Done."

"A fully equipped operating room."

"Done."

"I need to be indemnified in writing if anything goes wrong."

"Done. Done. It's all done." He waves his arms impatiently. "Do you think we thought about doing this an hour ago? Let me also make it clear that we know you're in heavy debt. So is your sister."

Maggie is no longer surprised at what he knows. He works for a top-level Russian oligarch. There is little doubt that whoever is behind this has made sure to check all the angles before making this request.

"So?"

"So the moment you agree to do this," Brovski continues, "that debt will be gone. Yours. And your sister's. The malpractice suit filed against you? It will be settled."

"How?"

Ivan Brovski just shrugs.

Maggie swallows. No more crushing debt. No more trials and depositions. How much is that worth?

A lot.

"Why can't your client just go to a discreet clinic like this one?" Maggie asks.

"He doesn't like to leave the house."

"But he'll have to leave it to go in for surgery."

Brovski shakes his head. "We've built an operating theater in his home. It's state-of-the-art."

That term again.

Maggie takes her time, tries to play it cool.

"What do you say, Doctor McCabe?"

"I'll need to stay for two weeks post-op."

"Yes, of course."

"That's a fair amount of time for me to be away."

"Ah," Brovski says with the hint of a smile, "very good."

She says nothing.

"Let me guess, Doctor McCabe: You're not sure our paying off the debts is adequate compensation."

Maggie shrugs. "What you're asking me to do is pretty risky."

"It's not, not in the least, but fair enough." Brovski checks his watch and feigns boredom. "We are in a bit of a rush, so let me cut to it. If you come with me to the airport right now, on top of getting you and your sister out of debt and settling your malpractice case, how about we pay you..." He pauses and looks up purely for effect. Then he just drops the bomb.

"...ten million dollars?"

If Maggie ever had a poker face, it's gone now. He almost laughs.

"Five million put into your account at Merrill Lynch right now. The other five million when you're done."

Maggie is not sure she can speak. Ivan Brovski grins.

"So we have a deal?"

CHAPTER FIVE

Maggie stares out the window of what could inadequately be described as a "private plane." Not that she's had a lot of experience with private planes, of course. When she boarded, the flight attendant introduced herself as Hannah and then proceeded to give Maggie an orientation tour of a full-size 180-seat Airbus A320 renovated for private use. The new interior more resembles an upscale Manhattan penthouse than anything in the aviation family. The décor is gold with leopard prints. Flight Attendant Hannah leads her through a curving open floor plan with two lounges, a dining room, a gourmet kitchen, a theater room with a 65-inch contoured TV ("One of our four large-screen TVs," Hannah had told her), and a primary suite with a king-size bed and a marble ensuite bathroom, including one of those oversize rain showerheads.

In the primary bedroom, there is a Matisse oil of a woman reclining on a couch.

"Is this a real Matisse?" Maggie asks.

Hannah's reply is a simple smile.

———

Two hours earlier, she and Ivan Brovski finish their meeting at Barlow's, and Ivan leads her back toward the elevator.

"Before we leave," Maggie tells Ivan, "I'd like to speak to Doctor Barlow."

"He's in surgery."

The elevator opens. Maggie gets inside.

Alou and the Mercedes await them in the basement garage. Alou opens the back door. She slides in. Her phone is there. Ivan gets in the other door and sits next to her. She picks up her phone. No service in the garage's underbelly. When the Mercedes finally reaches street level, six notifications for unanswered calls pop up, all from Sharon.

Ivan sees the notifications over her shoulder and smiles.

"What?" Maggie says.

"Your sister," he says. "Call her back."

She does. Sharon answers immediately, before the first ring finishes, and asks in a harried voice, "What the hell's going on, Mags?"

"Meaning?"

"The bank called. My debts have been paid. All of them."

Sharon keeps babbling excitedly as Maggie looks up at Ivan and that no-teeth grin.

When Sharon stops to take a breath, Maggie explains. "I was just hired for a job."

That silences Sharon for a moment. Then: "And this job paid off my debts?"

"Yes."

"What kind of job?"

"A high-paying one."

"Well, I knew that already."

"I'll be gone for a week, maybe two."

"Doing what, Mags?"

"Don't worry, okay?"

"Good thing you said, 'Don't worry,' because no one ever worries after someone says that."

"I can't say more."

"Why not?"

Maggie switches the phone from her right hand to her left. "It's confidential. There are privacy clauses and HIPAA and all that."

"So, wait, you're working as a physician again?"

"What part of 'it's confidential' is confusing to you?" Maggie half snaps. "Look, it's all fine, trust me. Please just let me do this."

Sharon has more questions, but Maggie dodges and weaves and gets her off the phone. When she hangs up, she tells Ivan, "I need to go back to the hotel to check out and pack—"

"Done."

"That 'done' stuff," Maggie says. "It's getting annoying."

Ivan Brovski sits back and smiles. The car turns north on the Henry Hudson Parkway.

"Suppose I change my mind," Maggie says.

He tilts his head the smallest amount.

"Suppose I want out."

"Your phone," Ivan says, pointing at it with his chin.

"Yes."

"You have your banking app, no? Check your balance."

Maggie knows or at least suspects what's coming when she uses facial recognition to open the app, but her eyes still bulge.

The five million dollars are already there.

"Call your financial advisor before we get to the airport," Ivan says. "He may have to report such a large deposit."

"She."

"What?"

"*She* may have to report, not *he*," Maggie says. "My financial advisor is a woman. I would have thought your research would have told you that."

"The first name Leslie threw me off," Ivan says.

Man, they really do know everything.

"Also call your attorney," he says. "The suit against you is being settled as we speak."

Maggie sits back. The implications are overwhelming. No more malpractice suit. Wow. "You didn't answer my question," she says.

Ivan glances out the window, then back at Maggie. "The 'suppose I change my mind' question?"

"Yes."

He shrugs. "You can give us the money back, I suppose. The debt relief and the malpractice settlement might make the rest of the recompensation unwieldy and arduous, but let's not go there quite yet, shall we? I want to assure you that this is all on the up-and-up. My client is a very important man. Because he has the means and craves secrecy, he is hiring you as"—Ivan looks up as though again searching for the right words—"the ultimate concierge physician. Please don't worry."

"Good thing you said, 'Don't worry,'" Maggie mutters, echoing Sharon.

"Pardon?"

But there it is—that whole thing about recompensation being unwieldy and arduous. It's too late. She is in it now. There is no way out. It is how they do it. Ivan Brovski might smile a lot, but that smile never reaches his eyes. You don't cross these people. She should have learned that a long time ago.

Marc's voice: *"I have a bad feeling about this . . ."*

She should have listened. Or maybe not. Nothing has changed. Ivan is right. It is a job, a good one, ridiculously well paid, and really, she had heard rumors about this kind of private surgery for years. Like he said: She is being hired as a concierge doctor. It's not uncommon.

In the end, this patient, like any other patient, is hiring her to perform specific services, and—not to toot her own horn—he can afford the best.

It's a win-win.

"Once you board the plane," Ivan Brovski says, "we will insist on no communications with the outside world. This was explained to you before, but to reiterate: No calls, no emails, no FaceTime, no messaging apps like WhatsApp or Signal or Telegram or—"

"Yeah, I know what a messaging app is, thanks."

"Wonderful. So if you have any more calls, you should make them now."

Sure, she thinks. *Make more calls now so Ivan can hear every word.*

She hits the call button for Porkchop's payphone and is surprised when the man himself answers.

"Talk to me," Porkchop says.

"I have a job."

She again vaguely explains that she will be traveling and will be well compensated for a work assignment she can't disclose. She throws in the HIPAA and confidentiality talk. Porkchop says nothing. He doesn't interrupt. He doesn't ask follow-up questions. He doesn't argue.

That surprises her.

When Maggie finishes, Porkchop finally breaks his silence and says, "Put me on speakerphone."

"Why?"

Silence.

That's Porkchop. She bites back a sigh and hits the appropriate button and says, "Okay, you're on speaker."

"M47-235," Porkchop says.

Ivan smiles.

"What's that?" Maggie asks into the phone.

Ivan answers. "This car's license plates."

On cue, two motorcycles, one on either side of them, roar past the Mercedes. Pinky buzzes them from the driver's side, Bowling Pin Guy—she never caught his name—from the passenger's.

"I expect my daughter-in-law to remain safe and happy," Porkchop says. "Are we clear?"

Ivan says, "Of course, Mr. Porkchop."

"Don't make me have to find you."

"And vice versa," Ivan says.

Porkchop disconnects the call.

Ivan Brovski is still smiling. "Your father-in-law has a flair for the dramatic."

You don't know the half of it, she thinks, but maybe he does. Still, it is comforting to know Porkchop is on this.

On the plane, Maggie takes a seat in an oversize leather-stitched recliner with a built-in massage function. She has learned something very fast and obvious in the past twenty-four hours:

It's good to be rich.

Flight Attendant Hannah comes over and offers her "traveling sweats" from Brunello Cucinelli. Maggie accepts. Hannah asks whether she'd like a drink from the bar. Maggie is tempted, but for right now she wants to keep her wits about her, so she takes a water with a slice of lime.

She sits back and watches as the plane takes off from Teterboro Airport. Again she is met by the spectacular skyline of New York City. They don't tell you this on tour websites, but if you want the best view of Manhattan, you have to go to New Jersey. The plane reaches its cruising altitude of, according to the pilot over the speaker system, thirty-seven thousand feet. The flight time, he tells them, will be eleven hours and twenty-three minutes.

"We have a large selection of films and television programming," Hannah tells her.

"I just want to get on the Wi-Fi, thanks."

"Oh, sorry, the Wi-Fi is currently unavailable."

"Why's that?"

Another nervous smile. "Here's a menu of gourmet dishes we serve on board. Let me know if there is anything else I can do for you."

There is only one other person on the plane—a large man with a scowl who speaks no English. He sits up front, near the pilots. Security, she assumes. Package delivery—and she's the package.

Maggie heads back to the primary bedroom. The bed looks inviting. She decides—why not?—to lie in it and watch some television. There is no way, she figures, that she will actually sleep, but the blend of exhaustion and stress must be playing games with her. She falls asleep in minutes.

At some point, Hannah wakes her. "Are you hungry?"

She blinks her eyes open. "I am."

"Our chef Gregor makes wonderful omelets."

Remembering the Aman, she half jokingly says, "Florentine?"

"Of course."

"How long was I asleep?"

"I'm not sure. But we land in about an hour."

No way. No way she slept that long.

"Your luggage is in the corner, but there is a change of clothes waiting for you in the closet if you prefer. There is also a warm coat, hat, and gloves for you. You will need them."

Hannah leaves, sliding the door closed behind her. Maggie manages to sit up and stumble to the bathroom. She sees the empty glass of water on the night table.

Did they drug her?

In the closet, she finds Loro Piana cashmere loungewear and puts it on. She can't tell whether the full-length coat is real shearling fur or not—she suspects that a Russian oligarch doesn't buy fake furs—but ethics aside for the moment, it's too warm in the plane, so she carries it with her out of the bedroom. She sits at the plane's dining room table, and Hannah serves her the omelet. It's delicious, and she can't help but wonder how Plane Chef Gregor's compares to the one she refused at the Aman. Inane thoughts like this circle her head because, as the kids say on social media, it's about to get real.

They touch down at a small airport. Private, she assumes. No other planes in the air. Nothing lands immediately before them or after. She spots only a handful of other planes on the ground, all looking like rich people's toys. They taxi to a stop. Maggie reaches into her purse. She has her passport with her. She always carries it, a habit she picked up during her many years working humanitarian crises overseas, when you never knew when you'd be traveling on a moment's notice.

When the plane door opens, Maggie feels a crushing burst of cold air. She buttons up the coat—definitely real shearling—and slips the matching hat over her head. She finds fur-lined leather gloves in the coat pocket and slips them over her hands, flexing the fingers into place.

Hannah shouts over the howling wind, "Thank you for flying with us."

"Thank you," Maggie shouts back.

She expects a black car to be waiting, but across the tarmac there's a helicopter instead. A man waves her toward it. She climbs into the back. It's a six-seater, but she's alone. Two pilots sit up front. One turns around, hands her a black aviation headset, and mimes that she put it over her ears. When she does, she hears the pilots converse in Russian with a woman she assumes is an air traffic controller. In moments they are up in the air. They fly over a vast landscape, a forest really, blanketed in snow.

Maggie has not been in a helicopter since she was crammed into the medevac ones during the war. It feels absurd to be so comfortable in one. There's a twinge of something like guilt here.

Through the headset, one of the pilots switches over to broken English and says, "Flight time just six minutes, Doctor."

He turns and looks at her to make sure she understood. Maggie gives him a thumbs-up in reply.

She sees very few buildings, even in the distance, which is odd. Rublevka, she knows, is only a few miles outside of bustling Moscow. That's part of its draw for the überwealthy—it is private and protected and ultra-exclusive, but it is not remote.

At least, not remote like this.

The copter veers toward a snow-capped mountain. When it makes its way over the fir trees, Maggie sees a clearing in the distance. Not a natural clearing. It looks to be a perfect rectangle cut out of thick woods and taking up acres.

In the middle of the rectangle, equidistant from the property's borders, stands a palace out of some long-ago fable. She looks down on it. "Palace" is really the only word for it. A term like "mega-mega mansion" is inadequate here. The palace is too sprawling, with too many interconnected branches to be anywhere near the mansion family.

The copter starts to descend about a hundred yards from the front door. The lawn isn't just green—it's perfect green, flawless, seemingly painted green. Maggie wonders whether it's real grass or something artificial. The copter sets down gently, the rotor blades decelerating to a stop. When the pilot opens the door, the frigid air hits her in a rush. She steps out, the wind biting her face.

The palace gleams—actually gleams—in the sunlight. She wonders whether the entire edifice is marble, though that seems unlikely. The architecture is overwhelming and heady, much too much, a garish and almost grotesque blend of Italian Renaissance, French Rococo, and mostly Russian Baroque. The windows are tall and thin. There are reliefs and carvings on the walls. Overly ornamental domes and gold-trimmed cupolas line the roof.

It all feels, if not fake, not authentic either. The beloved palaces Maggie has been lucky enough to visit in her lifetime—Versailles, Pitti, Abdeen, Buckingham, Mysore, the Alhambra—none of them are this pristine. None gleam like this, probably because they have aged and been ravaged by time and history. People have lived and died there, history has happened, and when you visit, even if you stand at a safe distance or are surrounded by clamoring visitors, you can feel the ghosts that still haunt the place. This palace feels more like what it is—a reproduction, a showpiece, unblemished in every way.

Maggie stands there, unsure what to do, when the front door opens. A man steps into the doorframe. She is at a pretty good distance, at least a hundred yards, but she sees him raise his hand and beckon her toward him. She huddles up against the biting wind and starts down a green path. The grass feels real and even warm beneath her feet.

How?

There are white marble statues, lots of them, forming a gauntlet for her to head down. She recognizes many—Michelangelo's *David*, Myron's *Discobolus*, Puget's *Milo of Croton*, Rodin's *Adam*—all too white, all too pristine, all too obvious and soulless replicas.

The palace—she will just keep calling it that for now—has four soaring floors. Everything here is big and obvious and unsubtle—not so much an attempt to classily suggest opulence and power as to batter you with it.

The man at the door stands and waits.

Despite the frigid cold, the man is not wearing a coat. His shirt is gaudy maroon and silky and too tight. His belt line is hidden by an unapologetic gut. His jeans are skinny jeans in the sense that they seem much too small. His hairline is somewhere between receding and surrender, slicked back with something oily.

Oily.

If she was asked to describe him in one word, "oily" would seem apropos.

He smiles and waves at her with childlike enthusiasm.

"Come, come, Doctor, you must be freezing," he says with a thick Russian accent.

Maggie hurries her step. He whisks her inside and closes the door. Despite the massive entrance hallway—soaring ceilings four stories high, a grand marble staircase in the center that branches to both sides, a crystal chandelier the size of that helicopter—the warmth from the heating system is immediate. She quickly takes off the hat and gloves, and unzips the fur coat.

The man spreads his arms. "Welcome, Doctor McCabe!"

She is not sure of the protocol here—he looks ready to hug her—and when she puts out a hand to shake, he looks a little disappointed.

"Thank you," Maggie says. "And you are?"

He rubs the greasy stubble of his chin with one hand, uses his other hand to shake hers. "My name," he says, "is Oleg Ragoravich."

She can tell that he is scrutinizing her face to gauge her reaction. She tries not to give one, but she knows the name. Ivan Brovski had insisted that there was no need for her to know until arrival, but before the plane took off and she lost service, Maggie googled "Russian billionaires" and "Russian oligarchs" and then added words like "clandestine" and "reclusive."

Oleg Ragoravich was one of about a half dozen possibilities she crossed when doing this. She hadn't had time to do a deep dive, but there wasn't all that much anyway. Of the top ten Russian billionaires, he is listed as "one of the most reclusive" and rumored for many years to be in poor health. He looks fine to her, but that doesn't mean much. There are almost no photographs of him online, suggesting that he's had them scrubbed from the internet. Most people don't realize how easy it is for the über rich to do that, to control their online existence, how often you will google someone superpowerful and what comes up through search engines is only what that superpowerful entity wants you to see.

In Ragoravich's case, there are a few old grainy black-and-white photographs. His age is listed as "between 61 and 64 years old." Birthplace: Unknown but perhaps Tbilisi. As with many of his fellow Russian billionaires, the story of how he amassed his fortune is murky—something to do with the "chaotic privatization" of state-owned assets when the Soviet empire crumbled, along with currying favor with current government leadership.

Ragoravich's "source of wealth" is listed as "metals."

Vague enough?

"This isn't Rublevka," Maggie says to him.

"Pardon?"

"I was told I was going to Rublevka."

"No, no. I mean, yes, that's my main residence, but we thought it would be more comfortable and private at the Winter Palace. You like?"

She doesn't know how to answer that, so she just gives a nod.

"You must be exhausted after such a long flight. Would you like to see your room or—?"

"I'd like to inspect the medical facilities right away."

He grins. "You're no-nonsense. I like that. Come. I'll give you a tour on the way."

Oleg has a walk that proudly leads with his protruding belly, his arms behind him, chin high, a little bounce in the step. They head down a wide corridor lined with oil paintings, some of which she recognizes. When Maggie hesitates as they pass one set, Oleg spreads his arms and says, "You recognize them, yes?"

She does. Three Rembrandts (*A Lady and Gentleman in Black, Christ in the Storm on the Sea of Galilee, Portrait of the Artist as a Young Man*), a Manet (*Chez Tortoni*), and of course the pièce de résistance, Johannes Vermeer's *The Concert*.

"Cute," she says.

"How so?"

"Reproductions of the masterpieces stolen in the Gardner Museum heist."

"Very good." He looks pleased. "May I tell you a secret?"

She gives him a baleful eye. "You're not going to tell me that they're the real thing."

"No, no," he says. Then he leans toward her. "Well, except for one. I bought it from a Connecticut mobster five years ago."

"So one is genuine," she says, trying to keep her sarcastic tone to a minimum.

"Yes."

"Which one?"

"I don't tell."

"Uh-huh, sure. So you could be pulling my leg."

"I could be, yes." He starts up again. "You're a fan of art, no?"

"Truth? I'm more a fan of art heists."

"True crime," he says.

"Yes."

Oleg is almost giddy as he stops by a closed door. A blank screen of some kind is mounted to the right of it. "I want to show you something. I think you will find it compelling."

He sticks his face near the screen and stays still. Facial scan, Maggie assumes. She hears the click-click-click of a lock's tumblers. Then a buzzing noise. Oleg grabs hold of the knob and pulls the door open.

Total darkness.

They step in. Oleg waits a moment, as though building suspense, then he flicks a switch against the wall inside the door. The lights come on. And there, on the far wall, hang three identical—or at least identical to her eye—reproductions of the world's most famous painting.

The *Mona Lisa*.

Maggie frowns at him. "Let me guess," she says. "The *Mona Lisa* in the Louvre is a forgery. One of these is the real one."

Oleg can't stop smiling. "You find that so hard to believe?"

"Pretty much."

"You know, of course, that the *Mona Lisa* was stolen from the Louvre in 1911."

She nods. "By Vincenzo Peruggia. It was also returned in 1913."

"Very good, Doctor McCabe, and yes, that's the official story."

"Official story." She again tries to keep the sarcasm from her tone. "But, uh, you know better?"

"Better, worse, who's to say? But here is what we both know: The *Mona Lisa* was stolen from the Salon Carré at the Louvre on August 21, 1911, by Vincenzo Peruggia. For the next two years, there wasn't a clue what happened to the *Mona Lisa*, despite an obviously thorough police investigation. You know all this, correct?"

"Correct."

"So how does Peruggia, who had been so *so* careful, get caught? The official story, I mean: Two years after stealing it, Vincenzo Peruggia travels with the *Mona Lisa* from France to Italy, where he contacts an art dealer named Alfredo Geri. Peruggia says to Geri, 'Oh, I have the *Mona Lisa*.' Just like that. Out of the blue. After being so careful for two years, Peruggia just up and tells someone he stole it. And what happens next—after Peruggia shows Geri the *Mona Lisa*? Alfredo Geri asks permission to contact the director of the Uffizi Gallery, a man named Giovanni Poggi, to authenticate the stolen painting. Can you imagine this conversation? 'Hi, I stole the world's most famous painting, what do you think?' 'Oh, is it okay if I show it to the director of the famous art gallery in Firenze?' The utter stupidity."

Oleg shakes his head. Then he asks her, "Do you know what happened next?"

"They call the police," Maggie says. "Peruggia is arrested. The *Mona Lisa* is returned."

"Precisely." Oleg tilts his head. "Does that sound plausible to you, Doctor McCabe?"

"So you don't buy the official explanation," Maggie says.

"I don't, no."

"You think Peruggia made a perfect forgery and gave that back instead—and now the original is hanging in your home."

"No." Oleg grins, rubs his hands together as though warming up for his tale. "Again, let's stick to facts. In 1932, Karl Decker wrote an article for *The Saturday Evening Post* after speaking to an Argentinian con man named Eduardo de Valfierno. Valfierno claims that he was the mastermind behind the theft. He hired Vincenzo Peruggia to steal the painting and then he commissioned an art forger named Yves Chaudron to make six identical copies of the *Mona Lisa*. The genius here is that with the real painting gone, potential buyers had no original to compare with it. According to Decker's article, Valfierno sold the forgeries to über-rich collectors who believed it was the stolen masterpiece for a total of ninety million US dollars. It was the perfect crime."

"I know the Decker article," Maggie says. "It's a conspiracy theory. Decker has long been discredited."

"Correction," Oleg says, raising a finger. "Decker *was* 'discredited' because none of the six forgeries has ever been found. The logic went that if six forgeries were out there, surely one of them would have surfaced in the twenty years between the time of the robbery and the time of Decker's exposé. But now..."

His eyes slowly move back to the far wall.

"You're saying these are three of the six Chaudron forgeries?"

Oleg nods. "One of these was in the hands of a Saudi prince. He kept it on a yacht. Another was kept in a safe by an American oil magnate's grandfather living in Tulsa. I had both paintings examined with modern technology. It's been confirmed that despite attempts to make them appear older, they were both very good forgeries painted in the early twentieth century."

"What happened to the other three?"

Oleg shrugs. "I haven't found them yet, but I have a theory. Once Vincenzo Peruggia was arrested and the 'real'"—Oleg makes quote marks with his fingers—"*Mona Lisa* was returned and those superrich buyers realized they'd been easily swindled, they either destroyed the paintings or hid them out of embarrassment."

Maggie steps closer. She stares at the three paintings, looking for differences. She can't see any. She notices the familiar craquelure in all three paintings. These forgeries are indeed well done. "So if Decker's theory is true," Maggie says, "you have three excellent and perhaps famous forgeries."

Oleg could not look more pleased with himself. "No," he says.

She turns to him. "No?"

"According to Decker's article, the forger Yves Chaudron took his massive share for the crime, changed his name, and vanished into the French countryside, where he lived out his days in quiet luxury."

"Okay," she says.

Oleg gestures toward the paintings with his chin. "One of these three *Mona Lisas* was found in a château near Chamonix. According to what I learned, a sketchy French art restorer named Philippe Canet hung it over his fireplace for years. When Canet died, his daughter took it down, finding it tacky to be hanging up what she thought was just a normal reproduction of the old masterpiece. She sold it to my dealer. But you see, in 1913, when the *Mona Lisa* was returned to the Louvre, the science behind authentication was far more primitive, especially in terms of the aging process. Now we have pigment analysis, X-ray fluorescence, Raman spectroscopy, ultraviolet lights, chemical analysis, carbon dating, all that. I was able to test all three of these *Mona Lisas*. Two of them, as I mentioned before, date back to the early twentieth century, which fits Decker's time period for when the forgeries were being created."

He takes a step closer to the wall.

"But one of the three, the *Mona Lisa* hung above art restorer Philippe Canet's fireplace, dates back to the early sixteenth century—the time that Leonardo da Vinci painted the *Mona Lisa*."

He turns and looks back for Maggie's reaction. She tries to keep her expression neutral.

"So what's the most likely theory on what really happened? Vincenzo Peruggia stole the *Mona Lisa*. How he did it has been well documented. He brought the stolen masterpiece, per Valfierno's plan, to

Yves Chaudron, so Chaudron could use it to make the best possible forgeries. But instead of giving Peruggia back the original, Chaudron gave him one of his forgeries and kept the original for himself. Who would know? Then he changed his name to Philippe Canet, moved to a humble château outside Chamonix—and hung the original *Mona Lisa* above his fireplace, where it remained for the rest of his days." He grins and shakes his head in awe. "Think about it. How marvelous that must have been for a master forger like Chaudron." He turns and meets Maggie's eye. "Every day, Chaudron stared up at the original *Mona Lisa* in his own den while the world clamored and still queues up for hours to glimpse—not a da Vinci but an Yves Chaudron forgery. That, my dear doctor, is magnificent. That, my dear doctor, is immortality."

Maggie's eyes move back to the wall. She steps closer, seeing whether her very amateur eye can spot any differences. She doesn't buy his story, but she also can't deny that she feels a deep chill being in this otherwise barren room.

Still staring at the wall, with her back to him, Maggie asks, "Which one?"

"Does it matter? You are one of the very few people alive who have seen the real *Mona Lisa*. The rest of the world gawks at a fake. It's like religion when you think about it: Only one faith can be correct. The rest of the world worships a forgery. You, my dear, now get to be the enlightened."

Maggie frowns. "So you're not going to tell me?"

"No, not yet."

"Why?"

He doesn't answer. He opens the door and leaves the room. Maggie stares for another moment, meeting the eyes of all three *Mona Lisas* as though one of them might reveal some inner truth to her. None do. She follows Oleg back into the corridor. The lights go out. The door closes and locks.

Maggie lets loose a long breath.

"Shall we continue?" Oleg asks.

He shows her other valuables on the way—more artwork, a Qian-long vase, a fifteenth-century tapestry, sculptures—but after the *Mona Lisa* story, the other collectibles seem almost passé. Oleg eventually leads her down a long corridor into a glass-enclosed walkway—no need to experience the elements. As they cross through the snow, Maggie notices a large pile of firewood up against the side of the glass. They are now in a see-through tunnel behind the palace. At the end of the tunnel, Oleg opens a door. Maggie senses a cavernous space. He hits a switch on the wall, revealing an enormous garage/showroom loaded with cars. Collectibles, she is sure.

"Look at my baby," Oleg says, walking serpentinely through the collection. "A 1962 Ferrari 250 GTO, the greatest Ferrari of all time, a grand tourer with a V12 engine, three hundred horsepower. Only thirty-six were ever produced over a two-year span..."

Maggie tunes him out. Men and cars. She has zero interest. She has also had enough with the estate tour. She wants to get to work and start prepping for the surgery. Oleg shows her the key is in the ignition. When he jumps in and says, "We can take it for a quick spin. Just open the sliding doors and we can vroom around the property," Maggie cuts him off: "You were going to show me the medical facili-ties, remember?"

Oleg's hand drops off the ignition key. "Ah yes, I do prattle on, don't I?"

Maggie chooses not to answer. Oleg slides back out of the car.

"Shall we?"

He exits the vast showroom through the same door where they entered. He takes her back through the glass walkway, past the fire-wood, and turns left at the foyer when they are back in the main house. When Ragoravich opens another door—she gets this is all to impress, but it's still difficult not to be floored—there is an Olympic-size indoor pool. Only one person is in the giant pool right now, someone who knows how to swim, slicing through the water with barely a ripple.

"Nadia!" Oleg calls out.

The swimmer—Maggie can only really see the bathing cap and the arms doing a picture-perfect crawl—does not slow down.

"Nadia!"

Still nothing as she glides through the water with a smooth stroke that is almost hypnotic to watch.

"Nadia," Oleg says to Maggie, "is your other patient."

"I'll need to examine her before the surgery. You too."

Oleg does the head tilt again. "We'll see."

"No, we won't see. I'm not performing surgery without examinations and consultations."

Oleg just smiles.

"What?" she says.

"Please, Doctor McCabe, can we stop the posturing? You are here. You are being well paid. I understand that there are certain protocols. I am paying a great premium to avoid some of them. Like when you flew here on my private plane. Did you have to arrive at the airport two hours early? No. Did you have to go through a metal detector or wait for your boarding group to be called? No."

"This isn't the same thing," she says.

"But it is, my dear."

"I won't do it then."

He doesn't bother replying anymore. He grabs a towel and waits for Nadia to reach the edge of the pool. When she does, he calls out her name again. This time she hears and stops. He barks something at her in Russian. She nods and makes her way to the ladder. When Nadia gets out, it almost seems like she's moving in movie slow motion. Nadia reaches up, pulls off her swimming cap, and shakes out her long black hair as though she were appearing in a shampoo commercial. Oleg hands her a towel. She takes it and then she turns and looks at Maggie.

Nadia is, no way around it, gorgeous.

Blue-aqua eyes that sparkle off her sun-kissed skin, raven-black hair, the lithe and long body of a swimmer. She also looks, Maggie can't help but notice, young. Very young. Oleg appears to be around sixty. Maggie pegs Nadia somewhere in her early to mid-twenties.

Does it surprise her that a billionaire oligarch has a young... girlfriend, bae, boo—what other bizarre terms had Porkchop used?

It does not.

When Oleg puts his arm around Nadia's back, Maggie cringes for her. Keeping his hand on her lower back, Oleg leads Nadia to where Maggie is standing. In the pool, Nadia was poetry in motion. On land, with Oleg touching her, Nadia's movements are more tentative and awkward—gangly even in a way that reminds Maggie of her teenage nephew.

When they stop in front of Maggie, Oleg doesn't introduce Nadia. He just says, "She's too skinny, no?"

"No," Maggie says.

Maggie steps toward Nadia and puts out her hand. Nadia looks toward Oleg as though seeking permission to respond. Oleg nods that it's okay and Nadia hesitantly sticks out her hand for a quick shake.

"I'm Doctor McCabe. You can call me Maggie."

Maggie locks her gaze onto the blue-aqua eyes, but Nadia quickly turns back to Oleg.

Oleg says, "She doesn't speak a word of English. But she's too skinny. I like a woman with a bountiful bosom." He gestures this with both hands in a hopefully exaggerated way. "You understand?"

"Oh, I understand," Maggie says. "Do you understand that I'm not performing any surgery on Nadia without her permission?"

"Permission?" Oleg repeats with a laugh. He starts waving his hand theatrically. "Of course! You must have her"—he laughs again—"'permission.' I wouldn't dream of having Nadia do anything against her will." Oleg rips off some Russian in Nadia's direction. Nadia listens

obediently. When he finishes, Nadia nods at him. Oleg says something else in Russian, a bit more animated now, and points at Maggie.
Nadia turns so that her entire body faces Maggie. Their eyes meet
again.

Nadia nods at Maggie and says, "Okay."

Oleg spreads his hands. "See?"

"See what?" Maggie says. "What was that?"

"You wanted Nadia's permission. I asked her if she wanted you to
give her bigger boobs—oh, and maybe a rounder ass. It's too flat right
now. Nadia is saying okay, that's what she wants."

"What she wants," Maggie says, "or what *you* want?"

Oleg looks perplexed for a moment. "Why does there have to be
a difference? She wants, I want—why can't we all get what we want?
Don't make life a zero-sum game, Doctor McCabe. That's how you
create losers. The world is a series of negotiations—and the best negotiations are when both sides win. We've made a deal, Nadia and me.
She gets, I get. Same as you and me, no?" Oleg grins again.

"Come, I want to show you your operating room."

He steps toward the exit. Maggie stays where she is. He waits a
moment. Nadia tightens the towel around her as though she wants
to hide. For a few moments, the three of them stand there in silence.
Oleg breaks it.

"Fine," Oleg says with a melodramatic sigh. "My personal physician is expected in an hour. He can tell you everything you need to
know about my medical history."

"And Nadia?"

"What? I told you what she needs." He arches an eyebrow and gestures at Nadia as though she were an appliance on a game show. "And
come on, you can see she's *very* healthy, no?"

Maggie crosses her arms. "I'll need to examine her. Alone."

"But Nadia doesn't even speak English." Then Oleg stops and raises
his hands in mock surrender. "Fine." He barks some more Russian at

Nadia. Nadia nods and scurries away. "I'll show you your operating theater. Then you can"—he makes quote marks with his fingers—"'examine' Nadia—alone—before my physician arrives. Okay?"

Maggie is about to accept, but Oleg sees no need to wait. He is already on the move. She follows him into a corridor with tile flooring. Their footsteps echo. When they reach the end, Oleg opens a door and steps aside.

"Your operating theater," he says with a deep bow.

She enters, blinks, looks again.

Oleg is enjoying her reaction. "I trust you find it satisfactory?"

Maggie swallows and manages to say, "It seems fine."

"Oh, it seems more than 'fine,'" Oleg replies. "It is an exact reproduction of the operating room you used at Johns Hopkins. Our people measured yours, took videos and pictures, asked your former staff for details. You'll find every instrument and machine in the exact places, though, not to boast, our equipment is more up-to-date."

He isn't exaggerating. It feels as though she were back in Baltimore. She wants to ask about the how and why, because she had just agreed to take this job, what, thirteen, fourteen hours ago?

How had Oleg built this so fast?

Answer: He couldn't have.

Had he already known—or at least, assumed—that she'd agree to come? That seems more likely. Dr. Barlow came down from New York City to Johns Hopkins for the award ceremony. He had to have known by then, at the very least, that he would be asking Maggie to go to Russia to do this surgery. Taking it a step further, it seems unlikely that Barlow didn't first consider Maggie for this surgery at least a few days before he came to campus. It probably took some time and thought on his part. Backing up even further for a moment: Ivan Brovski—or maybe Oleg Ragoravich himself—would have approached Barlow. Maybe they offered the job to Barlow first, but Barlow wouldn't need the money. Or maybe Barlow didn't want to go at his age or with his reputation. Whatever. They would have then discussed with Barlow who would be a good candidate for the job. Somewhere along the way, it would occur to Barlow that the perfect person—someone who desperately needed money, who would be discreet, who had the necessary skills, who would not worry about career repercussions—would be Maggie McCabe.

And continuing to follow this road, someone like Oleg Ragoravich or Ivan Brovski wouldn't just accept Barlow's recommendation without doing due diligence. They'd run a thorough background check. They'd have learned about her schooling, her surgical expertise, her finances, her malpractice suit, her work with WorldCures, her now-tattered (though once-pristine) reputation.

All of that, even with the power and money behind Oleg Ragoravich, would take time.

Time enough to build an operating room.

And if she had said no? Well, so what? The operating room would be at the ready for the next potential doctor. They could then quickly redesign, if need be, to suit the next candidate. Who knows? Perhaps Maggie wasn't their first choice. Perhaps this wasn't the first time they'd done surgeries out of Oleg's compound. Perhaps this room was originally bigger or smaller or the anesthesia cart was placed on the left instead of the right or was painted cool blue instead of the muted green Maggie preferred.

Or perhaps they knew she would say yes.

It all feels very surreal.

There are three men in the operating room. They all come toward her.

"Your two nurses per your request," Oleg says. "And your anesthesiologist."

Oleg's watch buzzes. He squints at the screen and frowns. "I must leave you now. Nadia should be in the other room waiting for you by now. Then my doctor will be here. I'm sure you'll then need to rest before tonight's ball."

"Ball?"

"Yes. A massive one, here at the palace. Five hundred people. I expect you to be there."

"I thought you were a . . ." She stops.

"Private?" Oleg finished for her.

She was going to say "recluse" but close enough. "Yes."

"I am. Very."

She doesn't ask the obvious "Then why a ball?" follow-up because it's already unspoken and he's choosing not to reply. She instead stays in her lane: "As your physician, I want to warn you that if you want to have surgery tomorrow—"

"I know, I know." He holds up his hand. "'Nil per os'—Latin for 'nothing by mouth.' So nothing to eat or drink after midnight." His watch buzzes again. Oleg heads toward the door. "We can talk more tonight at the ball. But now? I promised you could examine Nadia alone. She is waiting for you in the room across the hall."

CHAPTER SIX

Nadia stands in the corner of what looks to Maggie like a spare office. She wears a plush white terry cloth bathrobe that seems to be swallowing her whole and makes her look even more petite. Her jet-black hair is wet. Her skin glistens.

Maggie smiles at her. Nadia is expressionless.

Speaking very slowly, Maggie says, "Let me see if one of the nurses can translate for us."

"No."

Maggie watches as Nadia crosses in front of her and closes the door.

"I speak English," Nadia says. "I just don't want them to know."

"Oh."

There is no examination table. Maggie had debated bringing her into the operating room for a full exam, but it seems more important to do a private consultation—just talk to her alone—than do a physical yet.

"Is it okay if I call you Nadia?" Maggie asks.

"Yes, of course."

They both take a seat. Maggie isn't sure how to begin. She wants to say, "My God, you're gorgeous, don't do this to yourself," but that would be wrong and unfair and judgmental. But none of that lets Maggie off the hook as a physician and, well, a woman. There could be disturbing issues around this procedure involving consent, coercion, and power dynamics.

"How old are you, Nadia?"

"Twenty-four."

"Do you understand what Oleg has hired me to do?"

"Augmentation mammoplasty," Nadia says. Maggie tries to place her accent. There may be Russian or Eastern European, but she also hears something else. "In short, a boob job."

"Are you okay with doing this procedure?"

"Yes."

"I should go through the risks—"

"No need. I know them."

Maggie nods slowly, leans forward. "Anything you discuss with me is between us. I will keep it in the strictest of confidences. Do you understand?"

"I understand."

"You can trust me, Nadia."

For the first time, Nadia smiles—and it's radiant. "I do already, Doctor. You're the only one who knows I speak English."

"Thank you for that." Maggie shifts a little more toward her. "I need to make sure you're okay, Nadia."

Nadia says nothing.

"If someone is pressuring you to have this surgery—"

Nadia laughs. "You can't be serious."

"—I can refuse to do the surgery."

"Then Oleg would bring in someone else."

Maggie lowers her voice. "If you don't want to stay—"

"Who says I don't want to stay?"

"—I can get you out."

Nadia looks almost amused. "Do you really believe that, Doctor McCabe?"

"Believe what?"

"That you can get me out."

"I'll find a way."

Nadia mutters something in a foreign tongue. "How? You, like me, are totally at their mercy. You can't call anyone. Your phone won't work. Oh, and your bedroom? It will be bugged. Just so you know— this is one of the few rooms in the house that doesn't have cameras and listening devices. So how do we make our escape? Will you hide me in your suitcase?"

"Listen to me," Maggie says, moving closer. "I can find a way."

"You're being naive."

"Nadia—"

"And I don't want you to," Nadia says, her tone firm now. "I am here by choice. I can leave anytime I want. I understand the surgery. I know the risks. They are minimal, no?"

Maggie nods. "Most studies report a one to five percent chance of a complication."

"Between one and five percent," Nadia repeats. "That's an average."

"Yes."

"But I don't have an average doctor, do I?" Nadia says. "Oleg only hires the best."

They lock eyes.

"It's an easy choice for me," Nadia says. "I want to do it."

Maggie nods, giving herself time to think. "That's fine. It's up to you, of course. I just want you to know that I'm here for you. That I want to help you."

"Many girls," Nadia continues, "beautiful girls, would give any-thing to be in my place."

"I understand," Maggie says.

Nadia flashes the smile again. "I know what I look like, Doctor McCabe. I know the effect I have on men. But after this surgery, I will be, let's be honest, irresistible."

"You already are, Nadia."

"Don't be patronizing."

"I don't mean to be."

"You heard what Oleg likes. That's what I need to be."

"Got it."

"Will you help me?"

Maggie sighs but she also nods. "If that's what you want, I will, yes."

Then Nadia drops a truth bomb on her: "You don't know me," she says. "You don't know my life."

Which is fair. Maggie knows that. But she can't just let it go either. "You're right. I don't. But know this: I'm here for you. I'm on your side."

"I know," Nadia says. "Tomorrow you will operate on me. You will keep me safe."

"I will," she says.

"That's all I need." Nadia walks to the door. Then she says, "I bet you've made sacrifices for the man you love, haven't you, Doctor McCabe?"

Maggie feels the too-familiar pang.

"Doctor?"

"I have," Maggie says. Then she adds, "But not something like this, no. He would never..." She stops and reminds herself of an obvious truth: They aren't the same, Maggie and Nadia. As Nadia so aptly put it, *You don't know my life.* It's condescending to compare. Maggie gets that.

But then Nadia asks, "Are you married?"

Maggie feels the tears push into her eyes.

"I mean, you have someone special in your life, right?"

Maggie still doesn't reply.

"Doctor?"

And then, because Nadia deserves the truth, Maggie gives her the honest, heartbreaking answer:

"No," Maggie says, "I'm not married anymore. There is no one special in my life."

───────────

Nadia leaves. Maggie stays in the office.

She checks the door for a lock. There is none. No matter. She turns off the light and moves over to the couch against the far wall. She sits on it, pulls her knees up to her chest, hugs herself. Tears run down her cheeks. She lets them. She isn't crying, not by the medical definition. Crying involves facial muscles like the orbicularis oculi and mentalis. Crying involves the release of oxytocin and endorphins. Crying is usually accompanied by shortness of breath or increased heart rate.

But this is just tears sliding down her face.

For a few minutes Maggie doesn't move. She can't move. She just sits in the dark and hopes no one will knock on that door. This is her life now. The self-pity makes her sick. Still, she takes out her phone.

She hates this.

With a shaking hand, she clicks the blue icon.

Marc's face appears.

"Why is it so dark?" he asks.

"I'm sitting in a dark room."

"Why? I can barely see you."

She moves her face closer to the screen.

"You've been crying."

"I'm fine."

"Where are you? What happened at your meeting with Barlow?"

She stares at his face, scrutinizing his expression, as she often did, for a tell.

"Mags?"

Her eyes close. "He offered me a job."

"Oh, great."

"Not so great," she says. "I'm supposed to do surgery tomorrow."

"Hold up. Where are you?"

"Not sure exactly. Somewhere in Russia."

"Show me," he says.

"What do you mean?"

"Wait," he says, "I can't see your phone's location. How come I can't see your location?"

"I don't know. They blocked everything. There is no way for me to call out or be tracked—"

The door bursts open. Maggie startles back, almost dropping her phone.

A voice bellows, "What's going on here?"

Maggie looks up and sees the hulking form of Ivan Brovski standing in the doorway.

"Who are you talking to?" he shouts.

He steps into the room, flicks the light on, and closes the door behind him.

"You're not allowed to call anyone!"

Maggie backs up.

"Stay away from me."

"You made a promise! No contact with anyone!"

"It's not what you think."

Ivan is furious. He starts counting off on his fingers. "No phone, no email, no messaging app—"

"That's not what this is."

"I don't understand. How could you even call someone?" His face is red. "The Wi-Fi is set so nothing can go out or in or..."

Without warning, Ivan's hand shoots out with cobra-like quickness and snatches her phone away.

"Hey! Give me that back."

Maggie tries to grab the phone from him, but Ivan holds her off with one massive, powerful hand. With his other hand, he brings the phone up toward his face so he can see the screen.

"It's not what you think," Maggie says.

"I heard a man's voice."

"It's not—"

"Who were you talking to?" he demands. "What did you tell him?"

Maggie stops struggling. She sighs and gestures for him to have a look for himself. Ivan appears puzzled. He lowers his hand away from her. When he stares at the screen, his eyes widen.

"How . . . ?"

"Press the blue icon," Maggie says.

"What?"

"Just"—she lets loose a breath—"press the blue icon."

With a thick thumb pad, Ivan Brovski does as she asks. Then he looks a question at her. "Do you want to explain?"

"You know about my husband."

Of course he does. They investigated her financial situation, her sister's, her malpractice suit. They'd know everything about her.

Ivan nods. "Doctor Marc Adams, renowned cardiothoracic surgeon."

"And you know," Maggie continues, trying very hard not to let her voice crack, "about his death."

Ivan nods again, more solemnly this time. "He was on a humanitarian mission in Ghadames when a militia group raided a refugee camp. Your husband stayed behind to help a patient. It cost him his life."

"Yes."

Ivan lifts the phone. "But I just saw your husband on your phone."

"No."

"No?"

"You saw," Maggie says, "a griefbot."

He makes a face. "A what?"

"A griefbot. You've probably heard of rudimentary ones."

"I have no idea what you're talking about."

Maggie wonders how to explain this without sounding insane.

"When a loved one dies, and when someone misses that loved one, misses them so much that..." Maggie shakes it off, channels her sister, and tries a more analytical approach. "A griefbot is an artificial intelligence app that mimics a dead person via their digital footprint—for example, their social media content, emails, maybe videos online or photographs on their phone, whatever. The software then creates a lifelike avatar of the deceased, and a mourner can"—she hesitates—"a mourner can actually converse with it."

"You mean talk to it?" Ivan says.

"Yes. When done well, the humanoid AI can replicate the dead person's speech patterns, personality, temperament, mannerisms, intelligence, tics, gestures—everything that made the deceased unique. It can generate full conversations and even comfort the grieving."

It takes him a few moments to get it. "And in this case, you're the grieving?"

"Yes."

"So you were talking to a computer?"

How to explain this...?

"It's more complicated than that," Maggie says. Then when she sees the look on his face—part pity, part...disgust?—she quickly adds, "I'm not doing it for me."

"Oh?"

"It's for my sister."

"Sharon McCabe? But why would your sister...?" Then Ivan nods, remembering. "Her expertise," he says. "She specializes in creating AI people."

"That's an oversimplification too, but yes."

Ivan points at her phone. "So she created this...did you call it a griefbot?"

"It's a beta version. It doesn't have the last few months of his life on it. But it's still her most advanced."

"So you're, what, testing it for her?"

"Exactly."

Ivan stares at the phone for a few moments. "I see," he says, and the pity in his voice almost chokes her. "Do you find it comforting?"

She settles for the truth, because why not? "I don't know," she says. "It's weird. I feel embarrassed every time I talk to it."

Ivan gives her a half smile. "And yet here you are—telling your AI husband about your visit here."

"Like I said—to help my sister."

"And if your sister didn't need the help?" he asks. "Would you still talk to it?"

Enough, Maggie thinks. She doesn't want to discuss this anymore. The truth is, Sharon's griefbot would probably be less painful if it wasn't so damn close to reality. Sharon had found a way to perfect her creation by not only getting Marc's entire digital history, but by hacking into every database he ever visited. Do you have an Alexa or Siri or some other smart speaker in your house? It hears you, records the data, and stores it in clouds. Your iPhone's built-in microphone does the same. So does your home surveillance system and doorbell and motion detectors and monitoring feeds—they all spy on you and listen to every word you say, even when you think they are off. This isn't a shock—most people know this. The problem for big tech has always been what to do with all that stored raw data, how to sort it and make it profitable or at least useful.

Sharon had found a way.

She figured out how to use someone's life data to recreate a near-perfect digital duplicate of a human being. Even Maggie can't tell the difference most of the time. That's what's so incredible about Sharon's invention—and, of course, what makes it so terrible. The "Marc" griefbot isn't a comfort so much as a constant reminder that the real thing was hacked to pieces in a godforsaken refugee camp more than four thousand miles from his home.

And yet Maggie keeps opening the app.

Is that insane?

Or conversely, is it any worse than spilling your guts to a paid therapist—or talking to yourself? We all have constant inner monologues going on in our heads. We all have imaginary conversations with superior beings or dead loved ones. Is it any crazier to have these conversations with a nearly flawless AI replica of the man you loved?

These are either deep philosophical questions or delusional self-rationalizations. Maggie isn't sure which.

Either way, Marc is dead.

You've heard about the five stages of grief—denial being the first, followed by anger, bargaining, depression, and acceptance. *Those stages are wrong*, Maggie thinks—or at the very least, inadequate. When she first found out about Marc—when Porkchop knocked on her door on that terrible night, the devastation on his face impossible to hide—Maggie dropped to her knees and sobbed uncontrollably. There was no denial. She got it immediately: The only man she'd ever loved was dead and gone forever. *Forever.* She would never see him again. She would never touch him, never hold his hand, never feel safe and small in his arms, never pull him close when she couldn't sleep, never help him go back to sleep when he had a nightmare, never know the peace and solace of just being with her soulmate—the real definition of love—or see his goofy smile across the breakfast table or roll her eyes at his intentionally corny jokes or...

Never.

She got that all in a mad rush, instantly, in a split second, and the reality of that truth crippled her. That's when denial rushes in. Denial comes second, not first, because those first few seconds when you comprehend the awful truth—Stage One should actually be "total understanding"—are so devastating, so awful, so painful, so debilitating that your mind forces you to move on to denial in order to survive.

So total understanding is the first stage. Then denial. Anger, bargaining, depression arrived together, a toxic concoction, one overlapping and blending with the others. You spiral. And with that comes the need to numb.

Enter pills.

Maggie started taking them. Not many. Just enough to take the edge off. So she could sleep. So she could vanish. She still worked. She still performed surgeries and lived with Sharon and helped with her mother.

She had it under control.

But then her mother died.

So she took more pills.

She was still okay, she thought. The pills were there, a part of her, but they weren't all-consuming. They were just a temporary buttress to shore up an otherwise strong woman.

But one day, Maggie took too many pills before stepping into an operating room. Or she toxically mixed them with something else in her bloodstream. Or maybe she didn't get enough sleep the night before, so they hit her harder. Something. Something with the pills and her metabolism went very wrong that day.

And now she's here.

"I'm very sorry for your loss," Ivan Brovski says. "Your husband was a hero. I don't know if that's a comfort at all—"

"Thank you," she says, cutting him off. "Could you please give me back my phone?"

Ivan stares down at it for a moment. Then he puts her phone in his jacket pocket. "Tomorrow."

"What?"

"I can't let you have it. The features are too advanced. Perhaps you can reach a person in the outside world with it. Perhaps even your sister."

"The app is self-contained. That's how I've been able to use it."

"Is it? Are you sure? Doesn't AI keep learning? You and I don't know what it can or can't do. How about if I give it back to you after the surgeries?" Then, with an almost mocking tone, Ivan adds, "You don't *need* your griefbot, do you?"

She knows what he's doing—needling her like this—but the shame still hits her deep. It's just an app. It isn't Marc. Like an advanced computer simulation. Nothing more.

"Unless," Ivan continues, "I mean, if you *really* rely on it—"

"Fine, I get it," she snaps. "Keep it." And in truth he's right—Maggie doesn't know all of the app's capabilities. Perhaps Sharon could use the app to reach her or at least figure out where Maggie is.

That could put Sharon in danger.

Maggie checks her watch. "I have to go. I'm supposed to talk to Oleg's personal physician."

Ivan Brovski smiles and spreads his hands. "You are talking to him."

CHAPTER SEVEN

van Brovski brought her to yet another room.

"How many rooms does this place have?" Maggie asks.

"I'm not sure anyone knows." He gestures with his arm. "Please."

It reminds her of Barlow's conference room. Not an exact replicate like her OR, but then again, all these sleek rooms look the same. Ivan signals for her to take a seat. He moves around the table, sits across from her, and touches the tablet in front of him. The large-screen TV on the far wall comes to life in bright white.

"So you're a physician?" Maggie says to Ivan.

"Oxford trained."

"What's your specialty?"

"I'm a general internist. Nothing fancy. Like you, I served in the military. When I resigned my commission, Oleg hired me to be his full-time physician and liaison."

"Liaison," Maggie repeats. "I bet that term is pretty flexible."

A small smile comes to Ivan's lips as he taps something on his tablet. The white vanishes from the television screen. "This is Mr. Ragoravich's electronic medical records." He taps another icon, and the file slides to the left, making room for another. "And this one belongs to Nadia Strauss."

"Nadia's last name is Strauss?"

He gives her a noncommittal shrug and hands her the tablet so that she can control the screen. The first page for both patients displays what one might expect: height, weight, date of birth, gender. Unlike the electronic medical files Maggie was used to from the hospital, there are no spaces for billing information—nothing about insurance company, address, social security number, occupation.

"You met your surgical team," Ivan says.

"Briefly."

"Just so you are aware, it's not just the operating room we've duplicated."

Maggie looks up from the tablet. "Meaning?"

"We interviewed members of your surgical team in Baltimore."

"When you say interview—"

"For training purposes," he says. "So your team here has been schooled on your operating room preferences and protocols."

"You don't miss much."

"We believe in minimizing risk, Doctor McCabe. We want to assure your success."

"I see."

"Assuming you approve, the schedule for tomorrow is as follows: Meet with the team at seven a.m. to go over procedures. Personally inspect the surgical facilities and all implantation devices. We are told you usually do this three hours before a surgery. Is that correct?"

"Yes."

"Very good. So Mr. Ragoravich will go into surgery at ten a.m. He will undergo three procedures. One, a blepharoplasty. Two, a sliding genioplasty using fat transfer, so that his jawline more resembles the one in Photo A."

Maggie clicks on what is marked as Photo A. It offers up a black-and-white, oddly grainy view of the lower half of a man's face.

"And three, a rather unique open rhinoplasty. I think you'll find that most exciting."

"Why's that?"

"You'll be implanting an artificial nose scaffold."

Maggie makes a face. "I'm not familiar with that."

He grins. "I know."

"I'm familiar with nose scaffolding using cartilage and tissue."

"That isn't what this is, though there is a lot of overlap, and that's why it's an open rhinoplasty. You'll make the incision below the nose"—Ivan points with his beefy finger at the space between the upper lip and the start of the nose—"peel the skin up, do whatever you need to clear out space, and then insert the scaffold."

"An artificial scaffold?"

"Yes, that's correct."

She frowned. "I didn't know such a thing existed."

Again the grin. "It didn't. Until now. But I assure you it's been tested."

"Who built the scaffolding?"

"We did," he says. "Via AI on our MB Reps 3D printer."

Maggie sits back. "Are you serious?"

"I am."

"You have an MB Reps 3D printer?"

"That surprises you?"

They sell, Maggie knows, for nearly a quarter million dollars. "Not really, no. But like I said, I never heard of this before. What's the scaffolding made of?"

"It's a patented biocompatible polyethylene."

Maggie nods. That's a common and proven material for implanted medical devices. Trace and Marc had done their work with that too. "And it's a full nose scaffold?"

"Yes."

"And you know I've never done that procedure before, right?"

"Truth?" Ivan leans in conspiratorially with the same grin. "I'm not sure anyone has. Do you think that's a problem?"

She looks at the chart, considers the procedure, visualizes herself doing it. Her pulse picks up pace. She can't help feeling excited at the prospect. "Not really, no."

"It's why we picked you."

"Pardon?"

He settles back. "We didn't think it would be an issue for you."

"Who is 'we'?"

"Doctor Barlow, mostly. He says you're a bit of a risk-taker." Ivan quickly waves both hands in front of his face as though clearing away his own words. "No, no, not like that. He meant like a maverick. You understand the best way to improve medical care is to push boundaries, no?"

When she doesn't reply, he adds, "Anyway, Doctor Barlow thought you'd relish this challenge."

The truth is, Dr. Barlow was correct. Maggie had read tons over the years on building and creating custom implants via AI and 3D printing—Marc and Trace had been working on something similar with the THUMPR7—but the technology still felt like years in the future. A nose scaffold is not a heart or a liver—but it's a pretty exciting step.

You have to walk before you can run.

"In most ways," Ivan continues, "it works like any other facial implant."

"Except," Maggie says, studying the images, "it will more radically change the way Oleg's nose appears."

"Yes."

"Most people want a smaller nose."

"Oleg Ragoravich does not. Click Photo B."

She does. The image—grainy black-and-white again, which is strange—is of a nose that would politely be called "prominent." The vast majority of people go through plastic surgery to improve their aesthetics. This is fairly obvious. Some want to look like a favorite celebrity, but between this new nose, the chin implant, and the eye work via the blepharoplasty, Oleg Ragoravich clearly did not want that.

He wants to look like someone else.

Or at least, not like himself.

"We figure the three procedures should take you between three and four hours," Ivan continues. "Would you agree?"

She would. Probably three, but it pays to have extra time with the nose scaffold. She'd want to inject some fat and stem cells into the area, just to make sure the device wasn't rejected.

"Which brings us to Nadia," he says, tapping the screen. "Assuming we begin Mr. Ragoravich's procedures promptly at ten a.m., we will have Nadia prepped and ready for a two p.m. start. Does that work for you?"

"It does. I assume we are using silicone for the breast augmentation?"

He nods. "We can choose either round three hundred ccs, three fifty ccs, or four hundred cc implants, all on standby."

The four hundreds would be too big, but keeping three sizes ready for an operation was standard. Silicone was back in—saline was out. In the nineties, there were headlines about silicone leaks causing cancer and lupus, but after extensive studies, they found no link between silicone breast implants and an increased risk of breast cancer.

"What kind of incision are you going with?" Ivan asks her.

"I prefer the inframammary," she says. "Assuming that's okay with Nadia."

He nods. There are three types of incision used in breast augmentation: inframammary (under the breast), periareolar (around the edge of the areola, a sort of half-smile incision), and transaxillary (in the armpit). The inframammary is most common. The periareolar sometimes affects sensation, and the transaxillary is used only for saline and makes positioning difficult.

Maggie starts clicking through the pages, seeing if anything sticks out. "Can I keep these medical files to review in full?"

"Of course. That tablet is yours." Ivan checks his watch. "The gala ball is in a few hours," he says, putting his hands on the sides of his chair as though ready to push himself up. "So if there's nothing else—"

"Hold up a second," Maggie says. Ivan waits. She clicks back, then forward. She reads the history again. "It says here Nadia only has one kidney."

"Yes. She donated the other, what, six, seven years ago."

"To whom?"

"Her brother."

"Do you know what he had?"

"The brother?" He looks up as though trying to remember. "Nephrotic syndrome, I think. We ran a urine test and bloodwork on Nadia, of course. She has no signs of it."

Maggie mulls that over. Something isn't adding up. "Where is Nadia from?"

"Originally? I have no idea."

"How did she meet Oleg Ragoravich in the first place?"

"In a club in Dubai. What difference does it make?"

"Having only one kidney could be an issue."

"Could be, but it's not. Nadia has been medically cleared. She's in excellent health. As for the rest of your questions, Oleg Ragoravich is a private man."

"Which reminds me," Maggie says. "If he's so private, why is he throwing a huge party tonight?"

"It's a ball, not a party."

"What's the difference?" Maggie asks. Then, thinking better of it, she adds, "I'd rather not go."

"You should. For one thing, you're expected. For another, you will want to see the difference between a *party* and a *ball* with your own eyes."

"Would it be a cliché to say I have nothing to wear?"

"It would be," Ivan says, rising from his seat, "if that were true. But come on, my dear, you must know by now that we are prepared."

CHAPTER EIGHT

Maggie stares out her bedroom window and watches the guests arrive. A long tent-like walkway has been put out between the helicopter landing pad and the front door. The snow, which was still falling, is strategically gone, though she has seen no one shovel it away. She'd asked Ivan Brovski how they cleared it away.

"Heat coils under the ground," he told her.

But of course.

Other guests are pulling up in big black cars, either stretch limos or oversize SUVs. The men wear tuxedos. The women wear formal gowns.

Maggie's bedroom is, no surprise, larger than most apartments. Ivan had shown her the way to her room. The first thing he'd done when they arrived was open her walk-in closet with, she estimated, somewhere between thirty and forty outfits.

"All in your size and style," Ivan informed her, "including…"

He gestured to the three formal gowns suitable for, well, a ball.

Maggie shook her head. "I'm not even surprised anymore."

"I assume you like them."

She did. Very much. She pulls out a navy blue dress nearly identical to the one she'd worn at Johns Hopkins a few days ago. Same shoes in her size too. "Weird," she says. "I have this same outfit at home." Then it dawns on her: "But you already knew that."

Ivan shrugs. "Not me, personally. But yes, artificial intelligence made the selections—a new software program that scours the internet for all your photos and videos, sees what you wear to various events, and creates a wardrobe based on what it believes is your taste."

"Terrific."

But there is no way they could have done all this in, what, twelve hours?

Someone has been watching her.

For how long?

"There are a few nice diamond pieces on the bureau. Tasteful, I'm told. Feel free to borrow them."

"Okay."

"How about if I stop by at eight? We can go to the ball together."

She nods. He leaves. Maggie remembers what Nadia said about bugs and cameras. Not much she can do about it, she supposes. The room is fully stocked with a potpourri of dream products—Chanel perfume, Christian Dior makeup, every top-of-the-line skin product imaginable, all touting promises of youth via peptides and collagens. She takes a shower, letting the hot water steam up the room just in case of cameras, throws on a robe, lies in bed. She closes her eyes. No time for a nap. Instead, Maggie starts visualizing and even acting out the surgery. Her father had told her about Colonel George Hall, a Vietnam War combat pilot who spent over seven years in the notorious Hanoi Hilton prison. To maintain his sanity in the face of starvation and torture, Colonel Hall imagined himself playing golf in his tiny cell. He would feel the sun on his face, smell the green grass, take each swing with care. He would see the ball go up in the air, watch it land on the fairways and greens of his favorite courses. Supposedly he did this every day and actually improved his game just through this visualization. Maggie didn't know if that last part was exaggeration or myth, but that didn't matter. She got it. She lies back now, closes her eyes, raises her hands into the air, and uses the scalpel to make the first incision. In her mind's eye, she goes through the entire operation—her own virtual world of surgery. She does this a lot—or used to when she was licensed. It is her way of both meditating and preparing.

At eight p.m., there is a knock on the door. Maggie opens it. Ivan's eyes widen when he sees her all dressed up. He swallows back whatever comment he was about to make about her appearance, and says, "You chose the navy."

"Yep."

"It suits you."

"Thank you."

"Are you ready?"

Ivan looks stiff and uncomfortable in his tuxedo, the bow tie wrapped tourniquet-like around his neck. The house is oddly silent when they leave the bedroom. It's not until they leave the wing that she starts to hear voices, occasional laughter, string music. They stay on the third floor and enter the ballroom from a balcony above it. The ballroom is polished white marble with gold leaf. It is huge, the approximate size of a college basketball arena. Relief carvings of baby angels, a look Maggie never understood, line the ceiling's perimeter. There are probably three, maybe four hundred people mingling below. As she heads down the stairs, Maggie notices what appear to be food stations, a worldwide tour de cuisine on steroids. She wanders around and, for a moment, lets herself be a guest. She tries the abalone with liver and uni dipping sauce from Sushi Yoshitake, a three-star Michelin restaurant in Tokyo's Ginza district. Lung King Heen, another three-star Michelin restaurant in Hong Kong's Four Seasons Hotel, offers a scallop and prawn dumpling. Talula's from Asbury Park provides pizza slices with Calabrian soppressata and local honey. Fromagerie Cantin, the renowned Parisian cheese shop, offers Aisy Cendré, a semi-soft cow's milk cheese buried in oak ashes for a month.

A voice interrupts her midbite. "I know it's a cliché, what with being here in Russia, but you have to try the caviar."

The voice has a decidedly haughty American prep school accent to it. Maggie turns. The handsome man offers her a boyish aw-shucks grin. His tuxedo looks sculpted on, graceful, draping exactly where it should be and fitted where it shouldn't. The midnight-black fabric seems to absorb light more than reflect it. No need for a flashy tie or patterned cummerbund when you're seemingly fitted by a deity, just the shine of onyx studs against the pure white of his starched shirt.

He looks soft, pampered, privileged.

As the man and his polished shoes glide toward her, Maggie notices a moistness in his blue eyes, perhaps from drink.

"I'm Charles Lockwood," he says with a crooked grin, sticking out the unblemished, manicured hand.

She hesitates, not sure whether she should give her name. He picks up on it.

"And you're Doctor Maggie McCabe," he says for her.

His stubble is curated and on point. His black hair is long and wavy, the kind of unruly and ungroomed that often requires too much product. It all works in its own way, she presumes. Charles Lockwood cuts a striking figure, which is clearly the intended effect.

"Have we met?"

"No, but I knew your husband a bit. I'm terribly sorry."

"How did you—?"

"I dabble"—Lockwood lifts a manicured hand and shakes his fingers—"in cardiothoracic surgery too."

"No one 'dabbles'"—she imitates his finger gestures—"in cardiothoracic surgery."

"Fair enough. I don't say this with false modesty, but next to your husband? Yes, I dabble. Marc seemed a good man, maybe even a great man, I don't know. But he was the greatest surgeon I'd ever seen."

Maggie feels her throat start to close. She pushes on. "So what brings you to Russia, Doctor Lockwood?"

"I was going to ask you the same thing."

"Yeah, but I asked first."

"Probably the same reason you're here," he says.

"Hey, Charles, there you are!"

Two giggling women, both young and blonde and straight out of an influencer's social media page, call out to him in Russian and approach on either side. One takes one arm. One takes the other. Both look at him adoringly. Charles replies to them in Russian. Both women pout, let their grips slip, and sulk away.

Charles turns back to Maggie and gives her a what-are-you-gonna-do shrug of the shoulders, palms up.

"Yeah, I don't think we're here for the same thing," Maggie says.

He chuckles. "Sorry about that," he says.

"Don't let me keep you from your friends."

"They'll be around later."

"I bet. You speak Russian?"

"I dabble."

"Dabbling seems to be your modus operandi."

Charles Lockwood gives her what he is sure must be the most winning smile. "I spend a lot of time here. I enjoy the lifestyle."

"That lifestyle being?"

"A tad hedonistic. Nothing wrong with fun, Doctor McCabe, is there?"

She tries not to frown. "None at all."

"Perhaps you and I can get together during your visit."

"Yeah, no, I don't think so."

"Come now, Doctor McCabe, there is always time for a little fun along with our fundraising. Where are you staying?"

She ignores his question. "What's that about fundraising?"

His expression says he knows that she's dodging. "That's not why you're here?"

"No, are you?"

"As a matter of fact, I am."

"For?"

"A medical startup specializing in cutting-edge longevity treatments."

Again with the cutting edge, Maggie thinks.

Lockwood peers over her head. "Have you met our host?"

"Yes."

Charles Lockwood makes a face to indicate he's impressed. "Have you seen Mr. Ragoravich at the party?"

"It's a ball, not a party."

"Pardon?"

"Never mind." Maggie's eyes scan the ballroom. "No, not yet."

"I'm hoping to meet Oleg Ragoravich tonight." Charles Lockwood turns his attention back to her. "Your turn."

"Turn?"

"Why are you here, Doctor McCabe?"

"Maggie."

"Why are you here, Maggie?"

"I can't really talk about it," she says.

"Why not?"

She shuts him down with a face.

"Oh, my bad. I won't push." He throws up his hands in mock surrender. Again, Charles Lockwood probably thinks it's a charming move on his part, and maybe for others, it is. Maggie hates this kind of faux charisma, the playboy blend of privilege and drink and good genes and people around you telling you that you are God's gift.

Then Lockwood says, "Is Trace Packer here too?"

Maggie doesn't bother hiding her surprise. "You know Trace?"

"Let's just say we partied a few times together in our day."

"I bet."

"Trace knows how to party." He looks around. "I figured you're both here to fundraise."

"Our charity closed down."

"I'm aware," Charles Lockwood says.

"You seem aware of a lot of things."

"I like to be in the know."

"Do you know where Trace is?"

"No, why would I?" When Maggie doesn't reply, he asks, "So are you here to, what, thank your old benefactor?"

"I told you I can't talk about it," Maggie says. Then, realizing what he said: "What benefactor?"

"Are you serious?"

"Do I look like I'm joking?"

Charles Lockwood moves a little closer. "Aren't you one of the founders of WorldCures Alliance?"

"Yes."

"And who was your biggest donor?"

"The Kasselton Foundation."

"Operated by?"

"I don't know. I mean, the financial stuff was more Trace's area of expertise. I met a few board members—"

"Oleg Ragoravich," Charles Lockwood says.

She almost takes a step back.

"You really didn't know?" Charles seems amused now. "The Kasselton Foundation is funded by none other than our host."

Maggie just stands there and tries not to look surprised. She isn't sure what to say and doesn't want to make the mistake of saying more. She doesn't know Charles Lockwood. She doesn't get what's going on or why he's here or if she should believe him. In her peripheral vision, she spots Nadia making her way toward them, wearing a shimmery silver gown. The crowd parts Red Sea–like as she strides with runway grace toward them. All heads turn and follow.

Charles Lockwood leans closer to Maggie and whispers, "Take care of yourself, Maggie. Stay alert."

Then he slips away.

———————

Maggie debates going after him, but Nadia arrives before she can make a move. Maybe that's for the best. What else is there to know? Charles Lockwood would have no reason to lie about Ragoravich. Or would he? And if he wasn't lying, well, what did that mean? Was Oleg Ragoravich the man who gave the original seed money for World-Cures Alliance? And if he is a former supporter of WorldCures, does it matter?

Yes, it does.

Because if he is, it means Maggie's being here—her being chosen as their personal surgeon—is not a coincidence.

But maybe that makes sense. Maybe Ragoravich and Brovski already know and vetted her work with WorldCures. She would have been a known entity to them. Maybe that's why she was hired—a surgeon they had some knowledge about, some connection to and familiarity with, would be a comfort, no?

Nadia arrives. "Ivan says you have questions about me."

"I do," Maggie says. "About your health records."

She nods, her wide eyes scanning the room. "Can I ask a question first?"

"Of course."

"How long do I need to fast before the surgery tomorrow?"

"Twelve hours would be optimal."

A hint of a smile crosses Nadia's face. "So that gives us time to eat a little, no?"

"It does."

"Let's start with the caviar. But also? Gesture a lot. Like we don't speak the same language."

"Got it."

"And pretend you're speaking to other people when you can. Like don't always look directly at me."

Maggie agrees. For the next half hour, she and Nadia peruse the various tasting stations. The Tajimi-ushi-variety Kobe beef topped with Alba white truffles—the bite-size portion probably cost more than Maggie's car—melts in the mouth, forcing both closed eyes and some kind of involuntary vocal reaction. Maggie bides her time. She doesn't immediately ask about the kidney donation. There are two reasons for that, though they are somewhat closely related. One reason, the most obvious, is that she and Nadia are bonding in perhaps the oldest way known to mankind—breaking bread together. They enjoy the rare delicacies, relish them, close their eyes and savor every bite. Nadia's joy in the experimental tasting is childlike and endearing. Maggie can feel Nadia's trust grow with each bite. Maggie lets herself get immersed in this experience as well—Reason Two—channeling her father, who expressed his appreciation for modern life with gusto and enthusiasm.

"We live in the greatest era in human history," her father would tell his daughters. He would then explain that there was less war, pestilence, disease, crime, starvation than any time ever. Then he would move on to food. "The vast majority of humans have known very little variety in taste. Empires rose and fell, people were conquered and slaughtered, merely to add spice and flavoring to their palates. Think about it. A hundred, two hundred years ago, only the most elite of elite got to experience one or two other cultures' food. Now all of us can walk through any city and within a mile you can eat Chinese, Indian, Thai, French, Italian. You can have lamb from New Zealand, pompano from Florida, barbecue from Texas. If you told even the richest king that would be possible, he would have never believed it. What we take for granted is nothing short of a miracle."

So, keeping that in mind, Maggie and Nadia laugh. They share. They analyze the various delicacies. They stay with food, skipping the stations with "pharmaceuticals" and "gurus" to guide you through whatever psychoactive drug experience you might imagine. They also bypass the various alcohol tastings, though a few of the vodka ones tempt Maggie more than she wants to admit.

Finally, Nadia says, "Ask your questions."

A waiter takes Maggie's mother-of-pearl spoon. "Tell me about your kidney transplant."

"Why?"

"Because it could be relevant to your medical clearance."

"I was already cleared medically."

"Then humor me."

"It was for my brother," Nadia says a little too quickly.

"How old is he?"

"Now? Thirty-one."

"Is he your full sibling?"

"Yes."

"What did he have?"

"Why does it matter?"

"Your brother needing a kidney transplant at age twenty-five is pretty rare," Maggie says. "His illness is most likely something genetic."

"So?"

"So there's a decent chance that you, as his full sibling, especially one who was a genetic match for a transplant, might be susceptible to a similar illness."

"I've been medically cleared," Nadia says again. "The rest doesn't matter."

"I'm your physician. I need to know your complete medical history."

"No, you don't," Nadia says, and there is a little bite in her tone. "You're here to give me a boob job. I donated a kidney. That has nothing to do with this."

"I'm not sure why you're so defensive about this."

"And I don't know why you're so nosy," Nadia replies.

"This isn't idle curiosity. If you donated a kidney to your brother, he was obviously very ill. Like I said before, since you are a genetic match—"

"Stop please."

Nadia shuts her eyes and keeps them closed. One tear escapes and runs down her cheek. Maggie takes Nadia's hand and leads her through the room. Men stare at them, openly looking them up and down, inspecting them, nodding their approval. Maggie doesn't like it, but now is not the time to care or get caught up in the rich-man version of street catcalls. When they get out of the ballroom, Maggie turns left and leads Nadia to a quiet area down the hallway.

"Nadia?"

Her eyes are shut tight. "I've told no one."

"It's okay."

"It's been six years."

Nadia finally opens her eyes. They're wet and red.

"It's okay," Maggie says again, putting a gentle hand on the girl's arm. "I'm on your side. Always."

"You'll tell Oleg. Or Ivan."

"Never. Do you hear me? Never. I won't tell anyone. That's a promise."

Nadia releases a long deep breath. Maggie waits, gives her a little space.

"They gave me a totally new identity. Nadia isn't my real name."

"What is your name?" Maggie asks.

She shakes her head. "I can't tell you. I might trust you, but that doesn't mean my family has to."

"I don't understand."

"I'm Nadia Strauss now. That's all that matters. Please. I want you to call me that."

"Okay, sure, no problem."

"And I do have a thirty-one-year-old brother. And a mother. I had three other siblings and a father, but they're long dead. We were poor.

Not poor like Americans. You Americans don't really know poor. You have no idea what poor is. We wouldn't eat for days, until it feels like your stomach is stuck to your spine. We literally had nothing but each other."

"Where was this, Nadia?"

She doesn't answer. Her eyes stare past Maggie. It's a look Maggie sometimes saw in combat. The thousand-yard stare. Nadia's voice is distant now, detached.

"I was sixteen years old. My mother loved me. No one forced me. You do what you do to survive. You in the West think you have problems. I see it on social media now. People seeking"—she spits out the next words with pure contempt—"*self-help*, whatever that means. *Self-care*. Searching for, ugh, *fulfillment*. Whining, complaining, not feeling satisfied with their perfect lives." Nadia shakes her head in disgust. "How come starving people never need self-help or self-care? If you really want to cure your sleep anxiety over...over I don't know what...try not eating for five days in a row. Try sleeping on a dirt floor in the winter with no heat. Then let's see how much you worry about 'fulfillment' in your big house with two cars in the driveway."

Nadia turns her gaze back toward Maggie. Maggie stays still.

"You can figure out the rest, can't you, Doctor McCabe?"

Maggie probably can. "Tell me anyway."

"My mother woke me up one morning. She took me into the concrete building. No warning. No time to think or prepare myself. Probably for the best. They'd already run blood tests on everyone in my village. I was a match. They flew us out. They laid me down on a table. My mother took my hand. I had two kidneys when they put me to sleep. When I woke up, I only had one. Don't look at me like that."

Maggie tries to keep the horror off her face, but she doubts she's successful.

"You think my mother forced me."

"I didn't say—"

"She didn't. I understood. Even if they'd given me a choice, I would have done it."

Maggie swallows. "Your family sold your kidney." She doesn't mean to blurt it out like that, but if she offended Nadia, she can't see it from her expression.

"You don't understand," Nadia says. "We had nothing. Our family was mostly dead. That was our fate too. Starvation probably. Maybe slaughtered in war. My brother, my mother, maybe me. Or maybe my fate would have been worse. I don't know. So we made a choice. I gave up something I didn't need. In return, we were saved. We were given a new life. Money. New identities. They sent us...I won't tell you where exactly. But look at my life. Look where I am now. My mother and brother, they live in an American city. In the Midwest. I won't tell you which. My brother is in law school. My mother has her own apartment. Can you imagine? A real apartment with electricity and running water. She has a refrigerator and freezer. Do you know what she does every day?"

Maggie shakes her head no.

"She keeps a chicken in the freezer, and every night before she goes to bed she opens the freezer and just stares at the chicken. She can't believe it's real. She's worried one day she'll go to sleep and wake up and it will all have just been a dream. So you see? All of you who live in comfort can afford your ethics and morals. You want to judge me by them. How, you wonder, could I sell my own kidney? And I am here to tell you that it was the best thing that ever happened to me—and my family. My kidney is in someone else now. It probably saved a person's life—who knows?—but I know selling it saved three other lives. So don't you dare judge us."

"I don't judge," Maggie says softly.

But of course, it isn't that simple. Maggie knows that. You don't buy and sell human organs. It's immoral. It's exploitive. Selling organs commodifies human bodies, reducing individuals to their monetary value. It leads to trafficking and corruption and kidnapping and abuse.

And yet.

"I'm going to bed," Nadia says.

"Why are you here, Nadia?"

"What?"

"Why aren't you, I don't know, in the Midwest with your family?"

"My decisions are none of your business."

"That's true."

"You're not my psychiatrist or spiritual advisor. You're just a plastic surgeon."

"But I want to help."

"You can't," Nadia says. "I told you already. You don't know my life. Just do your job and leave me in peace."

CHAPTER NINE

Nadia says that she's going to say goodnight to Oleg before heading to bed.

"Do you mind if I come with you?" Maggie asks.

Nadia shrugs, so Maggie follows her up the stairs and around the corner. There is a gold door with two beefy bodyguards on either side. Nadia says something in Russian. One of the bodyguards barks something back and points at Maggie with his chin. Nadia explains who Maggie is, or at least, that's what Maggie assumes. The bodyguard talks into his watch. A few seconds later, the door opens. Nadia enters first. Maggie is right behind her.

The room is done up in a gaudy red velvet that a Vegas brothel might consider over-the-top. The floor is blanketed in beanbag chairs and oversize pillows and various low-level seating, all punctuated by glass-piped, multi-hose/multiuser hookahs. You could probably fit a hundred people in here for an orgy—that looks like the room's natural use—but right now there is only one person: Oleg Ragoravich. He stands by one long windowed wall. The windows are one-way and at an angle so you can look down at the ballroom, but the ballroom can't look in on you. Maggie remembers the mirrors lining the top of the wall where the crown molding is. She figures that this is the other side of those mirrors.

Ragoravich doesn't turn when they enter. He stares down at his ballroom not unlike an emperor at the Colosseum. Nadia says something in Russian. Maggie catches the end, "dobre noche," meaning good night. Oleg waves and mutters the same words back. Nadia doesn't wait. She turns and heads back out the door without another word or even a glance, leaving Oleg and Maggie alone.

Oleg still has his back to Maggie.

"Are you going down?" she asks him.

"Later." He points through the window below. His voice is suddenly soft. "I saw you."

"In the ballroom, you mean?"

"Yes. How's the food?"

"Eh, not bad. You could have spent a little more, gone for the upgraded appetizers."

He still doesn't turn around, but she can see a small smile from where she stands. "You saw the stage?"

"Yes."

"Do you know who's going to play?"

"No."

"Elton John. Are you a fan?"

Maggie nods. "He's one of my favorites."

He finally turns and faces her. "Mine too."

"I'm almost tempted to stay up," Maggie says.

"Please do."

"I have surgery tomorrow."

"True."

"So do you."

"Yes, but I'll be asleep for it," Oleg says.

"True."

He stares down at his guests. "Greed isn't what you think it is." His voice is thick with drink, or maybe that's just sadness.

"What do you mean?"

"The problem is, you can't go back. You can try. But human nature never lets you. Wherever you are, that becomes ground zero. Greed is not 'I need more'—it's the fear of losing what you already have. Of going back. So you hold on tighter and keep trying to climb up. Because that's the only way you can go. Life won't let you stand still. You are either on your way up or you're on your way down. And you'll do anything not to go down."

"That," Maggie says, "sounds like the very definition of greed."

He chuckles without humor. "Or a wonderful rationalization for it."

"That too. Are you all right, Mr. Ragoravich?"

"I'm fine," he says. "We all have our moments of melancholy."

Maggie thinks about what Nadia said, about the rich not having real problems and how their melancholy is a luxury. What must her reaction be when her oligarch gets gloomy?

"When did I first come on your radar?" she asks.

"You mean as a physician?"

"I mean in any way."

"I don't know. I leave these affairs to Ivan."

"I was his choice, then?"

"Why are you asking me this?"

"Have you heard of WorldCures Alliance?"

He frowns. "That was the charitable foundation you ran before . . . before your troubles?"

"Yes. Did you donate to it?"

"No. I don't think I ever heard of it until Ivan gave me your résumé."

"Have you heard of the Kasselton Foundation?"

"No, should I have?"

"You're not connected to it?"

"No." He turns back to her. "Did someone at the ball tell you I was?"

Maggie isn't sure of the right move here. She could lie, of course, or try to back away, but there is a good chance Oleg Ragoravich would figure out where she heard this. He told her already that he'd been watching her at the ball. He may have even seen her talking to Charles Lockwood. Even if he hadn't, the entire ballroom is probably under CCTV surveillance. He could search the footage for it.

Taking all of that into account, Maggie settles for a half-truth. "Someone hinted it, yes."

"Who?"

"An American. I didn't catch his name."

"From the ball?"

"Yes."

Oleg smiles. "Every American here is in the CIA." Then his eyes suddenly darken. "Does he know why you're here?"

"No."

"You didn't tell him?"

"Of course not."

Oleg Ragoravich takes a second, then seems satisfied with that answer. She should leave it there, let it go, but she can't.

"Why would someone tell me you finance the Kasselton Foundation?"

"Who? This sketchy American whose name you can't remember?"

"Yes."

"I have no idea." Oleg meets her eyes and holds them. "But I swear on the lives of my children, I don't know what the Kasselton Foundation is."

He may be a psychopath, but Maggie believes him.

"Do you mind if I ask you one more thing?"

He gestures for her to go ahead.

"Why are you getting this surgery?"

He frames his face with his hands. "You mean because I'm already so handsome?"

"Ten, maybe fifteen years ago," Maggie says, "I was part of a group of reconstructive surgeons who were invited to the Marshals Service headquarters in Arlington. They run the Witness Protection Program. You know what that is?"

"Of course."

"They wanted our opinion on what operations we could perform on the face, so that those who entered the program would be unrecognizable to their enemies."

"Makes sense."

"It does," Maggie agrees, "except our conclusion was, there really was nothing much you could do. You could change hairstyle and color. You could do some eye or ear work, try to give them a rhinoplasty, that sort of thing. But in the end, they mostly looked the same, just with a facelift."

"Interesting," Oleg says. "I assume you think this applies to me."

"Does it?"

Oleg doesn't answer. "It was nice talking to you, Maggie."

"And you."

"Are you going back to the ball?"

She shakes her head. "I have to be up early for surgery."

"We can push it back a few hours. For Elton's sake."

"Tempting."

"But?"

"But no."

Oleg Ragoravich turns so that his back is facing her again. "Will it be painful?"

"The recovery? You'll be a little uncomfortable for a few days. No activity for two weeks. That includes sex."

He says nothing.

"Anything else?" she asks.

"I see you're getting close to Nadia."

Maggie wonders what he means by that. She chooses to tread carefully. "She's a patient. I need to make sure she's cleared for this surgery."

"Seems more than that to you," he says. He points down to the ballroom. "I was watching."

"It isn't more. Why, is there a problem?"

"No, but you don't speak Russian, do you?"

"No."

"And of course, Nadia can't speak a word of English." His voice has some sarcasm in it, but his tone is closer to regret or even sorrow. "So I wonder—how do you two communicate?"

Oleg holds a hand up before Maggie can say anything. "I know. I've always known."

"Know what exactly?"

"That Nadia tells a lot of stories about herself," he says. Then he adds: "None of them are true."

CHAPTER TEN

God, how Maggie has missed this.

In medical terms, the suffix *plasty*—as in rhino*plasty* and blepharo*plasty* and genio*plasty* and mammo*plasty*—means "repair," "restore," "replace." It comes from the Greek word "plastia," which means "to mold"—and that is what it means to Maggie. Mold. Repair. Restore. It's science. It's art. The clay you create with is human flesh. There is no greater honor or responsibility than being a surgeon. For most of her career, Maggie dealt with soldiers and children with severe injuries and deformities. With her own two hands, she had the ability to mold, repair, restore them. Imagine that for a moment. Imagine what a privilege it is to do that kind of work, to make a living that way, to have people put that kind of trust in you and your abilities, to make them whole again.

How had she let herself betray that trust?

The obvious rationales—a butchered husband, a dead mother, whatever—none of that could ever excuse what she did. She had been given the greatest gift possible—the ability to heal through artistic creation—and she had squandered it.

Now she has been gifted this reprieve—for one day, at least.

Maggie goes through the same routine she's gone through hundreds if not thousands of times before—wash the hands, don the scrubs, tie the mask over the nose and mouth, snap on the gloves—but there is nothing routine about it. Not today. When she enters the surgical theater, emotions fly toward her hard and fast, nearly overwhelming her. Tears come to her eyes. She holds steady. She stops and takes a few deep breaths before approaching the table where Oleg Ragoravich lies unconscious. Her support staff—that's how she views them, as *hers*—are poised and ready.

This, Maggie knows, is where she belongs.

The operating room is her temple, her church, her sanctuary. Marc was home for her. She was home for Marc. But she and Marc both knew that here, in the cathedral they called an OR, was where they felt their most whole, their most complete.

She loved that about Marc. And he loved that about her.

They were the luckiest people in the world, weren't they?

Once Maggie asks for a scalpel, once she makes the mid-columellar inverted-V incision to access the underlying cartilage, her heart rate slows down. The calm enters her bloodstream. She settles back into this state of blissful creation. She would curse herself for not appreciating this feeling, this reverence, this calling, but she'd always understood and appreciated how special and extraordinary it was to be a surgeon.

And she'd blown it anyway.

That's what we stupid humans do. We carry the seeds of our own self-destruction.

She focuses now on the work to the point where she gets lost in it. Time passes. She has no idea how much. There are TV-like monitors so she can watch—they are in most operating rooms now—but she almost never needs them. It takes a little longer than she expects to clear away the nose cartilage so she can fit the marvel that is the artificial nose scaffold into place. She had hurried down three hours ago and geeked out when the technician showed the artificial scaffold to her. The material was, well, a nose—flimsy and stiff and malleable and brittle all at the same time.

She starts with this procedure because it is new and thus the most difficult. But it goes smoothly. She then moves on to the eyelids. She wants this feeling to last—to take her time, to remain in this state of pure contentment—but she knows it can't. It doesn't work that way. Surgery has its own organic, quasi-circadian rhythm. You can't mess with it to please your own needs.

She marks the natural folds around the eye and then uses a curved size 15 blade to make the incisions. She removes excess skin, muscle, and fat and closes the wounds up. The sliding genioplasty, a very specific type of chin augmentation, is next. She cuts through the mandibular symphysis—in layman's terms, the chin bone—and shifts it with her gloved hand. She harvests the fat from Oleg's abdomen via liposuction and transfers it to the face. Then she molds and shapes and shifts until Oleg's chin and jawline resemble the chin and jawline in the photographs.

Ivan Brovski is scrubbed and masked. He watches everything in silence. When he sees her close to finishing, he says, "Odd."

"What?"

"You're even better than your reputation."

Maggie should be above feeling pleased by the flattery, but the truth is, she's not. Maybe she would have been in the past. Not now. She closes up, and when she exits the operating room, Maggie sees that the total operating time on Oleg Ragoravich was three hours and fifteen minutes. Not bad. Maggie paces, feeling wired and jazzed. She can't wait to get back in there. The operating room is soon ready for Nadia's breast augmentation. Ivan Brovski is already there. Like before, she ignores him. Not out of malice or annoyance. She's just in the zone. She doesn't want anything interfering with that. If Brovski wants to watch, so be it. But she doesn't feel the need to facilitate or hinder.

Focus. Stay in the moment.

As with most surgeries, intermittent pneumatic compression

devices—think inflatable leg-squeezing machines or high-tech compression boots—are placed on the patient's legs. This is to regulate blood flow and prevent deep vein thrombosis or again, layman's terms, a blood clot. The Bovie pad is already stuck on Nadia's upper thigh. Put simply, it's a grounding pad used to channel electric currents away from the patient's body.

Maggie would have wanted to go with the most cutting-edge method of breast augmentation—using a patient's own fat—but Nadia didn't have enough fat to donate, and that procedure would have been too subtle a change for what she (or Oleg) wanted. Instead, they were going with the aptly nicknamed, state-of-the-art "gummy bear" implants—solid gel breast implants known for shape retention and realistic consistency. If you slice traditional silicone breast implants in half, the material will leak out like honey. That's not the case with the more solidified gummy bears.

Most people think they know how breast augmentation works: The surgeon makes the incision, creates a pocket behind the pectoral muscle, places the implant in the pocket, and then centers it behind the nipple. That's all true, but for the best work, you need to strap the unconscious patient to the operating table so that at some point, you can sit them up in a Fowler position. It is really the only way to evaluate the breast shape and assess the placement. Think about it. Do you want them to look natural only when you're lying down? Or do you care what they look like when you're sitting or walking? Duh. To not have the patient cranked up to a seated position because of hemodynamic concerns that have pretty much been laid to rest in study after study is, in Maggie's view, negligence.

The scrub nurse presses the operating table's button, moving the strapped-in Nadia into an upright position. Maggie inserts the various sizers and then stands back to see which ones are most symmetrical and appropriate for Nadia's frame. She has, as Brovski mentioned, the three sizes from which to choose. Dr. Deutsch, her mentor in this procedure, told her that when in doubt, go with the larger one because when it's over, almost every woman he's worked on says they wished they had gone a little bigger. Maggie keeps that in mind, but she also believes, perhaps wrongly, that Nadia is being somewhat coerced into doing this. In the end, the three hundred ccs, the smallest of the three sizes, provide the best aesthetic anyway, so Maggie goes with that.

At some point Ivan Brovski exits without a goodbye. Maggie idly wonders about that, but again this isn't about him. It's about the patient and the procedure.

A few minutes later, Maggie finishes up with sutures and steps back.

It's over.

Except it most definitely is not.

The scrub nurse turns off the ESU or Electrical Surgical Unit. Then she pulls the Bovie pad off Nadia's upper right quadricep.

And everything changes.

Maggie freezes and feels her world start to spiral.

"Doctor?"

Nadia has a tattoo on her leg. Maggie bends down for a closer look.

The tattoo is garish orange and purple. It's a cartoonish image of a goofily smiling serpent with a halo and a silly wink.

"Doctor McCabe, are you okay?"

Maggie has seen only one tattoo like this before.

On Marc's leg.

Maggie can't move.

The scrub nurse says, "Doctor?"

Her eyes finally move off the tattoo and up to Nadia's face. Nadia's eyes are closed. It'll be thirty to forty minutes before she's awake and able to converse. Maggie's gaze is drawn back to the tattoo.

There is no way this is a coincidence.

She thinks about that tattoo—how Marc regaled her with its college-spring-break origin story and how bad Marc was at handling his alcohol (which he was) and how his friends got him drunk (though it was his fault too, he'd admit) and how they stumbled down the French Quarter—and when he told the story, you could see the New Orleans night sky and feel the thick Creole humidity and touch the brick of the old buildings—and how he ended up in that small tattoo parlor and it was just a dare, no one thought Marc would go through with it, and how the artist, who was definitely drunk or stoned or worse, drew it in pen in mere seconds and that was it, it wouldn't go any further than that, surely, just a pen drawing, and then the artist— his name was Agent or something like that—took out the needle, and ha, ha, okay it's time to stop kidding around except no one did and it hurt like hell even with all the alcohol, and when he woke up, the area was all red and Marc thought it might be infected...

How can Nadia have that same tattoo?

"Doctor?"

She looks over at the anesthesiologist. "How long will the patient be out?" Maggie asks.

"An hour."

Maggie nods, turns her attention back toward the scrub nurse. "Where is Doctor Brovski?"

"He left in the middle of the surgery."

"Do you know where he went?"

"Perhaps he is looking in on Mr. Ragoravich?"

Maggie doesn't hesitate. She hurries out of the operating room and heads down the corridor. Post-op is the corner room. Maggie pulls up when she enters Oleg Ragoravich's recovery room.

It's empty.

That's wrong. She looks for the attending nurse. Nope, not there either.

Where the hell is Oleg?

He should still be here. The plan was to keep him in the recovery room for the next few hours at the very least before moving him to his bedroom upstairs.

So where is he?

Doesn't matter. Not right now. Right now, she wants to find Brovski and get her phone back. She wants to bring up the griefbot. She wants AI Marc to explain to her how the hell the twenty-four-year-old mistress of an oligarch has the exact same one-of-a-kind Serpent and Saint tattoo that he had.

This palace has workers everywhere, but suddenly Maggie can't find one. She heads through the abandoned indoor pool area, which is dark and humid, which again reminds her of Marc's tale about that humid New Orleans night. She still has on her scrubs. The heat from the pool is cloying. She rips off her lowered surgical mask and cap and tosses them in a bin.

When she exits by the other end of the pool, she's back in the corridor Oleg had led her down when she arrived . . . wow, was that only yesterday? . . . when he showed her the locked Mona Lisa room.

The door to the Mona Lisa room is wide open.

Maggie half sprints toward it. When she turns the corner, she sees three identical paintings on the wall, except they are all oil paintings of wildflowers.

No *Mona Lisas*.

What the . . . ?

No time to worry about it. She continues down the corridor. She passes the fake Gardner Museum pieces and notices that one, the Vermeer, is now missing.

Something is going on.

She isn't sure what to do when she hears a bellow from above. "Doctor McCabe?"

Maggie spins. It's Ivan Brovski.

"Where are you going?" he asks. "Why are you still in your scrubs?"

She moves back toward him and starts up the stairs. His face is set. She doesn't like that. "I need my phone," she says.

"You can't have it. You were told as part of your employment there was to be no communication—"

"And I told you that I wasn't communicating with anyone."

Ivan Brovski stares her down. "Then why do you want it back so badly?"

"That's not your concern."

His voice becomes soft. "It's not really him, you know."

"Yeah, no shit."

"It's an unhealthy crutch. You don't need it."

"What I really don't need," Maggie replies, "is mental health tips from an oligarch's lackey. Give me my phone, please."

Another man—Maggie recognizes him as one of the guards from last night—runs up to Brovski. The man is big, with a giant rectangular head. It's as if someone just dropped a cinder block between his shoulders. He looks Maggie over with disgust, as though she'd dropped out of the back of a dog's behind, and whispers something in Brovski's ear. Brovski's eyes close in what appears to be exhaustion. Then Brovski barks what sounds like an order in Russian. CinderBlock nods—tricky when you have no neck—and hurries over to another big man in another ill-fitting black suit.

"What's going on?" Maggie asks.

"It's time for you to leave, Doctor McCabe."

"Wait, what?"

"The helicopter will be here within the hour."

"I just finished the surgeries."

"An hour should give you time to shower and change."

"I told you up front. I need to stay with the patients—"

"No, you don't. I'm here. We have staff. The surgeries went spectacularly. As I mentioned before, you are as gifted as your reputation.

We will let Doctor Barlow know how pleased we were with your services. If you'll excuse me—"

"I want my phone."

"You'll get it when you depart."

Maggie is confused. Why the sudden rush? Why the change in demeanor? Maggie isn't big on vibes, but the whole vibe here has taken an unexpected turn for the worse.

"Oleg Ragoravich isn't in his room," Maggie says.

"That's not your concern."

She looks down by the front door. Two more men in ill-fitting black suits rush outside.

"Tell me about Nadia."

Brovski looks annoyed by the question. "What?"

"Where is she originally from?"

"I have no idea."

"Come on, Ivan. You know everything about me."

"Because you're a physician hired for discretion and ability. So yes, of course, we vetted you."

"And you don't vet the boss's mistress?"

"Exactly. He said not to, so we didn't."

More black-suited men rushing back and forth.

"I have to go," he says.

"Are you going to tell me what's going on?"

"Nothing. Shower, get changed. I'll bring your phone to your room. Then you can leave."

He rushes off then. Maggie isn't sure what to do. That garish tattoo— on Marc's leg, on Nadia's leg—keeps strobing through her mind. She can't stop it. Part of her wants to follow Brovski and demand her phone, but it's pretty clear that he's not going to give in on that yet.

So what next?

Stay calm. Think. Plan.

Okay, since Nadia is still unconscious, Maggie decides the best move forward is to shower quickly and change. If they are serious about her leaving—and they seem to be—is that really such a bad thing? Brovski was right—these surgeries are, in the end, fairly routine. The staff seem competent in handling the post-op, and if something goes wrong, they should be able to handle it.

So why shouldn't she head back to the United States as soon as possible?

Because she needs to know about that damned tattoo first.

One step at a time, she tells herself. Do your job. Shower, change, hurry back to the medical wing, find Oleg Ragoravich—they probably moved him to his bedroom already—check on him, make sure he's okay, and by then, Nadia should be waking up.

She hurries to her room, turns on the faucets, and steps under the spray. Funny thing: Even the shower gives her a nostalgic pang. That had been part of her old surgical ritual—the post-op shower—and she missed this feeling, the light exhaustion, the satisfaction of accomplishment, the clearing of the mind, the gentle cusp between her professional life and whatever awaited her (Marc) when she was done. Okay, yeah, it's just a shower, but even the tiny remnants of blood and tissue, the workday spiraling down the drain, had been her own sort of purification ceremony.

The shower is also a good place, perhaps the best place, to think, so Maggie tries to come up with a rational reason that Nadia has the same tattoo as Marc.

She can't think of a single one.

She needs more information. Simple as that. Ask Nadia when she wakes up. Ask the griefbot when she gets it back. Ask both.

Deep breaths.

She changes into loungewear and heads to the door. When she opens it, CinderBlock is standing there like a second door. She tries to move past him, but he blocks her.

"Please move out of my way."

"You stay," he says with a thick Russian accent.

"I need to check on my patients."

"Stay."

His eyes are on hers, and she doesn't like what she sees. It isn't anger or hatred or even determination in them. It's more...nothing. Lifeless. Like she's staring into the eyes of a filing cabinet.

She has a few options here, none of them good, but she tries the simplest. She channels the backyard touch football games of her youth. She loved them, especially on Thanksgiving. Her mother, a huge New York Jets fan, would play quarterback. Mom would imitate her NFL quarterbacks, shouting out nonsense. Maggie has always been quick as opposed to fast. That made her dangerous in the game. So, odd as it sounds, right now, with CinderBlock looming over her, Maggie fakes left like a running back. Cinder shifts his body to follow. Maggie pushes off her left foot and explodes past him on the right.

She doesn't know whether she can run faster than him. She doubts it. But she has now put him in an uncomfortable position. The only way to stop her is to use physical force. That's a big step up from blocking her path. CinderBlock would have to sprint after her now—perhaps grab or even tackle her. And she might resist. That would be forcing him to take this to a different level.

Maggie is hoping that he doesn't want to go there.

When he hesitates, Maggie keeps moving. "I'll be right back, I promise," she calls out, glancing behind her. "I just need to make sure my patient is okay."

She can see the wheels turning, even behind the lifeless eyes, but she doesn't give him time to weigh the pros and cons. He will either use physical force or not. If he does, so be it. She will deal with the consequences.

But there is no way Maggie is getting on that helicopter without talking to Nadia first.

She turns and sprints down the corridor.

CinderBlock doesn't follow. Or at least not yet. She sneaks a glance over her shoulder. No, he's not running after her. Of course there is more suited security around. He may be contacting one of them to get in her way. No point worrying about it. Better to just keep moving. The only way they should be able to stop her is to use force.

She doesn't *think* they will.

Think. Not know. *Think.*

But again, what are her options?

She runs past the Mona Lisa room. The door is closed again. Up ahead she sees three black-suited men running toward her. Reality hits. Doesn't matter how much hand-to-hand combat training she has. There is no way she will be able to get past all three of them.

But also, there is no way she's going to go down without a struggle.

She braces herself. But the three men veer away from her and run the other way.

What the hell is going on?

She sprints through the humid pool area and back into the medical wing. She checks Oleg Ragoravich's room. Still empty. She heads down two more doors to Nadia's recovery room. The door is closed. She knocks once, just out of habit, and reaches for the knob. She turns it and pushes in, worried now that Nadia will have vanished.

But she is there.

Nadia is in the bed, her eyes in that half-closed post-op way Maggie has seen a thousand times before. Maggie feels her heart beating wildly against her chest. She slows herself down, focuses on her breathing, steps into the room. No one else is here. Where the hell is all the support staff?

When Maggie closes the door behind her, Nadia stirs. Maggie waits. Nadia starts blinking open her eyes. Maggie sees the full water glass. She grabs a straw.

"Here," Maggie says. "Sip this."

She places the straw between Nadia's lips. Nadia sips.

"How do you feel?"

"Groggy," Nadia manages.

"That's normal."

Maggie has automatically switched into physician mode. She checks Nadia's vitals and stitching. All normal. Nadia starts waking up. Maggie can feel her eyes on her. It's always interesting to see how various patients react to their doctor. Some look away. Some watch with reverence or worry or even mistrust, as though trying to read what the doctor is really thinking versus what they are willing to admit out loud.

She hears someone run down the corridor past the door. A man shouts in Russian. Maggie doesn't understand what he's saying, but there is panic in his tone. Time is not on Maggie's side here. She gets that. She locks the door and sits on the edge of Nadia's bed. *More personal this way*, she thinks. Less intimidating.

"I want to ask you something."

Nadia's eyes are blue and wide and beautiful. "Is something wrong? Did the surgery—"

"No, no, you're fine. The surgery went perfectly."

Nadia just looks at her and waits.

"When I was doing your surgery..." Maggie isn't sure how to ask this. She reaches to pull back the blanket on Nadia's leg. It's the wrong move. Nadia jolts, cringes, holds the blanket in place.

Just dive in, Maggie tells herself.

"You have a tattoo on your upper thigh."

There is a brief flare in those eyes now. "You saw it?"

Maggie can hear the fear in Nadia's voice now.

"Yes."

"I don't understand. My leg. It was covered. You were supposed to be working on my chest—"

"I saw it at the end," Maggie says. "When the surgery was over. The nurse took off the Bovie pad."

Nadia looks terrified.

"It's okay," Maggie says, trying to reassure. "I didn't mean to..." She stops, tries again. "Could you tell me where you got it?"

Nadia closes her eyes and shakes her head no.

"Please," Maggie says. "It's important."

"Why?"

Maggie needs to keep this moving. "I've seen the design before," she says.

"What do you mean?"

"Please, Nadia. Can you just tell me where you got it? Why do you have it?"

Nadia pulls up her legs as though trying to protect them.

"Nadia?"

"Leave me alone."

"They're making me leave soon."

"What?"

"Something is going on. I can't find Oleg. They want me to leave. Please, Nadia, I need to know about the tattoo."

"But why?" Nadia asks—and now there seems to be a small accusation in her tone. "Have you seen that tattoo before?"

"Yes," Maggie says.

"On other young girls?" Nadia asks. "Or boys?"

"No," Maggie says. "On someone I loved very much."

Nadia blinks. "I don't understand."

"Nadia, please tell me how you got it."

Her voice turns stone-cold. "You know already."

"What? No, I don't."

"This loved one," Nadia says. "Did he also donate a kidney?"

"No. Why would you ask that?"

"Because," she says, "that's when I got mine."

Maggie makes a face. "When you donated your kidney?"

She nods. "He put me under for the operation. When I woke up, my kidney was gone, and on my leg..." She shrugs away the end of the thought.

Maggie tries not to look horrified. "The tattoo was just on your leg?"

"Yes."

"So they put it on while you were under?"

Nod.

"And you'd never seen it before?"

Tears push into Nadia's eyes.

"Nadia?"

"It was his sign."

"Whose sign?"

"I need more water."

Maggie puts the straw between her lips. Nadia lifts her head to sip. When she's done, her head falls back on the pillow.

"My mother told me that her grandfather used to brand camels," Nadia says. "Always on the left side of the face. Always. So you knew what tribe it belonged to. Here, with him, it was always on the upper right thigh. Where no one in my village would see it." Nadia winces and tries to sit up. "Who do you know who has it?"

"Like I said"—Maggie's head is swirling—"a loved one."

"No."

"No?"

"That's not good enough," Nadia says. Her voice has more edge now, bordering on anger. "What loved one?"

Maggie's mouth goes dry. She's right, of course. She has every right to know. "My husband."

"Did he donate a kidney too?"

"No. He was a surgeon."

Nadia's eyes lock on her. "Did he do mine?"

"No," Maggie says too quickly.

"How can you know for sure?"

Maggie says nothing. She feels lost.

"Where is your husband now?" Nadia asks.

"He's dead." Maggie hears the distant monotone in her voice. Then she adds, "He was killed."

Nadia doesn't look surprised. "They murdered him?"

The question throws her. An odd question. Or was it? "What do you mean by 'they'?"

"Who killed him?"

"I don't know."

Nadia shakes her head. Maggie feels cold inside.

"Nadia?"

"You're lying," Nadia says.

"What?"

"I see it in your eyes. Who killed your husband?"

Maggie isn't sure how to answer that. "Marc was on a humanitarian mission in a war zone. The camp was overrun by men with guns and machetes. It was a slaughter. He . . ."

She stops.

"How did he die?"

"What?"

"You said guns. You said machetes."

"I don't know," Maggie says, her voice soft. "I hope a bullet, but . . ." She stops. There is no reason to say more about that.

Silence.

"The surgeon," Nadia says, her eyes steady now. "The one who took out my kidney. He was a white man. They called him the Snake. I didn't know why. Until I saw the tattoo." Nadia looks away. "He was not kind."

And then Nadia says it: "Trace."

Maggie freezes. "What?"

"There was a man there. Someone called him Trace."

"He was the surgeon?"

Nadia shakes her head. "No. He tried to stop it."

The door bursts open then.

It's Ivan Brovski with CinderBlock and a nurse. They look at the bed behind Maggie. Maggie follows their gaze and sees that Nadia has her eyes closed, feigning unconsciousness. The nurse crosses the room and checks Nadia's pulse.

Brovski grabs Maggie's arm.

"Let go of me," Maggie says, pulling her arm free.

Between clenched teeth, Brovski says, "What are you doing in here?"

"I told you. I wanted to check on my patient. I was waiting for her to wake up."

"Why did you lock the door?" Before she can come up with a lie, Brovski shakes it off. "Doesn't matter. Nadia is in good hands. Let's go."

"Where's Ragoravich?" she asks.

But Brovski is not having any of it. "Please get your stuff. It's time to leave."

CHAPTER ELEVEN

Ivan Brovski escorts her back to her bedroom. CinderBlock follows a few paces behind. When Brovski opens the door to her room, she moves to the window and looks out. There are more suited men scouring the front lawn.

"What's going on, Ivan?" she asks.

"Nothing that concerns you," Brovski says. "Here."

She turns to him. Brovski extends his hand.

Her phone is in it.

Maggie resists the temptation to snatch it away. Doesn't want to look too eager. Her hand reaches out and closes around it. Ivan holds on for another second. Their eyes meet.

"Just so you know," he says, "we deleted your sister's app."

He waits for her to react. Maggie gives him nothing.

"Out of an abundance of caution," Brovski continues. "I hope you understand."

She doesn't reply.

"You'll be home soon. I'm sure your sister can provide you with a new one then."

Nothing.

"Also," he adds, "the battery is very low. Don't worry though. A charger will be provided for you on the plane."

Show him nothing, Maggie tells herself. "How long until the helicopter arrives?" she asks.

"Ten minutes."

"This outfit is itchy," Maggie tells him. "I'm going to change into something else for the trip."

"Of course."

Maggie heads into the bathroom and closes the door. The bathroom is what you'd expect—gold, marble, ornate. She waits to hear him leave. When he does, Maggie turns on the shower—and then she unlocks the phone.

Yep, the griefbot app is gone. Or at least, the little icon is.

Maggie doesn't know much about technology, but what Brovski's undoubtedly cocky experts don't know is that Sharon sets up her proprietary apps so that they can*not* be deleted without facial recognition from both Sharon and Maggie, plus a password. If someone else tries to delete them—like Brovski's experts—the icon does indeed vanish from the screen so that it appears deleted—but in reality, it just moves to a hidden folder.

Maggie swipes, hits the news app, which isn't really a news app, and accesses the hidden folder.

And voilá, the griefbot app is there.

She allows herself a small smile. *Sharon*, she thinks, *you friggin' overcautious, anal genius.*

She clicks the icon and AI Marc returns.

"Hey," Griefbot Marc says to her.

The battery is indeed low, maybe 10 percent. No time to waste. "Tell me about your tattoo."

"I must have told you a hundred times, but okay. I was in New Orleans—"

"That's a lie, Marc."

"What?"

"I need you to tell me the truth."

The bot even perfectly mimicks Marc's perplexed expression. Well, if Marc had indeed been genuinely perplexed when he was alive. Maybe that had been an act. Maybe it had all been a lie.

No, she tells herself, don't do that.

Don't start questioning everything about the man you loved.

"I need to know about the tattoo, Marc. I'm not angry or anything. You probably had your reasons for not telling me. But that's in the past. I need to know now."

"Maggie, I don't know what you're talking about."

"I saw a woman who had the exact same tattoo on her leg."

AI Marc grins. "Hey, maybe it's an ex," he says.

"What?"

"You know, like as a tribute. Someone who couldn't get over me. Come on, don't be jealous."

Maggie makes a face. The app thinks she's joking.

"Though in truth," he continues, "well, I show it to a lot of people. I mean, when I'm wearing shorts. Or at the beach or something. It always gets a laugh, you know that—"

"Marc, I need you to listen to me. I'm being serious here."

Sharon had warned about this. She had created a griefbot so much like the real Marc that it would also withhold truths that the real Marc might. "If Real Marc would have lied about it, so would Grief-bot Marc," Sharon had told her. "Like, if Marc really didn't like a dress you wore but would lie to spare your feelings, so will AI Marc. And to get more serious, let's say Marc secretly gambled or had another wife in Akron or whatever—something he would keep from you—so will AI Marc."

In short, if Real Marc wouldn't tell her the truth about the tattoo, neither would AI Marc.

"This is life and death," Maggie continues, because she needs to reach this...this artificial being. Not Marc. A hell of a facsimile but still just that. Not more. "Whatever reason you had for lying to me about the tattoo? It's not important anymore. Water under the bridge. You'd do anything to protect me, right?"

"Of course. Maggie, you know that."

"Then tell me about the tattoo. The truth."

"I was in college. I was in New Orleans. I had too much to drink—"

"The truth, Marc."

"That's the truth. I was on spring break—"

"I just did surgery on a patient," Maggie interrupts.

Griefbot Marc's face changes. He is now the serious, focused, great-listening husband-colleague she could bounce cases off of. "Okay. Give me the details."

"A twenty-four-year-old woman."

"Procedure?"

"Breast augmentation."

"Okay, right. So?"

"So when I looked at her upper right quadricep, she had the same Serpent and Saint tattoo you have. Not something close. Not like what Porkchop or the gang have. The exact same as yours. The same design. The same colors. The same location on the upper thigh."

AI Marc shakes his head. "That's impossible."

"Marc—"

"I'm serious. That makes no sense at all. That tattoo guy in New Orleans. I think he was more wasted than I was. That's where I got it."

"It's on her leg," she counters, trying not to shout with frustration. "It's real. I saw it. Marc—"

"Wait, I got it."

"I'm listening."

"It's a prank."

"It's not a prank."

"Has to be. I've done the calculations, Maggie. Wait, I bet it's Randi. She always made jokes about the tattoo—and she loves pranks."

Randi Edmunds had been Maggie's lead scrub nurse.

"Remember that prank she pulled on April Fools' with the ties on the surgical gowns. Randi has to be behind this. She drew a tattoo on your patient's leg to mess with you. It's just the kind of thing Randi—"

"It's not a prank," she snaps back.

Time is running low. Maggie knows that.

"It's not Randi Edmunds. She's not even here. Please, Marc, I need you to tell me the truth."

Maggie hears a knock on the door and then someone enters. From behind the bathroom door, Ivan Brovski shouts out, "Doctor McCabe?"

The shower is still on.

"Sorry!" Maggie shouts back. "I just wanted to rinse off again. I'll be out in a minute."

There is a small pause. Then Brovski says, "The helicopter will be here in five minutes. Please hurry."

"Right, got it."

She drops her phone hand to her side and wonders what to do next. That's when she hears Marc's tinny voice coming from the phone:

"Maggie, why are you with Ivan Brovski?"

Maggie's blood goes cold. She raises the phone back to her face, so she can see Griefbot Marc's face again. "You know Ivan Brovski?"

"Yes."

"How?"

"Where are you, Maggie?"

"At an oligarch's house somewhere in Russia."

"Oleg Ragoravich."

"Yes."

"What are you doing there?"

"Barlow got me a high-paying concierge gig."

"To do what?"

"The breast augmentation I just told you about?"

"That's it?"

"No, I also did three facial surgeries on Ragoravich."

"Why did he want that?"

"I don't know."

"Did I hear Brovski say something about a helicopter?"

"I've finished the surgeries," Maggie explains. "They're flying me home."

"On the copter?"

"Yes."

"Maggie?"

She looks at the screen and keeps it close. She recognizes that facial expression too.

Marc is scared.

"Whatever you do," he says to her, "don't get on that helicopter."

The cold rips through her. "Why not?"

"There is an abandoned iron ore mine two miles away. No one knows how deep the hole is. Five, six thousand feet at least."

"So?"

"So if you get on that helicopter, they will throw you into it."

"Marc—"

"You don't understand these people."

"And you do?"

"You performed facial surgery to change Ragoravich's looks, Maggie. They can't let you live. Do you understand what I'm telling you?"

The knock on the bathroom door startles her.

"Let's go, Doctor McCabe," Brovski says. "I'm losing my patience."

"Maggie," AI Marc says, "you have to run."

CHAPTER TWELVE

The alarm startles Sharon.

It is late, way past anyone rational's sleep time, but Sharon is awake. She usually is. She requires very little sleep, or at least, she gets very little sleep. Her mind has a tendency to run too hot. It is hard to shut it off. At one point, someone had suggested meditation, but just the thought of clearing the mind or turning off her brain or whatever stupid-speak people use merely to describe this awful experience caused Sharon anxiety to the point of a near panic attack. She doesn't buy it anyway. Asking any human to stop thinking is akin to asking them to stop their heart from beating. You can't. Not really. Sharon understands that better than most. Most people could control their thoughts in one way or another. Or experience mental fatigue and exhaustion.

Sharon could not.

She'd been reading a novel in the leather chair in her bedroom. Cole is in bed. Oddly enough, while she can rip through journals and manuals and technical books, she reads novels slowly, leisurely, making sure every scene comes to life in full color in her head. This is the closest she gets to shutting down—distracting her brain with fiction rather than problem-solving.

Sharon sits up when she hears the alarm. Her bookmark has Edward Hopper's *The Sheridan Theatre* on it. Sharon's favorite painting.

Maggie had bought it for her at the Newark Museum gift shop when they visited in May.

Sharon places the Hopper bookmark between pages ninety-two and ninety-three, closes the book, rises.

Her mind is a constantly whirring thing, her brain overheating—it makes life unbearable in many ways. It makes it impossible for a man to stay with her. To love her. Tad had tried. In the end it hadn't worked. Her... Is it a condition? Hard to say. Everything is called a condition now. You shake your leg, you have some big diagnosis. Sharon doesn't buy it all. Is she on the spectrum or autistic or something like that? Undoubtedly. Does it matter? She isn't sure. But this is how she was built and so her "condition" (let's just call it that for now) eventually drove Tad away. She hadn't expected him to become bitter. That had taken her aback. But she knows—and not in a pathetic, needy, pitiful way—that she is unlovable. She could be a decent mom and daughter and sister. She could be a pretty good friend. But her condition makes her unworthy of true companionship or love.

So be it.

The alarm sounds again, jangling her nerves. Sharon is a cautious person. You have to be in this business. Every software or AI enhancement she creates has backdoors and security traps, even the ones she's provided to the government. Especially those. She could destroy the programs at any time. She could see whether someone tampered with them...

... and she could see if someone tried to delete them.

That—Sharon can see immediately when she fires up her laptop to check the alarm status—is what happened here.

Someone has tried to delete the griefbot on Maggie's phone.

This is not good.

It doesn't take a genius to figure that out. Sharon had done as Maggie asked. Up until now, she has respected her sister's desire for privacy. Maggie had gone up to New York City to see Evan Barlow.

Barlow had offered Maggie some kind of high-paying but secretive work. Maggie had told Sharon that she couldn't say more because it would violate HIPAA and privacy clauses. Fair enough. Sharon let it go. Sharon accepted the financial good fortune that had come their way, even though she knew that there had to be a price to pay somewhere for it.

Is now the time to pay up?

Someone tried to delete the griefbot.

It couldn't be Maggie. Maggie knows that she can't do it alone. Sharon had wondered about that. She had built every app and software program so that the only way it could be altered, touched, or deleted in any way was via Sharon's direct involvement. She'd wondered whether this whole griefbot testing thing had been a mistake. The power of this particular griefbot is both enticing and destructive, but when you think about it, when you *really* think about it, that's true of every invention that makes an impact.

There is no such thing as a consequence-free discovery.

It is what man chooses to do with it.

Sharon is a scientist first. She sees things from that perspective, and again that makes her cold in too many ways. Still, Sharon remembers Tad's long body on the couch, the way he would lie behind her and spoon her, and now that same man hates her and wants to destroy her.

So be it.

Perhaps she shouldn't have pushed Maggie with the griefbot. Sharon had rationalized that it would help her sister deal with the grief. But had that really mattered next to Sharon's blinding drive for scientific progress? Marc's death had been so sudden, so brutal, so shocking, that transitioning with an experimental AI version could offer real comfort, Sharon rationalized. But at the very least, Sharon should have given Maggie the option of deleting the app on her own.

Now, staring at the alarm, Sharon wonders why someone would

try to delete Maggie's griefbot. She can't come up with an answer, but one thing is crystal clear.

Maggie is in trouble.

––––––––––

Ivan Brovski shouts, "It's time to go."

Maggie looks at the griefbot and turns off the shower.

"I need to grab some clothes from the closet," she calls back. "I'll meet you downstairs."

There is silence for a few long seconds. Then Brovski says, "I'll be right outside the door. Please hurry."

Maggie waits until she hears the door close. She peeks out.

He's gone.

From her app, she hears the Marc griefbot say, "I'm putting a phone number in your link. I need you to call it."

"There's no service here," Maggie says. "They've blocked it off."

"I know."

"How?" Then: "Have you been here?"

"Yes."

"When?"

"Get a few hundred yards away from the house, and you should be able to call."

"What the hell? Why didn't you tell me—"

"No time for that now, Maggie. Here's the number."

She checks the screen. The phone number is not one she recognizes. Does it even matter? How can she call? And what will happen when she does? Ivan Brovski is standing right outside the door. Does she hope to, what, run through the door, surprise him, run outside?

So what's her plan here?

She tests the bedroom windows. No special locks on them. She's on the third floor, but there's a short drop from the window on the far wall to the side roof. Snow is falling. She checks the closet. No heavy coat. One sweatshirt. She throws it on. It won't be enough. Not with this cold.

But again, what choice does she have?

No more hesitation.

She pushes open the window, and a blast of cold shoves her back a step. She closes her eyes against the wind and swings her legs over the sill. Her sneakers scrape against the stone roof as she drops out the window and closes it behind her.

Oh man, it's freezing.

The ground, except for the coil-heated part of the lawn, is blanketed with snow. She wonders how much time she has before Brovski starts knocking on the door. Not much, she imagines.

Time to move.

No way to go down the front. Not with the black-suited men still crisscrossing the lawn. She has to find another way. The wind is already biting her face. She can't stay out here too long. The exposure will get to her soon.

Keep moving.

A plan... Well, not really a plan. Almost a plan. A bare sketch of a desperate, impossible idea comes to her.

Head to the back of the house, she tells herself.

The roof tile is slick, and she nearly falls before regaining her balance. She ducks low and starts half sprinting, half skating toward the back of the estate. With a shaking hand, she sees the battery on her phone is down to 4 percent. Shit. She hits send. No response. She hits send again and jams the phone back in her pocket.

She needs both hands to keep her balance.

Maggie tries to remember that weird house tour with Oleg Ragoravich.

Man, was that really only yesterday?

It is too cold. She should go back. Maybe the Marc griefbot is wrong. Maybe Brovski and Ragoravich don't mean her harm. She did the work she'd been hired to do. People know she's here. Or at least, well, when she thought about it, only one person knows: Evan Barlow. So if she vanishes now, if she is somehow thrown out of a helicopter into a deep hole, somewhere in the forests of Russia, what would happen to her? Would Barlow come forward? And if he did, so what? What could anyone prove?

But the griefbot had said it best: She'd done facial surgery on Ragoravich. Why? None of it had been to improve his looks. She'd known that right away. It was clearly done to disguise him. To change his identity. The type of surgery she'd performed would fool any facial-recognition program at, say, an airport or border crossing.

But still. Would they kill her?

She starts slipping as she reaches the edge, nearly sliding right off the rooftop. She claws her way to a stop at the drainpipe. She sits up, her legs dangling over the side of the roof. She stares down.

Way too far to jump, even with the snowbank.

There has to be a way.

There's a fire ladder to her right. Perfect. She scooches toward it. When she reaches out and touches the top rung, she pulls her hand back. The metal is so cold it feels as though her hand might freeze-stick to it.

"Doctor McCabe?"

The wind snatches most of the sound away, but she knows it's Ivan Brovski.

She has no chance. Not really.

Surrender? Is that her best option?

Ivan again, calling from the window: "Maggie?"

She lays flat on the roof. Her head hangs off the edge. She looks down. No one is directly below her. She turns her head to the right. Nothing. She looks to the left.

Two black-suited men. They have guns out.

What the hell is going on?

Maggie hears a shuffling noise from behind her.

Someone else has come out on the roof. They're coming toward her.

No choice now. She pulls down her sleeves, so that the cuffs cover her palms. Makeshift gloves. She jumps on the ladder and starts down it. If her memory and geography are correct, she is over the indoor pool right now.

So what's the plan?

She'd considered working her way back indoors and then finding a place to hide. The palace is huge, with lots of rooms. It could take a long time to find her. But then she remembered that the place was loaded up with CCTV. There is nowhere she can go without being spotted and found.

Including probably this roof.

So the only way is to keep moving.

She still has one idea though. A dumb one. A desperate one. But if the swimming pool is where she thinks it is, then so should be...yes.

The glass walkway is right where she hoped it would be.

She is on the third rung of the ladder when she sees cords of stacked firewood. *Good*, she thinks. That might help. She climbs farther down the ladder. When she's halfway down, she looks up.

CinderBlock is staring down at her.

Maggie's eyes widen as she watches him take out his gun. He points at her. Their eyes meet and Maggie can see in his casual, almost bored expression what's about to happen.

CinderBlock is going to shoot her.

He isn't going to shout out a warning. He isn't going to call for her to halt or freeze or surrender.

He is simply going to pull the trigger.

Maggie sees it coming. By the time she hears the blast, she's already pushed off the ladder. She falls backward. The bullet whizzes past her leg, clanking a metal rung below her. There was no time to look down before she jumped, so she doesn't know how far the fall is. She tucks her legs in, braces herself, lands hard.

The momentum forces her into a roll through the snow. The cold bites her skin hard and deep, nearly paralyzing her.

Keep moving.

It's a funny thing. When she first pushed open the bedroom window, she wondered when her military training would kick in. When would the calm descend on her? When would her heartbeat stay under control? When would she be cool and detached and analytical?

Nothing had prepared her for this.

And yet.

And yet the training had kicked in—it just hadn't announced itself. It is a part of her. No, there is nothing routine or rote here. No, she'd never trained on how to escape an oligarch's mansion via a window on an icy rooftop. But time has indeed slowed down for her. Here Maggie is, with a man firing shots at her from above, freezing in the snow, and she has something that resembles a strategy and even a plan.

Using the momentum from the fall and roll, she jumps behind the firewood just as the next shot rings out. When you watch someone fire a handgun on television, it seems like a pretty accurate weapon. It is not. The truth is, CinderBlock is now a good forty to fifty feet away from her. The wind is howling in his face. The cold is numbing his shooting hand.

It's hard to be accurate.

He realizes it too. She can see him grab his phone to call in reinforcements. That gives her a chance to make her next move. She picks up a log from the firewood. It's frozen solid. Solid enough? She will find out. She sprints at the glass walkway where Ragoravich had led her on his tour. There is a small spiderweb crack in one of the panels. That might help. She rears back with the firewood and hits the window crack as hard as she can.

The glass shatters.

She doesn't look behind her. She doesn't look up. A bullet strikes nearby and more glass shatters, raining down on her. She ducks and covers her head and jumps through the shattered window and into the walkway. Then she turns left as another shot rings out. In the corner of her eye, she sees a black-suited man round the corner and sprint toward her. Maggie clocks that he's there, but that doesn't change her plan.

She just needs to pick up the pace.

The door to the car showroom is unlocked. She hurries through it, shuts it behind her, throws the deadlock. The room is pitch black. It had been that way when Oleg Ragoravich brought her here. He'd hit the light switch on the left. She does that now. The lights boom immediately on in shade-your-eyes bright. Maggie doesn't shade her eyes.

There's no time.

She looks for the switch to open the huge garage door. Her plan is a simple one. Oleg Ragoravich has a car collection. When he offered her a joyride, he showed her that he keeps the keys in a certain car.

So that's the plan. Get the showroom door open. Get in a vehicle. Drive out.

She finds the switch. The door is two stories high. It grudgingly starts to part like the Red Sea. It makes a lot of noise. It moves too slowly. Maggie stays on the move. She knows that black-suited men will be on her any second.

A voice yells out something in Russian.

Probably telling her not to move. She turns and sees the black-suited man aiming the gun at her. Her mind whirs, searching for a solution—but in the midst of the whirring, she notices something interesting.

The black-suited man doesn't fire right away.

Why? CinderBlock fired. This guy fired too when she was in the glass walkway.

Why isn't he firing now?

And then the answer comes to her. Oleg Ragoravich loves these cars. They are expensive, worth millions of dollars apiece. The black-suited men probably figure that they have her trapped now. No need to fire and risk harming something so valuable.

That gives Maggie the wiggle room she needs.

She keeps sprinting and ducking behind cars until she reaches the Ferrari. Two black-suited men follow. She fumbles with the door but manages to slide into the driver's seat. One of the men is on her now. He grabs the handle of the door as she starts to close it. With her left hand, Maggie keeps pulling the door closed. With her right, she fires up the ignition. The man keeps his hold on the driver's-side door. Maggie tries to hold on, so he can't get in. It's a draining game of tug-of-war.

The ignition is on, but the car isn't an automatic. It's an old manual with a stick shift. Maggie hasn't driven one since she was eighteen. But her dad had taught her. The man is pulling hard on the door. He has the leverage now. Another man is coming to join him. No way Maggie can fight them both off. She holds on with her left hand and tries to shift the car into gear with the right.

It's not working.

He's winning the battle. The other guy arrives and grabs the door too. Maggie waits until they have full pressure on her. Then she simply lets go. The door flings open. The men stumble back, lose their balance. That's what she's been counting on. But one of them recovers fast. He reaches out and grabs her by the hair.

He starts dragging her out of the car.

Maggie takes her right hand off the shift. She curls her fingers and delivers a palm strike straight into his groin.

The man's grip loosens.

Maggie pulls the door back closed. She shifts now, hits the accelerator, drags him a few feet before the man falls away.

The showroom doors haven't opened enough for her to get

through. Again: Doesn't matter. She slams the Ferrari through what-ever opening there is, pushing into the wooden doors and doing Lord-knows-what to the Ferrari's paint job.

The doors hold for a second before splintering and releasing the car. Maggie is out.

She feels something akin to euphoria—her plan worked!—when a bullet shatters the back window. Maggie ducks. The cold again rushes in. With one hand still on the gearshift, she pulls the steering wheel hard to the left. Another bullet whizzes above her head, shattering and knocking out the front windshield.

Now what?

Just keep your foot on the gas pedal.

She does. Up ahead she sees another black-suited man aiming his gun at her. She aims the car at him and stays low. He ducks away.

She hears bullets, but nothing hits.

Now what?

She checks her phone.

Are there enough bars?

She hits send again. No reason to look anymore. Just keep hitting the send button and hope for the best.

She can see now that the front gate is closed. Can she ram the car through? She doesn't think so. The car is old and small. The gate looks foreboding, built for security. A man stands in front of it, gun drawn.

She veers to the right and takes a road up the side of a hill.

A black SUV is following her now.

Shit. Another gun blast.

Her tire explodes.

She swerves, but she keeps her foot on the accelerator. The Ferrari still has enough firepower. She keeps her foot down. The car fishtails up. She has no front windshield anymore. The cold digs deep into her face. She can barely keep her eyes open.

The black SUV chases her, moves alongside. The tire is gone now. She's driving on the rim. Another bullet rings out.

Maggie feels something tear in her shoulder.

It's over now. A part of her knows that. There's nothing she can do to control the car anymore. She takes her foot off the accelerator, tries to hit the brake. But either her foot or the car won't obey.

The Ferrari veers off the road. Maggie's eyes are closed now. She feels rather than sees the plummet. She tries again to hit the brake or turn the wheel. But nothing happens. Nothing slows down. The descent continues until the car slams into a tree.

There is no seat belt in the Ferrari. Not that Maggie would have had time to put it on. But there is nothing to keep her in place. Maggie feels her body lift and rocket forward through what remains of the front windshield. Shards of glass slice her skin before she smacks into something hard.

Her body goes slack. Everything leaves her. Everything turns cold, so cold, a deep, hard, bone-crushing cold she's never experienced before.

And then, mercifully, everything turns black and there is nothing.

CHAPTER THIRTEEN

Porkchop spreads the printouts on the bar. Sharon stands over him. They are at Vipers for Bikers. It is eight a.m. Last year, Porkchop started opening for a Full Throttle Breakfast with specials like Rise and Ride, the Biker's Breakfast Slam, and the house specialty, Pit Stop Pancakes. It's proven to be a hit with the tourists.

"Okay," Porkchop says, "explain to me what I'm seeing."

"There is a proprietary beta UX app I created on Maggie's phone."

"Uh-huh."

"It contains certain features involving the Doppler effect, CDRs, GPS, triangulation—"

"Sharon," Porkchop says.

"Yes?"

"Are you saying you can track Maggie?"

"Yes. No. Well, I could. Maggie didn't explain what my new program can do, did she?"

Porkchop gives her a look. "You know I don't own a smartphone, right?"

"It's why I took the first train here," Sharon says.

"I'm sorry about that."

"So Maggie never mentioned an app?"

"An app to me is chicken wings," Porkchop says.

Sharon nods. "Of course she wouldn't," she says, more to herself than to him.

"I'm not following."

"It's . . ." Sharon shakes it off. "Never mind, it's not important. What's important is that the app was on her phone. It's an important app. For her. For me. It could one day also be worth a lot of money. She visited you when she came up to see Doctor Barlow, right?"

"Right."

"And then she took some job. Something very lucrative. All of a sudden, all my debt was gone."

Porkchop nods. "I know. He flew her someplace."

"Russia," Sharon says. "A remote region near Gelendzhik north of the Black Sea."

"She told you this?"

"No. Look at the printout. It follows her route."

"Your, uh, app does this?"

"Yes."

"Sharon, I don't know much about technology, but wouldn't you lose the ability to track when it's in the air or off Wi-Fi or whatever?"

"If you used strictly Wi-Fi or cellular services, yes. But I've been able to keep the app active by tying the frequency into governmental satellite LEOs—that's Low Earth orbit—"

"Sharon."

"Right, sorry. Here's the point. Someone tried to delete the app off Maggie's phone." Sharon raises her hand as though to stop him. "No, it wasn't Maggie. She would know that it couldn't be done this way. The most rational reason is that someone took away her phone, didn't like that app being on it, and tried to delete it."

"What's on the app?"

Sharon hesitates.

"Sharon?"

"You wouldn't understand. And it's not really important. What does matter is that someone took possession of Maggie's phone, undoubtedly against her will."

"So she's in trouble," Porkchop says.

"Yes."

"Can you use the L-E-whatever to tell us where she is now?"

"Here's where she was yesterday. I brought the satellite image."

She reaches over him and turns the page.

Porkchop studies the page. "I assume the red dot is her?"

"Yes."

"I only see trees."

"I know. I had to zoom out. There are roads, but whatever building is there, it's being blocked."

"What does that mean?"

"It means someone rich and powerful lives there. He doesn't want his house seen via satellite. He wants to stay hidden."

Porkchop says nothing.

"So at 2:13 a.m. local time yesterday," Sharon continues, "someone tech savvy found a way past Maggie's facial recognition and got into her phone. Forty-eight minutes later, someone tried to delete my proprietary beta app. It's tricked up so that the person who does it will think they succeeded, but they didn't. That triggered an alarm that reached me around three in the morning."

"What else do you know?"

"The app was later reinstalled."

"How's that?"

"I don't know. Perhaps the experts are better than I thought and figured it out. Or maybe Maggie got her phone back. I don't know. The estate has a cell phone jammer. In short, the phone has not been used at all since her arrival. No calls allowed in or out. No emails or messaging. No Wi-Fi or internet access."

"But your, uh, app. That still works?"

"Yes. Because it uses LEO satellites. That's how I can still track it. Most people believe that if you are off Wi-Fi or cellular service, you can't be tracked. That's not true. You can be. Even if a phone is off, you can be tracked." Sharon shakes it off. "Let me get to the point."

"That would be helpful, yeah."

"Someone took Maggie's phone. Someone broke into it. Someone tried to delete the app. That sent me the warning. Several hours later, the phone, which had been in a location where cellular access was blocked, moved out of that bubble long enough to make a call."

"Who did Maggie call?"

"We don't know it was Maggie," Sharon says. "But it's a Lithuanian phone number. It's the kind designed to be untraceable."

"Okay, so where's Maggie's phone now?"

"That's another issue," Sharon says. "I can't trace it anymore."

"So, what, it ran out of batteries, or someone turned it off?"

Sharon shakes her head. "I told you. Even if a phone is off, you can track it."

"So?" Porkchop asks.

"So," Sharon says, "someone destroyed it."

———

As he does most mornings, Dr. Evan Barlow says goodbye to Hector the doorman at his apartment building on Fifth Avenue between 61st and 62nd Street and slides into the back of his Mercedes-Maybach.

From down the block, two men on motorcycles watch. One is a big squat man known to his friends as Pinky. The other is Porkchop.

Porkchop nods and then they both follow. They stay back, but Porkchop isn't particularly worried about being spotted. When they get within six blocks of Barlow Cosmetics' main office, Porkchop becomes certain that that's Barlow's destination. He sees no reason to stay behind. He and Pinky speed up, find parking, wait inside the expansive lobby.

There is security, of course. No New York City building is without security nowadays. But the guards leave you alone on the ground floors of most buildings as long as you don't loiter too long. It's if you want to get on an elevator that all the security and badges and passes and IDs kick in.

Five minutes later, Barlow's car pulls up to the front. He steps out of the back and enters the lobby. Porkchop doesn't hesitate. He approaches Barlow from the back and slaps his shoulder in a gesture that may look friendly from a distance but is hard enough to intimidate. Barlow startles at the blow and looks behind him.

"Remember me?" Porkchop says.

Barlow's eyes narrow as he looks the old biker up and down. But only for a second. Yep, he knows. Still, Porkchop adds the reminder.

"You were at my son's wedding."

"I remember," Barlow says. "You're Meatloaf or something."

"Don't try to piss me off, Evan."

"What do you want?"

"We need to talk."

"I have a full schedule this morning."

Porkchop throws his arm around his shoulder and neck area. Two good buddies. "This won't take long."

Barlow shrugs him off and straightens his shoulders. "You don't scare me."

"No?"

"No."

"Not even a little?"

Barlow raises his chin, sticks out his chest. "There's security everywhere."

Porkchop nods and then punches Barlow deep in the stomach. It's a short jab, no fuss, no big windup or any of that. The hand forms a fist near the waist and shoots up fast. You don't need that much power to make this effective. It's more placement than strength. Porkchop's knuckles land flush on the solar plexus, knocking the wind out of Barlow. Barlow bends at the waist. His mouth is open in a silent scream because the air is gone from his lungs. Porkchop grabs him and gently leads him to the ground. Pinky steps in front of them, blocking the security guard's view.

"Just relax," Porkchop whispers. "Your breath will come back in a moment."

No one saw the blow. No one rushes over. Part of that is the speed and relative stillness of Porkchop's move. Part of it is that you don't expect something like this on the ground floor of a fancy Manhattan high-rise. Whatever, no one reacts at first, but with Barlow on the floor struggling to regain his breath, a security guard finally notices. He starts to hurry over.

"If you tell him anything other than you're fine," Porkchop says in his calmest voice, "you'll need a doctor better than you to put you back together."

The guard, a bony guy with a prominent Adam's apple, arrives. "Doctor Barlow?"

"He slipped," Porkchop says.

The guard ignores him. "Doc?"

Barlow finally catches his breath. "I'm fine, Darryl," he manages. Then: "I'm going to need a security pass for my friend here."

Darryl ends up getting a pass for Pinky too. They use the barcode to get through the turnstile and into the elevator. All three step inside. When they do, Barlow snaps, "What do you want?"

"First off, I'm sorry," Porkchop says. "Not about the punch. You deserved that. But the 'you'll need a better doctor than you' line. I can't believe I said that."

Pinky says, "It was bad."

"I know. Way too arch."

"Even the delivery was off," Pinky adds with a disappointed shake of his head. "I expect better from you, Porkchop."

"I know," Porkchop agrees. "Just know that I let myself down too."

The elevator opens with a ding. Barlow's assistant, Mrs. Tansmore, greets him as he comes into the office. Porkchop, decked out in full biker garb, winks at her and kisses her hand. You can't get away with this anymore. But Porkchop can. Mrs. Tansmore blushes.

"They call me Porkchop," he says.

"Nice to meet you, Mr. Porkchop," Mrs. Tansmore says.

"I bet Doc Barlow never told you he used to be in a motorcycle gang."

"No, he never did."

"We used to say Barlow set the Bar Low, if you catch my drift."

She doesn't. Pinky frowns and shakes his head at Porkchop. Then Pinky raises both his hands. One is a fist. The other is two fingers. This is signaling 0-2, meaning that between the "you'll need a better doctor" line and the "Bar Low" pun, Porkchop is one strike away from being out.

Porkchop nods. "Fair."

Porkchop follows Barlow into his office. Pinky stays out with Mrs. Tansmore and guards the door. No one in, no one out.

"What do you want?" Barlow snaps.

Porkchop frowns. "Can we skip this part?"

"Skip what part?"

"The part where you pretend you don't know I'm here about Maggie."

Barlow nods. "There's nothing for me to tell you," he says.

"You hired her for a job."

"Do you understand what HIPAA violations are?"

"I do."

"Do you understand patient confidentiality?"

"Again: I do. So who hired her?"

"If she wants to tell you—"

"She's in Russia. She's in trouble."

Barlow blinks. "What makes you think she's in trouble?"

"Four days ago, you travel down to Baltimore. You tell Maggie you have some big reason to see her. She comes up to New York. You two meet. Suddenly debts are paid. Lawsuits are settled. She gets on a private plane at Teterboro. She ends up in Russia. I get it. It's some kind of surgical concierge service. Off the books. I don't know whether it's all legal or not, and I don't much care."

"I'm not going to confirm or deny—"

"Don't make me punch you again, Evan."

"Look," Barlow says. "She's safe. She's fine."

"I have reason to believe otherwise," Porkchop says. "But you can allay my fears. Call the client. Get Maggie on the phone."

"I can't do that."

"She's in trouble, Evan."

"How can you know that?"

"Call the client. Say there's an emergency at home, that I have to talk to her."

"How can you know something's wrong?"

"Tell them you need to speak to her for a moment. I want to make sure she's okay."

"You do know I care very much about Maggie," Barlow says. "That she was a prized and beloved student. That I was very close to her mother."

"Yeah, I know all that," Porkchop says.

"Do you really think I'd do something to put her in harm's way?"

"If you did..." Porkchop stops. "Wait, I don't want to come up with another arch threat. So let me state this plainly. If you did indeed put Maggie in harm's way, I'm going to kill you. Not sure how. I may throw you through that window. I may strangle you to death. I don't know. I don't care. I lost my son. You know that, right?"

"Of course."

"I'm not losing Maggie. Do you hear me?"

Barlow nods. "We're on the same side here."

"Good. Then call. I want to hear her voice."

Barlow heads over to his desk and sits down. Porkchop takes the chair across from him. Barlow opens his phone and checks phone numbers. He puts speakerphone on and calls one. No answer. He calls another. The same.

On the third number, a voice answers with one word. "What?"

Porkchop jolts up. He recognizes the voice. It's the guy who was in the car with Maggie.

"It's Evan Barlow," Barlow says.

"Yes, I know. My phone has caller ID. What do you want?"

"I'd like to speak with Doctor McCabe for a moment."

Silence.

"Hello?"

"She can't come to the phone right now. Don't call back."

The call disconnects. Porkchop has Barlow try again. No reply. One more time, the same. Porkchop says, "Tell me everything."

Barlow stands up and starts pacing. "Why are you so sure something is wrong?"

"Someone destroyed her phone."

"How can you possibly know that?"

"I don't want to waste time explaining this to you. Tell me what you know."

"It's not that complicated. Or uncommon. It's like you said. Über-rich people come to me. They want the best, and they want full discretion. I've traveled on my own a few times. A Saudi prince once. A rich man in Brunei. They fly you in on private jets. They pay you a fortune. It's all off the books."

Porkchop nods for him to continue.

"I'm sorry about your son. I met Marc several times. He was a brilliant surgeon. And I know, well, when he and Maggie were together, you could feel the connection, you know what I mean?"

Porkchop gives him nothing.

"So when Maggie lost him and then her license . . . I wanted to help. She's a brilliant surgeon too. You probably know that. I figured this was a good opportunity. They wanted the best plastic surgeon money could buy. Maggie needed money and wanted to get back in the game somehow."

"What kind of surgery?"

"Cosmetic. There would be two patients, so at least two surgeries. The client's mistress would be getting breast augmentation. And the client himself wanted some facial work. I don't know the specifics."

"Who was the client?"

Barlow shakes his head.

"What?" Porkchop says.

"I don't know who the client is."

"How can you not know?"

"That's part of the discretion. They all have middlemen."

"That was the middleman on the phone?"

"Yes. He calls himself Ivan Brovski. I doubt it's his real name. He's the one who contacted me. He's the one who spoke to Maggie."

"And you don't know who he works for?"

"Right."

"So before you send a doctor overseas like this, you don't vet the client?"

Barlow says nothing.

"Then how can you know if they are legit?"

"None of them are 'legit,'" Barlow half snaps. "That's sort of the point. How did I vet him? A million dollars was deposited for me in an overseas account. Just for taking the meeting. That's the vetting. I got another million dollars when Maggie agreed to take the job."

"So they pay you that kind of money to, what, find a top-notch doctor who will work discreetly?"

"Yes."

"And that's what happened here?"

Silence.

"Evan?"

"No. This case was a little different."

Porkchop doesn't like the way Barlow is starting to squirm. "Different how?"

"Like you said, most of the über rich, they trust me to find them excellent medical care in the most discreet manner possible. That's how it works—and it works well for all. It's in all our interests to keep this as clandestine as possible. I'm sure you understand."

"So what was different this time?"

Barlow opens his mouth, closes it, tries again. "I was going to suggest a surgeon," he says. "A man I've worked with before. He's an excellent physician right here in New York City."

"And they didn't want this guy?"

"No. They wanted Maggie McCabe."

"They asked for her specifically."

"Yes."

"So you weren't the one who recommended Maggie to them?"

"No. Ivan Brovski came to me. He said he needed a doctor—but that they already knew the perfect one."

"Maggie?"

"Yes. His instructions were pretty specific. Maggie was the doctor they wanted. Period. They knew I was her trusted family friend."

"So you didn't recommend Maggie," Porkchop says. "It was all a setup."

"I don't know if I would call it a setup—"

"This client. The oligarch or whoever. He requested Maggie personally?"

"Not the oligarch," Barlow says.

"Who then?"

"His mistress. A woman named Nadia. She's the one who specifically requested Maggie McCabe and only Maggie McCabe."

CHAPTER FOURTEEN

The end of the dream, if this is a dream, is always the most painful.

She is with Marc again. Somehow, she both knows he is dead and yet completely accepts that he is alive. Yes, this makes no sense, but that's true of most dreams when you analyze them. Or maybe it's different this time. In the past, Marc has always come to her. This time, maybe, just maybe, she is coming to him. Either way, Marc is there. They sit at an old wooden table in the middle of a vineyard. There are two glasses of red wine in front of them. Neither has been touched. The sun is setting, the sky a burnt orange. She and Marc sit side by side. He looks out over the vineyard. She stares at his profile. She can't look away. She fell in love with that profile. It belongs on a Roman coin, she would joke. A tear runs down Marc's cheek. *"I promise you that your life will be extraordinary,"* he says to her. Those had been the closing words of his wedding vows. She remembers how overwhelmed she'd been when he said it, standing in front of everyone they loved and cared about, that line, that final line. *"I promise you that your life will be extraordinary."* Damn, she'd thought at that moment, such a good line that when she finished her own vows, she'd repeated it. *"I promise you that your life will be extraordinary."* Not happy. Not fulfilling. Not complete. *Extraordinary.* They were not going to buy that suburban house and work in private practice and do the work of married physicians with two-point-four kids and a barbecue in the yard and a basketball hoop in the driveway. In the dream, a tear runs down Marc's cheek, as it did when he spoke on their wedding day. But that tear had been one of joy. This one is not. She takes his hand. His hand is real, she notices. She can feel it. She wouldn't be able to feel it if it was a dream. It's flesh. It's Marc's hand. This is reality. Marc is alive. So why is her heart sinking? He finally turns to look at her and when he does, his grip slackens. *No, no. Stay. You're here. With me.* But Marc is pulling away. She reaches out and grabs the hand tighter. But the hand is gone. He's still there. The tear is still on his cheek. Comfort him. Love him enough so that he would never ever go. She throws her arms around him, pulls him close. *Don't go. Please, Marc, stay.* This isn't a dream. This is real. Except now she is starting to awaken. There is nothing crueler. She tries desperately to swim back down, to stay, to cling to this old wooden table in this dream vineyard. Marc is alive here. That's all that matters. But something is pushing her to the surface. She fights it. But she knows she can't win. Marc begins to fade away. She is in that crest now, that strange crest between the dream world and full consciousness. There is clarity here, terrible clarity— this is only a dream; Marc is still dead—and it crushes her anew. She feels the tears on her cheeks, real ones, and she knows.

Marc is gone. Marc is dead.

When Maggie blinks her eyes open, a man's face is staring down at her.

It's not Marc, of course. It's Charles Lockwood. The playboy from Ragoravich's ball.

"You're okay," he says to her. "You were hurt in a car accident. But you're okay now."

The dream flees. It is amazing and merciful how fast that happens. The only remnants are the tears on her cheek. Maggie opens her mouth to speak to him, but nothing comes out.

"Here," Lockwood tells her. "Take these."

He scoops some ice chips into a cup and puts them in her mouth. Maggie knows the move—it gives someone water but won't let them take in too much at once. Charles wears a white dress shirt, the sleeves rolled up on his knotted forearms. He checks her vitals. The playboy is gone now. The physician has emerged.

"Don't try to talk yet. Just tap your finger once for yes, twice for no. Do you remember the accident?"

It takes a second and then the memories of her escape rush in— opening the bedroom window, the biting cold, the roof, the gunfire, the Ferrari. It's all there. Jumbled maybe. But enough.

They'd chased her. They'd shot at her. They wanted her dead.

She had tried to get away. Something hit her. She lost control...

She signals yes. She does so with the finger tap, but she also tests out a head nod. The pain is minimal.

"How...?" she manages to say.

"You reached out to me."

She gives him a confused face.

"The phone number you called. Our emergency line. It came through. We moved fast."

Emergency line. She tries to remember. Her head is swimming. The phone number. The one the Marc griefbot had given her. When she tries to speak, Lockwood shakes his head and tells her that she should rest. She ignores that and tries again to shake her vocal cords free. When she finally gets out a few words, they sound muffled and far away. "You knew Marc."

"I did, yes. I assume he gave you my phone number?"

How to answer that...? She can't. Not really. So she just nods.

"There's a lot to tell you, Doctor McCabe," Lockwood says. "I need your mind clear for that. It's not yet. I know, I know. You think you're ready. But you're not." He moves his chair closer to her. "First though, I need to know why you're here."

How to even explain it all to him?

"I need to know why you're staying with Oleg Ragoravich."

He waits. She lets her head fall back on the pillow. Her eyes close. Does she trust him?

Marc—or the griefbot version anyway—had given Maggie his phone number and told her to call. That means when he was alive, Marc trusted Charles Lockwood. Shouldn't that be enough? Maybe. But then again—and it may be because her head can't stop spinning—how does she know what Charles Lockwood just told her about getting a call is true? Everyone has been playing head games with her. She knows that now. None of this is accidental or coincidental. Ever since Dr. Barlow approached her at Johns Hopkins, Maggie has felt the thing she hates the most—out of control. She feels manipulated, lied to, like she's fighting against too strong a current. So is Charles Lockwood another part of that? Is he telling the truth or another liar?

There is one way to know for sure: Ask the griefbot.

She sucks on more ice chips. There's an IV in her arm. She takes a second or two to scan herself and assess her own injuries. There are places of soreness and pain, but she feels pretty damn good. She wants to ask him about that, about her injuries, but she gets that right now Charles is focused on his own questions. When the chips melt and her mouth is moist enough to speak, she says two words: "My phone."

"What?"

"I need my phone."

"I don't advise you calling anyone," he says. "They'll be monitoring anyone close to you."

"Who will be monitoring?"

He shakes his head and scooches a little closer. "Maggie, listen to me. I will explain everything when you're ready. It's a lot. But right now—and I can't stress how important this is—I need to know why you were staying at Oleg Ragoravich's house."

"I need my phone first."

"I don't have it," he says. He leans back, blinks, runs his hand through his hair. "Your"—he stops, searches the air for the word—"extraction—it was not easy. Do you remember the crash?"

She nods.

"A bullet grazed your upper back. Wait, are you in pain? I should have asked you that first."

"I'm fine," she says.

"The old Ferrari didn't have seat belts and luckily, I guess, your windshield was shot out. So you didn't slam into it on impact. You rolled down a ravine. That's what saved you. You were hard to reach. Ragoravich's men couldn't get to you right away. They figured the exposure would kill you anyway. You have frostnip, by the way—you're lucky it wasn't full-on frostbite. That will hurt for a while. Point is, they saw no point in rushing to you. The ravine is tricky in the snow. That gave us time to get there." He looks off, his eyes welling up. "Do you remember an SUV chasing you?"

She nods.

"There were two men in it. They're both dead."

Silence.

"So I don't know where your phone is. In that Ferrari, I guess. Maybe in that ravine, I don't know. It's not important. We can get you another. If you're too tired to answer questions—"

"I'm not."

"You had my emergency phone number," Charles says.

"Yes."

"Only one way: Marc gave it to you before he died."

That wasn't the way, of course, but it would be too much to explain the griefbot right now.

"And if he gave you the number, then you know you can trust me."

She doesn't know that, but it makes sense. And what choice does she have? She doesn't even know where she is. She only knows that Marc had warned her that Ragoravich or Brovski would try to kill her, that they had indeed tried, and that someone, probably Charles Lockwood, had saved her.

So why not? She had to trust someone.

"I was hired to do plastic surgery," Maggie says.

Charles Lockwood frowns at that answer. "On?"

"Oleg and a young woman named Nadia."

"That's the mistress I saw you talking to?"

She nods.

"So how did they end up hiring you?"

She explains in spurts about Evan Barlow, about Nadia's breast augmentation, about the facial surgeries on Oleg Ragoravich, about Ragoravich disappearing from his recovery room, about the sudden panic, about the attempt on her life. She doesn't go into the griefbot. As she speaks, exhaustion wedges its way into her bloodstream and spreads. It takes everything she has to stay awake.

"You know it's not a coincidence," Lockwood says. "You being hired for this job."

She does now, doesn't she?

"Who are you?" she asks.

"My name is Charles Lockwood. Just as I said."

"Are you CIA?"

"Let's just say something like that."

"Where am I?"

"You're safe," he says. "And to answer your next question, you've been here two days."

Two days. Her head drops back on the pillow. She wants to ask a million more questions, wants to stay awake, but her eyes are starting to flutter closed.

"I want to know..." She stops speaking.

"You will. I'll tell you everything soon. But one last thing for now."

Her eyes are closed now.

In the dark, she hears his voice: "Where is Trace Packer?"

"Bangladesh maybe," she tells him.

"No, he's not. Trace is missing, Maggie. We think he may have intentionally gone off the grid."

"I don't understand."

And then, as Maggie sinks under, hoping to head back to that dream in the vineyard, she could swear she hears Charles Lockwood say something that makes absolutely no sense: "We think Trace is trying to find your husband."

———————

Maggie doesn't see Charles Lockwood the next time she wakes up. Or the time after that. She is being looked after by two women in hospital scrubs. The women are kind and quiet. Maggie feels her strength returning. She asks them questions—where am I? where is Charles Lockwood?—but they give her a lot of tight smiles and no answers. She is soon able to get out of bed, walk around. Her recovery may seem remarkable, but her injuries ended up being more superficial than serious. There is some pain near her shoulder where the bullet grazed, and her head aches from the aftermath of a concussion.

But she also feels antsy and ready to go.

That night, when Maggie wakes up in her dark hospital-like room, she senses someone is with her. Her eyes adjust enough to see the silhouette, and then the face comes into focus. It's Charles Lockwood. He stares at the wall.

She speaks first. "Why did you say Trace is trying to find Marc?"

He doesn't move.

"Marc is dead," she says.

"I know." Charles Lockwood leans back in the chair. "I shouldn't have said that."

"Why did you?"

"How are you feeling?"

"Like I want some answers. Like I want them now."

He nods. Her eyes are adjusting. She can make out his face now. The gloss and polish she'd seen at Ragoravich's have been wiped away. There are lines etched on his face. His hair has a touch of gray. He looks weathered, worn.

"There's a lot to tell you," he says. "I also don't know how much you know already. I don't know how much you knew at the time or how much you figured out later." He turns to her. "Do you know who Eric Hoffer is?"

"No."

"An American philosopher. He has this quote I love: 'Every great cause begins as a movement, becomes a business, and eventually degenerates into a racket.'" He smiles. "Good, right?"

She doesn't reply.

"Corruption starts small," he continues. "My uncle was a pastor. He had this pious parishioner, a sweet widow, to handle the church's budget. Mrs. Tingley. She devoted her life to that congregation. She worked long hours. One night, when she stayed late yet again, she got hungry and wanted to get a sandwich. She'd forgotten her wallet at home. That's what she said. Who knows, right? Anyway, Mrs. Tingley ordered a sandwich from the local sandwich shop and used some of the petty cash from that week's tithing to pay for it. No big deal. Easily justified. Then she did it again. Then she ordered two sandwiches and brought one home for her son. That's it. Just an extra sandwich. Ten years later, the parish realized Mrs. Tingley had embezzled almost half a million dollars."

"I assume there's a point to this story," Maggie says.

"There is. And I think you know what it is."

"Why don't you just tell me?"

"You were the pretty face of WorldCures Alliance. Sorry, I know you're more. But the media loved you. The combat surgeon. Devoted her life to helping the poor in dangerous hot spots. You're pretty and telegenic and yeah, that shouldn't matter, but we both know it does." He pulls his chair closer. "Why did you end up leaving WorldCures?"

"My mother was sick. I came home to be with her."

He tries to give her a probing look. "That's all?"

Silence.

"What else happened, Maggie?"

"Do you go by Charlie or Chuck, or should I call you Charles?"

"Most people call me Charles."

"Great. Let's not worry about me, Charles, okay? Tell me what's going on."

"Fair enough," he says with a nod. "You know about the Kasselton Foundation."

"Of course."

"But you never worked with them directly?"

"No, never."

"They were WorldCures' biggest donor."

"I think so, yes."

"So here's how it plays out. One day, the Kasselton Foundation gets in touch with a new charity desperately seeking funding. In this case, WorldCures Alliance. Maybe they called you. Maybe they called Marc or Trace."

"It was Marc."

"Okay, fine. So Marc goes to woo them. Maybe you go too. Doesn't matter. They seem impressed by your passion and presentation. They claim to love your idea of advanced, cutting-edge treatments for refugees and the poverty-stricken. They offer to make WorldCures a sizable donation, probably in chunks. Like Hoffer said: It begins with a cause—and you had a great cause. The Kasselton Foundation was going to help you save lives. So, of course, WorldCures took the money. Who wouldn't? None of you knew it was connected to Oleg Ragoravich via back channels and shell companies. And even if you did suspect, well, so what? Ragoravich is just a businessman. How he makes his money isn't your concern. And hey, better he donates his money to a worthwhile cause like WorldCures than using it to, I don't know, spread his corruption or buy another megapalace. There's a lot of ways to justify it. And again, you're just nonprofit employees looking to do good. So you take the money. Maybe a million dollars to start. My God, you think, the patients you can save with that. And you do. You save lives. You develop new medical technologies and techniques. It's great. And then, a few months later maybe, the Kasselton Foundation comes to you again. They want to make another donation because they realize WorldCures has a lot of needs. You need to hire staff. You need trucks and drivers and construction workers and paper clips and beds and medical equipment and whatever else. And guess who has vendors for you to use?"

"The Kasselton Foundation," Maggie says to keep things moving.

"Precisely."

"Straight-up money laundering," Maggie says. "That's what you're saying."

"Nothing straight-up about it. But yes. Money laundering seems complicated, but I'm going to make it very simple in this case. Let's say I'm a criminal. I donate my ill-gotten money into a nonprofit. The nonprofit uses my donation to purchase legitimate goods and services from a company owned or controlled by me. Period, the end. I also overcharge. I mean, who would notice? Maybe the truck rental is normally a thousand dollars. Your charity will get invoiced for five thousand dollars. The point is, my money gets laundered—it came back to me via a respected nonprofit—and you, the altruistic charity, still get a lot of money via my donations. It's why you look past it—it's in your interest to do so. Yeah, sure, you may think that price seems too high for a truck rental, but so what? You aren't footing the bill. You are making out. If someone else is also making out, that's not your concern. It's a win-win, if you think of it that way."

"And this is what you claim happened with WorldCures?"

"Yes. And I don't claim it. You know it."

"Do me a favor, Charles. Don't tell me what I know."

He puts up his hands in mock surrender. "You're right," he says. "And it doesn't matter. I'm not here to prosecute anyone for that. For what it's worth, I don't think any of you three did know at first. You, Trace, Marc—you're physicians. Healers. You don't do the books. When you got the first check, the Kasselton Foundation probably insisted you hire one of their own under the pretense of making sure their money was spent in a proper way. So I think for a while, yeah, like I said, this kind of corruption grows slowly. You may have had some inklings which you subconsciously ignored. Doesn't matter if you did."

"So where do you fit into this, Charles?"

"What about me?"

"You said it wasn't a coincidence I was chosen to do Oleg's surgery."

"Right."

"It also wasn't a coincidence you were at the house for Oleg's party."

Lockwood grins in the dark. "Didn't you say it was a ball?" His hand goes up. "Kidding, kidding. Just looking to add a bit of levity here."

"Yeah, pretty hilarious."

"I'm trying, Maggie, because this story is grim, and it gets grimmer." He runs his hand through his hair. "Or maybe, I don't know, maybe there's hope at the end of this too."

"Hope how?" Maggie thinks about what she heard before she fell asleep, about Trace searching for Marc. She knows, of course, that it's impossible. But the fact that he would voice that . . . "And what did you mean about Trace searching for Marc?"

He takes a few moments. His hand is on his chin. Exhaustion emanates from every part of his body. "Let me tell it my way, okay?"

She doesn't reply. She just waits.

"You want to know why I was at Oleg's, but you've probably figured it out by now."

"You're investigating him."

"Yes."

"And you're, what, undercover?"

"That makes it sound sexier than it is. But yes. I am a physician from a rich, well-connected family. It's easy to pass me off as a ne'er-do-well who relishes the Russian party life. Do you know that was the first time Oleg Ragoravich has had any kind of event in the past three years? He's been ultra-secretive about his movements. He'll show up somewhere, like in Dubai, but he never lets anyone know ahead of time. I've been on this case for the past two years, and I've still never seen him in person. Not even at that crazy ball."

"Why do you think that is?"

"Not sure. There are rumors of bad health. There are rumors he pissed off some powerful people and fears assassination attempts." Then: "Can I ask you a question?"

"Go ahead."

"When did Marc give you my number?"

"He didn't."

"How did you get it?"

Maggie wants to get information, not give it. "Maybe we could start with how you knew Marc."

Charles nods—this is going to be a bit more give-and-take than he'd expected.

"Marc realized that they were in way over their heads with no way out."

"Because of the money laundering?"

"That was part of it, but do you want to know a hard truth?"

"Sure."

"I don't think Marc cared all that much about the laundering. I don't think any of you did. All three of you are brilliant surgeons and researchers. You all also have, sorry, a bit of a god complex. Sure, Marc wanted to save lives and all that. But I also know he—and let's be honest, you and Trace too—have the surgeon's ego. You are ends-justify-means types. A lot of do-gooders are. That's just a fact. So my guess is, if it was simple money laundering, Marc would have used all the justifications I just gave you and looked the other way."

"You're saying it didn't stay that way?"

Charles smiles but there is no joy in it. "Nothing ever stays stagnant in life. The world is in constant motion. Corruption, like everything else, either gets worse or it gets better."

"And this got worse?"

"Very much so."   .

"How?"

Charles shakes off her question. "The point is, Marc wanted out. So did Trace. They asked for a face-to-face with Ragoravich. Oleg loved doctors. He thought they could help him. I don't think it's a coincidence that he chose to sink his fangs into WorldCures of all charities. From day one, he saw the potential for more than just cleaning his money."

"Potential how?"

Once again, Lockwood shakes off her question.

"Stop doing that," Maggie says.

"Sorry, but you have to let me tell it my way, okay?"

She gives him a reluctant suit-yourself-continue gesture with both hands.

"So Marc and Trace are flown in to Ragoravich's palace. They tell Oleg that they're grateful and appreciative, but they plan on leaving WorldCures Alliance, and they wanted Oleg to be the first to know. Ragoravich shakes their hands and thanks them for their time. Then they got back on the helicopter with some other visitor. An overweight bald man. That's how they described him. We still don't know who he was. They flew the helicopter over an abandoned iron ore or salt mine, something like that, and Oleg's men threw the bald guy out. Just like that. No warning. Not a word said. Right in front of Marc and Trace."

Maggie looks at him in pure horror.

"Then they grabbed Trace. Like they were going to do the same to him. They dangled him upside down outside the copter for five minutes, holding on to him by one ankle."

"My God."

Charles nods. "Anyway, message received. There was no leaving WorldCures. They were in too deep. Trace, I think he surrendered to that fate. But you know your husband. He was a problem solver. He kept looking for a way."

She nods to herself at that. Marc believed that he could indeed find a solution to every problem. There was no quit in her husband, just a road not yet taken.

"That," Charles says, "is where I come in."

"Marc became your, what, informant?"

"Something like that, yeah. He put out feelers. Quietly. I came to him. I told him the only way out was for him to help us take down Ragoravich."

"Did he agree?"

Lockwood says nothing.

"Did he agree, Charles?"

"Yes."

Maggie feels the tears come to her eyes. "You said Trace is missing."

"Yes."

"And you also said he may be looking for Marc."

Charles shakes his head. "I shouldn't have said that."

"But you did."

"Yes." Charles lets loose a long breath. "There are three theories about your husband's death. Would you like to hear them in order of believability?"

She wouldn't. But she still gives a small nod. She knows where he's going to go with this. She needs to hear him say it out loud.

"Theory One: Marc got caught up in the violence of a volatile region. That's the most accepted theory, of course. It's also, for the record, the one I most believe. It's backed up by evidence and logic."

"What's Theory Two?"

"I think you can probably guess now."

Maggie nods. "Oleg Ragoravich killed Marc."

"Yes."

"He found out that Marc had turned on him. He set it up to have him killed and made it look like he was a casualty of war."

"Yes."

"And Trace, what, he got away?"

"And that's why he's in hiding, yes."

Maggie thinks about it, tries to stay detached, unemotional. "That actually seems almost as likely as Theory One, don't you think?"

Charles doesn't respond.

"I mean, Marc risks going up against this powerful, rich, evil man—and then he ends up dead."

"I don't think that's what happened."

"Because then it would be in part your fault," Maggie says. "My husband comes to you for help, and he ends up dead."

"That's not it."

"What then?"

"Because if Oleg Ragoravich wanted them dead, he wouldn't have had to jump through so many hoops. Did Oleg plan the slaughter at the refugee camp? Thirty-three people were murdered in that rampage. Seems like a lot of unnecessary collateral damage. And of course, he didn't want to just silence Marc. There was Trace too. Trace, if you believe this theory, got away. Do you think Oleg Ragoravich would be that sloppy?"

All good points. But of course, Maggie already knew that.

"So," Maggie says, "let's get to it, shall we? What's Theory Three?"

"It's ridiculous."

"But?"

Lockwood looks at her. "Did they spare you the details?"

"About?"

"About how Marc was killed."

She feels her chest tighten. "I know about the"—Maggie is never sure of the right word to use here—"savagery."

"To some people that seems odd."

"A lot of victims got hacked to death."

"I know."

"And yes, maybe he was hard to identify. But a DNA test was done."

Charles Lockwood tilts his head. "By whom?"

Maggie is not sure who did it.

"Did the local authorities do it?" Charles asks. "I mean, there's no American embassy in that area. The closest was in Tunisia. So who ran the DNA test?"

"There were people," she says. "Reliable people."

"Right then. I mean, sure. It's why that last theory is ridiculous."

"So what's your third theory, Charles?"

"It's obvious, isn't it?"

"Not to me."

"If Ragoravich found out what Marc had done, he would kill him, of course. And just to make sure the lesson stuck, Oleg would probably kill anyone and everyone close to him. Especially you, Maggie.

Best-case scenario: Marc would have to look over his shoulder the rest of his life."

"Did you tell Marc this? I mean, when you recruited him."

"No."

"Why not?"

"You know why."

"Because you didn't give a shit about him. You cared about your case."

"Yes," he says calmly. "I put him in an untenable situation—after he put himself in one. But there was a way out. For you, at least. If Marc ended up 'dying'"—he makes quote marks with his fingers—"in a refugee camp in Tunisia, then, well, you'd both be in the clear."

Maggie feels the cold down to her bones. "You're saying Marc faked his own death?"

"No, I'm saying that *didn't* happen. I'm saying it's a ridiculous—"

"That he, what, found another body that got hacked up there. That he pretended it was his, bought off whoever ran the DNA test. And now, what, he's in hiding?"

"I'm saying the theory is ridiculous."

"But that's Theory Three?"

"Yes."

"And to follow it through, Trace, what, ran off and hid—and now he is meeting up with Marc? And what's the plan after that, Charles?"

"I don't know," he says. "Theory Three, I admit, is pretty weak."

"It is," Maggie says.

"But one thing is true either way."

"What's that?"

"You're very close to Trace."

"Yes."

"You've known him a long time."

She nods. "We served together in combat."

"Whatever theory you believe—One, Two, or Three—Trace Packer is missing. So my question is, How far would you go to find him?"

"As far as I have to," Maggie says.

He nods, slaps his legs, stands. "When you're strong enough—"

"I'm strong enough now."

He thinks about it. "Okay. We leave tomorrow."

"Where are we going?"

Charles smiles. "Someplace much warmer."

CHAPTER FIFTEEN

Dubai

The Dubai heat starts in your lungs.

The sun is relentless, merciless. It finds you. It beats down upon you. It's just you and the sun. You have a personal, one-on-one relationship with the sun. There is no middleman, no filter, no cloud cover, no escape. You get the purest hit of the sun. The sun love-bombs you. It's dry and heavy and clingy. It swarms with an all-consuming furnace-like heat. It suffocates you from within and from without. It saps your energy first, then your spirit.

Maggie had experienced this kind of desert heat too often during her military service. She'd be walking on the tarmac where she could see the squiggly waves from the heat and feel it burn her feet all the way through her combat boots. She had experienced every kind of malady from this kind of heat—dehydration, rash, headache, dizziness, fatigue—during her WorldCures missions. The cold of Russia may have been deadly and awful. But this blazing sun? Maybe worse.

Fortunately, Maggie only experienced the Dubai heat for a minute, maybe two, walking from the private plane to the sleekest-looking super-fancy sports car. A man giving off serious Viking vibes—long blond hair and a beard to match—holds the door open for her.

"Welcome," the Viking says.

The sports car only seats two, so Maggie slips into the front seat, the blast from the powerful air-conditioning more than welcome. The Viking circles around and gets low into the driver's side.

"Is this a Bugatti?" Maggie asks.

She doesn't know cars, never had any interest in them, never understood those fascinated by them. Cars aren't her baby or friend; she doesn't think they're cool. They get her from Point A to Point B. Period, the end. She only guesses it's a Bugatti because it just feels like money and because Charles Lockwood had told her that she'd be staying at the new ultra-exclusive Bugatti Residences by Binghatti, which is supposed to somehow combine Binghatti luxury living (whatever that means) with, well, Bugatti luxury automotive design. Didn't make much sense to Maggie, but not much about the innovatively decadent (yet decidedly throwback) Dubai lifestyle did.

The driver answers in American English. "It's a Bugatti Tourbillon."

"A Tourbillon?"

"Yes."

"It's really called that? A Tourbillon."

"It is."

Maggie frowns. "Name seems a little on-the-nose, doesn't it?"

"*Billon* not *billion*. It's French for 'whirlwind.'"

"Yeah, but still."

"Fair point," the Viking concedes. He adjusts his sunglasses and strokes his thick beard. He hits the gas pedal and in seconds they are traveling ninety miles an hour. "This car," he says, "cost 4.1 million dollars."

"No way."

"Yes way."

"I think your voice had a typo in it," Maggie says. "It moved the decimal point to the right a spot or two."

The Viking likes that. "It did not. Only two hundred fifty of them will ever be manufactured."

"Two hundred fifty Tourbillons," Maggie says.

"Yep."

She's surprised Oleg Ragoravich didn't have one in his showroom. "How old is it?"

"Old? The Tourbillon debuted this year. It's brand spanking new."

"Wow."

"Nice ride, right?"

"Not 4.1-million-dollars nice."

He grins.

"I'm Maggie McCabe, by the way."

"Yeah, I know. I'm Bob."

"Nice to meet you, Bob."

"Same."

She notices the telltale lump in his suit jacket. Bob is carrying a gun. He also has that calm, that stillness, Maggie has seen only in the best trained of soldiers.

"What can you tell me before we arrive?" she asks.

"Not a thing," he says.

"Is Bob even your real name?"

His answer is just a smile.

Charles Lockwood had flown down with her on the private plane, but he stayed on board, explaining that he had to return immediately to Russia. The flight time was six hours. He'd spent almost all of it with her going over the "plan"—as generous a use of that term as Maggie had experienced—yet again:

"Your cover is one you're already playing: concierge surgeon for the superrich, this time for a family in Dubai. I can't give you their name. That's part of the discretion. But the client is described as a 'retail magnate.' Here are two passports. Yours, of course. Use that. The other is made out in the name of Emily Sinclair, a pseudonym, just in case. When you arrive, they'll give you the details on what cosmetic work they want. Your mission—man, I hate that term: I sound like I'm M in a Bond film or something. But the mission is pretty simple. We are trying to find Trace Packer."

As the Tourbillon revs closer to the city, the famed skyscrapers of Dubai start to come into view, like shiny mirages rising from the desert sand. The site is like something out of a futuristic movie—a blend of nirvana and dystopia, which, when you think about it, can appear to be the same thing from a distance. Maggie had been to Dubai maybe a dozen times during her years in the military and with WorldCures. She and Marc had tolerated the visits, while Trace dove into the city and all its excesses.

She remembers Trace explaining the appeal to her and Marc:

"You can't have an up without a down. You can't have a left without a right. You can't have good without evil . . ."

"Are you getting to the point?" Maggie had interrupted.

She had heard these philosophical musings from Trace many times over the years. It's one of the things she'd most enjoyed about Trace's company—he always said something that made her think. What they don't tell you about serving in combat zones is that the rare spikes of adrenaline are made far more potent because of the hours of mind-numbing boredom—which, when she thinks about it now, is a lot like what Trace was saying with this no-up-without-a-down stuff.

"And," Trace finished, with his rakish smile, "in my case, there can't be altruism without debauchery. You two, well, you have each other. You'll spend the night in some high-rise hotel bed with a billion-count threads and do what you should do. Me? I plan to visit a risqué nightclub and imbibe and ingest and flirt and end up with a strange beauty in my bed, one who will see my innate wonderfulness and not charge me and it'll be passionate and romantic and even love—no, not what you two have because, well, almost no one has that—and then, poof, it'll be gone with the morning sun."

Maggie just sits in that memory for a moment.

Trace Packer.

From the driver's seat, Viking Bob asks, "Are you okay?"

"Fine."

The car makes a sharp right turn. In her head, Maggie rehearses the "plan"—again, the word deserves quote marks—remembering her first question when Charles Lockwood had told her the destination:

"Why Dubai?" she asked.

"Before I answer, I just want to remind you," Lockwood began. "You don't have to do this. This isn't your fight. You don't have to help—"

"Why Dubai?"

"Okay, fair enough. Several reasons, but I'll start with the main one. Oleg Ragoravich's plane is there. It left four hours after we rescued you. We don't know who is on it, but Dubai is important to both of them."

"Both of them?"

"Oleg and Nadia met in Dubai. Nadia was a lead, uh, hostess at Etoile Adiona. It's an ultra-exclusive nightclub. Oleg frequents a lot of big nightclubs. Anyway, they met there. Fell in, well, whatever you fall into with these kinds of relationships. And here's the big thing— according to our intel, Nadia was spotted there last night."

"At Etoile Adiona?"

"Yes. You'll be able to get in tonight. It's been arranged. Look, people will know who you are, but in this case, it works for your cover. WorldCures had a footprint in Dubai—I don't have to tell you that— so your past may help open doors."

"And that's reason number two?" Maggie asked. "The WorldCures connection?"

"Yes, but let me be more specific: Dubai was the last place Marc and Trace were seen before they left on that final humanitarian mission. I assume you know this?"

She nodded.

"Not only did they launch their final humanitarian mission from Dubai—Trace Packer went back there *after* Marc died. Did you know that?"

"Yes."

"Did that surprise you? That Trace didn't come for the funeral or something?"

There had been no funeral for Marc. Marc hadn't believed in them. The Serpents and Saints had done a ride in missing man formation—leaving a space for where Marc's motorcycle would have gone. Porkchop was the lead bike, of course. Maggie was on the back of the bike. She never saw Porkchop cry, not even on that day, but she could feel his shoulders heave as she pulled in close.

"No," she said. "It didn't surprise me. If you wanted to honor Marc, the best way would be to get back to work."

"Okay, yeah, I guess that makes sense. So anyway, all roads lead us to Dubai. That's why you're going there. The plan is for you to stir things up so we can find Trace. Go to Etoile Adiona. Talk to Nadia. See if she knows where Oleg Ragoravich is. Everything here is connected. We just don't know how. We just know there's a lot of bad people in Dubai doing bad things." Charles Lockwood hesitated. "Maybe you shouldn't do this. After all, they just tried to kill you. Maybe it's too risky—"

"Shh," Maggie interrupted, raising her palm, "the patronizing is getting on my nerves."

Bob the driver breaks the spell. "There's home. Be it ever so humble."

It does not look humble in any way, shape, or form, but of course, that's the point. The Bugatti skyscraper looks more like modern sculpture than a residential tower. Everything is dynamic curves and fluid lines, sensual even, as though the building can't quite stay still. It's wrapped in a shiny metal facade, and with the desert sun reflecting off it just so, it's as though the high-rise were both a crashing wave and a rolling sand dune.

"Hang on," Bob says.

Bob rips up the drive. She expects a valet or maybe just parking in the front. But that's not what happens. He veers the car down an entry bay into an underground garage. The parking spot, she notices, has glass walls on three sides. Odd. When Bob turns off the engine, Maggie reaches for the door handle, but Bob reaches across her and shakes his head.

"Not yet."

The car, with them inside of it, starts to rise.

"It's an elevator," Bob tells her.

"An elevator for your car?"

He shrugs. "A Bugatti should live in the Bugatti. Every penthouse has a parking spot."

"For your car?"

"Yes."

"In the actual apartment?"

"Yep. It's perfect symmetry. Integrating automotive passion with French Riviera luxury. Merging Bugatti's automotive-inspired aesthetics with the highest standards of living."

"You didn't just make that up," Maggie says.

"No, you sit around a lot in this job. There's a brochure."

Maggie can't help but shake her head. The sports car rises above the city, floor upon floor, the view outside the windshield and glass door jaw-dropping, until they stop, yes, in the middle of a spectacular apartment. After Bob nods that it's okay now, they both slide out of the Bugatti and enter the heart of the penthouse. The décor is a bit like the car—sleek, aerodynamic, stunning—but the space is all about the windows: floor-to-ceiling, very high, glass so clear you could easily walk into them. You don't feel as though you are in a high-rise with a spectacular view. You feel at one with the view, the unassuming marble floor vanishing, as though you were floating.

Maggie stands there and flashes back to Charles's final instruction:

"You're going to want to call your family and tell them you're all right. Don't. They still think you're on your original job, so it's not like they are unduly worried. The last thing you want to do is pull them into this by making an errant call."

She'd promised that she wouldn't call.

But that is a promise she has no intention of keeping.

The penthouse is silent.

"Is anyone else here?" Maggie asks.

"The family owns three floors."

"Of course."

"You'll be the only one on this one."

"Of course."

Bob leads them to her room, which is minimalist and off-white and unassumingly decorated because again it is all about the cityscape. Every wall is done in gentle curves with no corners or harsh edges. It makes you feel as though you're on a boat in the middle of calm seas. There is a kidney-shaped swimming pool on the expansive deck outside her window.

"The full patient medical records will be here within the hour," Bob says. "They should provide you with all the information you need. Surgery will be scheduled for tomorrow unless there's an issue."

She wonders whether she will need to make up an issue to stall for time, so she can stay longer. Probably not. Charles or whoever had already informed the "retail magnate" that Maggie's strict patient protocol was to stay at least four days post-op—and if you wanted the best, which Maggie is, you understood, accepted, and paid for that.

"Impressive, no?" Bob says.

She nods. The view reminds her of that skyline shot of Oz from the original *Wizard of Oz* movie. It looks enchanted, magical, make-believe—a place where fantasies come true. But if you take a second look, it also looks artificial, futuristic, slightly nightmarish. The skyscrapers sparkle and glitter and they're all glass, almost fragile looking, so that you could imagine hurling a giant stone and watching it all crash down in shards.

"Is there a bar nearby?" she asks.

"A bar?"

"Yes."

"As in a pub?"

"Sure."

Bob frowns. "You want to go out for a drink?"

"Yes."

"The day before you perform surgery?"

"I need to move around," Maggie says. "I get antsy before a surgery."

"You probably won't be surprised to hear this," Bob says, "but this tower has some pretty spectacular amenities."

"Gasp oh gasp, label me surprised."

Viking Bob smiles. "The penthouse has two private pools. You could get a massage or a holistic healing session or something like that. There's a fitness center, a gym, a spa, a wellness retreat—"

"What's the difference between a fitness center and a gym?"

"Damned if I know."

"How about between a spa and wellness center?"

"Same answer."

She smiles at him. "How did you get this job, Bob?"

"Served in the military. Same as you. In fact, I think we were both at Camp Arifjan."

"And then?"

"And then I got offered a boatload of money to work here. It's not a complicated story."

"You like it?"

Bob shrugs. "We can make fun of the overindulgence," he says, "but my wife and I like luxury. It's safe, no violent crime, tax-free, good health care, high standard of living. The kids seem happy. Why? You looking to move?"

"Hard pass," she says. "With all those amenities, I assume there's a bar downstairs."

"They'd never use the word 'bar' here. There is however a wood-paneled exclusive club that offers an upscale social setting for elite and like-minded individuals to mingle."

"You really memorized that brochure."

"It looks bad to be scrolling on your phone."

"Can I go to this club?"

Bob shrugs. "Suit yourself. This isn't a prison."

"Kinda feels like one."

"It does, doesn't it? Third floor."

He leads her to a glass elevator. There are no buttons inside. She steps in, and he says "Private club" out loud. The elevator doors close and it whisks her down. It moves fast, silently; Maggie feels a little pressure in the ears.

The private club is varnished wood and low lights. The barkeep is tall and female and looks as though she just came off a Paris runway. The premium liquor bottles behind her are lit from below, which makes them appear even more premium. The men strewn about are a variety pack, but they all look middle-aged or older. The women are, no surprise, younger, far younger, and probably use social media euphemisms like "influencer" or "fitness model." They are, no question, hot, but extremes—their hair is either jet-black or white blonde, their skin is either darkly tanned or completely pale, and—no judgment here—they've all been surgically enhanced or rejuvenated, which, come to think of it, are two more euphemisms.

Maggie gets it. Dubai is a playground for the rich and their most hedonistic urges. It's Disney World for grown-ups who don't want to be grown-ups. It wants to be salacious and gritty, but it is hard to blend that with the baser need to be safe and comfortable. There is nothing wrong with having fun, as Charles Lockwood and Trace Packer had pointed out, as long as it's victimless. Is this? Victimless, that is. Maggie doesn't know. The other issue for Maggie is based on something very simple she's observed over the years—no one looks happy the day after. It all feels a tad desperate and sad. These people are rich and successful and powerful and have everything, but it isn't enough. That's the problem. It is never enough. Human nature sees to that. We get used to every luxury. Even the richest men in the world, we've seen over the past few years, can't be satiated, no matter how much money or power or yachts or women or offspring or hero worship or attention or whatever they have. Maggie's parents had introduced her and Sharon to the music of Bruce Springsteen, constantly playing his vinyls on their old record player, and there was a line in the song "Badlands" that the poor man wants to be rich, the rich man wants to be king, and the king ain't satisfied until he rules everything.

That.

At the bar—yes, it's still a bar; dress it up, use premium liquors and crystal decanters and upscale glassware, it's still a bar—Maggie is surprised to see more women than men. Very few of the women appear to be building residents, though perhaps that's sexism or ageism on her part. She doesn't know the deal, but what seems to be happening at first glance is that the young women sit at the bar. Alone. There is at least one stool empty next to them. A man approaches, chats them up for a few minutes, and then they move into a darkened booth.

Hmm, Maggie thinks. *Change of plans.*

She'd hoped to find a man seated alone and make her approach that way, but perhaps this is better. As she heads to the bar, she notices three men against the walls in a triangular formation, all with, yep, the black suits and sunglasses, even in this low lighting. Security. Even in here. Maggie takes a seat next to a too-young, coltish woman with a heavy foundation of makeup. The young woman—okay, can we be honest and call her a girl?—stares at her in surprise. Her fake eyelashes are oversize, like two tarantulas lying on their backs in the hot desert sun.

Maggie gives her a big smile and sticks out her hand. "Hi, I'm Maggie."

The young woman looks suspicious but returns the shake. "Alena."

"I need a favor, Alena."

Alena waits, still giving off the wary.

"Can I borrow your phone?" Maggie asks.

Alena looks puzzled. Maggie wonders how fluent her English is. Then Alena says, "I don't have one."

"You don't?"

"I mean, I *have* one, but . . . Are you a resident?"

"No. I'm visiting someone."

"Oh, that explains it."

"Explains what?"

Alena leans in closer. "They take away our phones."

"Who does?"

"Downstairs. When we come in. You go through a screening. They take your name. They take your photograph. They do a background check. And they lock your phone in a vault."

Odd, Maggie thinks at first, but then she realizes that it makes perfect sense. Big-time security at places like this. People pay big bucks for privacy and anonymity. Heck, Maggie doesn't even know the names of her hosts. Naturally, they wouldn't want any woman coming into their exclusive lair and snapping pics or uploading videos to social media.

Damn. She'd counted on finding a phone down here.

Alena puts her hand on Maggie's arm. "Are you okay?"

The young girl's voice is suddenly older, more mature.

"I'm fine, Alena."

"Why do you need a phone?"

Maggie wonders how to answer that and goes for the truth. "I need to call someone at home."

"You're American?"

"Yes."

"And you don't own a phone?"

"I do. It's complicated."

Alena moves a little closer and whispers, "Do you need help?"

"No, I'm okay."

"Are you sure?"

Her concern is so authentic, so touching.

"I am, Alena. How about you?"

"Oh, I'm fine."

"Where are you from?"

"Ukraine. But I've been here two years now." Then: "You really need a phone, don't you?"

Maggie isn't sure what to say.

"Are you in danger?"

"No."

"But you need to make this call?"

"Yeah, I do."

Alena nods. "Order a drink. Watch me. When I go to the ladies' room, wait a minute and then follow me in."

"Wait, what?"

But Alena is already up and moving toward a dark booth. The modelesque bartender saunters over and asks Maggie what she'd like to drink. Maggie asks if there's a bourbon she'd recommend. The bartender says they have a Pappy Van Winkle 23 Year Old. Maggie is about to nod, but she has a distant memory of seeing one on display at a museum or something.

"Do you have, I don't know, Maker's Mark or something?"

A hand reaches over her shoulder, holding a very fancy-looking credit card. She looks to see who it is.

Viking Bob.

"Get her the Pappy Van Winkle," he says, handing the bartender the card. "In fact, make it two."

Maggie says, "You don't have to—"

"Your host insists," Bob interrupts.

"How much is it?"

"If you have to ask, you don't belong here."

"But I don't belong here," Maggie says.

"Fair point. Just be glad they ran out of the Old Rip Van Winkle 25 Year Old."

"Why?"

"In stores it sells for fifty K a bottle."

"Fifty thousand dollars?"

"Yep."

"For a bottle of bourbon?"

Bob shrugs.

"Does it come with a sex act?"

He laughs. "I guess it should at that price."

She laughs back, making the quasi-bawdy joke to keep the mood relaxed and casual so he doesn't interfere with whatever Alena is planning. Bob has clearly been sent down from ahigh to keep an eye on her.

"On the rocks or straight up?" the bartender asks.

"Oh, you can't put Pappy Van Winkle over ice," Bob says.

The bartender nods, pours the drinks. They clink glasses. Maggie brings the glass to her lips. The smell is ambrosia. She tilts a sip into her mouth, leaves it on her tongue for a moment, and even with everything that's going on, she lets the bourbon warm the back of her throat.

Oh man.

Bob smiles. "Good, right?"

"Nectar of the gods."

Alena reappears from a dark corner.

She heads down the side of the bar, not so much as glancing toward Maggie. Maggie carefully takes another sip. She smiles at Bob while, behind him, she sees Alena stroll past one of the guards and disappear into the bathroom.

Maggie waits. She doesn't want to rush this or do anything that might be clocked as suspicious.

Count to sixty, she tells herself. Count to sixty and then excuse yourself.

She makes it to twenty-five. That seems like enough. She takes another sip and slowly rises from her stool.

"You okay?" Bob asks.

"Yeah, fine. I'm just going to go—"

Bob suddenly clasps her forearm with a firm grip. She can feel the power in his fingers as they close talon-like around her skin.

"What are you doing?" she asks.

"Just a warning."

"Take your hand off me."

"We know about your past."

"Let go of me." Then: "What are you talking about?"

"You've had problems," Bob says. He releases his grip. "You had"— finger quotes—"'issues.'"

"Why did you make quote fingers around the word 'issues'?"

"What?"

"I had issues. It's how I lost my medical license. It's why I'm here. No need to put that in quotation marks."

"So you get my concern?"

"No."

"You had *issues*—and what's the first thing you want to do when you arrive? Seek out a bar. You feel me?"

"I wouldn't feel you with oven mitts," she says. "My issue wasn't alcohol."

"Still, Maggie. Maybe you and I just have this one drink and go back up?"

So Bob had been sent down to keep an eye on her, but not in a way she'd worried about. "Sounds like a plan. Now, if you'll excuse me, I have to pee."

She heads down the bar, gives the security guard a quick half smile, and pushes open the bathroom door. Alena is waiting. She has a phone in her hand.

"Where did you get it?" Maggie asks.

"It's one of the men's," Alena tells her. "He's with my friend. We, uh, distracted him. She still is. I don't know how much time you'll have. Use WhatsApp. Delete the call from his recent list when you're done and leave it on the toilet in the second stall. I'll come back to get it."

"Thank you," Maggie says.

But Alena is already pushing open the door. "Hurry," Alena says before disappearing back into the bar.

Maggie steps into the second stall. The phone is unlocked. WhatsApp is up on the screen. She holds the phone in her left hand and is about to dial a number when she realizes something.

She doesn't remember anyone's phone number.

She has used her mobile phone and contacts for so long that she can't remember Sharon's number. The house's number, yes, that she remembers from her childhood, but when the bills started stacking up, Sharon got rid of those phones. Porkchop doesn't have a mobile. He uses the payphone at Vipers for Bikers.

Wait, hold the phone. So to speak.

The payphone. It's old. Porkchop had been able to pay more to get the number personalized. She knows the final six digits correspond with the letters V-I-P-E-R-S.

What are the first?

The area code is 201. So it's only one number.

It comes to her now.

How long does she have? Between Bob at the bar and Mr. Alena-and-Friend Distracted, she can't stay on very long.

What are the odds Porkchop is at Vipers and by the phone anyway?

She doesn't know. But what other choice does she have? Plus if what she thought was happening at home *was* happening, well, Porkchop could be resourceful.

She quickly loads the digits in with her finger and presses send.

Porkchop answers on the first ring. "Where are you?"

"Dubai."

"More precise?"

"The Bugatti residence."

"Do you need to be extracted?"

"No, I'm good. Listen, I don't have much time. I went to Russia. Barlow hired me—"

"I know this," Porkchop interrupts, because he listened when she said she didn't have much time. "The mistress. Nadia Something."

"What about her?"

"She specifically requested you for the surgery."

Maggie makes a face. "What do you mean? She doesn't even know me."

"You said you're short on time."

"I am."

"So don't waste it. It wasn't Barlow's idea to hire you. He was just a go-between. Nadia wanted you in Russia. Any idea why?"

Maggie's head spins. Nadia? Nadia requested Maggie as her surgeon? "Who told you that?"

"Barlow."

"It makes no sense."

"Make it make sense. This Nadia knows you. She wanted you in Russia. We've researched her and found nothing significant."

We.

Interesting choice of words on Porkchop's part. She gets his hidden meaning here.

"Why are you in Dubai?" Porkchop asks.

"They think Trace is missing," she says. "They want me to help find him."

"Would I be sexist and belittling if I said it sounds too dangerous?"

"A little, yeah."

"So?"

"So I need to follow this through, Porkchop."

"No, you don't," Porkchop says. Then: "Okay, what can I do?"

"They have a theory," she says. "This CIA guy. His name is Charles Lockwood."

"We'll look into him."

Again with the "we."

"He told me not to contact anyone from home," Maggie continues. "That it could be dangerous for you."

"It's handled. We're safe. What's the CIA guy's theory?"

There's a commotion outside. Maggie lowers the phone for a second. Then she hears a man shout in English. "What did you do with my goddamn phone?"

No time to stall, Maggie realizes. So she just dives in. "That Marc is still alive."

From outside in the bar, she hears the voice of a placating woman: "Calm down, Arty. We'll find it."

"I'm not calming down! What did you do with my phone?"

Maggie puts the phone near her ear. "I don't have much time, Porkchop."

"We know that theory can't be true," Porkchop says.

His voice is almost too steady, but she still hears the slight hitch of Porkchop fighting back the choke.

"Maggie?"

"I'm here."

"Marc was hacked up in North Africa. They're lying to you. They're trying to manipulate you."

Porkchop's words make her heart sink.

"Maggie?"

"They believe it's possible."

"Doesn't matter what they believe."

"They think maybe Marc faked his death," she says, speaking fast now. "A violent Russian oligarch named Oleg Ragoravich was using WorldCures to launder money. Marc became an informant—"

"Maggie—"

"Ragoravich found out. That's the theory. His people would have killed Marc—and me and probably you too. So Marc faked his own death—"

"Maggie—"

"To escape him."

"And, what, he never told us?"

"Yes. To keep us safe."

There's more commotion outside. The American man is furious now, demanding that they turn on all the lights.

Time's up, Maggie thinks.

"Porkchop, I have to—"

"So he's been alive this whole time?" Porkchop half rants. "And he chooses to stay silent. Even now? He never tries to reach out to his wife or father and tell us..." He stops. "Maggie—"

"I know," she says. Tears run down her cheeks. Her heart plummets deep in her chest at what is so obvious. "Marc is dead."

"Then what are we doing here? It's not our fight."

The bathroom door bursts open.

"Bye."

Maggie disconnects and deletes the Vipers number. The screen-saver comes on. The center image is a man with a fake tan and blin-dingly white teeth in some kind of dark club surrounded by young, curvy women holding a huge birthday cake with the message "HAPPY BIRTHDAY TO THE ARTSTER." The Artster. Maggie shakes her head. My God. Men. She flushes the toilet, puts the phone on top of it, and then hurries out. Alena rushes past her, not so much as glancing at Maggie. When Maggie gets back to the bar, she spots the Artster in a dark suit and blindingly white dress shirt with one too many buttons open. He is still ranting about someone stealing his phone while a young woman tries to calm him—"It's okay, Arty, it's here, Arty, we'll find it, Arty"—and another digs through the cushions. *Look at this clown,* Maggie thinks. Arty the Artster. Another faux Master of the Universe. Arty shouts for someone to turn on the goddamn lights, but that doesn't happen. Another young woman joins the search. Then a secu-rity guard. Alena hurries back out of the bathroom and immediately gets on her hands and knees to "help" in the search for Arty's phone.

A few seconds later, in an acting performance that deserves Oscar buzz, Alena shouts in stop-the-presses style: "I found it!" and lifts Arty's phone into the air.

The other women clap and cheer. Arty scowls.

From across the bar, Alena meets Maggie's eye. There's a small, knowing smile on the young woman's lips. Maggie mouths a thank-you. Arty snatches the phone from Alena's hand and heads to the exit. He snaps his fingers—actually snaps his goddamn fingers—and two of the women follow.

Then Alena heads to the exit too.

She doesn't look back when she leaves.

Bob taps her on the shoulder. "Do you want to finish your drink?"

What she really wants to do is follow Alena and make sure she's safe and okay and take her back home with her, and even while thinking all of this, Maggie knows how condescending she's being. Alena had offered her help. No strings, no quid pro quo. It's a moment in time. Maggie will never forget it. She will never forget Alena. Appreciate the connection, as fleeting as it might have been. It's so damn human.

Man, Maggie thinks, *I'm being awfully deep today.*

"Maggie?"

She throws back the rest of the bourbon and puts the glass back on the bar. "Let's go," she says. "I need to review those medical files."

CHAPTER SIXTEEN

Maggie can't stop thinking about what Porkchop said about Nadia.
Nadia is the reason she ended up at Oleg Ragoravich's palace.
Nadia is why Maggie nearly got killed.

Nadia is the reason she is here right now in Dubai.

Why? How?

Lots of questions. No answers. Which makes the "plan" even more relevant.

Maggie has to visit Etoile Adiona tonight and find Nadia.

Back in her room, Maggie sits on the king-size bed and opens the first patient medical record. The bed, of course, faces the floor-to-ceiling windows. Night has fallen. The city is still a mirage, but now it's one of glitz and shadows. The Burj Khalifa, the famed tower, pierces the night like a silent sentinel. The Dubai Fountain shimmers and glistens. Dubai feels remote and endless from up this high. It sparkles like polished diamonds against a jeweler's black velvet. It dazzles and explodes. It beckons and holds you at bay with a firm hand.

She goes through the medical files. Two patients. One is a five-year-old girl who needs otoplasty—ear pinning surgery. Prominent ears are often an aesthetic concern, particularly so in this world. The human ear is about 80 percent of its adult size by the age of five, so that's often when this is done—before the age when a kid will be made fun of in school.

The second surgery...Oh man, this is so in her wheelhouse. Maggie can't help but feel a huge adrenaline kick when she sees it: a four-year-old boy in need of cleft lip and palate repair—the quintessential reconstructive procedure for a plastic surgeon. As she reads through the file, Maggie starts rehearsing the palatoplasty in her head, her fingers subconsciously moving in sync with her thoughts— separating the palatine muscles, isolating them, creating the flaps along the roof of the mouth to reconstruct the soft and hard palate.

Damn. How she missed all this.

Half an hour later, she puts the files away and turns her attention back to the Nadia situation. She wishes she could ask the Marc griefbot about her, but then again, Maggie's strong guess is that Sharon probably had and learned nothing important. Porkchop had used the "we" several times during their conversation. That hadn't been an accident. That had been his way of warning her in case someone was listening in.

She'd figured that Porkchop would be ready for her call—and he was. Porkchop had answered the payphone himself, on the very first ring, which was not how it usually worked. That told her that things had gone pretty much thusly: When Oleg Ragoravich's people tried to delete the griefbot from Maggie's phone, Sharon got sent an alarm. Sharon realized that something was very wrong and went to the only person she knew Maggie trusted one hundred percent.

Porkchop.

From what Maggie now put together from the brief phone call, Porkchop had paid Dr. Evan Barlow a visit, probably demanding reassurances that Maggie was okay. Barlow told Porkchop about the concierge surgical work—and more importantly, about Nadia.

Again the key question: What is Nadia's deal? What is her goal?

It has to be connected to WorldCures.

That much is clear to her now—and something about that keeps niggling at the base of Maggie's skull. She's missing something. It's right there, right in the sweet spot (sour spot?) where she can't stop thinking about Theory Three, the one where Marc is somehow still alive, and while she knows that theory is utter bullshit, knows that Marc is dead, knows that his beautiful body was hacked up into pieces by a machete in that refugee camp...

But now she wonders: Why did they hack him up?

It's something she couldn't really face before for obvious reasons, and true, Marc wasn't the only corpse left in that state. There had been others. But not a lot of others. And of course, if you wanted to pull this off, if you planned to fake your death—and yes, she knows *knows* that he didn't—you'd make sure your "corpse" wasn't the only one mutilated beyond recognition, right? If it was only you, that would look suspicious. So you'd make sure that other dead bodies were also left in a similar, awful, gruesome state.

Stop.

But she can't because something isn't adding up. She knows that now.

Nadia.

There is a laptop in the room. Maggie figures it's being monitored, but she doesn't care. Not for this. It's a long shot, a tremendous one, and yet...

Using Google, Maggie finds Ray Levine's website. The top title reads:

Pulitzer-Prize-Winning Photojournalism of Ray Levine

Maggie met Ray Levine when he'd been embedded with her unit during four combat missions. That's where he'd taken the famous photograph of her and Trace on that copter over Kamdesh. Ray Levine had battled some strange demons in his life, and perhaps that made him so able to capture the "beautiful awful"—to use Ray's term—in conflict, suffering, and heroism. You took your time with Ray Levine's photographs. You felt the color and the texture. They made you slow down.

Maggie skims down the left sidebar menu: Afghanistan, Iraq, Rwanda, India, Gaza, Kosovo, Pakistan, Israel, Chechnya, Indonesia, Sudan, Ukraine. Ray has ones closer to home—his home—like Asbury Park and Atlantic City. Then he lists topics too, like Famine, War, Crime and Punishment, Refugee Care.

She braces herself and clicks on the Refugee Care link. There, in black and white, is a photograph of Marc and Trace, taken the day before Marc died. Marc sits in front of a makeshift tent, his head back, his eyes open, his surgical mask half untied and dangling from his neck.

Damn.

Marc. On his last full day of life. And Ray had captured him. The fatigue, the fire, the passion, the exhaustion, the commitment—it's all etched on Marc's craggy, beautiful, worn, tormented, celestial face.

How can such a life force be extinguished?

Easily, she knows. She had seen it in the men—boys, really—she'd served with, some not even twenty years old. They were all strong, funny, smart, bright-eyed, with smiles that could cleave your heart in two—colorful, powerful life forces that were vibrant one moment, and dust the next. It isn't hard to die. It doesn't take much. That's the worst part of it. There is a saying: "When one man dies, a whole universe dies," and while the implications are obvious—the death of even a single soul is like destroying a world, that human life has profound value—dying is also routine, mundane, almost tedious.

Marc, the gorgeous soul in this photograph, is dead.

Happens every day.

She looks now at Trace standing next to Marc, hands on his hips, squinting into the sun. *The stages of grief*, she thinks. The anger one. She never admitted this to anyone, barely to herself even, but a small part of her had been bitter at Trace for, well, surviving. Trace breathes,

Marc doesn't. Simple and as awful as that. Trace had done the right thing on that day, according to everyone who was there. He listened to Marc. He saved lives doing so.

Maggie understood all that, but the anger stage of grief didn't.

She clicks the right arrow. A seemingly blank page comes up. Maggie scrolls down to the bottom. There are two text input fields—one for a username, one for a password. After Marc's murder, Ray had sent her an email offering his condolences and the one thing he could offer that no one else could: his art. He had taken hundreds of photos at the refugee camp that day and stored them online. "When you're ready," Ray had written, "you can access them with the username Thalalatha and the password Hududu." Maggie understood. Thalalatha Hududu is an Arabic phrase that roughly translates to "Three Boundaries."

That's the Arabic name of the TriPoint refugee camp where Marc had been murdered.

She clicks into the username text box and types in Thalalatha. She tabs over to the password and types in Hududu. Her hands, she realizes, are shaking. Ray had written "when you're ready" because he knew she wasn't. She isn't sure she is now. The pain is still so deep and raw. She doesn't need to probe that wound.

But now there is a reason.

So with a deep breath, Maggie clicks the blue Sign In button.

Photo thumbnails quickly populate the screen, dozens of them, at least a hundred on the first page. On the bottom is one of those page count things. It reads:

1...17

Ray's raw footage. This could take a while.

But it doesn't.

Maggie doesn't know exactly what she was looking for—but she finds it anyway.

Right there. On the bottom of the first page. She spends the next hour going through the rest of the thumbnails. Twelve photographs in total tell the story. When she finishes, she realizes that there are tears on her cheeks. She sits back. She has answered one question, but it just leads to deeper ones.

There's a knock on her door.

Maggie closes her laptop, gives her tears a quick sleeve wipe, and says, "Come in."

Bob opens the door and steps inside. "Hell of a view, right?"

"Yes."

"You wanted to see me?"

"I'm meeting a friend tonight at a club in the Burj Binghatti."

He doesn't like that. "What club?"

"What's the difference?"

"Burj Binghatti is a residential building. It doesn't have a club."

"Not one that's open to the public," Maggie says.

"Oh, I see."

"I need a ride or I can call an Uber or—"

"You're doing surgery tomorrow."

"I'm aware."

"You're not here to go clubbing, Maggie."

"And you told me this wasn't a prison, Bob."

"You're being handsomely paid to be here."

"I'm being paid to perform a service. I'll perform it."

Bob shakes his head. "I don't like it."

"Don't care," she says. "I'm going."

"And if I say no?"

"Seriously?" Maggie shrugs. She checks her watch. "Fire me then."

Bob stands there for a moment, looking a little lost.

Maggie makes a shooing motion with both hands, palms down. "I need to shower and get changed. I plan on leaving in an hour."

Not sure what else to do, Bob reluctantly leaves.

Maggie takes a shower and grabs a simple black dress and sandals out of the essentials Charles has given her. She checks her look in the mirror, trying her best not to be self-judgmental. She isn't sure she's ready for an exclusive Dubai nightclub, but then again, she supposes she never would be. She steps out into the main room. Bob is standing there.

"Wow," he says when he sees her. "You look really nice."

"Thank you."

He gestures with his hand to the Bugatti still sitting in the middle of the living room. The rich can be so bizarre. "I'll drive you," he says.

"But you won't follow me in."

"If you say so," he says.

"I say so."

"I'll wait downstairs."

"I might be late."

"I'll be okay."

The drive is a short one. Charles Lockwood had given her very specific instructions about how to get into Etoile Adiona. The Burj Binghatti is currently the tallest residential tower in the world. Like every skyscraper in Dubai, it is sleek, space-age, and shiny. The most notable feature is the diamond-like crown on top. Bob drops her off in the elevator below ground on the C level past a facial-recognition security station. Maggie steps into the opulent elevator with some kind of purple quartz, amethyst maybe, lining the walls. There is a burgundy leather love seat in case you feel the need to sit for the ride. Again, no buttons to push, no bouncing lights telling you the floor. Nothing. The doors close, and the elevator shoots you rocket-like into the night sky.

The ride up the Burj Binghatti's hundred-plus floors takes less than a minute.

Not much time to use the love seat.

The entrance to Etoile Adiona is a shimmering portal, tucked away on the 110th floor. No sign announces the club's presence—if you need to be told where it is, you don't belong. Maggie steps out of the elevator and stands in front of a mahogany door. She knows there is a camera. A well-dressed man opens the door. He says nothing. Maggie sighs at the theatrics, but per Charles's instructions, she whispers the password, "Roman Goddess," before the well-dressed man steps aside and lets her enter. *Silly*, Maggie thinks, but it adds to the mystique, and places like this thrive on mystique.

The music assaults when you enter. No other way to put it. Maggie loves music, but she doesn't understand the need for it to be this hostile. The main room pulses with frenetic energy. It's a kaleidoscope of lights and mirrors and strobes. Nothing feels real, but that's probably the point. She sees dancers packed so tight they can only hop up and down rather than actually dance—human pogo sticks with spring necks, sweat glistening on their faces. Everyone is dressed in black and white. Some partiers are wearing capes and those Venetian masquerade masks. The room rumbles from a custom-engineered sound system.

Maggie tries to swim through the sea of revelers. A man with a masquerade mask half grabs her and starts to dance. She pushes past him and looks up. Above her head, a retractable roof reveals the inky expanse of an Arabian night. Neon drones paint the sky via intricate aerial choreography. The spectacle is mesmerizing. The drones fly with marching-band-like precision. It reminds Maggie of the Christmas light shows her parents would take her to as a kid, only raised to the tenth power.

She continues to trudge through the dance floor. The DJ, a woman with a sleeveless top showing toned arms, is on a giant swing above. She's rocking out loud while her platform sways back and forth, one hand on a turntable, the other pressing a single headphone to her ear. The bass gets into Maggie's bloodstream, making her chest vibrate like someone had jammed a tuning fork into her heart.

The basic VIP area is always easy to spot because, well, what's the point in being a VIP if you can't let others know they're excluded?

They sit in balconies so they can look down at you Roman Colosseum–style. It's dark up there, but from Maggie's vantage point, she can see a lot of men dressed in the more traditional dishdasha, big in the United Arab Emirates, a robe-like, single-piece, long-sleeved, ankle-length garment, which is white, simple, practical, comfortable, and—especially in the desert heat—cooling. A ghutra headdress with a classic black-corded agal. Marc often sported one when he came to this area, once the locals insisted that it was considered respectful and not any sort of appropriation.

Damn. Marc again. The constant stream of Marc-related pangs.

Up ahead she sees two beefy security guards with dark sunglasses standing behind, in a hackneyed move on the club's part, an actual red velvet rope. Maggie steps up to one of the security guards. The music is still loud—don't people just want to talk without screaming sometimes?—so she has to shout: "I'm looking for Nadia."

She expects him to come back at her with some stupid rejoinder like "I don't know any Nadia" or "Who's asking?"—a line like that. But instead, the guard nods and says, "We know."

"You do?"

He nods and unclasps one side of the velvet rope to allow her to pass. "Take the elevator to the Ecstasy Level."

Maggie gives him flat eyes. "Ecstasy Level?"

The guard shrugs as though to say, "Yeah, what can you do?"

Maggie moves toward the elevator. Ecstasy Level? Why not just call it something more subtle like Orgasm Floor or something? She gets in the elevator. Again no buttons, nothing saying Ecstasy or any of that. The doors close. The elevator heads up. The ride takes seconds, but to Maggie, it feels longer.

Because she's about to come face-to-face with Nadia.

Her hands flex into fists. She rocks back and forth on her heels, feeling a bit like what a boxer must feel when he's in his corner and waiting for the bell to ring for the first round. When the elevator door opens, the first thing Maggie sees are the stunning crystal chandeliers, a lot of them. They give off a soft, warm glow over a marble floor and plush seating. There are twenty, maybe thirty people—a celebrity or two Maggie thinks she may recognize—and while there is a perfume in the air that reeks of opulence and luxury, the main difference between the regular section of Etoile Adiona and the VIP section is that most people aren't allowed into the VIP section. That's it, really. Same music. Same dance floor. Same beverages. Slightly more attentive staff. Sure, it's less crowded, but if you don't want a crowd, why go to a nightclub?

The appeal is entirely about who is allowed in—and who isn't.

Life is always a high school cafeteria.

This has never been Maggie's world. The only time she'd go to clubs like this was when Trace would drag her as a wingman (wingwoman?) of sorts. "Stand near me," Trace would tell her.

"Uh, why?"

"Nothing appeals to a hot woman more than a man who is already with a hot woman."

"I don't know if I should be flattered or insulted on behalf of the sisterhood."

"Maybe both? But it's true. If I'm normally, let's say a seven—"

"A seven, Trace? Oh, look at you being all modest."

"—when they see me with you, it ups me to a nine, maybe a ten, in their eyes."

"Aren't you worried they'll think you're taken?"

"Even better. Forbidden fruit. It's a tremendous turn-on for women."

"It's not, Trace."

"It's not *to you*," he says. "But I'm not after a woman like you."

"More flattery."

"You know what I mean."

"Sadly, I do." Then, watching Trace obviously scope out a nearby woman: "You're a pig, Trace. You know that, right?"

Trace would spread his arms and smile. "Love me for all my faults."

She shakes away the memory. A waitress in what looks like tuxedo lingerie hands Maggie a smoky beverage, like something out of an old horror film, covered in glitter. The music is still too loud.

"What is this?" Maggie shouts.

"Our signature drink. Starry, Starry Night."

"What's in it?"

"Mango, yuzu, coconut, Dom Perignon—and our secret sauce."

Sounds gross, Maggie thinks, but she takes a sip. Not bad. "I'm looking for—"

"Nadia is behind the curtain."

Everyone here is prepared. "Like the Wizard of Oz."

"Pardon?"

"Which curtain?"

She points. Maggie has had enough. She hands the drink back to the waitress and storms toward the curtain. A man gets in her way, says "Hey, babe," and starts dancing for her. He's doing the middle-age Dancing Douchebag move of biting down on his lower lip. Maggie is about to maneuver past him, but she stops a second.

How does she want to come into this?

Would it be smarter not to show Nadia all her cards right away? *Slow down and think a sec.* Nadia has been playing her. Would it be wiser to let Nadia think she's still in control, not letting on that Maggie is on to her?

Should Maggie play it coy?

Before she gets to the curtain, it flings open.

Nadia steps out of some back room. The two women lock eyes for the briefest of moments. Nadia moves with the grace of a trained Bolshoi ballerina—her head high, shoulders back, clothes draped perfectly on her petite frame. She knows how to draw the eye and yet it's all organic. There is an intensity to Nadia, a focus, a fiery intelligence, a magnetism that you can't quite escape.

Nadia breaks into a run and when she reaches Maggie, she throws her arms around her and pulls her close.

"I'm so glad you're okay," she whispers in Maggie's ear.

Maggie surprises Nadia by pulling her even closer. Aggressively. Oddly enough, Maggie can feel the new breasts press against her own. She had forgotten about that for a second, that Nadia was a patient, that she'd recently had surgery. She must still be tender to the touch, but Nadia doesn't wince from Maggie's grip or back off. Still in an embrace, Maggie push-walks Nadia back toward the curtain. Nadia's lips remain near her ear. She can hear Nadia's breath catch. Maggie keeps Nadia's body pressed against her with one arm. Her other hand now slowly travels down Nadia's back. Anyone watching from a distance—or heck, even close up—would see something on the sensual side.

When Maggie's hand reaches her waist, Nadia stiffens, and then her body seems to totally surrender into Maggie.

"Doctor...?"

Maggie's hand slides to Nadia's hip bone, then down the side of her leg, and—should Maggie do it?—up her thigh. Nadia's breath quickens. Maggie is leading them back through the curtain, moving them away from prying eyes. The back room is empty and lined with plush sofas.

Maggie changes up now, pulling up on the fringe of Nadia's dress so that it's over her waist.

"Doctor," Nadia says again.

And that's when Maggie pushes Nadia back onto the couch. Nadia's face is flushed. Maggie is about to follow her down, but there's no need. Nadia's dress is still up over her waist. As was Maggie's wont, Nadia's thighs are exposed.

And unblemished.

Maggie looks back and makes sure no one is coming toward them. No one is. Anyone who saw them vanish back in here probably thinks they want to be alone, private, undisturbed. Good. That's what Maggie wanted.

Nadia's eyes flare for a moment, and Maggie can see she realizes what's going on.

Nadia pulls her skirt back down.

"Too late," Maggie says.

Nadia stays still. Maggie reaches out and grabs the hem of the dress and pulls it back up, once again baring her upper thigh.

"No tattoo," Maggie says, before letting go.

Yep, screw playing it coy.

"Time to cut the shit, Nadia, and tell me what's going on."

Nadia opens her mouth, a lie undoubtedly coming to her lips automatically, but Maggie cuts her off by holding up the phone Charles Lockwood had given her. She took screenshots from Ray Levine's website and has the photos lined up and ready to go. She only needs one, the first one, to make Nadia go still. Using her index finger, Maggie swipes through them, just to emphasize the point. The photographs are black-and-white, taken by Ray the day before the incursion that killed Maggie's beloved.

Marc is in many. Trace is in many.

And in the background, trying hard it seems not to be the object of attention, is Nadia.

"You're Salima," Maggie says. "You're the guide who led Marc and Trace to the TriPoint refugee camp."

CHAPTER SEVENTEEN

Maggie sinks into the plush sofa next to Nadia.

The two women sit side by side in silence, both staring out at the curtain. The music thumps into the room, but it seems hushed now, respectful almost, as though the entire club is receding into the backdrop.

"I know you asked for me," Maggie says.

"Asked?"

"To be your surgeon. You requested me."

"Yes." Nadia stares out. A sad smile comes to her face. "We met before, you know."

"I don't."

"No reason you would. I was eleven. In Libya. You probably treated a hundred girls that day, maybe more."

"Salima—"

"I prefer Nadia, if that's okay. I was both for a while, but Salima is dead now. She died in that refugee camp too."

"You've been lying to me," Maggie says.

Nadia doesn't answer.

"That tattoo," Maggie says.

"It was temporary, yeah." She shakes her head. "I should have kept it on longer, I guess."

"I'd have figured it out anyway."

"I guess that's true."

"Why did you do it?"

"The tattoo? Why do you think?"

"To mess with my head."

"Yes." Nadia still stares out, so that Maggie has the profile view. "Most of what I told you is true. I grew up in Libya during a time..." She stops, closes her eyes, opens them again. "That's not important. There were refugee camps. There were humanitarian crises. You were there. I don't need to explain to you how bad it was. And yes, I sold my kidney. Just as I told you. The World Health Organization claims over two thousand kidneys were sold in India alone last year. That's a small part of the worldwide black market. I have no regrets. I explained my reasons for doing so. It saved my family."

"Nadia?"

"What?"

"Are you in any pain right now? I mean, from the surgery."

Nadia chuckles at that. "A physician first."

"I should probably examine you."

"No, I'm fine. Really." Then: "Charles sent you, didn't he?"

"You know Charles Lockwood?"

"I work with him."

"He didn't mention that."

"He doesn't trust me right now. It's why he sent you. He told you about the money laundering?"

"Yes."

"Did he give you his whole theory on corruption—on how it starts small and it either grows like a cancer or it dies?"

"He didn't use a cancer analogy."

"But you get it. And if it starts with money laundering, you can probably guess the next profitable step."

Maggie nods. "Selling organs."

"I was in that refugee camp when I was recruited to donate my kidney. WorldCures was there too. After I agreed to be a donor, I was flown here. For the surgery."

Maggie is puzzled by this. "To Dubai?"

"Yes. To a place called Apollo Longevity."

Apollo Longevity.

Nadia is trying to read her face. "You've been there, right? At Apollo Longevity."

"You already know I have."

Nadia gives her a slow nod. "WorldCures has a relationship with Apollo Longevity."

"*Had*," Maggie says, correcting her. She tries to keep her voice controlled, even, though the memories are starting to rock her. "We had some space in their facility." And then, because Maggie wants to change the subject and is tired of Nadia's cute evasions: "Are you going to tell me my husband removed your kidney?"

"I wouldn't care if he did, but no, I don't know. What matters is that I got my family out. At a cost. Not just my kidney. The organ brokers, they would only provide two of us with identities to get into the United States. I gave them to my mother and my brother. They do live in the Midwest now, just like I told you. They are prosperous and happy."

"And what about you, Nadia? What happened to you?"

"I stayed here. In Dubai."

"On your own?"

"Yes."

"That must have been difficult."

"Not really, no," she says, but the words feel forced. "I, Salima, became Nadia. I did well here. I worked in clubs like this. Someone—a man usually—was always willing to take care of me. One Ukrainian benefactor gave me access to online education. He opened the door, and I walked through it. I learned quite a few languages, including Russian and English, which helped when I met Trace Packer one night at this club. He'd been drinking heavily. You know Trace liked night-clubs, right?"

"Yes."

"He told me I looked familiar. I figured it was just a line—"

It probably was, Maggie thinks.

"—and I was going to tell him he was mistaken, but I, well, I remembered him. He was kind at the refugee camp. He was so nice to his patients. So I told him who I was."

"You told him you were Salima?"

"From the refugee camp, yes. He said he remembered me. The next day, we met for coffee. He told me about WorldCures' latest missions. So I volunteered to help out."

Maggie tries to sort this all out in her head. Some of it she had figured out already. Charles Lockwood had hinted that laundering money was only the start—that that crime alone would not have been enough to make Marc flip on someone as deadly as Oleg Ragoravich.

But harvesting organs?

That would have been the proverbial straw for Marc. The money laundering—again, it was bad but once you cross that line, there really is no going back. Even if Marc wanted to flip on that, everyone who worked at WorldCures—especially their three founders—would be subject to prosecution or, at the very least, have their reputations destroyed. More than that—much more—Oleg Ragoravich would never let them sell him out and just walk away. If Marc or Trace had any delusions about that, one quick helicopter trip would have straightened them out.

"So you accompanied Marc and Trace on that last mission," Maggie says to her.

"Yes. I knew the area. I speak all the dialects."

"So what happened?"

"We got overrun. A surprise attack. Just like you heard. It was a slaughter. Trace and I tried getting people to safety. We were mostly successful. But Marc"—she stops, shakes her head—"he was so brave. Just like you heard. He insisted we go without him. He stayed behind, tried to save more. But still..."

Nadia stops.

"Still what?"

"The situation was dangerous, sure, but the invaders let the medical staff live."

Maggie swallows. "Except for Marc."

"Yes," Nadia says. "He's the only one they killed."

"You have a theory why?"

Nadia nods. "I think someone sold Marc out."

She lifts her head to look at Maggie now. Nadia's eyes are on fire, hot with anger, full of hostility even.

"And I think that someone was you, Maggie."

————————

Maggie doesn't even know how to respond to Nadia's words, so she goes with the most obvious:

"You think I had something to do with my husband's murder?"

Nadia stays quiet for a beat, but for Maggie, the pieces are slowly starting to, if not come together, at least fall out of the box and onto the table.

"Is that why you asked specifically for me to do your surgery? You wanted to get me alone. At that house. All those weird conversations, Oleg's ball, the hints something was wrong. And then, boom, the tattoo." How had Maggie not seen it? "You were trying to mess with my mind."

Nadia finally speaks. "Yes."

"You were hoping— Jesus, what were you hoping for?"

"That you'd slip up," Nadia says. "That you'd reveal the truth."

"The truth that I, what? That I would..." She can't even say it.

Nadia doesn't reply.

"Why the hell would you think I had something to do with...?" Maggie still can't articulate the thought.

Killing Marc?

Nadia stands as though she's about to leave. *Uh-uh, no way*, Maggie thinks. She blocks her path.

"You don't just lay down an accusation like that and walk away."

"I'm not walking away."

"What then?"

Nothing from Nadia.

Maggie gets up in her face. "I lost the man that I loved," she says. And Nadia replies, "So did I."

Silence.

"What are you talking about?"

Maggie almost takes a step back. She shakes her head. *No way. No way.*

"Wait, if you're trying to say that you and Marc..."

"No," Nadia says.

Maggie stops. "What then?"

Maggie looks Nadia over as though looking for a clue—and finds one. She hadn't focused on it before, but once Maggie's eyes latch on to it, she can't wrest her gaze away.

Nadia is wearing a ring on her left hand.

She hadn't been wearing it in Russia, that's for certain. But she's wearing it now. Maggie slowly reaches out for Nadia's hand. Nadia pulls back at first, but then she lets her.

It's a square-shaped emerald.

The one from that faded photograph in Trace's apartment.

The same one Trace had clutched at his mother's funeral.

Oh, damn.

Those puzzle pieces on the table? They start to shift into place.

Maggie meets Nadia's eyes. "You and Trace...?" Her voice drifts away.

Nadia nods.

Maggie closes her eyes.

"Trace is missing," Nadia says. "Do you know where he is?"

Oh man, she should have seen this. Maybe not immediately. Not when she first got to Ragoravich's or even when she met Nadia—but as soon as Maggie realized that Nadia was, in fact, Salima, she should have figured it out.

"We're in love," Nadia says.

More pieces drop into place.

"Where is he?" Nadia asks.

"I don't know."

"You claim he went to Bangladesh," Nadia says.

"Whoa, I don't claim anything. That's what Trace told me."

"Told you how?"

"On the phone. He called me. After Marc was murdered. He'd thought about coming back to the States. Pay his respects. That kind of thing. He wanted to make sure I was okay."

"Were you?"

"Okay? No, of course not. But he couldn't help with that. No one could. But Trace, well, he wasn't the best with death or grieving. Have you seen that side of him?"

"Yes," Nadia says.

"Then you know."

"It hurts him too much. Other people's pain. He has to deflect, channel it into something more constructive."

That isn't it, but Maggie sees no reason to go into that right now.

Nadia asks, "When did you last communicate with Trace?"

"When I was in his apartment the day before I came to Russia."

"Why were you in his apartment?"

"Because that's what we used to do. Trace asked me to look in on his place if I was in town. A long time ago, Marc and I lived in that building too."

"And you talked to Trace a week or so ago?"

"Texted."

"A text can be faked."

"What?"

"It could have been anyone on the other end. What did your text to him say?"

Okay, Maggie thinks, *that's enough.* "It said none of your goddamn business. Let me ask you the same thing: When was the last time you talked to Trace?"

"Here. In Dubai. Five months ago. The day you called him."

Maggie frowns. "I didn't call Trace five months ago."

"That's what he told me." A tear runs down Nadia's cheek. "He was upset. He said he was going to fly to Baltimore. That he had to see you in person."

Maggie shakes her head.

"I went with him to the airport," Nadia says. "I kissed him good-bye at Terminal 1. I watched him walk through security..." Nadia stops and looks away. "And that's it. Trace never came back. He never called me again. He just...vanished."

Silence.

"What did you say when you called him?" Nadia asks.

"I didn't call him, Nadia."

"And what happened when you met with him in Baltimore?"

"I didn't meet with him in Baltimore."

"So Trace was lying to me?"

Maggie doesn't know how to answer that.

Nadia lifts her hand and points to the emerald ring. "He proposed, you know."

"I had no idea."

"We were going to get married."

It made no sense. It made perfect sense.

Trace had always professed to be a confirmed bachelor, that he wasn't built for long-term relationships, and his past actions more than bore that out. So had Nadia changed him?

Could be.

Nadia made for a pretty amazing package. Maybe Trace had fallen for real this time. He gave her his mother's ring, for crying out loud. Maggie couldn't get over that. Trace's mother's ring on Nadia's finger. *Wow.*

So maybe, in that way at least, Trace had changed. What do they say in finance? Past performance is not an indicator of future results.

"Then suddenly," Nadia continues, "after Trace goes to see you—"

"He didn't see me, Nadia—"

"—my fiancé vanishes and supposedly ran off to help people in Bangladesh or somewhere else too remote to reach him. Not one word to me. Not a goodbye. Not a breakup. Nothing. Don't you find that strange?"

Maggie doesn't reply.

"And no one knows any details about his whereabouts. If he's working for a relief organization, no one can tell me which one. No one sees him or communicates with him. Meanwhile the last place he said he was going was, well, to visit you. So I start to wonder."

"Wonder what?"

"You left WorldCures—"

"My mother—"

"I know. She was ill. But come on, Maggie. You *left* WorldCures. You had some idea of what was going on. Let's not pretend."

That accusation again. What's the old joke her father used to tell? "Denial isn't just a river in Egypt." Had she intentionally looked away from the finances? Probably. And yes, she knew that Marc and Trace were risk-takers, that they were pushing boundaries, that they were frustrated by the normal protocols that slowed down medical advancements. They wanted to speed up their progress, ends-justify-the-means kind of guys, and when those two were both together, when you blended Marc's and Trace's passion, the result bordered on the toxic.

And there had been that surgery, that awful surgery here in Dubai...

"Do you see how it looks?" Nadia continues. "You leave WorldCures—and then on his very last humanitarian mission, someone sells out your husband."

"Oleg Ragoravich probably."

"That was my thinking too," Nadia says. "At first. Which is why I made it my business to get close to him."

"How?" Maggie asks, and as soon as she does, she realizes how stupid the question is. No need for subtlety. "You, what, seduced him?"

"The man I loved had vanished. I would do anything to get him back."

Sounds like a yes. "So how did it happen?"

"Like a lot of oligarchs, Ragoravich had made Dubai a big part of his life. I made sure we crossed paths. At this very club, as a matter of fact."

"Jesus."

"Are you judging me again?"

Maggie shakes her head. "No, go on."

"I wanted him to take me back to Russia."

"Which he did."

"Yes. I thought I would find answers there."

"And did you?"

"No, not really. I searched Oleg's computers and files. I don't think he had anything to do with Marc or Trace. So I kept asking myself: If Oleg isn't behind all this, who else could it be?"

Maggie makes a face. "And the answer was me?"

"I couldn't forget Trace's face getting on that plane. He was so shaken. Scared, even. I'd never seen him like that. Don't you see how it looked? Trace gets a call. He's upset. He drops everything and flies to you and then, poof, no one ever sees him again."

Nadia gives Maggie a challenging look. Maggie shakes it off.

"I had nothing to do with that," Maggie says. "Trace is my friend. We were in combat together."

Nadia's eyes continue to bore into hers. "I just want to find the man I love. You can understand that, can't you?"

"Of course."

"So now I'm in Russia, with Oleg. I'm learning about how he had his hand in all these medical charities. But I'm getting nowhere with my original mission."

"Finding Trace."

"Yes. But I'm starting to wonder what you're hiding."

"I'm not hiding anything."

"Meanwhile Oleg, he keeps saying how he loves me, but I'm too skinny. When a man says you're too skinny, well, you know..."

Maggie knows. They both know. Most women know.

"So Oleg, he was already looking into finding a discreet surgeon for some plastic surgery of his own. When I heard that, I suggested that at the same time, hey, I could get bigger boobs. He loved the idea."

"Big surprise," Maggie says.

The two women share a knowing smile. Men. They don't change much.

"So now I put myself in charge of finding the surgeon."

"And you made sure that I got selected?"

"Yes."

"So you could get me to Oleg's weird palace and hope, what, I'd crack?"

"Yes," Nadia says. Simple as that. "I'd control the environment. You'd be isolated, out of your element, off-balance. I wanted to confuse you, make you question everything. The tattoo was a big part of that. By the way, I saw the tattoo on Marc in a pool here in Dubai. He and Trace told me the story about how he got it in college. I had other things planned for you, and if they didn't work, I planned on directly confronting you—like I am now."

"You had other things planned?"

"Yes."

"More head games?"

"Yes. You were supposed to stay longer. Your first demand was two weeks."

Maggie remembers. "So what went wrong, Nadia? Why was everyone suddenly in a panic after the operations?"

"I don't know. But it had something to do with Oleg."

"What?"

"From what I could make out, he ran after the surgery. I heard gunfire. A couple of guys got shot and killed, I think. Ivan wanted me out of the way, so I asked them to fly me back home."

"You're lucky they didn't kill you."

Nadia smiles. "Not luck. I took precautions. Killing me would have made it worse for them."

Maggie thinks about it for a moment. They're missing something...

"Wait, why would Oleg Ragoravich want facial surgery anyway?"

"Oleg kept making jokes it would make him prettier."

"But we don't believe that."

"We don't," Nadia agrees.

"Oleg wanted to disguise himself. Why?"

"I don't know."

"And if that was the plan, why would he run?"

"I don't know," Nadia says. "I also don't know how you escaped. How did you get out?"

Maggie shakes her head. She's not ready to go there just yet.

A man dressed in, yep, a black suit opens the curtain. He says something to Nadia in Arabic. She nods.

"I have to go."

"So now what?" Maggie asks.

"I'm not sure. I don't even understand why you ended up coming to Dubai."

"The same reason you did," Maggie says. "To get answers. To find Trace."

"And maybe also find...?" Nadia asks, her voice with a little tease in it.

Maggie isn't about to go there. "And maybe also find a way to bring down this whole enterprise."

Nadia still has a hint of a smile on her face. "So the two of us should work together?"

"Yes."

"Except, Maggie, I don't trust you."

"Perfect," Maggie says, "because I don't trust you either."

CHAPTER EIGHTEEN

Maggie makes two calls before she gets back in the VIP elevator. The first is to her former classmate and suck-up student Bonnie Tillman. She needs to ask for a quick favor because Bonnie was class president and will definitely know.

Maggie gets right to the point.

"I need Steve Schipner's mobile number."

Bonnie groans. "Sleazy Steve?"

"Yep."

"The Boob Whisperer? Do you know he calls himself that?"

"I do, yes."

"Gross," Bonnie says, in case the groan hadn't been obvious enough. "Look, Maggie, I know you're going through a tough time out there—"

"It's for a medical consult."

"And only Steve can help? Come on, Maggie."

Maggie doesn't have time for this. "Do you have his number or not?"

With a theatrical sigh, Bonnie gives it to her.

It's midnight here in Dubai, but Maggie is hardly worried about waking him. The phone Charles gave her has Maggie's name on the caller ID. She figures that there's an excellent chance Charles or one of his people is listening in on the calls, but at this stage she doesn't really care.

Steve picks up on the third ring. His voice doesn't hide his surprise. "Well, well, well, is this really *the* Maggie McCabe?"

"Hey, Steve."

She hears classical music in the background. One of Chopin's preludes. A bit of a surprise for Steve. She'd expected something more like Van Halen's "Hot for Teacher" or Mötley Crüe's "Girls, Girls, Girls."

"To what do I owe the pleasure of a late-night call?"

Maggie tries not to roll her eyes. "I'm in Dubai—"

"What, now?"

"Yes."

"I hear music. Are you at a club?"

"I am."

"Which one? I know them all."

Big surprise. "Etoile Adiona."

Steve gives a low whistle. "Exclusive."

"Yeah, there's only like a thousand people here."

"It should start filling up now."

"With lots of young tail, I'm sure."

"What?" He laughs. "Oh, Maggie, I was only kidding with that. Look, give me ten minutes to get ready—"

"I'm on my way out," she says, "but I do need your expertise."

"Oh?"

"Will you be at Apollo Longevity tomorrow?"

Steve's voice grows a touch wary. "I should be, yes."

"I have a patient. A twenty-four-year-old woman. I performed a breast augmentation on her."

"Wait. Wasn't your medical license revoked?"

"Can I bring her to see you in the morning?"

"If you did something illegal—"

"It's nothing like that. Can we meet first thing in the morning? I'll explain everything then."

There is a long pause. Then: "What's the patient's name?"

"Nadia Strauss. Can you see her?"

Steve tells her that he can squeeze her in at ten a.m., right when Apollo Longevity opens. He then tries to convince Maggie to stay at Etoile Adiona or perhaps, if it would be more convenient, his apartment building has a members-only club in it, which would be the perfect place for a quiet drink. Maggie gets off the phone with as much kindness as she can muster.

She finds Nadia on the way to the elevator. "I found a way for us to get into Apollo Longevity."

They agree to meet in the lobby a few minutes before ten in the morning. Nadia walks Maggie to the elevator. When the doors open, Maggie is caught off guard when Nadia gives her a big hug.

"I still don't trust you," Nadia whispers in her ear, "but I trust them even less."

Nadia doesn't say who "them" refers to—Ragoravich, Brovski, Lockwood—but she assumes, the same as Maggie herself, all of the above.

"Uh, ditto," Maggie manages as she steps inside the elevator.

The ground floor of Etoile Adiona is in full swing now, and full swing here is defined as complete pandemonium. Maggie has no idea how many new people have come in during the half hour or so she was gone, but it feels like one more and the club would collapse a level or two. The dance floor is dark, lit only by the flicker from the strobe lights. The DJ is rocking out to something super-loud with a super-deep bass—so deep that Maggie can feel the lining in her lungs quake.

She tries to cross the dance floor, but it's slow going. There are simply too many bodies crushed together in too small a space. She squeezes herself between any cracks in the crowd, but there aren't many. She ends up making karate-chop hands and crowbarring her way through. The music transitions into something even louder and more aggressive. Maggie wants to cover her ears, but she needs both hands to slice through the crush of flesh. The entire dance floor has been transformed into a manic mosh pit now. The partygoers wearing the creepy Venetian masks are made more nightmarish by the strobe lights.

The whole effect is beyond dizzying.

Near the stage is what looks like a diving board. Patrons climb the ladder, spread their arms, and fall back into the heart of the dance floor. The crowd catches them and carries them along like waves at the ocean. Maggie can't quite get her footing. She's jostled to and fro, blindly pinballing closer to what she hopes is the exit.

Do people really enjoy this?

Maggie has never been claustrophobic, but she's finding it a little hard to breathe now. How often, she wonders, does someone have a panic attack in a place like this? Worse, if you do have one, there is no real reprieve or recourse. You are trapped. Maggie wonders how many of these nightclubbers are on a pharmaceutical hallucinogen. A fair number, she'd guess. She wonders, too, whether that would make this experience easier or harder, and the answer is probably both.

When Maggie was a college sophomore, a boy she had a crush on gave her a pill at a two-day outdoor music festival in western Massachusetts. She still doesn't know what was in the pill, but it made her freak out with paranoia. A paramedic took her and the boy to the "Chill Out Tent," where they were fed oranges and activated charcoal and had saline pumped into their veins.

Strange memory.

Maggie is wedging herself through two beefy men when someone grabs her arm.

It's not a casual or accidental grab. The grip is a straight-up iron claw. She tries to pull away. Nothing. She turns to see who it is, but through the mass of partygoers, she can only see a big, meaty hand on her forearm. Without warning, the big hand jerks her hard toward him. Maggie nearly loses her balance. The big hand pulls harder, dragging her back in the other direction.

Maggie isn't sure what to do here. She's being pulled through a human car wash. She tries to dig her heels in, tries to stop her momentum, but the pull is too strong. She yells out to stop, to let go of her, but the music is so loud she can't even hear her own shouts.

With her free hand, Maggie finds the man's index finger and tries to pry it off. His grip doesn't waver. His fingers clutch like eagle talons to the point she fears he may break skin. She thinks about spearing his hand with a fingernail—breaking his skin rather than hers—but her nails are all cut down to surgery length, which means there is nothing to spear him with. She sees the back of him now, the broad shoulders and big back, but with the crowd, with the crush of people, she can't rear back and kick him. She'd been taught pressure points that could possibly free her here, but pressure points never seem to work in the real world or on moving targets. She's just about to try one anyway when the man suddenly stops.

He turns around and takes off his mask.

Maggie freezes.

His eyes are bloodshot and blackened. His face is swollen. He has a thin bandage across the bridge of his nose. She's about to strike him—one shot to that new nose will finish him—but her eyes meet his and what she sees surprises her.

Fear.

It's Oleg Ragoravich.

With a head tilt, he signals for her to stay with him.

Maggie isn't sure what to do here, but curiosity gets the better of her. She nods and stops fighting him. His grip is lighter now, though it remains firm. She's good with that. She needs this hand on her arm so that she doesn't lose him in the crush.

The music's volume lowers a bit, the frantic beat decelerating as the DJ transitions the crowd into a slow song. The patrons quiet like particles when you turn down the flame. Everyone remains packed together, but now instead of rapid, frenetic movement, the bodies gently sway back and forth.

When Oleg and Maggie reach a bit of a clearing, Maggie frees her arm with a sudden tug. Oleg Ragoravich spins toward her. She again sees the fear in his eyes before he lowers the mask back into place. He puts his hands on Maggie's shoulders. She shrugs them off, but her first thought comes from her physician lizard brain: She needs to examine her patient and make sure he's okay. She needs to make sure the surgery took hold, especially the experimental 3D-printed scaffolding in his nose.

"How are you feeling?" she asks. "I should take a look—"

"I warned you," he says, and his voice chokes up. "I told you not to believe a word Nadia says."

"What's going on?" Maggie asks. "Why are you here?"

"You need to help me."

"Help you how?"

"They're trying to kill me."

"Who? What happened? Why did you run?"

His head is on a swivel now. "You don't understand."

"Yeah, I know," Maggie says, trying to keep the sarcasm out of her voice. "That's why I am asking. Why did you run?"

"You have to get me out of here."

"And take you where, Oleg?"

"Maggie, listen to me. You can't trust anyone."

"That I know."

"It's all a lie. All of it."

"What's a lie? Why did you run away?"

"I'm—"

And that is when several things happen seemingly all at once.

The music picks up the pace again. It grows louder—louder and more aggressive than ever. The room goes dark, and the flicker strobes turn everything into time-warping, dreamlike bursts of light. A group in Venetian masks swarm around them, separating her from Ragoravich, their dancing fevered and fast. Maggie loses sight of Ragoravich for a moment. She reaches out and finds his hand.

Her grip tightens. He holds on too.

She is staring into Ragoravich's eyes when she sees them go wide. Too wide.

His grip on her hand slackens. Maggie tries to hang on to him, to grasp his hand even tighter. She tries to pull him back toward her, but she's losing him.

His hand slips away.

"Oleg!"

But her cry is lost in the music. The masked crowd moves between them, pushing them apart. Ragoravich is tumbling away from her, almost out of sight.

"Oleg!"

She desperately tries to get back to him. There are too many masked people in the way now. Maggie shoves them hard, throwing punches even, anything to find Oleg.

There.

She sees him. Oleg is only a few feet away. She's almost back to him, close enough to touch. She reaches out to him.

That's when she sees a gloved hand pull a blade from Oleg's chest.

Blood spreads across his white shirt.

Maggie screams. But the music—the damn music—swallows the

sound away. Out of nowhere, someone delivers a body blow, almost knocking Maggie off her feet. She starts to spin, tries to regain her footing. But she can't quite steady herself. Through the flickers from the strobe, she can see that everyone around her is wearing a mask.

She can't find Oleg.

"Help!"

Nothing.

"A man's been stabbed!"

She can barely hear her own voice.

Where the hell is Oleg?

She lashes out now, panicked. But she can't find him. She starts throwing punches again. She searches frantically for Oleg or for blood or for a gloved hand carrying a blade—anything—but the room is too crowded, too dark, too filled with stuttering strobes.

She looks up, toward the open roof and the serenity of the night sky, and in her periphery, she sees a man being carried above the crowd mosh-pit style.

It's Oleg.

He is already at least ten, maybe twenty yards away from her. She starts flesh-swimming toward him. A beefy man in a black masquerade mask gets in her way. When she knees him in the balls, he folds like a lawn chair. Another dancer bumps her. Hard. Maggie throws an elbow. It lands in his rib cage. Someone else rams into her. And then someone slams her with an open hand on the side of the head.

Maggie staggers and sees stars.

The music still blares. The party patrons surround her, consume her. She reaches out blindly toward the man who just slapped her. Her fingers find his mask. She grabs hold and pulls it down.

It's CinderBlock.

What the...?

He shoves her hard and turns to hurry away. Maggie bounces

against someone behind her, and using that momentum, she leaps on CinderBlock's back. She's still screaming for help, but no one is paying attention. Even now, even with her leaping on a man's back, she doesn't stick out in this crowd. No one does. Everyone is in constant motion—jumping, dancing, leaping, raising their fists in the air, shouting along with the music.

From her new vantage point on CinderBlock's back, Maggie scans the dance floor. She sees two people surfing the crowd.

Neither is Oleg.

He's gone.

CinderBlock tries to buck her off, but Maggie wraps her legs around his waist and then ankle-locks them into place. Her right arm snakes around his nearly indecipherable neck.

Then she squeezes for all she's worth, choking him.

CinderBlock's hands start reaching behind him, flailing to grab her. She lowers her face into the back of his head—close enough so he can't get to her eyes, close enough so she can move with him if he tries a back headbutt.

She regrips and squeezes harder on his windpipe.

His hand movements grow more frenzied, more desperate to reach her, to get free for even a moment so as to get fresh oxygen.

But she has him.

She keeps squeezing. His knees start to wobble. She shuts her eyes and holds on. She will not let go. She will not let go until...

Whack.

A fist slams into Maggie's lower back, just beneath her ribs. The knuckles land flush on her kidney. The pain is a white-hot piercing stab. A coppery taste flows into her mouth. The blow shuts down muscles, organs maybe, incapacitates her. Maggie tries to hang on through it, tries to finish this off.

But then another punch lands in the same place.

Maggie feels everything in her close down.

Someone grabs her shoulders from behind and pulls her off Cinder-Block's back. Maggie crashes to the floor. People dance all around her, some stamping on her legs and back. She tries to fight through them, to get back up, but there are just too many people. She keeps battling, keeps trying to get up, keeps getting knocked down.

She screams and then screams again. But no one hears her. No one stops.

The crowd parties on.

CHAPTER NINETEEN

Sharon slides into the corner booth at Vipers.

Porkchop is already there. He looks up, sees the expression on her face, and waits. Sharon puts both hands on the table in front of her. She stares at them for a bit—her hands—and then sits back. Sharon's eyes are everywhere but on him. Her left leg has the jackhammer shakes, but that's pretty standard for her.

Porkchop knows Sharon is working up to something, so he just gives her space.

A few more moments pass. Then Sharon says, "Do you know what a griefbot is?"

The question is unexpected. But so is his answer. "Yes."

"You do?"

Porkchop nods.

"I always thought you were the ultimate Luddite."

"Pinky told me about them after Marc died. I guess he tried one with his mother."

"What did he tell you?"

"He said it's some kind of software program where the dead, I don't know, they text you? Supposed to help you cope with losing a loved one. It's like a digital replica of them or something."

Someone hits the jukebox. Tears for Fears start telling everyone to shout, shout, let it all out.

"Did you try one?" Sharon asks. "A griefbot, I mean."

"No," Porkshop says. "I don't want a digital replica. I want my son."

Sharon nods slowly. Then she says, "But you know that will never be."

"I do. Death is final." Porkchop gets that Sharon can sometimes be clumsy with her words or overly blunt. "Is there a point to this, Sharon?"

"I created a griefbot of Marc for Maggie. But it's not like any other griefbot."

Sharon takes the next ten minutes explaining the machinations, details, ingenuity that have gone into the AI development of the Marc griefbot. Porkchop listens and tries not to react. Sharon talks fast. She rambles a bit. She loses him when she gets too deep in the woods with the technology, but he just rides that out. Again, this isn't atypical with Sharon. Her mouth is always trying to keep up with her brain, and that's an impossible task.

Toward the end Sharon veers into the economic realities of her potential startup. "Unfortunately, I've concluded that as of now, my griefbot is not a viable marketplace product, fiscally speaking."

"Why not?"

"It took me two months of working full-time to gather the information on Marc—coding, hacking, researching, development. This is a beta version, a prototype, but I don't see how I can mass-produce it to the point where it would ever be profitable. It's too time-consuming to extract and organize the data."

"If your griefbot works the way you say it does—"

"Oh, it does."

"Then some people will pay anything for it."

"That's probably true," Sharon says. "But I have no interest in spending two months digging up information on, say, a billionaire's father, no matter what they'd pay. I want everyone to have access to whatever I create."

Porkchop sits back. "How long has Maggie had your griefbot?"

"Two weeks," Sharon says. "She didn't tell you about it."

"She did not."

"She thought it would hurt you."

Again with the blunt words. Behind them, Tears for Fears are singing that if they could change your mind, they'd really love to break your heart.

"You don't approve," Sharon says.

"Not my place."

"But it's not something you'd be interested in."

"The dead are dead," Porkchop says. "You're not supposed to get over it. You're supposed to live with it."

"Other people may feel differently."

"I'm sure that's true."

"Suppose it offers comforts?"

"It would be a false comfort."

Sharon shrugs. "All comfort is false, when you think about it. That's almost the definition."

"I'm not looking for comfort," Porkchop says. "It's not about me. It's about my son. It's not about what I miss—it's about what he missed, what was stolen from him. I don't care about my pain. I can live with that. It's the least I can do. What I can't live with—what I can't get past, what I *don't want* to get past—is what was taken from my boy."

Sharon says nothing.

"Do you think your griefbot can help with that?"

"No," she says.

"I don't mean to sound harsh."

Sharon puts up her hand. "I get it."

"What made you decide to do this?"

"Make a griefbot?"

"Make one of Marc for Maggie."

"Selfishness maybe. I wanted to see if I could do it."

"And you thought it would help Maggie."

"Yes."

"Why?"

"She needed answers. Do you remember when you and Maggie flew over to Tunisia?"

Porkchop does, of course. "She wanted to see where it happened."

"That would have taken you a day, maybe two," Sharon says. "You two spent three weeks there. Visiting patients in the hospitals. Talking to every TriPoint camp survivor you could find. Maggie immersed herself in all the horror. She didn't want to be spared. She wanted to hear how awful that day had been. Maybe Maggie thought hearing it all would be cleansing or healing or help her move on. But it was the opposite. When she came back, she wasn't the same. I could see it in her eyes. She started self-medicating. She almost killed a patient during surgery. She lost her medical license. She spiraled."

Porkchop just sits there. His expression doesn't change, but Sharon's words are shards of glass ricocheting through his chest. "So you tried to help with this griefbot."

"Yes."

"If I'm being kind, your invention is a crutch."

"Sometimes a crutch is all you need."

"In the short term. You can't keep using a crutch."

Sharon tilts her head. "Why not?"

Porkchop doesn't have an answer to that.

"We all have crutches," Sharon says. "We all have something to numb or distract or get us through the day. You have Vipers and your members. You have your bike rides. And..." Sharon points to the center of the room. "Do you think I don't know what that is?"

Her finger is aimed at Vipers' display area—more specifically, at the 1996 Honda Blackbird. Porkchop had bought it for Marc as a graduation present. After he died, Maggie had insisted Porkchop take it, ride it himself or give it to another Serpents and Saints member. But

Porkchop couldn't. He tried, but he couldn't bear seeing someone else on his boy's favorite bike. So Porkchop put it in here, in Vipers for Bikers, and every day, he stops in front of it and just stands there.

Yeah, who needs a crutch?

Porkchop stares at the bike now. "Did it help her?"

Sharon knows he's talking about the griefbot. "I don't know."

"But Maggie's been using it?" He wrests his eyes away from Marc's bike. "She was talking to . . . ?"

"Yes."

Porkchop thinks about that for a moment. It stings. The thought of Maggie talking to some computer-generated version of Marc. It stings more than he wants to admit, but what doesn't? Part of him gets it. Part of him finds it infuriating.

"No wonder Maggie believes Marc might be alive," he says.

"What?"

"She's been 'talking' to him," he says with more disgust in his voice than he intended. "Not him. Not her husband. Not my son. Just whatever Frankenstein version of him you created."

"It's not like that," she says.

"I said *at best*, it's a crutch." He tries but he can't keep the bitterness out of his voice. "But more likely, your griefbot is a delusion. It's a full-on lie."

Sharon sits back. Porkchop immediately regrets his words.

"I'm sorry," he says. "I didn't mean—"

"No, no." Sharon waves him off. "Don't do that. You do mean it. And I get what you're saying. It's fair." She tilts her head. "Why did you say Maggie thinks Marc is still alive?"

"She doesn't. Not really."

"But someone is giving her hope?"

"Yes."

Sharon shakes her head. "That's cruel."

Nothing crueler, Porkchop thinks. He turns his head and looks at his son's bike again. He flashes back to the smile on Marc's face when he rode it. That smile. His son's perfect, joyful, life-affirming smile. Gone. And not just gone, but intentionally extinguished.

Intentionally.

Premeditated. A conscious decision someone made to snuff out his son's existence.

His hands tighten into fists. Again. And again. It is an unbearable outrage. It cannot stand. If Porkchop stops and thinks about it for too long, he will go mad. He will start screaming, and he's not sure that he'd ever be able to stop. Still. Even now. Even after all he's done to quiet his own screams.

He's lied to everyone to quiet the screams.

Even Maggie.

CHAPTER TWENTY

Viking Bob drives Maggie back to the residence.

No one believes her. Or at least, that's what they claim.

A few hours ago, Maggie managed to crawl and claw her way from the dance floor and the crowd. There was no sign of Oleg Ragoravich. There was no sign of CinderBlock or any of the other masked men. Or maybe they were still there, right near her or still partying at Etoile Adiona. Maybe with those masks on, they stabbed a man and just melded back into the crowd and kept on dancing.

Maggie found a waitress and told her she saw a man being stabbed. Suddenly, the waitress's English wasn't very good. The waitress sends Maggie to the other side of the club and says to look for a man in a blue suit. There are dozens of men in blue suits in that area.

No one knows anything. No one can help. No one is sure who she should talk to. The music still blares. The party keeps going.

She finds the red velvet rope VIP area. Two new guys are working there. Neither one knows Nadia. Neither lets her through. She takes out her phone and dials 999 for the Dubai police. They are dubious too. She doesn't let up. She insists that someone come. With great reluctance they agree to send an officer, but she's to meet him outside.

They are not to disturb the Etoile Adiona guests.

Maggie heads outside, where a police detective with a big mustache waits for her. Bob is there too. "Don't do this," he tells her. "It won't go well."

She should have listened.

Big Mustache gets right into it:

"So you say you saw a stabbing, is that right? On a crowded dance floor? But no one else saw it? No one else reported it? Has anyone been reported injured? No? How come? Is there a body anywhere? Has anyone been reported missing? You say it was dark, only a strobe light—yet you saw all this clearly and no one else did? Are you sure? Are you sure you didn't hallucinate it? By the way, how many drinks have you had? Did you take any drugs? Should we run a blood test to be certain? Oh, and please tell me—why are you here? Alone. In Dubai. What is the purpose of your visit to Dubai? Where did you fly in from? Oh, I see—you flew in on a private plane from Gelendzhik in Russia. Why would an American be in Gelendzhik? And are you in Dubai on your own? Are you here as a tourist? On business? What exactly are you doing in Dubai?"

At some point, Maggie sees the futility—and the danger. Big Mustache keeps asking what she is doing in Dubai, and the real answer, which she is now actively evading, is "probably something illegal." She hasn't looked up the rules, but most countries require licensing and authorizations to perform surgery, and there is no reason to think Dubai does not. So she stops talking to Big Mustache.

In the car, Bob says, "Not really smart."

"What, I should have said nothing?"

"What did you think was going to happen, Maggie? That they'd close down the club and turn on the houselights and, what, search everyone in it?"

"I saw a man stabbed."

He shakes his head. "Charles vouched for you, but I should have known."

"You know Charles Lockwood?"

"Of course."

"Do you know—?"

"That's all I'm going to say on the matter, Maggie."

The car vrooms back up into the glass elevator.

Maggie asks, "What time are the surgeries tomorrow?"

"Today."

"What?"

"Not tomorrow. Today. You know it's four a.m. The surgery was originally scheduled to be today at two p.m."

"I'll be ready."

Bob shakes his head. "No, that isn't going to happen."

"Why not? I've done surgeries far more complicated on no sleep while the enemy dropped bombs. I can handle—"

"I'm sure you can do them standing on your head," Bob says. "But I'm going to advise the family against it."

"Why?"

He turns to her. "You have to see that there are big-time repercussions for what you did tonight."

"I reported a crime."

"And in doing so, you're now on the Dubai police's radar. There are reasons why we demand discretion, one of which is that practicing medicine, especially surgery, without proper local UAE licensing is prohibited—even if the surgeon has the necessary licenses in their home country, which, let's face it, you do not."

Maggie has no reply to that.

"So here's the thing," Bob continues. "As long as you don't do the surgeries, no laws have been broken. You're just a houseguest. That's what I'm going to remind the family—that currently there is no exposure. However, the moment you slice open a patient..."

"I get it," Maggie says.

Bob gives her a tight smile as the car reaches the apartment. "Thank you for understanding." He opens his car door. "I have to make a few calls, but I should be able to get you on a plane in the next two or three hours."

"No," Maggie says.

Bob turns and looks at her.

"I'm not done in Dubai," Maggie says.

"You plan on staying?"

"I can get a hotel room—"

"No, that'll look weird too." Bob shakes his head. "So what is your plan?"

"I'm meeting a doctor at Apollo Longevity at ten a.m."

———————

When Maggie gets into her room, she calls Charles Lockwood to fill him in on what happened. Charles listens and then says, "Sounds like Ivan Brovski is making a move against his boss."

"Doesn't add up," Maggie says.

"How do you figure?"

"If Ivan Brovski wanted Oleg Ragoravich dead, why wait until after the surgery? Why not, I don't know, bring in your own anesthesiologist and poison Oleg during it?"

"Jesus, you're dark."

"I'm just trying to think like these guys."

"Maybe Brovski acted *because* of the surgery."

"How so?"

"Can we both agree that Oleg Ragoravich wasn't getting cosmetic surgery to start male modeling?"

"We can," Maggie says.

"So Ragoravich wanted to disguise himself."

"And then, with his face still not healed, he runs away?"

"Hmm, you're right. It makes no sense."

They come up with no better theories for now. Charles promises to investigate and see what he can find out about Oleg Ragoravich's current whereabouts.

"Let me know how it goes at Apollo Longevity," Charles says.

When they hang up, Maggie heads into the shower. After she towels off, she stands in front of the full-length mirror and does a little medical self-examination. Her kidneys hurt. A lot. But there's no blood in her urine. Lots of bruises from the scuffle, but no broken bones or internal injuries. At least, none she sees. It's still early. There isn't much pain right now, but there probably will be in a few hours. Nothing she couldn't handle with some light medication.

She slips under the covers, but her nerves are too raw and jangled to sleep. Soon she will be back at Apollo Longevity. She hates that place. She swore she'd never go back. But there's no choice now.

Or is there a choice?

She doesn't need to do this. She could just go home. Her conversation with Porkchop still echoed:

"...I need to follow this through, Porkchop."

"No, you don't..."

Porkchop was right.

She could just leave right now. Her crusading days are over. She didn't come into this fight on her own—she was dragged here by lies and manipulation.

Nothing good will come of this in the end.

At least, not for Maggie.

She knows that nothing she does now will bring Marc back. She can just go home and live her life—life? what life?—and forget all about this.

But no, not anymore. Like it or not, there is no way she can walk away.

She has to see it through.

CHAPTER TWENTY-ONE

W ow," Steve Schipner says, "this is really great work, Doctor McCabe."
They are in an examination room. Steve wears a white lab coat. His name is stenciled in below the Apollo Longevity name and logo. To his credit, Steve examines Nadia with professionalism, discretion, and respect. It's as if he's a completely different person in here. His voice when he speaks to Nadia is kind, understanding, inviting. He listens to her, pays attention, responds appropriately, asks the right questions. Despite Nadia's stunning looks—and what could be viewed by some as the salacious medical reason they are here—Steve never, not once, hints at an ogle. He might as well be inspecting two lawn chairs. Maggie is surprised, and she is not. She has seen this before with physicians. It's not an act on Steve's part. You don the lab coat, you remember your oath, you get the importance and responsibility of what you are doing. You are everything to a patient—and they have to be everything to you.

Even Sleazy Steve understands that.

When they first met up in the lobby, Maggie had filled Nadia in on the Oleg...stabbing? Maggie isn't sure what to call it. Nadia had listened raptly. She'd been up in the VIP section and had no idea of any of it. "The one you call CinderBlock. His name is Akim. He was on the plane with me. So was Ivan Brovski. But they aren't in Dubai anymore."

"How do you know?"

"On the plane, I got hold of Ivan's phone when he fell asleep. I turned on his location services and dropped a pin to me."

Brilliant and yet simple, Maggie thinks. "So you can track him?"

"Yes. Last night, I could see he was at Etoile Adiona, but"—Nadia opens up her phone and clicks on the app—"it hasn't been active since 5:06 this morning."

Maggie looks at the screen. "Is that Dubai International?"

"Yes."

"So Ivan flew out. A location tracker won't follow him in the air."

Steve continues his exam with patience and skill. Maggie remembers the first time Trace brought Marc and her to Apollo Longevity. She had scoffed at the excess, at the exaggerated "fountain of youth" promises, constantly touted with the fascinatingly contradiction-in-terms phrasing of "anti-aging." The wealthiest people in the world flew in just for whatever treatment was currently in vogue, and—Maggie's personal opinion—even if well-intentioned, the vast majority were modern-day snake oil of one sort or another.

"You can get dressed," Steve tells Nadia. "We can talk more in the consultation room, but I can tell you now that the operation is a complete success. I see no reason to be concerned."

"Thank you, Doctor."

Nadia meets Maggie's eyes. Her eyes move to the computer monitor on the desk, then back toward Maggie. Maggie nods.

"We'll wait in the other room while you get dressed," Steve says. "Doctor McCabe, a word outside?"

Perfect, Maggie thinks. "Of course, Doctor Schipner."

Nadia's plan is simple, though a long shot. There is a computer terminal in the examination room. Nadia knows Trace's username and password. While Maggie stalls and distracts Steve, Nadia hopes to log on and see what she can find.

Of course, there are a thousand things wrong with this plan. Trace

Packer's login may not work anymore. There is probably nothing important to see—do they think there's going to be a message saying, "We've kidnapped Trace Packer. Here is his current location"?—and there might be trip alarms when she signs on or something like that.

But then again, who knows? She and Nadia are "spies" now, right? This is what spies do.

Steve escorts Maggie down the corridor. Up ahead she sees the one elevator that led down to the WorldCures floor.

"I wasn't kidding in there," Steve tells her. "You did great work with her."

"Thank you."

"And we both know you could have done this exam yourself. You didn't need to bring her in."

"I wanted to make sure," Maggie says.

"Make sure what?"

"I wanted a true specialist to back up my work," Maggie says. "And who better than the Boob Whisperer?"

Steve grins. "That's just marketing."

"Okay, sure." Then with a shake of the head she says, "Boob Whisperer."

"You're making jokes," Steve says, "because you don't want me to ask the obvious."

"That being?"

"Why did you do this surgery in the first place?"

"I could ask you the same question," she says.

"Pardon?"

"This is a longevity clinic, not a cosmetic surgery center."

"You don't see the natural partnership? I mean, when you think about it, what I do here is one of the things that actually does reverse aging."

"What about ozone therapy?"

He laughs. "Ozone therapy is old news. We have twelve rooms that do EBOO therapy now."

"EBOO?"

"Extracorporeal Blood Oxygenation and Ozonation Therapy," Steve says. "Doesn't that sound good for you?"

"It does." She needs to stall for Nadia's sake—and she's also sort of interested. "How does it work?"

"You lay back on the most comfortable recliner imaginable. Your blood is drawn from a vein into a tube and through a dialysis filter where it gets exposed to medical-grade ozone and oxygen. As the blood circulates through the EBOO machine, it removes heavy metals, pathogens, debris—"

"Debris," Maggie says. "I love that term."

"Me too."

"So all-encompassing. And meaningless."

"Exactly. Oh, and EBOO also rids your bloodstream of my other favorite all-encompassing term."

"What's that?"

Steve smiles. "Toxins."

"Oh yes."

"Nice and vague. Anyway, after this, your same blood is returned to your body via another vein. So it cycles. Then you throw in some buzzy terms—immunity support, detoxification, inflammation reduction, enriching, regeneration, infusion..."

"Sounds perfect for the jet-setter who has everything," Maggie says.

"Except immortality."

"Which is what they sell here."

"And *we* sell, to be fair."

"Yeah," Maggie says. "But what we sell is real. It isn't quackery."

Steve mulls that over for a moment. "I'm not sure it's fair to call it quackery. There are some quality physicians who swear by these treatments, but here's the problem: All of them profit from it. That's not to say that they are charlatans—they'll cite iffy studies and anecdotal evidence—but none of us think clearly when it comes to our wallets."

"We are all the hero in our own story," Maggie says.

"Exactly that." Steve reaches an office door. "Are you done stalling?"

"What are you talking about?"

"You're still not licensed, are you?"

"I'm not, no."

"So how did you end up being Nadia's surgeon?"

"You've probably guessed."

"You were paid," Steve says. "A lot."

"Yes."

"So some rich guy thought Nadia was too skinny."

Maggie smiles. "I guess you've dealt with this before."

"I have."

"How do you handle it?"

"I insist on talking to the patient alone. If they say no, I flat-out refuse to do it. If I feel she is being coerced, I try to help her find a way out."

"How?"

"First, I try to persuade the rich man in her life that he doesn't want her to have bigger boobs."

"Does that ever work?"

"Almost never," Steve admits. "It's like trying to convince a man he wants a smaller flatscreen."

"What's second?"

"I take a lot of photographs. I keep a lot of records."

"Why?"

"Do you want to hear the ugly truth?"

"That's always better than the pretty lies."

"I'm not sure about that," Steve says. "But let's take your Nadia as an example. Nadia is a mistress to a rich man. The rich man wants her to have a larger chest. I don't like it. You don't like it. But there's not a lot to be done in that case. So we just do it. But other times, well, the mistress is being discarded."

Maggie swallows. "Discarded?"

"The rich man grows tired of her. If the girl is lucky, he just breaks it off, maybe gives her a few dollars. But sometimes—the rich man wants the woman to disappear."

"I'm not following."

"The world is about making a buck. We both get that, right?"

"Sadly, we do."

"So if the rich man wants to get rid of the mistress and make a profit, what's the best way to do that? You traffic the girl. Coming here is like turning in a leased car. They get her refurbished and send her back out."

"Oh my God!"

"Or maybe that's an inept analogy: They just do whatever they can to make their property more desirable. And we both know that a trafficked woman with bigger breasts or buttocks—"

"—is worth more," Maggie finishes for him.

"Yes."

They both stop and let that hang in the air for a moment.

"What do you do when you see that?" she asks.

"There's a charity I can call. They'll come to the back door. I try to get her to sneak out. But most of the time, well, the patients don't want that. They think it will be okay. They'll use their new body to get another rich man. So I keep their DNA on file. In case it's needed for later."

She shakes her head. "It's a messed-up world."

"Dark," Steve agrees.

Silence.

Then Maggie says, "WorldCures used to have offices here."

"Yeah, I know. On the lower level."

"Can you take me down to see them?"

Steve wants to ask why, but he doesn't. He brings her to the elevator and then uses the ID on his lanyard to access the elevator. They head down in silence. When the doors slide open, Maggie knows the way. Steve lets her lead. The place feels abandoned. Their footsteps echo in the quiet.

"We don't do much down here anymore," Steve says. "Just EGF facials."

"EGF?"

"Epidermal Growth Factor."

"Meaning?"

"They use a foreskin extract."

"Pardon?"

Steve nods. "They buy foreskin from neonatal circumcisions."

"Please tell me you're joking."

"I'm not. Hospitals sell baby foreskins to biomedical companies."

She shakes her head. "I thought selling human tissue was illegal."

"It is in a lot of places. But—and don't ask me to explain why—it is legal to sell products derived from human tissue. EGF is also called the penis facial, but uh, that nickname is problematic for a lot of reasons."

Maggie slows when she gets to the door. It's ajar. She slowly pushes it open. The room is empty. She steps inside. The tile floor has been replaced with hardwood. There used to be a drain in the center. That's gone now too.

She thinks back to that terrible day, her last one in Dubai. The three of them had tried to save a life. That's what they told themselves. It had been a long shot. A sixty-two-year-old man named Kabir Abargil. Kabir had been brought in from a refugee camp—failing heart, weeks to live. Kabir was poor. He was on no waiting list for a heart.

Enter the THUMPR7.

Maggie wanted to exercise more caution—walk before you run—but Trace and Marc insisted that this was the perfect opportunity to launch their new technology. There are two major new research avenues focused on making heart transplants not only safe but more readily available. One school involves improving artificial hearts so that they are more than a temporary, stopgap measure. At Baylor St. Luke's Medical Center, five patients have successfully transitioned from the BiVACOR artificial heart to donor hearts, but in Australia, one patient lived with the BiVACOR TAH for over a hundred days. There have been amazing advancements in robotics using AI, much of which they used in creating the THUMPR7.

The other school is made up of cell therapies and regenerative medicine. The idea is that one day we will be able to repair the damaged cells or even grow new ones. This regenerative technology is, of course, being worked on for all organs. There are many scientists who consider this the footpath to a potential fountain of youth. Think about it—once perfected, you could create new hearts, lungs, livers, and constantly (and safely) replace your own. To use a car analogy, if you keep replacing the engine, transmission, tires, brakes, suspension, body, a car could theoretically run forever.

Marc and Trace—and to a lesser extent, Maggie herself—believed the answer lay in blending these schools: taking the latest in robotics via the THUMPR7-TAH and inserting regenerated cell tissue that has gone through the proper DNA sequence coding so it can not only help prevent rejection but also make the transition inside the body seamless.

Yeah, it's a lot.

In short, scientists could add cell tissue and certain DNA sequencing to make artificial organs integrate in the human body to the point that the recipient's immune system does not recognize them as foreign and avoids attack.

The first step, which they weren't able to do with Kabir Abargil, should have been to use a donated heart—that is, a *real* heart—and implant it inside the scaffolds of the THUMPR7. It would be better still if they could make it a "beating-heart" transplant—that is, where the donor heart never stops beating, eliminating ischemic time and reducing cell damage. If that worked, yes, in a few years' time, they could move on to doing transplants with just the THUMPR7 and regenerative tissue. But first, try it with a donated heart.

Walk before you run.

But that wasn't possible here.

The ethical lines on such operations are iffy at best. We all know the slow but crucial rules of the FDA and the dangers in rushing experimentation and implementation. But if a patient gives informed, voluntary, and competent consent and no other remedies are left, isn't it ethically permissible to try something experimental, especially if the alternative is certain death?

Hard to say. Probably not. But they were going ahead with it no matter what, and Maggie knew that the best-case scenario, which was still a terrible-case scenario, would be if she participated.

So she did. In this very room.

"Maggie?"

"'Every great cause begins as a movement, becomes a business, and eventually degenerates into a racket.'"

"What?"

"I did a surgery down here," Maggie says.

Kabir Abargil, the so-called "poor man," had no chance—and still he survived another twenty-one days. But they were awful days. And after that, Maggie wanted no part in any of this. Her mom had taken a turn for the worse. She headed home.

"I've heard rumors about that," Steve says.

She looks at him.

"I started working here a year ago," he continues. "WorldCures wasn't the only one down here."

"What do you mean?"

"I mean, there were other, shall we say, secretive medical research facilities? All in separate offices in this building."

"So where are they now?"

"They vanished. Overnight. Packed up and moved."

"All of them?"

"Yes."

"Where to?"

His phone buzzes. Steve checks the screen and frowns at what he sees. "I have no idea, but after what happened, they felt like this location was compromised."

"What happened?"

He glances up from his phone's screen and meets her eye. "You really don't know?"

"Why would I?"

The phone buzzes again. "Shit."

"What?"

Steve gives her a baleful eye and leaves the room. "Damn it, I should have known."

Maggie quickly follows. "Steve?"

"Oh my God." He stops, turns to Maggie, and now she can see the fear in his eyes. "Did Trace Packer send you?"

"What? No. Wait, do you know where Trace is?"

He turns and starts back down the corridor. "Jesus, how could I have been so stupid?"

She hears the ding of the elevator. The doors open. Two beefy men in blue blazers step out. Between them is Nadia. One man is holding her left arm, the other her right. Her wrists are held together by what looks like a plastic zip tie.

What the . . . ?

Both men, Maggie can see, have weapons strapped to their waists. The beefier one also has Nadia's passport and some other kind of ID in his hand. Keeping a grip on Nadia's elbow, he gives them both to Steve. Steve studies the ID and then starts paging through the passport.

"Let go of her," Maggie snaps. "And cut that tie off her wrists. Now."

When they don't, Maggie storms over and pulls at Less Beefy's arm. The arm doesn't move, but Less Beefy does look over at Steve.

"I got this," Steve tells the two guards.

Both men reluctantly let Nadia go, though she remains zip-tied.

"She broke into your computer," More Beefy says.

Steve holds up his phone. "Yeah, I know. I got the report."

"We've contacted Malik," Less Beefy says. "He wants to handle this personally."

Steve swallows. "I'll watch them."

"I think we should stay."

"I got this. Go upstairs and wait for Malik."

More Beefy doesn't like that. He looks at Less Beefy. "You stay right here. No one gets on or off that elevator."

Less Beefy nods.

"I'll head back up and wait for Malik."

More Beefy steps in, and the elevator doors close. Less Beefy gives them all hard eyes.

"I'm going to take them to the EFG room," Steve tells Less Beefy.

Less Beefy responds with more hard eyes. Maggie wants to roll hers, but there's no reason to make this situation any worse.

When they are back inside, Steve closes the door and says, "Tell me everything. Fast."

"Who's Malik?" Maggie asks.

"Head of security. Ex-military. He's going to want to know why Nadia was trying to break into my computer—and he's not going to ask nicely." He opens a desk drawer, rummages through it. To Nadia, he says, "How the hell did you get my password anyway? Never mind, I don't care."

Steve pulls out a large pair of scissors. He moves toward Nadia. She sticks out her wrists. Her hands are turning blue. The zip tie is too tight. Steve carefully eases the tip of the scissors through the gap and cuts the plastic.

Nadia rubs her wrists. "Thank you."

"I don't get it," Maggie says. "Nadia is a patient who sneaked a look at her doctor's computer. Why would they go so crazy?"

"Are you serious? She didn't just sneak a look. She tried to sign in as Trace Packer. Trace Packer, for crying out loud. Oh man, I'm totally screwed."

"Why?"

"They suspected me of helping him the last time."

"Helping Trace?"

"Yes."

"Helping him how?"

"Why did you come back?" he asks Maggie.

"Steve, please, listen to me. Trace is missing."

"I know. They've been looking for him."

"Who?"

"Everyone. Look, when I first got hired, WorldCures still had an office here, but, I mean, with Marc dead and you out of the picture, there wasn't much to it. But Trace Packer still showed up every once in a while. You know this, right?"

"Pretend I do."

"Trace and I hung out a little. We weren't friends or anything, but when it all went down, well, people thought I was involved, because of my connection to you."

"I'm not following. What went down?"

"One night, I'm lying in bed, dead asleep, and suddenly Malik is there. In my locked apartment. Sitting on the edge of my bed. He starts asking me if I know where Trace Packer is. I say no. He doesn't believe me. So then he starts with the interrogation. He says stuff like

'You went to medical school with Maggie McCabe, right? When did you last talk to her?' Like that. I found out later that Trace broke in here after hours. He stole, I don't know, something to do with World-Cures research—and then he flew out to Washington."

Washington. Nadia and Maggie share a glance.

"When was this?"

"Five, six months ago. Hold up. You live, what, an hour or two from Dulles. Did Trace go to you, Maggie?" Steve snaps his fingers. "Of course he did. That would make perfect sense. Oh shit, this is bad. This is really bad."

"He didn't come to me. Steve, listen to me. Trace is missing. That's why Nadia and I are here. Yes, he flew to Dulles five months ago. But I never saw him. In fact, as far as we can tell, no one has seen him since."

"If that's true—"

"It is."

"—then maybe they found Trace."

"No," Nadia says. "Trace is smart, resourceful. He'd have found a way."

Nadia's words sound hollow with false hope. Maggie's mind starts racing. She remembers the bill for the Wells Fargo safe deposit boxes she opened in Trace's apartment.

Whoa. Slow down a second. Maybe that's it.

Maybe whatever Trace had snatched from this building before leaving Dubai is now in those boxes.

That's why Trace had to come back to the United States. Not to see Maggie. But to make sure he kept control of their innovations. So, okay, Trace goes into Apollo Longevity at night. He nabs the THUMPR7 and accompanying machinery. He heads to Dubai airport, flies back to the United States, and then...

What?

Steve's phone buzzes again. An incoming call. He puts the phone to his ear and says, "What's up?" His face loses color. "Wait, what, right now?" Pause. "Hold on a second." He looks over at them. "What have you gotten me into, Maggie?"

Maggie offers up an elaborate shrug. "No clue, Steve."

Steve heads to a monitor on the desk. He leans over, still standing, and types into it. As he does, he keeps glancing at the door behind him. "Someone is at reception asking for you by name." He finishes and turns to her. "Do you know who he is?"

He flips the monitor so Maggie can see the live CCTV footage he's brought up. The camera is focused on a man with a . . .

Big Mustache.

The cop from last night. He is in plainclothes but flanked by two men in olive-green police uniforms with matching berets.

Steve says, "Well?"

"I saw someone stabbed on the dance floor last night. He's the cop who showed up."

"Are you serious?"

"No, Steve, I'm making it up."

"No time for sarcasm, Maggie."

"Always time, Steve. Anyway, he didn't believe me."

"Well, he believes you now. I recognize him. He's tight with Malik."

"Maggie." Nadia taps her on the shoulder. "Take a look at this."

Maggie turns. Nadia shows her the screen on her phone. It's the headline from a new article:

OLEG RAGORAVICH, RUSSIAN OLIGARCH, FOUND DEAD

"We have to get out of here," Nadia says.

———————

Steve takes the lead. Maggie stands on Steve's left, Nadia behind him so that Steve blocks Less Beefy's view of her hands. She keeps them together at the wrists so as to sell that she's still zip-tied. Less Beefy gives them tough-guy vibes by the elevator. Steve smiles and says, "Hey, I need a favor."

There is no hesitation.

That's the key. Maggie learned this in military training. There are many things that make a great fighter—size, skill, athleticism, quickness, adaptability, experience, heart—but one thing can often overcome all that.

Surprise.

Maggie smiles. Casual as can be. She doesn't call out. She doesn't offer up or even hint at a warning. She doesn't tense up or slow down or rear back or any of that. She just keeps walking, arms swinging, almost breezy.

Less Beefy isn't worried. He's a big man. She's a small woman.

No threat to him at all.

The whole thing takes less than five seconds.

Maggie picks up speed as she gets closer, her smile grows into something almost flirty. It throws him off, distracts him, and then, before Less Beefy can react, Maggie attacks.

The Web Strike—also called the Y Strike—uses the web between your index finger and thumb. Coming from below, Maggie bends her knees, powers up pistonlike with her legs, and drives the "Y" with as much force as she can muster into his trachea.

It's a dangerous blow, designed to incapacitate. Maggie doesn't relish hurting anyone—the physician in her cannot stand to see a person in pain—and yet there it is, the grin on her face, the undeniable thrum in her blood, the adrenaline spike she knows she will never stop craving.

Hello, darkness, my old friend . . .

Her blow lands clean, unimpeded. Maggie can feel his windpipe give way a little. A gurgling sound escapes his lips. He staggers back, both hands protectively on his throat. But now it's Nadia's turn. They had planned this in the seconds before coming out here. It isn't a complicated plan. It relied on the three S's—speed, simplicity, surprise.

Nadia jumps toward him like a feral cat. With both his hands out of the way, the path is free. Nadia's hand darts toward his waist, unstraps the holster, and pulls his gun free. She steps back and points the weapon at the man.

Steve puts his hands up too. "Please don't shoot me."

Maggie tries not to make a face at Steve's overbaked performance. It's her turn again now. She opens the pouch on the other side of Less Beefy's belt. According to Nadia, that's where he keeps his zip ties. She pulls them out. Nadia puts the gun hard against the big man's temple. There is crazy in her eyes.

"Put your hands behind your back," Nadia commands.

The man complies. Maggie throws on the zip tie and tightens it. She uses her knee to make his collapse so that he's now sitting on the ground.

Nadia moves in closer. "Make a sound. Please. Because then I can pull this trigger and blow your head off. I'll have the excuse to kill you, see? And I want that. So go ahead. Call out."

Less Beefy seems to be holding his breath.

Nadia gives him one final smile before she turns the gun toward Steve. Steve throws his hands even higher in the air. "Don't shoot!"

"Call for the elevator," Nadia orders him.

Steve nods to please and uses his lanyard to get the elevator. He knows, of course, Nadia isn't going to shoot him. This act of pretending to hold Steve at gunpoint is to peddle the fiction that Steve didn't cooperate with them, that he too was taken by surprise.

Nadia may be acting, but that gleam in her eye is enough to make

Steve glance at Maggie and make sure that they are all on the same side.

The elevator arrives. Only one elevator comes to this floor—this one—so once it is occupied, it will take whoever wants to reach them that much longer to use the stairs and figure out exactly where they are.

"Move," Nadia says, pushing Steve in the back with the barrel of the gun.

The three of them enter the elevator. Once inside, Nadia points the gun at Less Beefy until the doors close.

When they do, they hear him shout for help.

CHAPTER TWENTY-TWO

Inside the elevator Nadia keeps the gun pointed at Steve's head. "Zip-tie him," she tells Maggie. "Take his phone, just in case."

Maggie is about to ask what's going on—why does Nadia still have the gun up and in Steve's face?—but the answer is frighteningly obvious.

The elevator has a camera.

It probably has sound too. Nadia is continuing to sell it. Steve plays his part too: "Please, don't shoot me." Maggie is about to take out the zip tie, but the elevator stops.

They are already at the garage level.

When the doors open, Maggie expects there to be men with guns or police cars or sirens or something waiting for them. But there are not. There is nothing. The garage is silent. She gives Steve one more look, trying to say thank you with her eyes. He answers back with the most imperceptible of nods. Maggie doesn't know Steve's fate. Will Malik and Big Mustache believe whatever story of abduction he comes up with—or will they realize he was in on this?

No time to worry about it.

Nadia grabs Maggie by the arm and pulls them out of the elevator. They hurry-walk (not run because that would draw attention) toward the car ramp. No one stops them. Again the element of surprise.

Whatever Big Mustache or Malik had in store for them, there would have been no need to surround the perimeter of the building or get men to the garage. The elevator, like every elevator in Dubai, was superfast. It had been only ten, maybe twenty seconds since Less Beefy started to call for help. Even if he was heard immediately, they'd have to figure out where the cries were coming from. Once they did, they'd probably call for the elevator. But of course, the elevator was already taken. So it would take time to get up to their floor. Maybe some of them would choose to run down the stairs...

All of that takes time.

Maggie and Nadia slow their steps as they reach the ramp. They stroll up it and out. Simple as that. No one gives them so much as a second glance. The sun is at full power, blinding, debilitating, unbearable, but right now Maggie feels fine with it. Nadia is speaking Arabic into her phone. They move quickly down the street and enter the palatial shopping mall next door.

As they walk, Nadia pulls the phone away from her face and says to Maggie, "You told me Charles gave you a second passport."

"Yes."

"Give it to me."

Maggie does. Without slowing, Nadia opens it to the front page, takes a photograph with her phone, hands it back to her.

"What's going on?" Maggie asks.

"I saw the news report right before they caught me. Oleg's body was found in the Dubai Water Canal."

"Wow."

"Yes."

"Maybe I should just go talk to the police—"

"No."

"Why not?" Maggie asks. "I'm the one who called them. They can't think I'm involved."

"You're being naive," Nadia says.

"How so?"

"You fly into Dubai for sketchy reasons. On your first night here, you, a single American woman in her forties, go to a nightclub alone. You claim you saw the stabbing of a rich man who no one else saw, who you happened to bump into and whose house you happen to have just been staying in before you arrived—and this all happened right after you met with his mistress at the same club . . . Do I need to go on?"

"You do not," Maggie says. "You're good at this."

"I've had some practice."

"You want to explain?"

A small smile plays on her lips. "Another time. Now give me your phone."

Maggie does. Nadia presses it up against hers, transferring data from one to the other. "I've uploaded a mobile boarding pass in the name Emily Sinclair into your phone's wallet. It's for the Emirates flight to London—that's the next international flight out of Dubai. It leaves in an hour."

They rush through the corridor, take the escalator down the steps and past an ornate fountain into the parking garage. There is a sign with an arrow for Uber and Bolt riders. Nadia gestures toward it.

"I ordered you an Uber to the airport. It'll be downstairs in two minutes. The ride should only take fifteen minutes. There won't be time for the police to have covered the airport yet. They may have time to put your real name in the system."

"But not Emily Sinclair's."

"Exactly."

"And what about your name?"

"I'll definitely be in the system," Nadia says. "That's why I'm not going with you. I'll figure another way out and meet you when it's safe."

They head down toward the rideshare pickup zone. Three vehicles are waiting. Nadia checks the license plate on the app. "That's yours," Nadia says, pointing. "The blue one."

"Got it."

Maggie slides in, and Nadia closes the car door. The Uber pulls away. When the Uber hits the highway, Maggie takes out her phone and calls Porkchop.

He answers on the first ring. "Where are you?"

"On my way to London."

"Flight number?"

She tells him.

"Once you land," Porkchop says, "I'll have you covered."

"How?"

"Let's pretend you didn't ask me that. No contact until you arrive."

He hangs up.

Porkchop.

But he's right. Every word she says is being heard by Charles Lockwood. Does she care? Who knows? But the thing is, Porkchop doesn't want Charles Lockwood to hear. He isn't saying why. Not yet. But right now, that's enough for her.

As promised, the drive takes fifteen minutes. The Uber drops her at Terminal 3. She hops on what they call an APM—Automated People Mover—though Maggie has no idea what the difference between an APM and a small train is, and gets to Concourse A in three minutes. The security line is short and moves fast. Maggie is on full alert as she makes her way through it, sure that every employee is looking at her. She feels exposed. She wishes she had a hat or sunglasses or something, though that just usually makes a person stand out more.

When she reaches her gate, her flight to London is already boarding. She gets on the queue. Part of her keeps waiting for someone to
grab her arm and pull her out of the line. There are, of course, plenty
of security officers walking about the gleaming terminal. When she
scans her boarding pass, the Emirates employee at the gate asks to
see her passport. Maggie has it opened to the right page. It's the same
photo as the one in her real passport—Charles had just had it duplicated to create "Emily Sinclair's"—but the agent seems to be taking a
longer time than she should studying it. The gate agent looks at the
photo, then at Maggie, then back to the photo.

"Have a nice flight, Ms. Sinclair," the agent finally says, handing
her back the passport.

Maggie hurries to her window seat. A man in a "groutfit"—gray
sweatpants, gray hoodie—drops into the seat next to her. He says
"Well, hello there" with a little too much enthusiasm. Maggie isn't
a plane-engager under the best of circumstances. Engaging with a
plane passenger is up there with her major phobias, the most terrifying being when you get an aisle seat at a Broadway show and the
actors come offstage for audience participation.

Shudder.

Still, she gives the man a tight-but-polite nod back. Then she
stares out the window and doesn't relax until the plane taxis down
the runway. She closes her eyes and flashes back to one of her first
flights with Marc. In a surprise move, Marc gripped her hand tightly
and asked her:

"Why do we say we 'taxi' down the runway?"

"Good question. Well, not good, really. Pretty inane as a matter of—"

*"I mean, when else do we use the term 'taxi' as a verb to describe move-
ment? Why only with air travel? What else besides airplanes 'taxi' and why
do we use that term for it? Sorry, I babble when I'm nervous."*

"You're nervous?"

"*Maybe a little.*"

"*But you ride motorcycles.*"

"*Which, you may have observed, stay on the ground for the entire ride.*"

"*I didn't have you pegged as a nervous flyer, Marc.*"

"*It's kind of sexy, right?*"

"*Would you settle for barely cute?*"

"*I would, yes.*"

She shakes her head, and a sad smile, the only kind she had known for the past year now, comes to her face. The next time she and Marc flew:

"*I looked it up, Mags. Why they use 'taxi' for aviation.*"

"*God, you're a dork.*"

"*So in the early 1900s, two French aviation pioneers named Blériot and Farman started using the term 'taxi' to describe how primitive aircraft moved slowly across an airfield because it seemed similar to the way a taxi moves through city streets. Ergo 'taxiing' on a runway and whatnot. What do you think?*"

"*Barely cute. But also, okay, kind of sexy.*"

The pang—that ever-present Missing Marc pang—strikes deep in her chest. This is how grief works, isn't it? Grief doesn't attack her on Marc's birthday or their anniversary or any of that. Grief knows you are expecting it on those days. So Grief bides its time. It lulls you, makes you think it's not such a threat anymore, and then when your defenses are down—when a plane simply starts down a runway, for example—boom, it attacks.

Marc.

When the plane's Wi-Fi comes up, Maggie tries to read all she can on the death of Oleg Ragoravich. They don't call it a murder yet. Just a dead body. They don't even say foul play suspected or any of that. Like maybe Oleg was taking a swim and drowned.

Dubai just being Dubai, Maggie figures.

But some of the details bother Maggie. The articles note, for example, that Ragoravich was "positively identified by close colleagues." That seems an odd thing to mention. It's not like the body was found after years underwater. Why mention that? The article also notes that "hundreds of guests recently saw the normally reclusive Oleg Ragoravich at an extravagant ball"—yep, they actually use the word "ball"—"he hosted at his private residence in Russia."

Again: Why mention that?

The wording was odd. Something about it gnaws at the back of her brain.

She'd done a quick search on Oleg Ragoravich during her flight from Teterboro when she still wasn't sure of his identity, and found very few photographs of him. At the time, she'd figured that was a normal, rich-guy privacy issue. The rich, especially those who have reason to stay in the shadows, often paid to have their online presence scrubbed or manipulated.

Which led to a host of related questions:

Why are there so few photographs of Oleg Ragoravich online?

Why would Oleg Ragoravich have wanted plastic surgery now?

Why would he have decided to throw a "ball" the night before his surgery?

Why had he stayed up in the hidden room at the top of the ballroom? How had Charles Lockwood put it?

"I've still never seen him in person. Not even at that crazy ball..."

Something isn't adding up.

Her phone battery is low. She doesn't know what brand of phone this is—it isn't Apple and doesn't seem to be Android. The better for Charles to bug her, she figures. Still, she signs on to her email and sends Sharon a short message. Porkchop, she assumes, has been keeping Sharon in the loop, so Maggie keeps the email short:

> There are very few photographs of Oleg
> Ragoravich online. Maybe scrubbed? Can you

use internet archives or wayback machines to
locate more?

Something is starting to click.

Maggie turns off the Wi-Fi for a bit, trying to preserve battery. Does that work or is that a myth? She doesn't know. Every half hour she checks to see whether Sharon has written her back. Eventually, Sharon does:

> You are correct. Oleg Ragoravich actively
> scrubbed a year ago.
>
> He did not want any photos of him out there.
>
> I have only found seven so far. More to come.

But Maggie doesn't need more photographs. She sees it right away.

"Oh, shit," she says out loud.

The Groutfit next to her stirs.

The photographs Sharon found are on the older side. At a quick glance, there's nothing to see here.

Superficially.

It's the third photograph, the clearest facial shot, that seals the deal for Maggie.

She's seen this picture before, albeit in a very different form.

It's an official-looking black-and-white portrait from the military. Maggie would guess that it's thirty or forty years old, maybe more. Oleg Ragoravich is in uniform. He stares straight into the camera, his expression blank, a stone.

Oh, no. It can't be.

It's then that Maggie feels her phone vibrate with a text. It's from Nadia:

Ivan Brovski just landed. He's in France.

Nadia included a screenshot of a map. Maggie zooms in with her fingers. When she sees Brovski's exact location, Maggie's head starts spinning anew.

Damn, Maggie thinks. *I had it wrong the whole time.*

CHAPTER TWENTY-THREE

Maggie cannot believe what she is seeing.

For the first time in so long, her heart bursts with joy.

An hour later—an hour spent putting so much of it together—she lands at Heathrow Airport. If you are one of those people who want to make sure you get your ten thousand steps in every day, Maggie suggests you fly into Heathrow. You walk left and right. You go upstairs and down. You use escalators and moving walkways. It's also a "tease" walk—every time you think it's over, there is just one more turn, one more set of stairs, one escalator, one more moving walkway to go.

Several flights landed at the same time, the passengers disembarking and first flowing and then clogging up the main Terminal 3 artery that leads to the passport and immigration heart.

Maggie felt alone, adrift, and yet there is finally a real sense of purpose. She is putting it together. Not all of it. Not yet. But she thinks she has a big-time lead. Fatigue radiates from every pore in her body as she gets through passport control, bypasses the baggage carousel and customs, steps through the exit door...

She freezes when she sees him, half worried it's just a mirage.

Cue the bursting heart.

There are a ton of people in the arrivals hall. Chauffeurs with various name signs—some handwritten, some on touchscreen pads—are scattered everywhere. There are loved ones with welcome balloons and friends standing on their tiptoes, craning their necks to see who exits next. There are tour representatives and airport staff—maybe a hundred, two hundred people in all—but Maggie sees him right away.

Porkchop!

When she looks his way, Porkchop lifts his sunglasses and wiggles his eyebrows. Maggie shouts—shouts out loud—"Porkchop!" and breaks into a run. She wonders whether she's ever been so happy to see someone, and no answer comes to her. He spreads his thick arms, and Maggie jumps into them. Porkchop swallows her up in a bear hug. She welcomes the smell of Marlboro and leather, and then Maggie just lets everything go. She collapses into the bear hug. Her smile gives way to tears. She digs her face into the leather and for a few moments she just cries. Porkchop lets her, holds her up. He cups the back of her head with his big hand. His voice is uncharacteristically choked up as he mutters, "It's okay now, Mags, it's all okay."

She manages to say, "How...?"

"I was flying to Dubai," he says. "There was a change of planes in London so..."

"I'm so happy to see you." She hugs him harder. Then: "I think I know where we have to go now."

"Where?"

"Bordeaux. A vineyard called Château Haut-Bailly."

———————

"I did some research on the plane," Maggie tells him, as they stroll out of the arrivals hall. "There are no nonstop flights from Heathrow to Bordeaux."

"You don't want to fly anyway," Porkchop says, heading for the stairwell. "Too much scrutiny. Come on. Do you have anything that can track you?"

She thinks about it for a moment. "The phone Charles Lockwood gave me."

Porkchop gestures toward a trash can. She dumps the phone in it and keeps on moving. A sign reads HEATHROW EXPRESS. They follow it, walking side by side.

"So why Bordeaux?" Porkchop asks.

She quickly explains how Steve had told her that the medical researchers had packed up from Apollo Longevity and moved to a secret location. When she finishes, Porkchop says, "And you think the secret location is on a Bordeaux vineyard."

"Yes."

"Tell me why."

Maggie had spent a lot of the flight working out the angles. She is eager to try out her theory on the only person who might get it. "You remember the last time I called Trace?"

"Of course."

"I know you remember. It wasn't a question."

The Heathrow Express arrives, and they hop on. Porkchop sits and waits. He isn't the type to say I told you so, but he had warned her about making that call. She hadn't listened. Porkchop had been against reaching out to Trace. *"You don't want to tip him off,"* he'd told her.

And, of course, Porkchop had been right.

"Trace was in Dubai when I called him," Maggie says.

"How do you know that?"

"I've met his girlfriend. Fiancée, actually."

"The Nadia who wanted you to do the surgeries?"

"Yes."

"And you told her you called Trace?"

Maggie shakes her head. "She confronted me about it."

"What did you say?"

"I denied it." *Denied it*, Maggie thinks. A polite way of saying *I straight-up lied to her face.* "I said I never called him."

"Does she believe you?"

"Hard to know."

Porkchop nods. "Go on."

"So after I called, we know Trace vanished. You figured he had something to hide and ran off."

"Me?"

"Okay, I did too. But not like you."

Porkchop's face is set. "You know what we learned at the TriPoint refugee camp."

She nods. "One witness—and only one witness—claims they saw Trace leaving the camp *after* Marc was killed. That's it. And the witness could have gotten the timing wrong, whatever. Anyway, I called Trace because I wanted to hear his explanation. Not over the phone. Face-to-face."

"And he ran instead," Porkchop says, spreading his hands. "Gee, that doesn't seem suspicious."

"The point is, we figured he'd gone to Bangladesh or some other remote area."

"Made the most sense. Easier for him to hide."

"Either way," Maggie says, "you've been searching for him ever since. And you're good at this kind of thing, Porkchop."

"Not that good."

"No, you are. And you're—shall we say—highly motivated. Yet you've come up with nothing."

"The point being?"

"Maybe we got it wrong," Maggie says.

"How so?"

She sits up and turns to him. "Okay, so right after I called Trace, he broke into Apollo Longevity and stole the THUMPR7, the DNA sequencing machine, all of it. At first, I figured his plan was to fly to America and hide that stuff in those safe deposit boxes."

"Makes sense."

"It did, yes."

"It doesn't anymore?"

"Let me try this theory on you," Maggie says.

"I'm listening."

"Suppose Trace never planned on coming to America."

"Because he planned on running?"

"Not like we think."

"I'm not following."

"I think Trace flew that day from Dubai—not to the United States but to Bordeaux. I think that's where Oleg Ragoravich built in secret his new 'fountain of youth' headquarters. Trace was fascinated by that vineyard. Château Haut-Bailly. His apartment has a ton of wine from it. He even sent Marc and I there on vacation."

Porkchop allows himself a small nod.

Maggie shifts in her seat. "Nadia says she kissed Trace goodbye outside Terminal 1. But Emirates, the only airline that flies nonstop from Dubai to Dulles, leaves from Terminal 3. Air France uses Terminal 1. Not that he couldn't have taken a connecting flight, but..."

The Heathrow Express stops at London Paddington. Maggie and Porkchop rise and follow the signs for the Hammersmith & City Line. The train is packed so they stand for the five stops to King's Cross St. Pancras.

"Sharon just did some digging for me," Maggie continues. "An abandoned vineyard adjacent to Haut-Bailly was bought three years ago by someone using a double-blind trust. Sharon says there are satellite photos showing what looks like massive underground construction."

"Suspicious," Porkchop agrees.

"And do you want to hear the big kicker?"

"I'm all ears."

"Nadia has a tracker on Ivan Brovski's phone."

Porkchop crosses his arms. "That's the, uh, gentleman who took you on the plane."

"Yep. The one you told to keep your daughter-in-law safe and happy. I think your exact words to him were, 'Don't make me have to find you.'"

Porkchop lets himself smile. "Shows the power of my threats," he says. "What does Nadia's tracker show?"

"Ivan Brovski landed at Bordeaux-Mérignac Airport a few hours ago."

Porkchop arches an eyebrow. "You don't say."

"Oh, but I do."

"So maybe I'll have the chance to 'find' him, after all."

Porkchop makes a few calls on the platform—someone had clearly given Porkchop a mobile phone before he headed overseas—and then he and Maggie board the Eurostar for the journey to Paris. The train can travel 186 miles per hour and includes a thirty-one-mile railway tunnel that goes under the English Channel.

As they board, Porkchop says, "Did you know that the term 'Chunnel' is a portmanteau of 'Channel' and 'Tunnel'?"

"If you say so."

"'Portmanteau' was on my New-Word-A-Day calendar last month."

"I figured."

"It means a word blending the sound and combining the meaning of two other words."

"Great."

"Other portmanteaus include 'brunch'—breakfast and lunch—and 'motel'—motor and hotel."

"Yeah, I get it, Porkchop."

"First time I've gotten to use the word."

"You must be very proud."

They find their seats.

"You have more to tell me," Porkchop says.

"I do."

"But we are both exhausted. We have two and a half hours on the Eurostar before we get to Paris. Then we go from the Gare du Nord to Montparnasse to take a TGV train to Bordeaux. That's also over two hours."

"How do you know all this?"

Porkchop gives her the eyebrow arch. "Trace isn't the only Francophile, you know."

"We're going to need a place to stay in Bordeaux."

"Already taken care of." He holds up his phone. "We will be staying at the owner's private guesthouse at Château Smith Haut Lafitte. I told them we'd be fine at the Les Sources de Caudalie—that's their five-star hotel—but Florence insisted we'd be more comfortable in the guesthouse."

"Florence?"

"The vineyard's owner."

"Uh-huh."

"She's an old friend."

"I bet." Maggie shakes her head. "I shouldn't be surprised anymore."

"And yet you continue to be."

"How do you know, uh, Florence?"

"I spent a lot of years riding through Europe." Porkchop folds his leather jacket into a pillow and places it against the window. "Anything else before I...?"

She shakes her head. "Take a nap. I need to check something out anyway."

He closes his eyes and leans back on his leather pillow. Maggie spends the ride following up on some leads. She debates what she should tell Nadia, but for right now, she figures it's best to stay no contact. Once the Eurostar arrives at Gare du Nord, they take the

Paris Métro to Montparnasse, where they grab the high-speed train. It's when they arrive at the Bordeaux Saint-Jean station and walk outside that Maggie gets another reminder of who Porkchop is and what he means to people.

The street is lined with motorcycles.

Maggie can't even guess how many. Fifty riders? Or a hundred, decked out in classic biker garb, greet Porkchop. There is a magic to Porkchop. She's always known this. When Maggie's parents first heard how Marc had been raised, they'd been, to put it politely, wary. When they met Porkchop, the wary vanished. He had an ease, a confidence. You want to be near Porkchop. She sees it again now, the way people are drawn to him. It's not an act on his part. It's not something Porkchop turns on and off. It's not something he needs or cultivates. He makes people feel seen and secure, maybe because he doesn't try to work on it. There is, if you look closely, a coldness to him too. Porkchop loves very few, just his inner circle, but those he does he loves with a ferocity that both frightens and exhilarates. You know those stories about a parent lifting a car to save their child? It takes little to imagine Porkchop performing such a feat. His family is his world—the rest of the planet's inhabitants are in the periphery, deep background, scenery.

Porkchop goes down the leather-clad receiving line, offering hugs, double-cheek kisses, handshakes, backslaps, whatever. He introduces Maggie to the leaders. They hug her too. A woman with spiky gray hair introduces herself as Élodie and invites Maggie to hop on the back of her bike. Porkchop gets on with a man named Guillaume. The other bikers follow. It's an impressive sight. Ten minutes in, the other bikers peel off because it's getting late, and the bikes make too much noise. Thoughtful.

Guillaume and Élodie drive them through Château Smith Haut Lafitte's entrance and past the main hotel. They wind their way through the vineyard to the guesthouse. The guesthouse is rustic in the best of ways. Stone walls, tile floors, worn leather furniture, plain wooden furniture. There's a chess set on the coffee table. There are four bedrooms on the second floor. Porkchop's stuff is already in the corner suite. Maggie has no idea how. She takes the opposite corner. There are toiletries, but Maggie realizes, with the suddenness of her departure from Dubai, she has no clothes.

Ten minutes after arriving, a striking, elegant couple come by with a bottle of wine. The woman is the aforementioned Florence. She is with her husband, Daniel. They, too, greet Porkchop and Maggie with double-cheek kisses and warm hugs. Florence hands Porkchop the bottle. He studies it.

"The Rouge 2015," Porkchop says with a nod of approval.

Daniel opens it with a smile. "We also brought the Blanc 2022 if either of you prefer the white."

Porkchop looks over at Maggie. Maggie says, "I'm good with the red."

Florence and Daniel are, as one might imagine, charming hosts. They had just gotten back a few hours ago from a two-week cruise from Amsterdam to Basel, doing both the Dutch canals and the Rhine. A dream trip, they told them, but they are happy to be back.

"I assume," Florence says to Porkchop, "that you've been enjoying your stay?"

"Of course," Porkchop says. "But I do have a favor to ask."

He tells them that the airline has lost Maggie's luggage and he wonders whether they might have anything in either their manor or maybe the hotel's lost and found that she could use for the next day or two. Florence and Daniel both look Maggie over before Florence says, "You're about the same size as our daughter Alice. We'll send some garments down to you."

After Florence and Daniel depart, Maggie and Porkchop remain on the porch, staring out into the Bordeaux night, sipping the most heavenly of wines. The vineyard smells of soil and fruits, of earth and lavender. The moon puts the grapevines in silhouette. The silence, like the dark, wraps itself around them. Under any other circumstance, it would be perfect here, timeless and profound, and she tries to remember her father's advice about easing into the moment even in the midst of chaos. But that's not working tonight.

She looks at Porkchop's profile and thinks she sees a tear on his cheek.

"You okay?" she asks.

He nods. "Guillaume and Élodie tell me that there is no way into that abandoned vineyard. The area is remote and very well protected. CCTV. Motion detectors. Barbed wire. Round-the-clock armed guards."

Maggie takes another sip. "I'm not surprised."

"Everyone knows that it's more than a vineyard. The most prevalent rumor is that it's a secret military base. Some of the more conspiracy-minded think it's housing biological or chemical weapons."

"Even better to keep people away."

"Do we have a plan?"

Maggie thinks about it. "I think so, yeah."

They both sit back and stare out.

"There are things Marc didn't tell me," Maggie says.

"Which reminds me." Porkchop grabs hold of his satchel, puts his passport in the side pocket, and starts to dig through the main pouch. "Sharon told me to give this to you." He pulls out a phone. "Your griefbot."

He hands it to her. Maggie takes it. Porkchop turns and stares out again.

"You never told me about it," he says.

"No."

"Why not?"

"You know why not."

He nods. "Because there are things you don't tell me."

"Yeah, I thought you might be going there. It's not the same thing."

"Actually, it is. You trust me, right?"

"With my life."

"And yet you keep things from me. And I keep things from you."

"What do you keep from me?"

"You're missing the point."

"Also you're not my husband."

"Marc told you what he knew. What he could."

"He didn't tell me about Oleg Ragoravich."

"Do you think that means he loved you any less?"

"Now who's missing the point?"

"Part of the human condition is that we all think that we are uniquely complex—no one knows what we are *really* thinking, what we are capable of—and yet we are convinced we can read other people. We think that we know what's going on inside others, what they are really feeling or experiencing or thinking, but they can't tell the same about us. That's obviously impossible. You and Marc..." Porkchop stops and shakes his head. "You guys were the best couple I'd ever seen. But you weren't"—he puts his palms together—"'one.' That's new-age bullshit. It's also undesirable. Marc didn't tell you everything about Ragoravich because he wanted to protect you. Like you and me with the griefbot. Only yeah, fair—more so. Marc knew that if he told you the full truth, you wouldn't go home and take care of your mother. You'd want to stay by his side and fight with him. And then maybe you'd be dead now."

Maggie gets it. And doesn't. "Do you really think Trace had something to do with Marc's murder?" she asks him.

He just stares out.

"Porkchop?"

"No one knows what we are really thinking, what we are capable of."

"Quoting yourself?"

"Who better?" Porkchop lets loose a deep sigh. "It's late. I'm going to bed."

"You slept the whole train ride here."

"But you didn't. Get some rest. We have a big day tomorrow."

"Suppose Trace is there?" she asks.

Porkchop's eyes close.

"What will we do then?"

He opens his eyes, leans down, and kisses the top of Maggie's head. "We'll cross that bridge if we get to it."

CHAPTER TWENTY-FOUR

When she's left alone, Maggie opens the griefbot app.

AI Marc appears on the screen with a smile. But it's different to her now. Less potent. She's not sure why. It's like she sees the cracks and wires.

"Hey," AI Marc says. "Where are you?"

"In a vineyard in Bordeaux."

He smiles. "I wish I was there."

"You've been here before," she says.

"With you," he says. "I'll never forget."

Neither, Maggie thinks, *will I.*

"Who picked this place for us?" she asks.

"It was Trace."

"You knew back then that Oleg Ragoravich was building a facility here," she says.

His honest answer surprises her: "Yes."

"But you didn't tell me."

"No."

"Why?"

"Did you enjoy that weekend?"

She nods. She remembers the morning sun coming into their room, the way it bathed his beautiful face in the yellow glow. Marc opened his eyes and looked into hers and they just lay there, in the bed, side to side, and Maggie remembers an old Joan Baez lyric, "Speaking strictly for me, we both could have died then and there."

"That's all I wanted for us," Marc says. "A weekend together."

It's a good answer, a nice line, but there is no way to know whether it's true or not. In that sense AI Marc is no different from Real Marc. This answer might be Real Marc's truth, interpreted through data and overheard conversations. But what had Porkchop said about the human condition? You can't really know what another person is thinking deep inside.

And neither could any AI program.

"Is Trace in Bordeaux, Marc?"

"I don't know."

"Did he kill you?"

The screen glitches. Maggie expected that. The griefbot doesn't know it's dead. It can't comprehend its own death any better than a human. Sharon had warned about this.

As if on cue, AI Marc says, "I don't understand."

Maggie changes up. "This is a hypothetical. Let's say you're not Marc Adams. You're an AI creation of him. You were created by my sister to comfort me because the real Marc Adams was murdered. Your data dump ended three months before your death, so you can't know for certain. But you can look up the stories online. About your death. Study them, crunch the data, add in what you already know about Marc's life. And then tell me. Did Trace Packer kill you?"

The screen freezes.

Maggie sighs and stands. Then from her phone, she hears Marc say, "The most likely scenario is that Doctor Marc Adams was killed as reported—during the terrorist massacre at TriPoint."

"What's the second most likely scenario?"

"That Trace Packer was involved."

"How about...?" She stops, swallows, tries again. "Based on what you see, is there any chance that you're alive..."

The screen freezes up again. Maggie pushes on.

"...that you faked your own death or, I don't know, that you're still out there somewhere, alive?"

She waits. But the screen doesn't unfreeze.

In the morning, Guillaume and Élodie drive Maggie and Porkchop to Château Haut-Bailly. When they arrive, Guillaume says, "We have guns, if you want."

"Will they do us any good?"

"Only if you want to get killed. We will wait by the road with our top people. If you give the word, we can be there in minutes."

Porkchop thanks them. He and Maggie walk the path in silence. She leads. Her plan is a simple one. When they get to the fence, Maggie signals for Porkchop to stop. He does. There are no visible buildings, just overgrown grapevines as far as the eye can see. Maggie moves along the fence line until she reaches the gate.

She stands there and stares up into the camera.

Enough with the pretense.

Trace is either here or not. The answers are either going to come or they are not.

Whatever is going on, this is it. The end of the journey.

So Maggie stands there and stares up at the camera and waits.

It doesn't take long.

She hears the crunch of footsteps before she sees the hulking form of Ivan Brovski come into view. He walks to the gate. Porkchop eases himself a little closer to Maggie. Ivan doesn't so much as glance at him. His eyes are locked on her eyes and only hers.

"Come with me," Ivan Brovski tells her. "He's been waiting for you."

Ivan Brovski finally shifts his gaze toward Porkchop and then brings it back to Maggie.

"Just you," he says to her. "No one else."

Three armed men come out from the brush. They keep their weapons at their sides, but the meaning is clear. Maggie looks back at Porkchop. She gives him a nod that she's fine with this and he should stand down. Porkchop doesn't nod back.

The gate slides open. Maggie steps through. Porkchop stays where he is.

Brovski greets her with a handshake and a smile. "It's good to see you again, Doctor McCabe."

She says nothing. Brovski leads her down a path of unruly grapevines, leaving Porkchop and the fence in her rearview. Ivan starts off by her side but as the path narrows from the overgrowth, they're forced to move single file. Up ahead, half hidden by the heavy foliage, is a building Maggie assumes was once a wine cellar. The exterior is scarred and worn limestone. Moss clings to the walls for dear life. The stones look weak, wet, spongy, as though you could push your fist right on through them.

There is a heavy iron-banded wooden door with rusted hinges. Brovski opens it to let them in. The interior is musty, dingy, lit dully by a string of yellow lights tied to the ceiling beams. Two-tone oak wine barrels are stacked on their sides along the right-hand wall. Brovski heads to the back and pushes a stack of barrels away, revealing a blue door. He puts his hand on a control panel, and the blue door slides open with a Star Trek whoosh.

They head down a set of stairs to a matching blue door. When Brovski opens this one, Maggie is greeted by a sudden cold gust. The air has a stale, metallic tang to it. They step into a strange bunker or tunnel—a sterile underground artery of white tile and polished chrome. Humming LED lights form a stripe down the ceiling's center. Brovski leads the way. His shoes clack and echo. Maggie looks down at the shiny floor and sees her own distorted reflection staring back.

As they make their way down the artery, Maggie begins to see faceless people dressed in white lab coats—faceless because they all wear oversize surgical masks and caps and opaque goggles, and Maggie wonders whether the getup is to protect or disguise. She keeps walking. Walls become windows to laboratories of some sort. Various faceless lab-coated people perform various experiments.

At least, that's what it looks like. Maggie doesn't really know. She also doesn't really care.

She wants to see him.

This bunker is trying very hard to look—time to say it again—"cutting edge" and "state of the art." And yet it doesn't. The "hidden lair" has something of a faux vibe to it, the feeling of an overwrought reproduction, as if this is a Hollywood version of what a secret medical science lab should look like. She, Marc, and Trace were all involved in cardiology—and right now, this place may be well-kept and clean and sterile and sleek and even beautiful, but there is no beating heart. That's how it feels to her.

The people in lab coats—doctors? scientists?—startle when she walks past. They look up furtively, not wanting to make eye contact, even through the opaque goggles.

Maggie wonders about that.

Ivan Brovski stops at a metal door. No windows. No door handle—handles carry germs. Yet another faceless individual approaches her with a blue isolation gown, disposable gloves, and face shield.

"Put them on over your clothes," Brovski orders.

"What about you?" she asks.

"This is as far as I go. Put them on."

Maggie does as he asks. When she's done, Brovski waves his hand in front of a screen. Everything is touchless. The door opens with a sucking hiss. Maggie tentatively steps inside, and the door reseals behind her.

A deep voice says, "Hello, Doctor McCabe."

A big man sits in some makeshift throne on a riser in the middle of the room. A nasal cannula—the kind of mask you always see on television shows—delivers oxygen. There's an IV in his arm. A medical monitoring device displays his vitals—heart rate, blood pressure, oxygen saturation. He wears what is either a smoking jacket or a velvet robe—hard to know which—like something from a Playboy Mansion documentary. His is appropriately enough bloodred.

There is a *Mona Lisa* on the wall behind his head.

Oleg Ragoravich.

He smiles and spreads his thick, soft arms. "Surprised?"

Maggie takes a step toward him. "Would it hurt your feelings if I told you I'm not?"

"It would indeed." Ragoravich's breathing is labored, his chest rising and falling with a little too much drama. "Tell me how you knew."

"Lots of little things—why you threw the ball, the timing of the surgery—but the big thing is, I found an old photograph of you online."

"They're supposed to have all been deleted."

"Yeah, but you know there are always ways."

Ragoravich nods. "I do. Which photo?"

"Your military portrait."

"That has to be forty years old."

"I was given two photos to replicate before the surgery—Photo A and Photo B. Both were grainy black-and-whites. Photo A was the chin. Photo B was, well, your prominent nose. Both, I know now, were blowups of that military portrait. You wanted me to think the surgery was to change your identity. But in reality—"

"It was the opposite," he finishes for her. "You were making him look *more* like me, not less. Fattening him up for the kill."

Awful way of putting it, Maggie thinks, *but not untrue*. "The Oleg I knew—the one I did surgery on and got murdered in Dubai—he was some kind of imposter or body double."

"Body double," he says. "Or decoy. Not an imposter. His real name was Aleksander, by the way. He was my cousin. We look alike, no?"

Maggie nods. "Similar enough. From a distance."

"Aleksander has been my double for the past twenty-three years. Can you believe that? He played the part well."

"He did," Maggie agrees.

"Lots of powerful men have had doubles. Stalin. Noriega. Saddam Hussein. Some say Putin, but I think he's too paranoid to allow someone who looks like him that close. I had two others over the years, but Aleksander, he was the best. I loved him, really."

"And yet," Maggie says.

"And yet he had to die, yes. I need the world to think I'm dead—too many people are after me."

"So you sacrificed your cousin?"

He grins and steeples his hands. "Let me ask you something, Doctor McCabe. Is life about quality or quantity? It's a question you physicians ask every day, no? Do we measure life by the years—or the quality of those years? Aleksander grew up in poverty. Without me, he would have spent his life in drudgery, as a low-level factory worker, barely scraping by. Instead, Aleksander lived a life of luxury even kings couldn't dare have imagined—big mansions, private planes, fancy cars, the finest cuisine, and of course, beautiful women. So you tell me. Was I a curse in his life—or a blessing?"

"I guess we would have to ask him."

"None of us get to decide how we die, Doctor McCabe." He separates his hands, points the palms toward the sky. "Why should Aleksander be any different?"

Maggie nods. "Fascinating albeit sociopathic rationale," she says. "I assume you didn't share your plan with Aleksander."

"I did not, no."

"But he figured it out. Too late. After the surgery was done, when he saw the work I'd done, he realized you were—how did you so poetically put it?—fattening him up for the kill. That's why he ran."

"Yes. I think he deluded himself into believing that Nadia had true feelings for him. So we had people watch the club, figuring he would show up."

Oleg Ragoravich—the real one—tilts his head back, closes his eyes, struggles to swallow. She can see he's in pain. Maggie waits for him to continue.

"My main passion has always been in medical innovations because I have spent so much of my life in poor health. Health is everything—but we know that, don't we? You can have all the riches in the world, but if you don't have your health... Well, it's an old saying, but that's because it's so true. I've always had a congenitally weak heart in the physical sense—but the heart of a lion when I want something. And I wanted to find a way to cure me—and in the process, help others like me to live longer."

"Others like you," Maggie says.

"Yes."

"You mean the rich and powerful?"

"Don't be naive. It's always been that way. Medical research is held back by archaic rules. I don't have time for any of that. Mankind doesn't either. And you Americans especially have grown so lazy and stupid. You think you'd be healthier if you relied on your"—Ragoravich shakes his head as he says in pure disgust—"'natural immunities.' Please. *Natural immunities.* It makes me laugh." His voice goes up an octave in mimicry: "'Oh, we don't need modern medicine, we just need to meditate and trust our "natural immunities" like in the old days!' Bah. Do you know what the global life expectancy was in 1900? Thirty-seven years. Thirty-seven! That's what your natural immunities got you. Do you know what life expectancy is today? Seventy-three. Think about that. And do you know why? Of course you do. You're an intelligent physician. We live longer because of modern medicine—antibiotics, vaccines, control of infectious disease, new treatments for cancer, stroke, and yes, cardiovascular disease. We live longer because we *stopped* relying on our 'natural immunities.'"

He is panting by the time he finishes the rant. He takes a second, starts breathing again, looks at her. "What do you think?"

"I think the other Oleg didn't talk this much."

That makes him chuckle. "Very good, Doctor McCabe. But you know I'm right. Science and medicine work. The rest . . . They call me corrupt, but these so-called 'wellness influencers' preying on your gullibility, buying in bulk, repackaging junk as a 'health supplement,' jacking up the price . . ." He waves his hand dismissively in the air. "But you didn't come here to listen to a sick old man rant about humanity's innate stupidity."

"True, I did not," she says.

"Tell me what you already know, Doctor McCabe, and I'll tell you the rest."

Maggie doesn't hesitate—she dives right in. "Like a lot of your competitors, you laundered money through charities. But you did it with a dual purpose. You focused on charities that had connections to medical innovations, especially if they featured cardiology or cellular regenerative advancements. So-called 'fountain of youth' medicine. As you just explained, nothing with placebo supplements or scam therapies. Only charities involved in true medical innovations."

"Yes."

"It was common knowledge that WorldCures was doing major work on heart transplants via THUMPR7. You would have been all over that."

"WorldCures was my number one priority."

"So you donated to us and several other like-minded charities. You started the corruption with the money laundering. Then you moved on to black-market organ donation. And then, because you hated the—what do you call them, archaic rules?—some form of human experimentation. I assume that's what's going on down here?"

"Close," Ragoravich says. "You know we bought a kidney from Nadia when she was Salima?"

"Yes."

"And she thinks we sold it on the black market for transplantation."

"You didn't?"

"No. We needed a kidney with her DNA markings for a certain medical experiment. That's what I mean. Imagine how much faster you can make progress if you just buy real human organs instead of having to spend years trying it with pigs or in labs."

Maggie doesn't even know what to say to that.

"We've bought dozens of organs like this. Some, yes, we sold for transplantation. For profit. Others we kept for important experimentation. We took everyone's blood at refugee camps all over the world. You helped with that, as a matter of fact, for us. Now we have all that DNA stored in our own data banks. We can get exactly what we need when we need it—and when we see a match, well, everyone has a price."

"Who removed Nadia's kidney?"

"I wouldn't normally know. We did so many."

"Normally. But in this case?"

"You're wondering whether it was your husband."

Maggie shakes her head. "I know it wasn't."

"Because he was too good a man?"

"Because there are lines he wouldn't cross."

"Ah, but selling her kidney wasn't a bad thing. It was pure commerce. It saved the donor's—"

"Yeah, yeah, Nadia explained all that to me. I don't need to hear it again. Who removed her kidney?"

"You know now, don't you?"

She nods. "Trace Packer."

"Yes. Packer did many. He believed that innovation in organ donation was the future of medicine. He was willing to push the boundaries."

"In a dangerous way. I was at Apollo Longevity when we tried to implant the THUMPR7 in Kabir Abargil, a poor man—"

"A poor man who consented," Ragoravich interjects. "A poor man who was going to die and knew the risks and made an informed decision—"

"Yeah, okay, whatever."

"No, no, you listen." Ragoravich makes a fist and shakes it at her. "We have always sacrificed our fellow human beings for the greater good. Always. Wars, of course, but every advancement we humans have made—when we first created aqueducts for water, when we first traveled, built bridges, explored, pioneered, literally everything throughout history we ever did to advance civilization and—"

Maggie holds up her hand and says, "Oleg?"

"Yes?"

"I get it. You are extraordinarily creative with your self-justifications. But I don't really care."

"And in truth, neither do I. I want to live. That's all that matters to me in the end. It's why I focused on the heart. That's the immediate need. But we work here on every organ because there is overlap in the research—and because eventually I will need those too. Once we can replicate organs and tissues, a human could live theoretically for hundreds of years. And no, this isn't for the masses. We can't have everyone living that long. Even the knowledge that the possibility exists would end the world because, yes, people would kill to get it. That's not justification, Doctor McCabe. That's fact. God—if you are superstitious enough to believe in that man-made delusion—created a world where the only way to survive is to kill. You watch a lion take down a gazelle. The lion will try to keep the poor creature alive while he eats it so it stays fresh. The gazelle slowly dies in agony. That's the 'perfect' world designed by a just and kind deity." He chuckles. "And I'm the one delusional with self-justification?"

Maggie tries to catch him off guard. "Did you kill my husband?"

"No." There is no hesitation. "I needed him alive to work on that artificial heart. His death was a tremendous blow to me."

She tries again: "Did Trace kill him?"

"Could be," he says in too casual a way. "Marc found out about Trace organ harvesting. It upset him. Trace might have killed Marc to protect himself. But I don't know." Oleg's breath grows raspier. "I'm getting tired, so I need to get to the point. My latest heart is failing. I have run out of time. We have the latest THUMPR7 here. We have the DNA sequencing machine and all the other equipment. We both know what went wrong the first time you tried the operation on that 'poor man' in Dubai—you didn't have a heart. We have an ideal, healthy one now from a brain-dead man in a coma. The heart isn't being shipped either. I've paid to have the brain-dead man brought here. Your husband and Trace Packer wrote quite a bit on the advantages of 'beating-heart' transplantation when developing the THUMPR7. We will have the ultimate version of that. The heart will be taken out by a team just minutes before insertion. In short, the conditions are finally perfect for the transplant that can save my life."

"Why are you telling me all this?"

Oleg Ragoravich gives her a sharklike smile. "Why do you think?"

And then she sees it. "You want me to do the transplant?"

"Yes. Of course. That's why you're here."

Silence.

"Your husband is dead. Trace Packer, well, we don't know where he is. No Marc, no Trace . . . That leaves you, Doctor McCabe."

"But I'm a plastic surgeon—"

"Oh, you're more than that. Let's not play the false modesty card. I made a mistake back then. I relied on the two men. Old-world sexism on my part. I should have focused on you. You are the best surgeon of the group. Women often are better at focusing on what matters, at understanding the mission. They don't let their egos get involved the way men do. When you were around, Marc and Trace were better doctors, researchers, and humans. When you left, it all went to hell."

And if she hadn't left, Maggie thinks, *Marc would still be alive.*

"Whose heart is it?"

"I told you. A man in a coma."

"Someone from a refugee camp?"

"Does it matter?"

"Depends. Did you put him in a coma?"

"If I needed to, I would have. But I didn't. He's been brain-dead for months. If it makes you feel any better, I paid his caretaker a fortune to get him here."

"I need reassurances—"

"No, Doctor McCabe, you don't. You will do the surgery. You will be well paid. And after it is over, you will have both the satisfaction of completing your husband's work and the guarantee of safety. I have assembled the finest cardiothoracic surgery team possible—surgical nurses, perfusion technologists, a cardiac anesthesiologist, and two top heart transplant surgeons to assist you. This will all be over for you after you do this transplant tomorrow."

"It won't work," Maggie says. "The THUMPR7 isn't ready."

"The decision's been made."

"And if I refuse?"

"Do we need to play this game, Doctor McCabe?" Ragoravich sighs. "I showed you the carrot, so I might as well show you the stick." He steeples his hands again and rests his forefingers on his chin. "If you refuse, the other surgeons will still proceed with the procedure. But instead of the brain-dead comatose man's heart, I'll use your father-in-law's, which will be ripped out of his chest with no anesthesia while we make you watch."

He grins. "Do I make myself clear?"

———————

Porkchop can't help but laugh.

"He actually used those words? Ripping my heart out of my chest?"

"It's not funny."

"Except it kinda is. Oh, and without anesthesia? Did he really say that too?"

"While he makes me watch."

"That's a nice touch. Such a flair for the dramatic."

"Or the sadistic. What do you think we should do?"

Porkchop puts his hand to his chest. "Hell, Mags, I don't want my heart ripped out of my chest."

"Stop that."

They are back on the porch of the guesthouse at Smith Haut Lafitte, watching the sun set so majestically you figure it's showing off.

"You'll do the surgery," Porkchop says. "Like the man says, you have no choice. You do the surgery, we go home, we put this behind us."

"And Trace?"

"What about him?"

"We still don't know where he is."

"A problem for another day."

She takes a sip of wine. "None of this makes sense."

Porkchop says nothing.

"It's like they knew I was coming. It's like they led me here."

Porkchop still stares out in silence.

"Do you think Nadia set me up?" Maggie asks.

"How so?"

"She told me about Brovski landing in Bordeaux."

"How did she know where he was again? Oh right, she stole his phone and dropped a pin."

"Which is a little suspicious in itself, right? Maybe Nadia made that up. Maybe she's on their side. I don't know. But think about it. They were ready for us, Porkchop. Ragoravich had a surgical team prepared. He has the THUMPR7 and all our equipment. All he needed was me—and voilà, here I am."

Porkchop takes another sip. "You asked this Ragoravich guy if he killed Marc."

"Yes."

"And he said no."

"Right."

"Do you believe him?"

"I do. He only cares about the THUMPR7. He needed Marc for that."

"Did he?" Porkchop asks. "Or did he need you?"

"I don't get what you mean."

"Neither do I." Porkchop lifts up the empty wine bottle. "Probably a little too much grape."

"So what do we do now, Porkchop?"

"We finish our glasses. We stroll up the path to La Grand'Vigne. That's the vineyard's two-star Michelin restaurant. We sit at a little wooden table outside. We don't look at the menu. We ask Chef Nicolas what we should order and his sommelier for the proper wine pairing. We finish watching this glorious sunset, and we think about Marc."

The tears start pushing into her eyes again. "I shouldn't have gone home. I should have stayed with him in Dubai."

"Then you'd both be dead," Porkchop says. "You would have gone to that refugee camp with him. You would have stayed by his side during the siege. And whoever killed him would have killed you too."

"And whoever," Maggie repeats. Then: "You think it was Trace."

"Yeah, Mags, I do. But either way, you're alive. Marc is dead. He'd want you to move on."

"You don't believe in life after death, do you?"

Porkchop shakes his head. "We get one ride. This is it."

"So Marc is gone," she says.

"Yes."

"Forever."

"Forever."

"How do we accept that, Porkchop?"

"We don't," he says. "We can't."

CHAPTER TWENTY-FIVE

Before Maggie puts on her surgical gown, gloves, and goggles, Ivan Brovski enters the room and collapses into a chair.

"All okay?" Maggie asks.

"I need to deliver a message."

Maggie waits.

"Oleg Ragoravich has given us clear instructions: If he doesn't make it out of the surgery, neither do you."

He looks up at her.

"Hell of an incentive," Maggie says, because sometimes humor is the best defense mechanism.

Brovski stands. "I'll see you in the OR."

He leaves.

Half an hour later, Maggie is in the operating room and ready to go. Beads of sweat coat her forehead before she even starts.

"Doctor?"

It's the nurse to her right.

Deep breaths, Maggie tells herself.

"Scalpel."

Maggie begins by performing a median sternotomy to access the thoracic cavity. With the scalpel, she makes a vertical incision down the sternum and then, using the surgical saw, she divides the sternum to gain access. Maggie opens the pericardium, the membrane protecting the heart. They've already run the flexible tube down Oleg Ragoravich's throat and into the esophagus and now, using sound waves from the transesophageal echocardiogram, Maggie can see the heart on his monitor.

It's a mess.

The heart is gray and enlarged. She can see scars on the surface.

Man, this surgery is happening just in time.

The operating theater is, no question, fully stocked. The staff seems first-rate so far, even though Maggie did not meet any of them ahead of time. They, like Maggie, wear full-face masks and opaque goggles. Ivan Brovski, who, as promised/threatened, is also in the operating room, ominously explained that discretion is paramount in this strange hidden lair they vaguely call The Vineyard:

"They can't know your identity—and you can't know theirs."

Oleg Ragoravich lies beneath a sea of blue drape. His rib cage is split wide open now, held in place by retractors. It's gross to most, but Maggie finds it oddly beautiful, and yeah, she knows that's weird. Right now, only one assistant surgeon is in the room with her. She—yes, the other surgeon is a woman too—clearly knows her stuff. The third surgeon, Maggie is told, is in the adjacent theater with the brain-dead heart donor. That surgeon has opened the chest and will extract the donor heart at the same time Maggie removes Ragoravich's native heart and attaches the THUMPR7 in its place.

Beneath the glare from the surgical lights, Oleg's heart pulses in a weak, spastic rhythm. The tubes from the cardiopulmonary bypass twist away from the venae cavae and aorta. Maggie nods to the perfusionist, and the bypass takes over.

Oleg's heart sputters, slows, and then stops completely.

Time to move fast and disconnect the blood vessels.

Maggie uses scissors to part the aorta and pulmonary artery, their ends tattered by disease. She trims the right ventricle along the atrioventricular groove, preserving the tricuspid annulus. She does the same on the left side.

"Prepare the donor heart and THUMPR7," Maggie says.

The Vineyard has the latest cardiac retraction glove and sling, which are designed to lift the heart out of the chest without damaging surrounding tissue. Maggie does that now, carefully yet quickly. The native heart is seriously diseased—thinned and stretched, weak and so fragile that Maggie worries the heart muscle might rip or crumble or even disintegrate upon extraction.

"Need another set of hands?" the assistant surgeon asks.

Her voice is high-pitched, with an exaggerated Southern twang, and Maggie wonders whether the voice is a put-on for further disguise.

Maggie is a photo of focus. "I got it."

When the heart is clear of the chest, Maggie turns and drops it into a basin on the surgical back table. Normally a heart like this is sent to pathology for examination or disposal. What will they do with it down here in The Vineyard? Study it maybe. Use it for experimentation. Eat it. Who the hell knows?

Maggie lets herself smile at the thought.

In fact, she realizes, under her mask, she's been smiling the whole time.

Because even though she's scared out of her mind, even though she can almost feel the gun being readied if something goes wrong, Maggie loves this.

She loves being a surgeon. She loves operating.

"TAH," she says.

One of the surgical nurses hands her the THUMPR7 artificial heart.

"Donor heart ready?" Maggie asks.

"Coming in the moment you need it."

"Now," she says.

Maggie takes hold of the THUMPR7. She looks down at Oleg's vacant chest cavity. Where there should be a heart, there is nothing but a yawning, bloodless void. It is a sight to behold, this threshold between death and life, between an ending and a beginning, between emptiness and hope. This chest is the emptiest of vessels and a promise waiting to be fulfilled.

For the briefest of moments, Maggie considers ending that hope.

Her patient is a man with no heart, figuratively and, for the moment, literally. He is also, perhaps figuratively and literally, dead.

Only she can bring him back to life.

What would happen if she didn't? What would happen if she just let Oleg die on the table?

She glances to her right, toward Ivan Brovski. He may be goggled and masked up too so that she cannot read his expression, but his little headshake says it all:

Don't even think it. He dies, you die.

The door opens. The other assisting surgeon, his gloved hands covered in blood—it's a man—wheels an Organ Care System carrying the donor heart into the room. The OCS pumps an oxygenated blood base solution through the organ, keeping the heart viable.

The new surgeon stands on the other side of the table.

Maggie looks at him. He looks at her. But she can't really see him, of course. She can't see his eyes or his face. The shape of his body, too, looks pretty vague in the loose surgical gown. His hands are gloved.

He nods at her. For a moment, Maggie doesn't move.

Ivan Brovski says, "Doctor?"

Maggie snaps out of it. With her gloved hand, she steadily lowers the THUMPR7 artificial heart—the one created by WorldCures but mostly by Marc, Marc's brainchild, Marc's work, Marc's attempt to save lives on a massive scale—into the seemingly bottomless hole where Oleg Ragoravich's heart once resided.

"Suture," the assistant male surgeon barks.

His voice is gruff, muffled, and again she wonders whether this is his natural sound or if he is trying to mask his identity. With Maggie holding the THUMPR7 in place, her partner begins the delicate work of suturing the device's inflow connectors to Oleg's atrial cuffs.

Maggie joins in. Her adrenaline starts kicking into overdrive. She's nervous. She has never done anything like this.

Gruff Voice stops for a moment. Maggie looks up into the goggled face.

"It's okay," he says to her. "You got this."

Maggie is grateful for the encouragement. She swallows and nods.

The two surgeons—Maggie and Gruff Voice—work now in perfect tandem, threading the outflow connectors to the pulmonary artery and aorta, sizing the grafts with the precision of, well, cardiothoracic surgeons—too long and the lines will tangle; too short and blood won't flow.

"Left ventricle first," Maggie says, but Gruff Voice is one step ahead of her. He quick-connects—think "little snaps"—the heart to the Three A's: artery, aorta, atria. Maggie does the same with the right. The THUMPR7 has four flaps. They are all open.

"Now," Maggie says.

Gruff Voice opens the OCS or "heart box" and extracts a healthy, red, beating heart. He moves fast, guiding the donor heart into the THUMPR7. This, Maggie realizes, has never been done before. This, she realizes, would have been Marc and Trace's dream moment— the THUMPR7 in tandem with a healthy beating-heart transplant donation. With a nod, Maggie takes over. She uses forceps to maneuver the heart into place. She attaches the donor heart's pulmonary artery to the THUMPR7's plastic valve in only one place. If this works, that should be the only attachment they need. The DNA sequencing machine is normally used after surgery to detect graft rejection. Maggie uses a specially designed one now, one that offers immediate feedback. She checks the readout.

So far, so good.

This is what their technology is trying to do: blend the robotic wonders of an artificial heart with the idea of cell regeneration and tissue compatibility. The best way of doing that is via a full organ—as in a beating-heart transplant like this—but the future hope is that stem cells, rather than full organs, will be enough.

Gruff Voice says, "No leaks. Blood flow is strong."

Their goggled eyes meet again. They know this is the moment of truth. He gives her an encouraging nod. Maggie takes one more deep breath and turns to the perfusionist. "Turn it off."

"Wait, shouldn't we wean?"

"Not with the THUMPR7. It should kick in right away."

The perfusionist hesitates.

"Do it," Maggie snaps.

The perfusionist grudgingly switches off the bypass machine.

For a moment, nothing happens. Flat line.

Five seconds pass. Ten seconds.

The perfusionist says, "Doctor?"

"Wait," Maggie says.

"It's not working."

"Then he's dead either way," Maggie says, while that sarcastic inner voice adds, *And he ain't the only one . . .*

Ten more seconds pass, fifteen, twenty.

Ivan Brovski puts his large, gloved hands on both her shoulders as though to push her out of the way. "Doctor McCabe, what's happening—?"

And then, with an audible grunt, the THUMPR7 starts beating.

BEAT...BEAT...BEAT...
Steadier now.
BEAT...BEAT...BEAT...
It's working.
BEAT...BEAT...BEAT...
The room cheers.
BEAT...BEAT...BEAT...
Under the mask, Maggie's face breaks into a wide smile. She looks up to lock celebratory goggle-eyes with Gruff Voice.

But he's gone.

Maggie rips off her gloves, strips out of her gown, and steps into the shower.

The shower's jet stream is powerful. Marc had always liked that in a shower, maybe more so because the showers during any kind of humanitarian mission were set on what Marc called "light urination." When Maggie and Marc renovated the bathroom in their apartment, he offered the contractor no opinions on tiles, faucets, colors, toilets, design, only noting, "I want the water pressure to be so powerful I bleed."

The pang again.

Weird when it comes back. She hadn't felt him that much during surgery. Now, in the shower, with the powerful blast washing the blood and tissue of an evil man off her, once again grief makes its sneak attack.

She dries off and slips back into sweats. There is a full-size mask and goggles for her to wear on the way out. Forget it. If they recognize her, who cares? She enters that main tunnel again and heads to the makeshift ICU. She looks in the window. Ragoravich is still unconscious. There are monitors and six overly masked staff present. Maggie wonders whether any of these people had been on her team.

Through the glass, she hears it again.

BEAT...BEAT...BEAT...

From behind her, she hears Ivan Brovski's voice. "A tremendous success."

Maggie frowns. He sees it in the window's reflection.

"You don't agree?"

BEAT...BEAT...BEAT...

"I warned Oleg. I warned you. I don't think it's ready for human usage." She turns to him. "Who were the other surgeons with me?"

"I can't tell you that."

"To keep confidentiality?"

"Yes. You know now how we hire people. You know how we pay them. It's like you, in Russia."

"Speaking of Russia," Maggie says. "You almost killed me."

"Not really, no. You ran onto the roof. My men, they reacted. Aleksander was running away too at the time. It created something of a panic. We wanted to close it all down. We needed you alive, but the men didn't know the mission. And then, of course, there was Nadia."

BEAT...BEAT...BEAT...

"What about Nadia?"

He shrugs. "She was in many ways the lady of the house."

"Are you saying she wanted—"

"I don't know," Brovski says. "It doesn't matter anymore, does it?"

BEAT...BEAT...BEAT...

"Nadia led me here," Maggie says.

"What do you mean?"

"Can I see your phone?"

"Excuse me?"

She lifts her hand and beckons for him to give it to her. He looks as though he's about to protest but then, thinking better of it, he opens it with his face and hands it over. Maggie takes it and starts searching for the appropriate app. Brovski watches over her shoulder. Maggie doesn't care. When she opens the app, she scrolls down.

"Good timing," she says. "My being here."

Hmm. The dropped pin is there. Nadia had been telling the truth.

"What's that?" he asks.

"It's nothing."

Maggie hands his phone back to him. "It was good timing, I guess— my coming to France just when you needed me to do the surgery."

Brovski shrugs. "We could have grabbed you and brought you here anytime."

"So why didn't you?"

He shrugs again. "No need. You showed up."

BEAT . . . BEAT . . . BEAT . . .

"Yeah, I'm not really buying that, Ivan."

"And I'm not really selling it either."

"Do you know who killed my husband?"

Just like that. She holds his gaze.

"I can tell you what Oleg and I believed."

She waits.

"You are adrenaline junkies. You always took too many risks with your humanitarian missions, and while your medical care benefited some, it wasn't worth it. Many you saved ended up living short, miserable lives in squalor or getting killed in the next battle. You didn't have to take such risks. You could have played it safer. Instead, you chose to keep rolling the dice. Eventually the dice came up snake eyes."

BEAT . . . BEAT . . . BEAT . . .

"So it was just a matter of time," she says.

"I know you want there to be more. And maybe there is. Your husband died a hero. But he also died a fool."

Ivan Brovski starts to walk away.

"And Trace Packer?"

He says nothing.

"Do you know where he is?"

BEAT . . . BEAT . . . BEAT . . .

"You must be exhausted, Doctor McCabe."

"That's not an answer."

"It's the only one I'm giving you today." He nods toward the exit. "You know the way out."

She starts toward him, but he slips into a room and locks the door behind him. Maybe that's for the best. She's far too exhausted right now to come up with a new strategy to get the truth out of him. She turns left and moves down that massive white artery back to the stairwell. At the top of the stairs, she pushes the barrels out of the way. She's back up in the musty old cellar. She looks to the right, to the door, and she sees a man wearing a baseball cap exiting.

"Hold up!" she shouts.

He doesn't. The door closes behind him. Maggie hurries after him.

Of course, he could be anyone. He doesn't have to be the surgeon who stood across from her. But he's wearing a baseball cap. That might be meaningless, but you don't see a lot of men in France wearing them. In the United States, it's almost a staple, especially when someone doesn't want to be recognized.

But in France?

She opens the door and bursts out into the overgrown vineyard. It feels good to be back out of the bunker with its piped-in staleness. The air outside is both sweet and acrid, earthy and ethereal.

She looks left. Nothing. She looks right. Nothing. The only way out, as far as she knows, is to the right, to the gate where she has come and gone both times she's been here. She sprints toward it. When she makes the final turn she can see the gate, and through the gate, the man in the baseball cap is getting into the back of a car.

"Stop!"

He doesn't. He slips inside and shuts the car door. Maggie runs toward him, but it's too late. The car starts moving. The gate slides closed. Maggie bangs on the chain-link as the vehicle vanishes into the woods.

He's gone.

CHAPTER TWENTY-SIX

When the gate finally reopens, Maggie starts down the path. She finds Porkchop and his motorcycle in the clearing.

"How long have you been waiting here?"

Porkchop makes a production of checking the watch on his wrist even though he's not wearing one. "Since I dropped you off."

"That's twelve hours ago."

He shrugs. "Want to talk about it?"

"Not right now."

"Hop on."

Porkchop hands her a helmet. They drive back in silence—it's too exhausting to talk/shout on a motorcycle even if there was something to say. The wind in her face feels sublime. Maggie closes her eyes and lets it cool her. Porkchop plays no music. As always. It's just the bike and the road. Forget massages. Forget aromatherapy or hydrotherapy or saunas or body wraps or hot tubs. This is peace and isolation and freedom. The only place she loves more...Well, with Marc gone, there's only one now.

The operating room.

Her church, her sanctuary.

God, how she misses it.

As they pull in, Guillaume and Élodie wave from a big farmer's table covered in various wines and cheeses.

"Do you want to eat something?" Porkchop asks.

She shakes her head. "My social skills are out of order at the moment."

"Understood."

"You go. I'll walk down to the guesthouse."

"You sure?"

"Positive. I need time to decompress."

He nods, turns the bike off, heads toward the table. Maggie takes the path down through the vineyards. She heads into the guesthouse. She goes into Porkchop's bedroom and opens the side pocket of his satchel bag. When she's finished, she heads back outside. The golden haze is back. It touches everything. Colors are colors, but in a vineyard touched by this golden haze, colors are never stagnant; they become a living, breathing thing.

She stops at a quiet stretch near the guesthouse and leans against a tree. She stares out and soaks in the stillness. It's over now. She gets that. You don't get all the answers. That's part of life. Soon she will go back home to . . .

. . . to what?

No Marc. No surgery.

That's when she feels the cold steel press against the back of her skull.

A voice says, "You killed him."

Maggie's eyes close.

Nadia.

"I rechecked Trace's phone records," Nadia says through gritted teeth. She keeps the muzzle of the gun right up against Maggie's head. Maggie doesn't dare move, her eyes still on the golden haze and the pale blue sky. "You called him on your mobile phone the day before he left. You called him and told him something and suddenly he packed and flew to you."

Nadia circles so that she is now in front of Maggie. Her eyes are wide.

"If you lie to me, I'm going to pull the trigger."

Maggie doesn't speak.

"Did you call Trace? Yes or no."

"Yes," Maggie says.

The women are face-to-face now. Nadia aims the gun at Maggie's heart. "What did you say to him?"

A tear falls from Maggie's eye.

Nadia's voice is a snarl now. "What did you say to him?"

"I told him I visited the TriPoint refugee camp," Maggie says. Her voice is tinny in her own ears, as though she's speaking from very far away. "Or what was left of it. Most of the refugees had been relocated. I followed them. I found every survivor I could. They all told me that the militants who slaughtered them left the medical team alone. One woman named Aisha—she lost one arm and one leg. Chopped off with a machete. She'd been left in the sand to bleed out and die. But she didn't. She used her one arm and her teeth to rip her clothes and create tourniquets. She said she saw Trace come back to camp. Marc was alive when he did. She was sure of it."

Maggie looks into Nadia's eyes and waits.

"So you thought—" Nadia began.

"I didn't think anything. I told Trace I needed to see him. That there were discrepancies in what I was told happened to Marc. I said we needed to talk. In person. Eye to eye. Like this."

"And when he arrived?"

Maggie shakes her head.

"You killed him," Nadia says.

"No."

"Then—"

"Trace never showed. He ran instead."

Nadia lifts the gun. "Don't lie to me."

"I'm not lying. Trace was supposed to come. I waited for him. But instead, I don't know, he stole that device from Apollo Longevity and ran."

She shakes her head. "He wouldn't do that."

"Nadia, we both know he did. You heard Steve."

"And then what? Where is he now?"

Maggie shrugs. "I don't know."

"You're lying." Nadia pushes the gun toward Maggie's face. "You killed him."

And then Maggie hears another voice, a familiar voice, from behind them:

"She's not lying. She didn't kill Trace."

They both turn to see Porkchop.

"I did."

———————

Porkchop has a gun too. He tells Nadia to drop hers. She does. He tells her to kick it away. She does. Then Porkchop turns to Maggie. He doesn't so much as glance at Nadia anymore. It's as though she's not even there.

It's Maggie. It's Porkchop.

The rest of the world fades away.

Maggie feels her extremities go cold. She doesn't know what to do. She stands there, shaking her head.

"We didn't know," Maggie says to him.

"We did."

"Not for sure," she insists. "There were some discrepancies—"

"Not discrepancies," Porkchop says. "You didn't want to see the truth."

"So you..." Maggie shakes her head again.

"Trace flew into Dulles. Just like Nadia told you. When he arrived, Pinky was at the airport. He followed him. Trace bought a gun from someone on the street. Can you guess why?"

Maggie just shakes her head.

"When we grabbed him, Trace had phenobarbital and clonazepam along with that gun on him. We, uh, interrogated him. He planned to drug you. He planned to find out everything you knew—and then kill you. Stage your death to look like a suicide. You were depressed over Marc. Everyone knew that. He would tell the authorities that you called him, as the phone records would back up. You sounded suicidal and depressed. He caught the first plane over and came to your house and..." Porkchop shrugs away the rest of it.

Maggie can't speak.

It's Nadia who says, "So you just killed him?"

"Yes." Porkchop's voice is even, clear. There is no hesitation, no wavering. It's the most obvious thing in the world. He turns and faces Nadia. "And you knew he killed my son. When Maggie called Trace—and then he vanished—most people wouldn't leap to the conclusion that Maggie did something to him. But you did. Because you knew Maggie had motive. You knew what Trace had done to her husband."

Nadia says nothing.

Porkchop raises the gun and points it at her.

Maggie says, "Porkchop."

He ignores her. "Did you help Trace kill my son?"

"No," Nadia says. "I thought I saved him."

That slows him down. He keeps the gun up. "Explain," he says.

"On our way to the TriPoint camp, these young militants—the Child Army...Trace had hired them. To kill Marc. I didn't know until they grabbed us. I'm the one who convinced them not to go through with it. Trace and I talked after that. He promised me he would find another way."

"If that's true—"

"It is."

"Then Trace lied to you."

Nadia takes a moment and then says, "In the end, Trace saw the situation for what it was."

"What was it?"

"Either him or Marc. Marc was going to tell. It would have been bad for him and Maggie—but for Trace, it would have been the end. He was the one who harvested organs. He'd spend the rest of his life in prison. He tried to make Marc see that. He tried to make Marc see that what they were doing was actually good—it could change the world. Their work saved lives. They were on the cusp of making organ donation simpler and safer and more readily available. How, Trace kept asking himself, did Marc not see that? And still—*still*—I think Trace would have done the right thing. But then the massacre happened at TriPoint, and Trace went back. He said he wanted to save his friend. He said that an experience like this may make Marc see the light. So I didn't know. Not for sure. It wasn't premeditated. It was, I don't know, a crime of opportunity."

Nadia looks at Maggie.

"Doesn't make my husband less dead," Maggie says to her.

Nadia has nothing to say to that. No one does. For a while, they just stand there. No one talks. No one moves. Maggie turns away from them and stares out over the vineyard. The sun dips lower, bruising the sky a spiraling purple and orange. She finally has the answers. The truth will set you free, they say, but right now it feels as though it will forever hold Maggie captive. She hears Porkchop calling her name, but even he feels far away, unable to reach her. She doesn't want to hear. She doesn't want to reply. She doesn't want to think or process or assess or consider the repercussions.

Not right now.

Right now, she just wants to stare at the spiraling purple and orange and wish the world away.

EPILOGUE

Three days after Maggie gets back to Baltimore, she calls Vipers and asks to speak to Porkchop. She hasn't seen him since that last day in the vineyard.

The woman who answers the payphone says he's unreachable.

"Tell him it's Maggie."

"Porkchop is off the grid."

"So you don't know where he is?"

"No one does."

"Suppose I really needed him."

"He's off the grid," she says, "but we can put him back on it if there's an emergency." Then she adds in a kinder voice: "Give him time, Maggie."

A week goes by. She calls Vipers again. The woman tells her the same thing. Another week passes. Same thing.

No sign of Porkchop.

Three weeks after that last day in France, Pinky answers the payphone when she calls.

"Porkchop is still incommunicado."

"Tell him I know," Maggie says. "Tell him I know, and I don't care."

There is a long pause on the other end of the line. Then Pinky says, "You think you know. But you don't."

Then he hangs up.

Two days later, Charles Lockwood calls her. "Oleg is in a coma. But that heart is still beating in his chest."

BEAT...BEAT...BEAT...

"Thanks for letting me know."

"Also The Vineyard—the whole operation—has been shut down."

"Good."

"No great loss," Charles says. "Oleg never kept the best scientists and researchers in the end. The best scientists and researchers may complain about the rules and protocols, but they understand why they're there. They want to work in the sunlight, not cut corners in the dark. That's the part Oleg never understood."

"I appreciate the call," Maggie says. "Take care of yourself, Charles."

"Let's stay in touch," he says.

"Yeah, I don't think so," she replies, but he's already ended the call.

Maggie's phone rings again. The caller ID tells her it's the pay-phone at Vipers.

"Porkchop is back," Pinky says.

"I'll come up tomorrow."

She disconnects the call and steps outside into the crisp night air. She takes a deep breath. This time of the year, the neighborhood always smells of freshly cut grass and backyard barbecues. The Burroughs family—Mom, Dad, Son, Daughter—sit on their front lawn. They all wave at Maggie. Maggie forces up a smile and waves back. Someone across the street is blasting a surprisingly touching Nick Cave ballad. His voice is raw and vulnerable as he repeatedly reminds a loved one that he's waiting for them.

Maggie blinks, swallows, and lifts her phone into view. With a shaking finger, she clicks on the griefbot icon. The app comes to life.

Marc's face appears. He smiles at her.

"Oh man, Mags, it's good to see you."

She stares at the screen. Nick Cave is singing to that same loved one to sleep now, sleep now, take as long as you need. Maggie closes her eyes and makes herself listen to the rest of the lyrics. When the song is over, she takes one last deep breath and heads back inside. When she enters the kitchen, Sharon looks up at her.

"We need to delete this," Maggie says, pointing at the app. "For good."

———————

The train pulls into Penn Station.

Pinky waits for her out on 33rd Street. They drive in silence to Vipers for Bikers. It's closed. Pinky unlocks the door and lets her in. And there, pacing in the room alone, is Porkchop. No Zen-like patience today. He doesn't have his sunglasses on. He turns and looks at her with shattered eyes.

"You told Pinky you know," he says.

Maggie nods.

"Tell me."

"I saw your passport."

Porkchop takes a deep breath. "When?"

"Right before Nadia showed up."

They both stop.

Nadia.

"I had to let her go," Porkchop says.

"I know."

"Even if I'll have to look over my shoulder."

"It was the right call."

"What else could I do?"

No need to answer that. Porkchop had pointed the gun at Nadia, his finger twitching on the trigger, his face twisted in anguish. But he didn't pull the trigger. Instead, he muttered, *It stays with you,* and told Nadia to go.

"What made you check my passport?" he asks.

"Your clothes were already in your room, and then Florence asked you if you'd been enjoying your stay—even though we just arrived. Why would she ask that? Then I looked at the flight schedules. There was nothing from JFK to Dubai stopping in London until later in the day. So I started thinking about it. After I called Trace to come home, he broke into Apollo Longevity. He wouldn't do that just to get phenobarbital and clonazepam. He stole the THUMPR7 and the assisting equipment. Those would be his get-out-of-jail-free card. My guess is, he planned to put it in the Wells Fargo bank. But he never got the chance because, well, you killed him. That means *you* had the THUMPR7. How am I doing so far?"

"Pretty well."

"So what was the deal you made, Porkchop?"

"I contacted Ivan Brovski via Barlow. I told him I had the artificial heart they'd been looking for. I would bring it to him. I would get you to France and help convince you to do the surgery. In return, they would pay us an extravagant amount of money and promise to leave us alone. That was the key—you and I would be out. I already knew who killed Marc. I already knew what happened to Trace—"

"But I didn't."

"You knew enough."

"No, sorry, you don't have the right to make that decision for me."

"I was trying to protect you."

"Yeah, look how well that worked out for Marc."

Porkchop winces. "I know. I was wrong. I'm sorry."

"No more secrets."

"No more secrets," Porkchop says.

There is something troubling in his tone.

"You have more?"

He gestures at her with his chin. "Why don't you go first?"

Maggie says nothing.

"Do you want to tell me about your father's gun, Maggie?"

Everything goes still, as if the very room were holding its breath.

Porkchop takes a step toward her. "You went down into your basement. That's where your father hid his old thirty-eight. Sharon saw you. She was worried, so she called me." He tilts his head. "What were you planning on doing with his gun?"

She says nothing.

"Trace was supposed to show up the next day. He killed Marc—and he was going to get away with it. You knew that. So tell me, Maggie, what did you plan on doing with your father's thirty-eight?"

Tears run down her cheeks.

"When you kill a man," Porkchop says, "it stays with you."

"It stays with you . . . "

"And," Maggie says, "you didn't want that for me."

"I didn't want that for you."

"And that's why—"

"I wasn't lying. We followed Trace. He planned on killing you."

"And if he hadn't been?"

"There's no point in talking hypotheticals."

"I love you," she says.

Porkchop nods, his eyes now wet with tears too. "I love you too."

She runs toward him then. She wraps her arms around him and pulls him close. She puts her head on his shoulder. Maggie's eyes look to the left, to the center of the room, searching and finding that motorcycle, and for a moment, she is certain that Marc is right there, riding it, giving her that smile that always reached into her chest and gently twisted her heart.

It's over.

"No more secrets," she whispers again.

But she feels his body stiffen.

"Porkchop?"

He pulls away.

"What is it?"

"The deal I made with Ragoravich."

"What about it?"

"I didn't just bring him the medical equipment."

She waits.

Porkchop looks at her, blinks, then turns to the side. He too is staring at the vintage bike he'd gifted Marc.

"He murdered my boy," he says.

"I know."

"He murdered my boy. And there he is, running his mouth, handing me all the same bullshit he told Nadia about how he'd wanted more organ transplants."

The temperature in the room drops ten degrees. "What did you do, Porkchop?"

"I didn't kill him."

"What?"

"I gave him his final wish."

"What wish?"

He meets her gaze. "More organ transplants."

His eyes grow cold now, distant.

And then Maggie sees it.

"Porkchop?"

"First, he donated his corneas. Restored someone's vision."

Maggie starts to shake her head.

"Then he donated a kidney. Probably saved a life. It's what he believed in, right? It's what he killed my boy for. Then he donated part of his lung—not too much or he'd die. I didn't want that. Not yet anyway. Same with his liver. And then his pancreas. I don't remember what else." Porkchop swallows, but his voice stays steady. "And then in the end, when I realized Oleg Ragoravich would do anything to get hold of a beating heart . . ."

He doesn't say more. He doesn't have to.

They stand there. Together. Maggie has no idea for how long. Eventually someone unlocks the door. They come into the bar. Then someone else. Someone says hi. More people come in. Maggie and Porkchop break apart, greet people, accept hugs, but all Maggie can hear is the same sound she heard when she was leaving the operating room.

BEAT...BEAT...BEAT...

ACKNOWLEDGMENTS
FOR *GONE BEFORE GOODBYE*

First, I would like to thank my mother and father, Betty and John Witherspoon, who served in the Tennessee Air National Guard and US Air Force, respectively. Their forty years of service in military hospitals and then private health care were the background of this novel. Living on military bases as a child, surrounded by medical military families, I learned about the connectedness of communities dedicated to risking their own lives to help others. Every dinner table conversation about surgery and patient care, filled with thrilling stories of harrowing medical experiences, influenced me to write about Maggie and Marc's passion for health care. My childhood visits to hospitals and military bases instilled in me a powerful lesson that a life of service to others is the most noble life to lead. Mom and Dad, I love you.

Thank you to Reza, Kevin, Steven, Dasha, Nadar, and many others who helped me build out details of locations and worlds I could only imagine visiting one day. You added truth and humor to every story you shared with me. Thank you.

Thank you to Ben Sevier, Lyssa Keusch, and the whole team at Grand Central Publishing for believing in this idea from Day One. Your enthusiasm was the wind at my back during this whole experience.

Thank you to my book agent, Cait Hoyt, who never fails to be my biggest champion, especially when I am past deadline and feeling so nervous I could crumble. You always help put me back on track and convince me I am writing something truly original. That's the biggest compliment I could ever hope for!

Thank you to Kate Childs-Jones, Meredith O'Sullivan, Chelsea Thomas, Maha Dakhil, Gretchen Rush, Rick Yorn, Josh Dembling, and my entire team, who always make sure I am endlessly supported in every creative project. Your hard work and encouragement made writing my first novel feel a little less daunting—notice, I only said "a little."

Thank you to Hillary, Beatrice, Jenna, and Jeff, who keep my life in order and make me look much more pulled together than I am! Your organization, attention to detail, and deep loyalty mean the world to me.

Thank you to Rachel Bati, who has kept the many different crazy trains in my life running on time for over (gulp!) thirty years. The three hundred emails, five hundred phone calls, and at least seven pep talks a day have made space for my creativity to flourish and grow in every way. I will be forever grateful for all the little ways you motivate me, including lots of funny stories about your hair and my favorite surprise cheer-me-up cookies during long days at work. I love you!

I would like to thank Harlan Coben for agreeing to jump in and become my partner on this amazing journey. I have no idea how I managed to convince a writer of your esteem to agree to coauthor with me for the first time, but I will be forever grateful to you for taking my seed of an idea and building out this fascinating world. A novel filled with global medical intrigue and massive corruption, all centered around a woman whose superpower is her surgical prowess, seemed like a far-fetched dream. You brought Maggie McCabe to life with your ability to shape an idea into a fully fleshed-out, page-turning thriller. And you made the whole process so fun! I am enormously proud of our collaboration and the deep humanity inside it. Thank you for being the best partner in the whole world.

Thank you to all my favorite writers, including all my Reese's Book Club authors, readers, and booksellers who inspire me to explore the edges of my imagination and dream of more stories to tell.

Finally, to my wonderful children and family, there aren't enough pages in this book to tell you how much your love means to me. I am so blessed to have the most encouraging family in the world.

—Reese Witherspoon

Ditto what Reese said.

Let me list a bunch of people who contributed to this book in no particular order: Ben Sevier, David Shelley, Lyssa Keusch, Danielle Thomas, Beth de Guzman, Karen Kosztolnyik, Colin Dickerman, Jonathan Valuckas, Matthew Ballast, Quinne Rogers, Lauren Sum, Staci Burt, Tiffany Porcelli, Andrew Duncan, Taylor Parker-Means, Alexis Gilbert, Joseph Benincase, Albert Tang, Liz Connor, Rena Kornbluh, Rebecca Holland, Mari C. Okuda, Jennifer Tordy, Ana Maria Allessi, Nita Basu, Laura Essex, Melanie Schmidt, Venetia Butterfield, Selina Walker, Charlotte Bush, Olivia Thomas, Rebecca Ikin, Lucy Hall, Alice Gomer, Anna Curvis, Meredith Benson, Mary Karayel, Diane Discepolo, Jamie Megargee, Lisa Erbach Vance, Samantha Reiter, and Anne Armstrong-Coben, MD.

A very special shout-out to the genius that is Robert Silich, MD, FACS. Reese and I had a lot of help on the medical front from many physicians and scientists, but Rob really took the extra step and came up with some fun, clever, and twisted research for us. Thanks, my friend.

And of course, what can I say about my partner and friend Reese Witherspoon? I keep getting asked if Reese is as cool, kind, and smart as she seems—and the honest answer is no, she's even cooler, kinder, and smarter than you imagine. Taking this journey with you was an honor and a hoot. You are a generous, compassionate, insightful, and brilliant partner.

—Harlan Coben

ABOUT THE AUTHORS

Reese Witherspoon is an award-winning actress, producer, *New York Times* bestselling author, and founder. In 2016, she established the media brand Hello Sunshine, which puts women at the center of every story across all platforms—from scripted and unscripted television, feature films, animated series, podcasts, audio storytelling, and digital series. Hello Sunshine is also home to Reese's Book Club, a community propelled by meaningful connections with stories, authors, and fellow members. Witherspoon is best known for her roles in feature films like *Walk the Line*, *Wild*, *Election*, and *Legally Blonde*, as well as Emmy Award–winning TV series *Big Little Lies*, *Little Fires Everywhere*, and *The Morning Show*.

Harlan Coben is a #1 *New York Times* bestselling author and one of the world's leading storytellers. His suspense novels are published in forty-six languages and have been number one bestsellers in more than a dozen countries, with ninety million books in print worldwide. His Myron Bolitar series has earned the Edgar, Shamus, and Anthony Awards. Coben is also the creator and executive producer of many television shows, including adaptations on Netflix of the #1 global hits *Missing You* and *Fool Me Once*, *Stay Close*, *The Stranger*, *The Innocent*,

Gone for Good, Hold Tight, and *The Woods.* His forthcoming TV series include *Run Away, I Will Find You,* and *Lazarus.*

For more information you can visit:

X @ReeseW

Instagram @reesewitherspoon

TikTok @reesewitherspoon

HarlanCoben.com

X @HarlanCoben

Facebook.com/HarlanCobenBooks

Instagram @HarlanCoben

Netflix.com/HarlanCoben

TikTok @harlan_coben

RAISING READERS
Books Build Bright Futures

Thank you for reading this book and for being a reader of books in general. As authors, we are so grateful to share being part of a community of readers with you, and we hope you will join us in passing our love of books on to the next generation of readers.

Did you know that reading for enjoyment is the single biggest predictor of a child's future happiness and success?

More than family circumstances, parents' educational background, or income, reading impacts a child's future academic performance, emotional well-being, communication skills, economic security, ambition, and happiness.

Studies show that kids reading for enjoyment in the US is in rapid decline:

- In 2012, 53% of 9-year-olds read almost every day. Just 10 years later, in 2022, the number had fallen to 39%.
- In 2012, 27% of 13-year-olds read for fun daily. By 2023, that number was just 14%.

Together, we can commit to **Raising Readers** and change this trend. How?

- Read to children in your life daily.
- Model reading as a fun activity.
- Reduce screen time.
- Start a family, school, or community book club.
- Visit bookstores and libraries regularly.
- Listen to audiobooks.
- Read the book before you see the movie.
- Encourage your child to read aloud to a pet or stuffed animal.
- Give books as gifts.
- Donate books to families and communities in need.

BOB1217

Books build bright futures, and **Raising Readers** is our shared responsibility.

For more information, visit **JoinRaisingReaders.com**

Sources: National Endowment for the Arts, National Assessment of Educational Progress, WorldBookDay.org, Nielsen BookData's 2023 "Understanding the Children's Book Consumer"